PAST STORM AND FIRE

Emeline Rhys

Green Dragon Publishing

Front cover image by MiblArt

Book design by Christy Nicholas

First printing edition 2019.

Publisher: Green Dragon Publishing

Beacon Falls, CT

www.GreenDragonArtist.com

Dedication

This is for all those people who must push through the storms in their lives, either figuratively or literally. For those that keep their eyes on the sunshine, no matter how long the rain falls.

Acknowledgements

As always, I want to thank my husband, Jason, for all his support. I also want to thank my critique group and my beta readers, especially Ian Morris, Mattea Orr, and Scott Franklin, for all their help.

Pronunciation Guide and Glossary

People

Arnbjörg – ARN-byorg
Árni Magnússon – ARN-ee MAG-noo-son
Asgrimur – ass-GRIM-er
Astriðr – ass-TREE-ther
Bragi – BRAG-ee
Fennja – FEN-ya
Gaukur Trandilsson – GOW-ker TRAND-ill-son
Gísla – GEES-lah
Goði/Goðr – GO-thee/GO-thur
Hávaldr – ha-VALL-dur
Hávarr – ha-VAR
Hrolf Kraki – hrowlf KRAH-kee
Hjúki – HYOO-kee
Isveig – ISS-vayg
Mundilfari – MOON-dill-FAR-ee
Sigurðsson – SIG-urth-son
Skuggi – SKOO-gee
Tomirr – tow-MEER
Vigdís – VIG-dees

Places

Akureyri – ACK-yoo-RAY-ree
Corcaigh – CORK-ee (Cork)
Luimneach – LIM-in-eck (Limerick)

Stöng - stowng
Sturlunga – STUR-lung-ah
Þingvöllr – THING-vell-ir
Weiseforth – WEES-e-forth (Wexford)

Other

Allsherjargoði – The chief religious and political leader in medieval Iceland– ALL-share-yar-GO-thee

Alþing – A representative democratic assembly in Iceland – ALL-thing

Bara fínt, en þú? – "I'm well, and you?" – BAH-rah feent, en thoo?

Búðir – Small, temporary building – BOO-theer

Eiginmaður – The husband of – EGG-en-MAY-thur

Eirish – Of Ireland – EY-rish

Galdraskræða – Book of Runes – GAL-drass-KRAY-thah

Grágás – Book of Law – GRAH-gass

Halló, hvernig ertu? – "Hello, how are you?" hall-OH, HVAYR-nig air-TOO?

Hólmgang – Duel – HOLM-gang

Höslur – The area a duel is fought within – HOSS-ler

Huldufólk – Hidden folk/Fairies – HOOL-da-folk

Kæri eiginmaður minn – "My dear husband" – KAY-ree EGG-en-MAY-thur MEEN

Kæri kona mín – "My dear wife" – KAY-ree KOH-nah MEEN

Morgen-gifu – Bridal gift for the morning – MOR-gen GEE-foo

Skaal – A toast for drinking – Skahl

Skíta – Shit – SKEE-tah

Skora a hólm – Marking the duel area – SKOR-ah HOLM

Skrælingi – Wild people – SKRAY-ling-ee
Skyr – A mild, thin yogurt – SKEER
Sýra – cheese – SEE-rah
Þingmenn – Free men who follow a Goði – THING-men
Þings –Gatherings of Þingmenn for legal disputes – THINGS

Chapter One

August 24, 1992, Miami, Florida

No window or door let in a breath of air, and Val grew entombed within a sarcophagus of sweaty doom. The central air conditioner kicked on with a whine, working overtime in the hot, humid August night.

Karl entered with her glass of white wine. She smiled and gulped most of it down, savoring the sharp, cool liquid. "The news just upgraded the hurricane to a hundred and fifty miles an hour."

"Thanks, Karl. I really needed that update."

"We'll be okay, Val. It's not like we're on the coast or anything."

She flashed him a brave smile. They sat silent for a long time, staring at the talking heads on the news wax poetic about the impending disaster.

Val had considered evacuating, but leaving was like giving up. Besides, where would they go? Her father's house? He summered in Vermont and his house in west Florida stood empty. She had no guarantee her father's house would fare any better, and panicked refugees choked all roads north.

The wind rattled the boarded windows.

Val wished someone would tell her everything would be fine, but she was used to being the strong one, the effective one, the motivated one. At least Karl brought her booze. Alcohol helped a lot.

She resisted the temptation to crack the door open to look outside. The sky would be dark and she wouldn't be able to see much. For now, they still had power.

The weatherman's words became hypnotic, and Val drifted into a semi-dozing state from the constant drone of his voice. Her mind shaped the meteorological terms into exotic meanings, sentences that made a certain surreal sense. Puzzled, she jumped from half-understood statement to nonsense.

She startled awake when the sound stopped, along with all the light and the hum of the air conditioning.

"Damn it." She stood, fumbling to find the small flashlight she'd kept by her chair. No, that's a pen. Where did the stupid thing go? Ah, found it. She gripped the heavy cylinder, fresh with four new batteries, and clicked the light on.

"Karl? Are you awake?"

Neither of them had gone to bed as they'd propped the mattress against the sliding glass doors. They both sat in their living room chairs. Karl lay reclined in his, snoring. Val decided to be kind and let him sleep. She made her way to the breaker room in the garage and flipped each off. She didn't want any fires starting when the power came on abruptly.

The howling outside didn't sound like wind. Instead, a train rumbled next to her house. The walls rattled and shook and, suddenly, Val wanted to be somewhere else, anywhere else. Any place but here in this stifling space, waiting for Mother Nature to pluck this laughable cardboard box from its flimsy foundations and toss her into the air like a demented Dorothy.

With a gulp to keep from crying, Val walked to the bathroom and glared at the bathtub, the most secure spot in the entire house. They'd filled the tub with water so they could flush the toilet if they lost power. Unless she wanted to strip down and take a bath, the tub wouldn't be a good hiding place.

At least the bathroom had no windows. No place for the glass to shatter, covering her with a thousand shards, creating a sucking vacuum and pulling her out into the fury. The white noise of the storm outside became a blanket, a shield between her gibbering soul and the panic which threatened to burst through.

She sat on the bathroom floor and curled her arm around the pipes under the sink. They seemed secure and strong, and the comfort kept her tears at bay. She envied Karl his slumber and ignorant bliss.

A crash made the house shudder, and she whimpered. Val hadn't been a religious person for many years. However, her Catholic childhood resurged through her fear, and she prayed under her breath. Hail, Holy Queen, Mother of mercy, our life, our sweetness and our hope. To thee do we cry, poor banished children of—

Another crash heralded shattering glass somewhere. Had a window broken? They'd covered all the windows except the tiny ones in the back of the garage. They hadn't found enough wood, and the outside of the garage was stucco. To nail anything over that would have damaged the wall. If that window broke, not much would be damaged in the garage—unless the break let wind get in and yank their house from its foundations.

Val wished Karl would wake. She wanted him to hold her and tell her they'd be fine. But rousing him would be unfair. Let him sleep through the worst.

Crash! Slam! Val cried unashamedly now. She gave up trying to identify the sounds or analyze what they meant. She only prayed over and over they would survive this horrible storm.

With a bizarre suddenness, the noise halted. The pressure still pounded in her head, but the wind ceased. The stillness and quiet became unnerving.

Val kept waiting for something new to happen, but the stillness grew until the pressure became an oppressive weight upon her soul. The soundless air became a living thing, wrapping around her like a stifling wool blanket. The silence grew worse than the storm's din had been, more suffocating than she'd ever experienced before.

She needed to escape, to be outside. Surely the eye of the storm had arrived. With a curse at her idiocy, she searched for the small transistor radio they'd bought and turned the dial until the crackling resolved into sound.

The first station aired nothing but prayers. She moved the dial into the FM range and tuned to her favorite rock station, WSHE. They should be broadcasting news on every local frequency rather than music.

After fiddling with the dial, past the ironic tunes of "Rock You Like a Hurricane" and "Riding the Storm Out"—what psychopathic DJs had chosen these?—the somnolent tones of an older weatherman said something about pressure and storm surge, and she fine-tuned the dial until the signal came in clear.

"The eye just passed over Homestead Air Force Base…" Homestead lie miles south of her. Could the eye be that large? The eye marked the greatest swath of destruction from a hurricane. The sudden increase of full-speed winds on the opposite side of the eye-wall would be devastating, much worse than the gradual increase in wind speeds on the other side. If no wind blew outside, she must be in the eye. But how far from the edge? If they sat near the northern edge, the winds would return with ruinous speed at any time.

As much as she needed to get a breath of fresh air, she didn't want to risk opening her sealed house to the danger of the monster storm.

Instead of stewing about a decision she'd already made, she paced. Val walked from boarded window to boarded window, flashing her light on each one to ensure each board remained firmly in place. Thankfully, she'd double-checked Karl's work on the boards on Saturday; otherwise she'd worry herself sick over the possibility of them coming off. She would still worry, but at least she had confidence in their sturdiness.

She should have left the radio on, something to fill the dead silence. No, we should conserve the batteries. The power may not be on for days.

When the tempest returned, the storm roared with furious vengeance, pummeling the wooden sides of the house with violent rage. The freight train returned, barreling toward her with mindless menace. With a sudden panic, Val ran back to the bathroom and almost jumped in the tub, wet clothes be damned.

Another object slammed into the wall outside. The sickening screech of wood and metal filled the room.

Damn! How the ever-living hell did Karl sleep through this cacophony?

She'd best go wake him and bring him into the safer room.

With great trepidation, she emerged from the small, dark room and found Karl, still snoring in his lounge chair.

"Karl? Karl, wake up. We need to go to the bathroom."

He didn't open his eyes but mumbled. "What? What do you mean, we? I can go to the bathroom by myself. I don't need your help."

She shook him again. "Wake up, Karl! The storm is getting worse. We have to move somewhere safer. Get up!"

Reluctantly, he grumbled and tumbled out of the lounger, not bothering to push the footrest down. He stumbled into the bathroom with her and they sat on the cool tile floor.

He squinted at the full tub. "You woke me for this?"

A crash and a sickeningly long creak shut him up.

More crashes, and the freight-train wind hit again. A huge whomp made them both flinch, and they laughed off their reaction with a slight tinge of hysteria.

Karl held Val's hand and squeezed. "We'll be fine, Val. This is a good, sturdy house."

She sincerely hoped so, but neither of them were experts in housing construction. She worked as an accountant in a second-chance college, and he worked as a janitor at a different college.

Yet another horrendous crash and ripping sound snatched Val back to reality. Boards creaked and groaned and she smelled something which made her shiver despite the mugginess.

The scent of fresh air.

Somehow, somewhere, the airtight seal had been broken in their house. She held her breath, waiting for all to be blown away by the indiscriminate fury of the storm, away to some place in another world, like the Wonderful Land of Oz. With luck, she'd get dropped at Disneyworld, or better yet, Key West. They had plenty of parties and alcohol in Key West. She'd party her troubles away and forget stress from work, a destroyed house, and a marriage with more stress than love.

The air increased, and she squeezed Karl's hand more tightly. Why hadn't they evacuated? They might have headed north to safety. Karl's ex-wife, Marjoree, and his son, lived in Georgia. Val detested the manipulative bitch, but better staying with them than dead by drowning or a house crashing on their heads.

The wall of sound seemed to be moving away from them. She breathed a little easier.

Hours later, she painfully uncramped herself from a sitting position. More time passed before she mustered enough courage to open the bathroom door and survey the damage. Before she did, she sent up a brief prayer of heartfelt thanks for their survival. They weren't out of the woods yet, but they hadn't been blown away, either.

The wind had died to an almost inaudible whine. Did she want to see the damage? Did she want to open that door and see everything she owned in tatters? Perhaps nothing more than a couple roof tiles cracked, or the door from the garage broken open. She knew the window of the garage had broken earlier.

With a deep breath, she put her hand on the bathroom doorknob and twisted.

The door wouldn't open.

With a grunt, she shoved shoulder on the door. She gained an inch. Her panic rose. "Karl, I need help!"

Together, with several curses and yells, they pushed the bathroom door open about a foot and squeezed through the crack.

The rain fell in the house.

To be fair, the rain fell outside the house, too. But since she could see the clouds above, the difference seemed irrelevant.

Val didn't know why the bit of ceiling remained over the bathroom. Possibly the braces attaching the tile walls stayed stronger than those to the wooden outside walls. She didn't know and didn't care. The wind still blew, but the rain had almost stopped as she turned in a slow circle.

Ruin surrounded her.

Val crossed herself. "Hail, Holy Queen, Mother of mercy."

As far as she could see, nothing stood higher than her head, except for random wooden planks sticking up at rakish angles out of piles of trash. Her mind refused to grasp the swathe of destruction. Nothing looked familiar. Her living room didn't exist. Instead, a pile of furniture, bright swatches of clothing, naked wood, roof shingles, leaves, and unidentifiable debris cut a swath around her and beyond. She glanced down and realized she stood in a pool of water, the strong breeze making it ripple slightly in the dim iron-gray light.

Karl's recliner lay on its side, impaled by a large branch of wood. Val shuddered.

A gust of wind almost pulled her off-balance, and she grabbed Karl's arm. He stood, mesmerized by the complete transformation of everything they had known.

"Where's the car, Val?"

She glanced toward the driveway. Then she remembered she'd parked their car next to the garage for safety. With dubious hope, she gingerly picked her way through the junk to see around the piles. A gleam of red rewarded her. While it didn't look destroyed, the car remained buried under countless chunks of house. The debris might be hers; it might be someone else's.

Her purse. She should find her purse. What had she done with it? Right. They'd put the valuables in safe, presumably waterproof places. The dishwasher, the refrigerator, the stove. Without a proper iron safe, they'd gotten creative.

She searched for the kitchen. Nothing looked the same; she had no frame of reference for the rooms. A pile of electronic spaghetti next to the recliner might have once been the television. There, that looked like the fridge, under that fabric. She'd never seen that pattern. The garment had been ripped in many places, but the old-fashioned flower print flashed bright in the dim light.

She yanked it down and patted the fridge, thankful to find something where it should be. Next to the fridge stood the dishwasher, which she jerked open. She found her purse inside, safe and sound. Her wallet, social security card, passport, credit cards, car keys; all she needed to get by in modern life. If she'd been thinking more clearly, she would have kept her purse close.

She handed Karl his own wallet and surveyed the area. She couldn't even see their bed. It should have been twenty feet that way, under a pile of branches.

"Karl, I think we should excavate the car. If we can get out of here, we should head north. There's no way we can sleep here tonight, so we need a hotel room." Karl looked at her dubiously, frowning and wrinkling up his eyes. He always did that when he thought hard. "What?"

"I don't think we're driving out of here."

She turned to look where he pointed and let out a low whistle. He didn't exaggerate.

Country Walk had been full of tall trees. All of those trees, it seemed, now lie in the road. Big, thick pines crisscrossed the roads in all directions.

Val tossed her hands into the air. "Great. Just great! I have no idea what we should do."

She sat on the ground, squishing in the water, and burst into tears. Val sobbed hard, unable to stop, even when Karl came over and put his arm around her in awkward consolation.

She cried in frustration and fear. She cried for her future. She cried for all the things she had just lost, so many things she couldn't even take a mental inventory. Everything gone— everything. All her furniture, toys from her childhood, her photographs, her mother's favorite shirt. Everything destroyed in a thunderous maelstrom.

When she finally felt cried out, voices intruded upon her misery.

Her next-door neighbors, Jerry and Clara, picked their way over. "Hey, Val! Are you two okay?"

She nodded, pulling herself to her feet. Her bottom got soaking wet. She didn't care. Everything had gotten soaking wet. She gripped Karl's hand. "Safe and sound, at least our bodies. Our house, on the other hand… well, our bathroom is still standing!"

Her quip elicited laughter tinged with more than a bit of hysteria from them all. It went on much too long.

Val noticed Jerry held Clara's hand tightly. "Our garage came through fine, and we had that weird little cellar we used for wine. That's where we hid. Luckily, it's tile-lined, so no water came in."

Val surveyed the surreally blank horizon. "So, what's the plan?"

No one said a thing. They glanced back and forth at each other with blank expressions.

Clara snapped her brightly manicured fingers. "Well, they have to send FEMA in, right?"

Karl asked, "What's FEMA?"

Val rolled her eyes, but Jerry saved her from answering. "It's the Federal Emergency Management Agency. They take care of folks after disasters like this."

Val looked around, spreading her arms. "How the hell are they going to get anything to us?"

Clara smiled. "Good question. They'll probably set up some central distribution center. Maybe someplace like the Walmart down the road. Something with a big parking lot and easy access."

Karl's eyes lit up. "Maybe they'll send in helicopters!"

Val glared at Karl. "Easy access. Right."

With a chuckle, Clara shrugged and raised her hands, palms up. "Okay, relatively easy access. Sure, there will be a lot of work clearing the roads, and it may take a while for them to get out to us. But… can you hear that?"

They all listened while the unmistakable roar of a chainsaw cut through the neighborhood.

* * *

Two days before, Val had yanked the soaked hand towel from her belt and mopped uselessly at her face. She looked out through the Miami neighborhood at countless other would-be handymen sealing their homes. The endless tattoo of hammers rang through the humid, tree-lined suburban street.

Through sweat-blinded eyes, she squinted at her husband, who perched on a ladder and held a piece of plywood over the living room window. "About a foot lower on the right. No, Karl, lower! Don't drop the wood! Just hold it like that; I'll hammer the damn nails myself."

She snatched the hammer from where Karl had tossed it on the ground earlier, fished in the bucket for three thick, straight nails and hammered them in place along the bottom edge of the wood. They rented the place, but the landlord said he didn't care if they put up wood for the storm. He owned ten other properties in the complex, so she didn't expect him to do any preparations himself.

Val studied the edges. "Come on, get down. I'll take care of the top." The phone rang in the house. "Oh, damn." She handed the hammer to Karl and rushed inside. Her father had the flu so any phone call might be important.

The wireless receiver slipped in her sweaty hand. "Hello?" Her boss sounded flustered. "Val? I need you to come in to work today."

She swept back the strands of blonde hair which escaped her ponytail. "Kim, what the ever-living hell? Today's Saturday, and in case you haven't heard, we've got a huge damn hurricane barreling down on us!"

"Exactly. It's all hands on deck at the college. We're trying to secure everything in case the storm hits this far north."

Val considered all the things she still needed to do. Karl hadn't found nearly enough plywood to cover the windows. Home Depot and Lowes ran out quickly. The deck furniture should be pulled in. She had no water, no ice, no supplies. Hell, did she even have a non-electric can-opener?

"Fine, I'll be in shortly." She slammed the phone down with a twinge of guilt. This crap wasn't Kim's fault. No, this idiocracy would have come from the college administration. You'll never find a more wretched hive of scum and villainy.

Karl still struggled with the nails. "Hey, hon. I need to go into work for a bit. I'll be back soon. When you're done with that window, why don't you find a safe place for the deck furniture?"

She didn't live far from work, but the normal half hour commute took almost an hour and a half. Northbound routes looked stuffed with Floridians fleeing the storm. For a dreadful moment, Val considered blowing work off and heading north, damn Karl and damn work and damn the house. However, as a responsible adult, she had things to take care of.

She still needed to go to the store to get gallons of water, chlorine tablets, and canned food. Oh, and a manual can-opener. Val laughed at the people who bought all the bread and milk. When the power failed, milk would quickly go sour and bread? Who cared about bread? Soft bread got rock-hard quickly in south Florida humidity. She'd stock up on crackers, instead. They'd renewed all of Karl's medications on Friday.

Bryan Norcross on Storm Center nattered away on the radio, describing Andrew for the hundredth time as a category three storm, and if they hadn't already evacuated out of the zone, to go now. Val and Karl didn't live in an evacuation zone. Country Walk stood a good ten miles inland, far from any coast. They wouldn't have to worry about storm surge, just wind and rain.

Val pulled into her driveway in the Country Walk neighborhood and stopped just short of the basketball hoop hanging from the garage. The hoop came with the house and reminded Val every day of the children she didn't have. Ignoring the dull ache, she glanced at the front window. Karl had finally nailed the board up. She sighed at the half-dozen bent nails sticking out beside the good ones. Then she noticed the words. In neon pink spray paint, Karl had painted "Karl –n- Val" on the board inside a lopsided heart. Her husband's sweet sentiment melted away her annoyance at the bent nails and a little of her heart.

With a sigh and a half-smile, she juggled the food, drinks, her purse, and the keys as she kicked the car door closed.

She wished she'd asked for a drink holder, but too late for that now. With a few sways and close calls, she got inside and dumped the lot on the small empty spot on the kitchen table.

"Karl! I've got food!"

When she heard no response, she walked to the back door. She did not expect the scene before her.

With a full hurricane coming straight toward them, the common wisdom dictated bringing in or securing anything that might become a projectile in high winds. Karl hadn't taken in the deck chairs or table. Instead, he piled them together in the center of the yard. He'd just finished placing the last chair, turning to her with a look of pride upon his face. He flung his arms out in a satisfied flourish. "All done!"

Val closed her eyes and prayed for patience. She expected none. She didn't pray much, not since she'd escaped her grandmother's church.

"Karl."

He frowned. "What?"

"Karl, what will happen to your Jenga Tower of Plastic when hundred-mile-an-hour winds hit?"

He considered the pile of cheap deck furniture, his brow furrowed. "They'll fall?"

"No, they won't fall. They will fly with great speed and prejudice at our house and our neighbors' houses. They will likely end up in the Wonderful Land of Oz. You'll have killed some poor, innocent witch, and her little dog, Toto, too. Don't you think a safer place would be inside that great, stuffed landfill we call a garage?"

He scratched his stubbly chin. "But what if they don't fit?"

She smiled sweetly, careful not to lose her temper. "Then move boxes from the garage into the house."

He ran his hands through his short, brown hair and cocked his head. "Why don't I just move the furniture into the house?"

She kept calm. "You could. But the furniture is dirty and wet. I'd rather they be in the garage. There are plenty of clean, dry boxes in the garage to move into the spare room."

"Oh, okay."

He began dismantling his creation, but Val said, "Your lunch is getting cold. Eat first, move furniture later."

Some days Val deeply regretted marrying Karl. Other days he acted sweet, funny and romantic. The latter seemed more seldom lately.

She'd been so young when they'd met, just nineteen and a cashier in Walmart. She'd just gotten out of two horrible relationships with 'bad boys', guys who'd treated her like dirt. Karl saw her crying in the break-room one day and comforted her, bringing her a donut and a soda to drown her sorrows in.

Karl stocked the shelves and had a sweet smile. He continued to comfort her and bring her gifts. His pampering seemed so foreign to her that she quickly melted at his childlike charm, despite him being fifteen years her senior. He rarely argued against what she suggested, always doing what she asked. The choice to move in with him seemed easy enough. She basically did as she liked. Val enjoyed being able to control her relationship with Karl as opposed the relationship with her alcoholic parents. A quick, simple marriage became the natural next step. To the last minute, her mother urged Val to change her mind.

On days like these, Val wished she'd listened to her mother.

* * *

The roar of the chainsaws became a constant background growl for the long, humid day after the storm. Val stopped her labor and mopped the profuse perspiration from her brow. Why did such a thing have to occur at the height of the sweaty, humid summer? While she'd spent many hot summer days doing yard work, she always stopped for frequent air conditioner breaks. Now, however, no such breaks could be taken, unless she wasted the precious gas in her car for air conditioning.

She closed her eyes and imagined herself on a simple farm somewhere cool. No trees crossing every road, no sweat dripping from her face, only windswept rolling hills and some sheep grazing near a small farmhouse with grass on the roof. For a sweet, serene moment, she could just about feel that cool, caressing breeze, when the squawk of an annoyed bird snapped her back to reality.

Clara caught her attention and beckoned her over. A crowd of neighbors stood around a new stump, one with a notebook listing their inventory. Among the five closest families, they possessed three chainsaws, plenty of rope, and two big pickup trucks. They parceled out the tools and got crews for clearing a road to the outside world. The road went right by Val and Karl's house to the complex entrance and SW 152nd Street.

The pine trees were so massive it took at least an hour to cut through each one, even with all the crews working at once. Then the sections must be tied up and hauled, using the trucks, to the side of the road. The huge effort had everyone drooping by the time the sun dipped to the horizon.

They'd cleared exactly two trees away, or a half a block. At this rate, they might make it to the main road by Christmas.

After a short conference, they decided to organize a huge barbecue.

Val gave them a half-smile. "The meat we all have in our freezers will go bad soon. We can eat most of it tonight if we cook it on our gas grills, right? If we don't want to waste the propane, there's plenty of wood to burn." This comment elicited another slightly hysterical laugh.

Clara clapped. "We could have a big bonfire, sing, and make s'mores! Anyone have marshmallows?"

Jerry raised his hand. "I have chocolate!"

Val laughed. "Jerry wins! I sure hope someone has graham crackers, 'cuz Saltines don't cut it."

They sifted through piles of debris to find cans, dry wood, whatever they could use. It became sweaty, discouraging work. When she stopped for a rest to wipe her face, Clara sat next to her. "You're not beat yet, are you? Wimp."

With narrowed eyes, Val asked, "Can you put my hair in cornrows like yours?"

"What? You can't be serious. Blondes look silly with cornrows."

Val shook her head. "I couldn't care less about looking silly. I want cool. And I mean temperature cool, not fashion cool. It's either that or I shave my head. That would look a lot sillier, wouldn't it?"

Clara tapped her lip a few times and felt the ends of Val's hair, pulled back into a desperate pony tail. "I suppose I could. I'll need rubber bands. Tiny ones, special made."

Bleakly, Val looked at what used to be Clara's house. "The cornrows won't stay otherwise?"

Her friend shrugged. "For a while, yeah. But not with hard use or with your silky white-girl hair. And have you ever slept in them? It takes getting used to."

"I'll get used to it. Better than sweating so much."

"Right. Wait here and I'll see what I can find."

A half hour later, Clara returned with bits of string. "These'll do for now. I'll keep my eyes out for bands. Sit."

Later on, Val patted her hair, proud of her new 'do. Her head felt much lighter, letting the breeze hit her scalp and keeping her cool. Well, as cool as one can be in the south Florida summer, at least.

Struck by a thought, she looked up. Most summer afternoons in south Florida were plagued by heavy rainfalls, just about mid-afternoon, but no clouds appeared in the sky. The hurricane must have hogged them all. Val smiled at the smidgen of good news.

As they took another break, Val looked around at her neighbors, her friends. Clara and Jerry held hands as they shared a plate of ribs. Karl had brushed back his sweat-soaked brown hair and poured rationed fresh water for each person.

She felt pride in everyone who had pitched in to help. "So, where are we all sleeping tonight?"

Michelle, who lived around the corner, suggested the clubhouse. "We can't drive, but the building is only a few blocks away. The walls aren't in great shape, but they survived better than our houses did. At least the structure is still standing and has a roof. No air conditioning, though. God, I miss air conditioning so much."

Val put her hands on her hips. "Right. Well, we can't have what we can't get. In the meantime, let's gather our food. Anyone have any frozen veggies we can put in a soup pot? Uh, anyone have a soup pot that will withstand an open fire?"

A familiar voice behind her piped up. "Darlin' girl, your savior has arrived!"

Val recognized the voice of her best friend and co-worker. She jumped to hug him, noting his oversized cowboy hat with a colorful beaded headband. "Jorge! What are you doing here? You live blocks away. Did you walk? How's your house?"

"I'm always fine, my house is toast, and I brought wonderful treasures."

He turned and waved his arm in a dramatic flourish over a laden wheelbarrow. "Voila! The fruits of being an SCA member for ten years."

Clara asked, "SCA?"

Absently, Val said, "Society for Creative Anachronisms. They dress up in medieval clothes and hit each other with massive swords."

Jorge shook his finger at her. "How many times have I told you? The SCA is so much more than that. Luckily for us all, my gear remained in my van from the last event. I brought a cooking tripod, an iron pot, all sorts of eating utensils and gear, and three tents. Oh, and one cot, but I'm keeping that for myself. I do need my beauty sleep. I also brought a bunch of hats for everyone to use."

Val grinned. "That's only fair, after you're loaning us the other bounty! By God, for once I'm glad I know you, Jorge! But hats?"

He handed her a pink straw cowboy hat with a bright rainbow beaded band. "I'll remind you of that during the next audit. Hats to keep everyone's scalp from getting fried. I have a bunch because I make hatbands, so I'm lending my stock for the occasion."

She raised an eyebrow, trying the hat on for size. It fell to her nose. "Really. I had no idea you were an 'arteest.'"

He shrugged. "I have fun making them. I use one of those little Indian bead looms, and the work goes fast. You should come with me to one of my art shows. Get the full art experience."

"Too many people. Oh! I found something of yours while sifting through things today." She ran to the salvage pile and extracted a shattered photo frame, still holding the photo of him in a rainbow unitard and Elton John sunglasses. "I believe this is you?"

He grinned as he carefully took the fragile memory. "Ah, Fantasy Fest, Key West, three years ago. That was one hell of a party. Have you never been?"

She shook her head. "Looks like quite a party."

"Understatement of the year, chica. Fantasy Fest is a-ma-zing. Even more fun if you're single." He waggled his eyebrows at her and poked her in the ribs. "Why don't you dump your lump of a Karl and come down next Halloween? I'm sure I can find one or two straight guys for you. They aren't exactly thick on the ground during Fantasy Fest, but a couple come along for the spectacle. Some are on a mission to 'fix' the lesbians."

Val grimaced. "Yeah, like that's the sort of guy I'd date. Besides, Karl is sweet."

"Sweet doesn't always cut it, darlin' girl. Who says anything about dating? I'm talking sheer, unadulterated sex, no strings attached."

"Not for me, Jorge, my friend. I'm more the settle down and get fat type. Stop being a drama queen."

He turned his nose up in mock disdain. "Careful who you call a queen in this town, darlin' girl. Besides, you don't mess with genius."

Two of the women fetched their frozen foods while Clara helped Val and Jorge unload his Wheelbarrow of Wonder. The items seemed solid and well-maintained. Jorge brandished an old-fashioned twist can-opener in his gear, but Karl surprised them with a secret. He rubbed a can of corn against the concrete until he squeezed the can, making the lid pop off.

Val stared at her husband. "Where in the name of sweet Jesus did you learn that?"

He shrugged. "At a Civil War re-enactment."

Val tried to set up the tripod without success several times before Jorge laughed and took the iron poles from her. "You don't know the trick."

"Well, no duh! Show me."

"No need to get huffy with me, darlin' girl. Watch and learn."

He inserted one pole into the central ring and braced the metal against his leg as he inserted the second. Holding both steady at the top with one hand, he snapped his fingers for Val to hand him the third pole. She did so, and he put the end in the ring, made certain all three legs stood firmly on the ground and evenly spaced, and backed up with a flourish. "Ta-da!"

"Hmm. And what if someone trips over one end? Does the whole thing fall over?"

He grinned. "Yes, but that's what this is for." He held up a larger iron ring, and carefully placed the circle over the top, bracing the whole contraption. Then he pulled out a chain with two iron S-hooks and placed the addition in the center.

Val frowned. "The pot hangs on that?"

"No, the pot sits on the top. What do you think, Sunshine?"

She gave him a half-smile. "No need to get huffy with me, darlin' boy."

Just then, Karl returned, his entire body dripping with sweat and a huge smile on his face. "We got through to the corner! I'm starved! Where's the food?"

Val looked over the pile of wood, as yet unlit. A glance down the street revealed their two neighbors, each pulling a barbecue grill and a kid's red wagon full of packaged mostly frozen meat. "Dinner might be awhile yet, Karl. Why don't you go wash your face? Or better yet, a sponge bath. Use the water in the bathtub, but don't get in the bathtub."

As one of the few intact rooms left, Val and Karl granted use of the bathroom to everyone as a changing room and washroom. The momentary privacy gave them one tiny morsel of normalcy in the sea of strange.

Karl disappeared into the makeshift outhouse and Jorge began whistling. As soon as she recognized the tune, she scowled at him. "Stop that, Jorge."

"What? It's just a song."

She raised her eyebrows. "What if Karl realizes you're whistling 'If I Only Had a Brain?'"

He waved his hand. "Pfft. I wouldn't whistle where he'd hear."

Val glared at him as she fished in her purse for a pack of matches. She didn't smoke, but Karl did. He tried to quit, but she still kept backup matches for when he needed a cig. She bent to light the fire, but Jorge pulled her away.

The tall man brandished a long-handled lighter and shoved the tip under the pile, clicking several times. A few more clicks and the wood, despite its vague dampness, smoked and flickered.

Val stared at the increasing flames with intense interest. Who would have thought she'd want a fire in the hot Florida summer, even at night? Not that night had fallen yet. The sun drooped west, but darkness remained a while off. Mosquitoes rose with the darkness, dive-bombing each of them at frequent intervals. The deepening blue twilight blanketed the fragmented landscape, making the unusual shapes amorphous and vaguely threatening.

Leaving the fire-making to her friend, Val organized her area a little better. They'd agreed to let the other couples take the tents, as her bathroom had just enough room for her and Karl to sleep in. The dry blankets and pillow Jorge had brought, however, became a delightful luxury. She set them next to the bathroom and looked around at what used to be her kitchen.

Looters might be a distinct possibility. They'd already discussed what protection each person possessed. While Val and Karl owned no guns, she hefted her large cast-iron skillet. Heavy iron worked wonders for cooking, but also made a great weapon in case anyone tried to get into their bathroom during the night. She'd have locked it tight, but a new bathroom lock had been on their list of eventual repairs. Unfortunately, that repair list now grew a teensy bit.

The rest of the men filtered in from the chainsaw gang, also drenched in sticky summer sweat and needing a good wash. Val sent each of them into her bathroom, hoping each would show consideration and keep the room clean and dry.

Jorge stoked the fire and started the barbecues. The candy bars she and Karl shared for breakfast became a distant memory. She thanked God she'd found them in her purse. The canned goods they'd so carefully hoarded in their pantry had landed who-knows-where now. Probably in someone else's backyard. Or lodged in a tree. Since the can-opener also flew away, the point became mostly moot.

The savory aroma of the roasting meat made her mouth water. A full rack of ribs, bacon, and hamburgers sizzled on the grill. The sweet tang of barbecue sauce wafted around them, but she forced herself to wait. Others in the neighborhood thought as they did, from the plumes of fragrant, tantalizing smoke curling up into the still-cloudy deepening sky like the field at a Civil War re-enactment.

To keep herself busy, she sorted through the debris closest to her bathroom hut. Most items were trash, which she carefully piled near the curb. Some actually appeared to be salvageable items. More often she found ruined memories. A twisted bit of plastic that may have been a child's toy. Shards of colored broken glass.

She discovered a couple pieces of her clothes in a shard of her dresser drawer. Three precious pair of underwear, two bras and four pair of socks. Pure gold. She picked up an old-fashioned round tin of hard candy. The tin didn't belong to her, but she wouldn't turn down the unexpected prize. She placed the precious sweets near the communal food pile. Everyone collected any canned foods they found. They'd found mostly beans and canned soups, but those tasted great with barbecue.

After several heart-breaking trips to the trash pile, which now included a soggy mess of her old photographs, a tin box with several of Karl's meticulously painted Civil War miniatures, a cross-stitched pillow she'd made several years ago for her mother, and the shredded remains of her grand-mother's antique bedspread, Val needed to stop. She had no more tears, and the last two days had been a roller-coaster of emotions. She needed to do nothing for a moment. She found a newly cleared spot on the concrete slab and closed her eyes.

"Val! Val, I need you!" Karl's voice sounded panicked.

Great, just what I need right now. With a sigh and a curse, she pulled herself to her feet.

* * *

The silence of the night grew eerie. The normal soundtrack of city life, such as cars passing by or the hum of refrigerator and air conditioning, disappeared. She heard nothing but an occasional gust of wind, the buzz of mosquitoes, or the cry of strange birds. Sometimes other, less-identifiable noises crept through.

Val felt hot, miserable, dirty, and bone-tired from all the work. Karl, despite cutting his thigh with a hand-axe, fell right to sleep. She tossed and turned, trying to find a less miserable position in the hot enclosed space.

At least she had shelter. Most people walked to the clubhouse to sleep. She'd rather surround herself in a familiar place than share with forty people. Jorge set up his cot and tent in his yard. Jerry and Clara borrowed one of his tents. Val and Karl slept in their bathroom.

The barbecue created high hilarity touched with underlying desperation. Everyone became so determined to make the best of the situation, and none wanted to peer into the bleak future.

Jerry and Karl had walked out to the main road and reported trees blocked roads as far as they saw. Country Walk didn't lie near a metropolitan center. The complex nestled deep in the outer suburbs of Miami, miles from any commercial areas. They sat closer to the empty wilderness of the Everglades than anything else. Without a car and cleared roads, no one would drive anywhere for a while.

The pile of salvaged canned goods grew enormous. No one minded when Jerry, a retired cop, took charge of doling out the bounty. Val and Karl stacked their portion in their bathroom, under the sink. She reached out and caressed the cans. Precious food.

She shifted to her other side. Every muscle in her body screamed for comatose rest. Why wouldn't her mind just shut up and let her sleep?

Val pulled up one of her standard sleep scenarios. She'd built several stock situations to imagine herself in. Each scene portrayed innocuous tableaus without stress or danger, so they normally allowed her to drift off into sleep.

The most common one started in a traditional pub in England. She had an attractive young man buy her a drink, and they'd chat. He'd be a minor noble, and they'd fall in love and live happily ever after in a lovely manor house in the Lake District.

Others included sitting on a Caribbean beach and sipping tropical cocktails out of glasses with ridiculous umbrellas. Another dream involved planning how to spend some ridiculous amount of lottery winnings.

None of these worked tonight. The stress of the last few days became stronger than a simple escape fantasy would fix.

She returned instead to that humble farm nestled in cool, rolling hills covered in grass. Several sheep baaed at her, including a mother ewe with three lambs. She glanced around at the small rustic cottage with grass on the roof. Grass? Why grass growing on the roof? Perhaps the turf insulated the house. In her desperate longing for a cool breeze, her imagination made the wind too bitter. She pulled her shawl tighter and huddled against a sudden gale. She squinted into the distance at the mountains surrounding her isolated valley.

A crash and a curse outside made her sit up, cast-iron skillet in hand. She froze, waiting to hear if the intruder would try the door.

Her hand ached with the tight grip on the handle. She got to her feet, careful not to disturb Karl. If he could sleep, she'd be kinder to let him. He possessed no amount of courage or bravado, a characteristic she both liked and hated about him. He acted sweet and gentle, like a puppy. She took charge of their relationship and made all the decisions. Also, his loyalty remained absolute. Sometimes, though, she wished for her husband to take charge, to take responsibility from her shoulders. She wished in vain.

Tonight, she needed to take responsibility.

The intruder cursed again. The night looked pitch dark. No moon shone and even if power flowed to light them, the hurricane had destroyed the street lights.

Val swallowed, waiting for the unknown person to try the door handle.

Minutes later, the handle rattled and opened, revealing a dark outline against the starlit sky.

With a screeching battle cry, Val swung the skillet at his face. She aimed just short as she didn't want to hurt him. She wanted to give a warning and scare him away.

Her ploy worked. He turned with a yelp and ran, falling several times over the debris littering the ground.

With heavy breaths, she scanned for any other intruders. Other than the fleeing shadow, nothing moved.

Karl still slept.

Val shook her head at his enviable ignorant bliss and closed the door again.

How she wished they'd fixed the lock before the storm.

She made several attempts at retrieving her dream of the farm. Soon, Val realized sleep would elude her tonight. With a sigh, she rose, frying pan in hand, and crept outside.

After the stifling claustrophobia of the room, she breathed the fresh, clean air of the night. No matter it remained August in south Florida. No matter she felt sweaty, grimy, and would kill for a hot shower. No matter her life lay in literal shambles around her feet. She stood outside and she breathed.

The stars looked brighter. No electricity meant no light pollution, at least this far in the suburbs. The radio said downtown escaped with little damage, with the worst destruction down in Homestead and Florida City.

"They're pretty, aren't they?"

She whirled around to see someone sitting in the darkness. She recognized Jerry's voice. "I haven't seen the stars that bright since I lived in western Florida, to be honest."

"Come, sit with me and enjoy the night, Val."

She did, and they stargazed for several minutes before he spoke again.

"The guy on the radio said we got hit by a major tornado through here."

She giggled. "Tornado? Did he not know what a hurricane is?"

"No, no, he meant tornado, caused by the hurricane. A T3, I think he said? Regardless, that's why the destruction is so complete here. The rest of this area isn't so bad until you get to where the eye hit."

"But I remember a calm bit. Wouldn't that be the eye?"

"The eye of the tornado, maybe. Not the eye of the hurricane. That landed farther south. I've been in a hurricane eye before, and this didn't feel the same."

She turned to him, though she barely discerned his outline. "You've been in a hurricane before? Here?"

He shook his head. "No, not here. Haiti. Back in my childhood. My dad worked as a doctor. We didn't have much, but we owned more than most. When the storm hit, we had a real cellar to go to. Most folks clung to their clapboard walls. The storm left nothing, nothing at all."

"What did people do? After, I mean?"

He shrugged. "They left, if they could. That's what we did. We moved to Florida, and my dad worked for a hotel for ten years before he sat for his medical certifications here. Then he became a doctor again."

Where would she go to escape this disaster? Her father's house sat in western Florida, but he lived in his Vermont summer home. She didn't want to move back with him, but that may be her only option. She'd be damned if she moved in with Karl's family. They were mostly ex-cons living in Georgia. Or his ex-wife's place.

Val pushed thoughts of the future away each hour, each job, each task. Physical work kept her from worrying about bills. Would she have to pay rent? She'd have a car payment. They couldn't live here for more than a few days, so she'd need to pay rent somewhere. Without being able to even get to her car, how would she earn more money? Hell, she didn't even know if the college survived. She might not even have a job to go to.

She and Jerry sat for a long time, staring into the night. When dawn arrived, the rising sun brought rain.

Some intrepid genius ran from house to house in the sullen morning light with a stack of tarps. Where the tarps came from, Val didn't ask, but she thanked him profusely. The stuff they'd been able to salvage, mostly clothing and metal bits, they safely shut in the trunk of her car. However, endless junk piles remained to sift through, to search for scarce treasure. They might salvage more items if they minimized the rain damage.

She thanked God above her car remained almost unscathed. The small car had some serious dents and dings with one window cracked, but once they'd cleared the branches off, she realized one huge branch had protected the car. The limbs cupped the vehicle like a wooden hand.

Not that she'd drive anywhere yet. The complex remained boxed in.

What was today? Wednesday? Thursday? No word came yet of FEMA or supplies. Each person took a shift on the radio, hoping to glean information, but they only heard help would be 'on the way' and the National Guard would be mobilized. Supplies were available, but no one said where or how to get to them.

Several of the men embarked upon another scouting mission to the main road and possibly beyond. Perhaps they'd find road crews, or at least someone with more information.

In the meantime, everyone sifted through their shredded lives.

In the early afternoon, Val stopped and pulled open a can of tuna. Using a precious fork, she shoved the disgusting meat into her mouth, forcing herself to chew. She detested tuna, but the amount of physical work she'd been doing required lots of protein and lots of water. She needed carbs, too, but bread remained hard to come by. Cans of beans abounded, but she should share those with Karl. He worked harder and needed carbs as much, if not more so, than she did.

With a deep sigh, she saved the can and wiped the fork clean. She glanced at her current pile. Why did she think she'd find anything worth salvaging? The only clothes she'd found had been waterlogged and some had already mildewed. Still, she owned no other clothes. Rinsing the cloth with rain water would have to do, as clean water remained too precious to waste.

She wanted to hit something. She wanted to scream at the futility of this, at everything, at the world. And why shouldn't she?

While clenching her fists until her ragged nails cut into her palms, she let out a bestial howl, echoing across the complex. Several people stopped to watch her, but when she did nothing else, they shrugged and returned to their own tasks.

Everyone evidently understood her rage. Someone else might do the same a little later.

The scream did little good in the grand scheme of things, but at least she felt better for having screamed.

That evening, they organized yet another barbecue. Some frozen food remained, as folks carefully opened their freezers and refrigerators, but such sustenance would soon run out.

When Jorge handed her a plate of grouper, she curled her lip.

"Eat and be thankful, darlin' girl. I know you hate fish, but we need to eat the seafood first. Fish goes bad more quickly. Just be glad your neighbors made a good haul this spring."

"I'd rather he hunted so we feasted on venison."

Jorge laughed. "You'd eat Bambi? You cruel carnivore. Besides, when have you seen deer around here?"

She chewed a piece of her grouper. "What about Key Deer?"

"Those things that look like little lost dogs? They ain't got enough meat."

"Better that than this."

He waggled his finger at her plate. "Gift horse. Mouth."

She grimaced. "I'd eat a horse first."

Just then, Karl cursed and hopped around on one foot. "Ow! Ow! Ow!"

Val closed her eyes and prayed for patience. Now what?

Clara came to the rescue and poured water on his burning toe. He must have dropped a coal out of the barbecue somehow. He possessed a special talent for clumsiness. Val hoped she used dirty water and not precious drinking water.

"You need a break, Val."

Jorge stared at her with an unusually serious expression. "No shit, Sherlock. What's your first clue?"

"Yeah, yeah, I know, we all do. But not just from this." He swept his arm around the barbecue circle. "I mean from your dear, beloved husband, there."

She rolled her eyes. "Do you know what happens if I leave him alone for a week?"

"Anything worse than what's already happened here?"

Val tried not to laugh but the repressed sound became a slightly hysterical giggle. "Okay, fair enough. What do you suggest?"

"Come with me to the next SCA event. You might have fun."

"Really? You've invited me before. You know what my answer is."

"That your idea of 'roughing it' would be a hotel with no room service. This experience might change your attitude."

She glanced at the barbecue, the bathroom, and the makeshift meal. "Fair point. Not right away, though. Give us some time to recover, yeah?"

A raucous screech from behind them made Val jump. She grabbed a can of beans, holding the weapon ready, but no one emerged from the still-twisted, partially denuded bushes. Val glanced at Karl and Jorge, but they shrugged.

She'd finally relaxed when the form exploded from cover, heading straight for the barbecue. The scrawny chimp screamed and beat its chest. Faster than she could credit, the simian ran to the meat, grabbed a chunk, and disappeared into the trees again.

Karl asked, "What the ever-living hell was that?"

Jorge frowned. "That, my friend, is the advantage of living near the zoo. The wildlife is so close, it's surreal."

Chapter Two

The fifth day after Andrew, helicopters passed overhead. Karl identified them as Hueys, some with double rotors. The news on the radio promised airdropped supplies to distribution centers in Homestead. Val understood Homestead had been hit harder, but she still felt neglected. Homestead already had an air base with plenty of supplies.

Finally, news came that FEMA set up a supply depot at an elementary school nearby. However, "nearby" meant six miles east. Still, a six-mile walk for water, ice, and medicine didn't sound too bad. Matches ran low and Jorge's lighter broke.

Karl and several others traveled daily for their handout, pushing wheelbarrows and pulling wagons to return with the loot. One guy rigged his bicycle with a wheelbarrow like a semi-trailer contraption. Several National Guard Humvees came in with boxes of food, water, blankets, and other necessities.

They received checks for clothing but no bank existed to cash them and no store opened to sell anything. Postal service didn't come to collect bill payments, even if any mailboxes stood. Like everything else salvageable, the checks went into the car, the only secure place.

The one thing they didn't have, which Karl desperately needed, was medicine.

Her husband bore several conditions, including a wonky thyroid and a tendency for his spine to grow random polyps. He'd been in and out of the hospital for various surgeries most of his life. He needed his thyroid meds every day and they had used most of them already.

As she sifted through yet another pile of stuff, the neighbor down the street waved at her as he walked by, his kid's once-shiny red wagon filled with supplies. How did families with children even handle this? She found this difficult enough with only Karl to look after.

She'd wanted a family but now resigned herself to adopting someday. Karl had a son with his ex-wife, and the boy inherited genetic slush from Karl, including his thyroid problems. Karl decided a long time ago to keep that from happening again and got a vasectomy.

He only told Val about his surgery two months after their wedding, as they laid in bed.

"Didn't you think this information would be important to tell your wife?"

He shrugged. "You don't want to have my kids, Val. I have a crappy body and so does my son. I can't make healthy babies."

She shook with barely suppressed, white-hot rage. "That may be, Karl, but you should have told me."

"We're discussing this now, aren't we?"

She closed her eyes and counted to ten. "Before we got married, Karl. We should have discussed this before. Before we exchanged lifelong vows."

"Not much we can do about that now."

Val clenched her hands, wanting to punch something, anything. She gripped her pillow and threw the soft object at the wall. It fell with an unsatisfying flop.

With a clear memory of her rage, Val gripped the shard of pink plastic she held, the remnants of a pink flamingo yard decoration. She forced herself to relax and decided Karl's decision might have been a good thing at the moment. Val had plenty of time for momentous decisions when they emerged from this crap.

Would they ever emerge? Would they ever rise from the ashes of Andrew, like a bedraggled phoenix in an endless swamp? She cursed and smacked at the five mosquitoes that landed on her arm.

A move to her father's house seemed like the better solution every day. If they ever emerged from this sweaty swamp.

"Val, I made you lunch." Karl handed her a sandwich with real white bread. Sure, the sandwich was the dreaded tuna, but she got real bread. She now understood the need to buy bread before a disaster. She thanked him and savored the treat. The bread must have been part of yesterday's supply run.

"Karl, you've been to my dad's house in Alva. Would you be okay with moving there for a while? Until things get settled here?"

He thought about that for a moment. His eyes darted to their house, the car, and back to her several times before he asked, "Is your dad there?"

She shook her head. "He usually stays in Vermont until the end of September."

He nodded. "Then I wouldn't mind so much. But what about our jobs?"

She shrugged and took another bite of her sandwich. At least he'd put a slice of cheese on it to mask the fishy taste. "I doubt I have a job right now. The college probably has no power, so there's no work. Everything's a mess. You might not have a job now, either. When we get out of here, we'll check on that. If we can take leave, we will. What do you say?"

He nodded slowly. "You sure we can afford all that?"

"We aren't paying rent here, or at my dad's. I have enough savings to get us through a couple months' worth of the other bills. The money from FEMA will help. Then we can reset."

"Sounds fine. Want another sandwich?" He smiled, brandishing the bag of sliced bread.

"Do we have anything other than tuna?"

* * *

Once Val finally returned to work, she discovered things didn't work out as smoothly as she'd hoped. Yes, her college had no power, but she still needed to clean. Karl almost got fired for not coming in or calling, despite being unable to do either for several days.

Kim patted her on the shoulder. "At least the clean-up won't take long. You only got one broken window in here. All three of mine shattered, creating a mini tornado on my desk!"

Val placed a finger on her lip, surveying the damage. Most of the filing cabinets survived, but plant matter and debris draped every surface. Her wooden desk had water damage.

Ironically, Jorge's desk looked relatively unscathed on the far side of the room.

With a deep sigh and a black yard waste bag, she cleaned up yet more junk. Perhaps living in an apartment would be better. She never wanted to clean another leaf or branch again in her life.

Jorge helped her, and when their office appeared passable, they pitched in to help Kim. The job took all day and the weather had gotten no cooler. Since the only windows were on one side of the room, no cross-breeze broke the heat and humidity.

Kim sat on her now cleared desk. "Right. Who's ready for a drink?"

Val raised her hand. "Or seven?"

Jorge hugged her. "I vote nine. At least nine."

"Ah, crap. I've got to check on Karl first. When did they say the phones would get fixed?"

Jorge shook his head. "Not until at least Monday. Maybe longer."

Kim pulled open her desk drawer, waving her cell phone. "What's the number?"

Jorge narrowed his eyes. "That thing works up here? Mine gets no signal at all."

"Your tower must be down. We've got one north of here. Number?"

Val put her hand out for the large boxy object and glared at the device. She'd only used one of these once or twice. She flipped open the bottom, pulled out the thin stick antenna, and punched in the numbers from memory. Three tinny rings crackled as she put the chunky phone to her ear.

"University maintenance."

"I'm calling about my husband, Karl Masterson. When does he need a ride? He didn't know when I dropped him off today."

"Uh… Karl'll be busy 'til at least six."

"Okay, thanks." She hunted for a hang-up button and chose the little red phone icon. Evidently, she chose the right one. She handed the phone back to Kim. "I've got until six. Handy little thing. How much does the phone itself cost you a month?"

"For the phone? No clue. The college bought it. I pay twenty-five dollars a month and a dollar a minute."

Val grimaced. She didn't need another bill. Of course, she had no phone bill this month. They had no phone service. Or phone, for that matter. Or electricity. Or garbage service.

In reality, her car and car insurance were the only bills left until they found a new place to live.

She stood. "I definitely need those drinks. Karl's off at six, so that gives us what, three hours to get toasty?"

Jorge laughed. "More if he comes along!"

She glared at him. "Who do you think will drive our drunken asses home?"

Several vodka-and-cranberries later, Val made a toast. "To friends, to the end, through thick and thin and blowhard hurricanes!"

Jorge clinked his grasshopper to her glass. "Skaal!"

Kim sipped her wine. "What the hell is a skawl? Is that like a shawl?"

Almost snorting his drink, Jorge said, "Skaal is a toast the Norse used to make. They still use 'skaal' in places like Iceland and Norway. The word means 'cheers' or 'good luck'."

Val rolled her eyes and downed the last half of her glass. "Then why not say 'cheers' or 'good luck'? Why do you have to make a history lesson out of everything?"

He shrugged. "Because history is utterly fascinating, and I think everyone should get a piece, whether they like it or not! Hey! Speaking of that—you promised to try out the next SCA event. Trimaris will hold a small event near Zephyrhills in two weeks. You game?"

"Trimaris?"

"The local kingdom. The SCA has kingdoms all around the country, and each one has their own leaders, customs, themes, etc."

Kim caught the bartender's eye and pointed at their glasses for another round. "And they dress as Vikings? Or medieval? I'm confused."

Jorge swigged the last of his drink and pointed his finger at Val. "Medieval is an era, not a culture. But it depends. The general theme of each kingdom is different and can change based on who is in charge. Right now, we're on a Frankish theme, but many folks are getting into Viking kit, so that's probably the next focus."

Despite her scoffing, the details intrigued Val. "Kit?"

"Costume, weapons, feast gear, crafts, language."

"Language? They learn a whole new language?"

Jorge laughed. "Most don't—maybe a few phrases. Some do, though. They really immerse themselves. Language, customs, décor. They make their garb the old way, with bone needles and card weaving."

Kim perked up again at this. "Weaving?"

"I knew that would get your attention! You weave, right? There's an ancient Norse technique called tablet-weaving that's all the rage in the group at the moment. Care to join us in Zephyrhills and take a class?"

Kim narrowed her eyes but didn't say no.

If Kim went, it might be a more enjoyable trip. At least she'd have someone around to hang out with if the history nerds turned out to be insufferable.

The bartender returned with their renewed cocktails and they raised them in a toast. "Skaal!"

* * *

A week later, the move to Kim's in Boca Raton ended up being anticlimactic. Her dad's house in Alva wouldn't be practical, and Kim insisted she had a spare room they should stay in until they got things sorted out. Val hated the concept of living with her boss, even though they were great friends. It seemed wrong to burp and fart in the house of the person who paid her salary. Sex with Karl remained absolutely out of the question, especially on Kim's frilly hand-knit coverlet.

They didn't even need to rent a U-Haul for their stuff, as everything salvageable fit in their car. With a wave to Jorge, Val aimed north and drove.

With Miami traffic, she had a good hours' drive to Kim's house on the county border. Everyone had manicured gardens and pools. Val instantly felt like an interloper. Karl, they'd probably arrest on sight as a criminal element.

When they pulled into the complex, she punched in the security code, nodded at the ancient gatekeeper, and twisted through several wide streets named for trees until she came to Kim's house.

Kim's home appeared to be a typical south Florida house, with orange wavy tile roof and stucco walls. Obligatory palms stood guard in the front yard with a young orange tree to one side. Under the windows a row of sea grapes grew, their large, round leaves fluttering in the breeze. Either the storm had barely touched this place, or the groundskeepers were ninja.

As they still had no electricity at the office, Kim gave her several large projects and a computer, carefully packed on her back seat, so she could work from the house for a couple days and still earn her pay. Karl hadn't been able to get any leave from his job, so they'd needed a local place to stay. Still, Val had always been the main money-earner in their marriage, so at least she still earned a paycheck.

The community appeared practically deserted. Most residents had summer homes in the north and only came south when the snow fell. Labor Day signaled the switch for most "snowbirds." After the hurricane, thousands of people gave up the ghost and fled the disaster area.

Val supposed she fled as well, at least temporarily. Unless she found a much better paying job in Boca, she would have to return to Miami and her life, eventually. Just now, however, apartments were scarce and expensive with so many displaced people snapping up the few livable homes.

They moved their few things into the guest room and she started her laundry. All her things would benefit from a thorough wash. Once finished, she came into the kitchen where Karl had already heated some of their canned chicken soup.

While she craved something other than food from a can, she smiled and thanked him. The soup steamed, at least, and she didn't need to prepare it. Crackers from Kim's cupboard were a welcome addition.

Kim had been insistent that they help themselves to anything in the pantry, but Val knew she'd have to do some serious shopping. Her boss was a health-food nut, and most everything was organic this and soy-food that. After wrinkling her nose at the almond milk in the fridge, Val decided she would kill for a nice, juicy rare burger piled with cheddar cheese and dill pickles. How do you even milk almonds?

How strange that the tiny things in life, the simple conveniences everyone takes for granted, become a treasured luxury after a disaster. A privileged upbringing could create blinders on the possibility of poverty in the world. While she craved more, this chicken soup and crackers remained a better meal than a huge number of people across history got, even to the present day. Here she stood, ungrateful for the simple pleasure of a balanced, hot meal. Perhaps Jorge had it right, and a little bit of history would be good for everyone.

How would she do if she had to harvest the grain, pound it in a quern, mix it herself, and bake the cracker, like the folks in Jorge's group did? Or if she had to slaughter the chicken, pluck it, cut it and cook it? She'd lived in cities all her life, so she'd never done or even considered such chores. Sure, as a child, she'd gone on the obligatory field trip to a

Women hang tools from the brooches—needles, scissors, awls, whatever they might need during the day. Very handy."

"Very ridiculous. I'll snag on everything I walk by. These will fall off the first branch I pass."

He shook his head. "Everything is handmade and sturdy. Trust me."

Val narrowed her eyes. "How can I possibly trust you when you're wearing that? You look like an extra from a bad movie."

He wore a long, striped, belted tunic, breeks, and leather flat boots that wrapped around his calves and tied over his breeks. "No, I look like an extra in a good movie. Were you expecting a horned helmet, perhaps?"

She snorted, but he continued. "Horned helmets are a fabrication of Wagner, nothing historical. Besides, horns are quite impractical." He touched her brooch for emphasis.

"Yeah, whatever. So, what goes on at this thing, and what am I expected to do? Did Kim say she'd be there?"

"Your only duty is to smile and say hello when greeted. And Kim said she'd try; that's all I could get from her. She's working on some big project."

"Great. Is there some super-secret nerd greeting I'm supposed to use?"

"Sure, I'll teach it to you. It's Icelandic."

Her eyes widened. "Icelandic? Are you fucking kidding me? I can't learn Icelandic!"

Jorge cackled until she growled at him, finally relenting. "No, there's no super-secret nerd greeting. 'Hello' works fine. Though if you want to greet them in Icelandic, 'Hi' will do."

She crossed her arms, tangling them in the strings of beads. "Hi? That's Icelandic?"

"Well, it's pronounced 'Hi,' but it's spelled H-E-J." He shrugged. "Your choice."

"Does everyone do the Viking thing?"

Jorge shook his head. "No, that's just me and my group. And really, it's Norse, not Viking. Viking is something you do, raiding, not something you are. Some prefer Frankish, or Norman. Some prefer Japanese. One guy dresses as an American Indian. As long as it's pre-1600, though, any culture is fair game. No fantasy or Tolkien stuff, just historical."

"Any other rules I should learn?"

"You'll want to choose a persona fairly quickly, so folks can greet you with your persona name. I'm Ragnar." He puffed his chest up. "My character is based on a possibly historical Norseman that may or may not have been the first to raid England."

"Right. How about if I go by Valeria?"

He scowled. "That's your real name."

She put her hands on her hips and scowled right back. "Yeah, and? Is there a rule against that?"

"No, but it's unimaginative at best. Besides, you'd have to spell it differently in Icelandic. Hmm. How about Vigdís? That means 'war goddess,' I think. I'll check with Snorri."

She giggled. "What? Snoring?"

"Snorri is our lore-keeper and historian. His character is based on a real historian from twelfth century Iceland. He knows all the things about the period. Music, art, farm life, whatever. He even speaks fluent Icelandic. He'd be the person to ask about your name."

She took a deep breath. "I guess we'd best get this over with."

They signed in and paid at the gate. Val nodded in silent greeting to those Jorge enthusiastically introduced her to.

Val had lived in cities and towns all her life and her parents had never enjoyed camping. Her mother's idea of roughing it was a hotel with no room service. Before the hurricane, Val would never have even considered actually camping, with a real tent, sleeping bag, campfires, and all that. Now here she was, not only camping, but dressing up in costume for the occasion.

Perhaps she really was crazy, after all.

She had to admit, the site impressed her. Dozens of authentic-looking campsites dotted the glade, and they'd decorated the inside of the modern building with shields and tapestries, giving the décor a medieval flavor. Several clusters of people worked on crafts, cooking, and weapons-training. A forge billowed smoke and a dozen cooking pits exuded savory aromas.

After surveying the offerings and looking at the schedule, Val pointed to one listing. "Where's the tablet-weaving? That looked relatively simple to learn."

Jorge led her to a small group of older women. "Hej, all. This is Vigdís. This is her first hour of her first SCA event. She's interested in what you're crafting. Be kind to her."

Before Val could protest, Jorge scooted away with a cheery wave, and she turned to behold the sea of strange faces before her. One dark-haired woman in an apron dress patted her bench. "Come sit next to me, Vigdís, and velkominn. My

53

name is Astriðr Sægeirsdottir. I won't bite too hard. I'll show you what we're doing."

Astriðr held out the project in her hand. "The cards hold the yarn like this, and if I flip it so, it acts as if we're switching the threads in a loom, just on a smaller scale." She flipped her card several times, first diagonally and then horizontally. After four cycles of the same pattern of flips, she handed it to Val.

"Ready to try?"

Val took the proffered card and flipped it as Astriðr had. Before she realized, she'd completed several inches of the weaving. She held her creation up with much more pride than she'd expected.

"Well done! Want me to set up a new project for you? That way you can decide on the colors and pattern."

Val nodded. "I'd better stick to the pattern I've learned, or I'll get confused. Which colors are available? Should I have brought yarn?"

Astriðr pulled out a large basket of rolled yarn. "I've got plenty, all natural fibers. I'm happy to share." She had many muted shades of orange, red, yellow, green, and blue. None were bright or strong. It looked like a watercolor painting, something from one of the romantic English masters like Turner or Constable.

Val chose a pale yellow and a deep rusty red, handing them to Astriðr, who pulled the ends and set them into the card.

After several hours, Val decided she enjoyed this. Her new friend, Astriðr, showed her several variations on the tablet-weaving pattern. When she finished her first ten inches of trim, she grinned and handed the trim to Astriðr.

Astriðr held it up to show everyone else. "This would work well on the hem of the apron dress you're wearing now."

"Oh, this isn't mine. Jorge borrowed it for me."

"Then we must remedy that!"

Val jumped as Kim's voice spoke in her ear. "Always knew you had it in you. I guess you had to go old school to discover it yourself."

Val twisted her head around. "Even you might learn something. Have a seat." She patted the bench next to her.

"In a moment. Have you got a sec?" Kim's mouth set into a thin line, and Val got up with a quick apology to Astriðr.

After they'd walked from the group to the tree line, Val glanced at Kim. "What's up? You have news. Is it good news or bad news?"

She waggled her hand. "A little from column A, a little from column B. Good news for me. You might see it as bad news for you."

Val gritted her teeth and narrowed her eyes. She needed no more bad news. Enough was enough already.

"Remember when I called out most of the spring?"

Val clenched her fists. "Yeah, for your cancer treatments. But you beat it, right? That's not the bad news, is it? That it's back?"

"No, no—nothing like that. My scans are still clear. They won't rule it as remission until I'm clear for five years, but so far so good. But my news relates to my time off."

Val gritted her teeth and waited for the rest.

"The college wrote me up for 'excessive absenteeism,' and wants to dock my pay."

Val's face grew warm. "Are you fucking serious? You had cancer, for God's sake! You could have died!"

"That doesn't matter to them. They want to squeeze me out, and this is how they're trying to do it. I've never really gotten along with the dean. It's all a cover story, anyhow. Well, I'm doing three things. First, I'm resigning. Second, I'm moving to my parents' farm in Alabama. Third, I'll be opening an alpaca farm and fiber shop."

Val couldn't get her head around that surreal list. Instead, she focused on her rage. "And four, you'll be suing the crap out of the college for wrongful termination. Right? Tell me I'm right."

Kim sighed. "Yes, I'll be suing them. But that's still a shot in the dark. This is an employment-at-will state. They really don't need a reason to fire me, but they want things to appear fair."

"This is anything but fair. Wait, did you say alpaca farm? What the ever-living hell?"

Kim chuckled and patted Val on the back. "Yup, alpacas. Fuzzy animals, like soft llamas. They're fur is all the rage in weaving circles."

"I've heard of them, I've just never heard of anyone farming them. Alabama. Huh. Oh, crap."

"Yeah. That leaves you alone without a guardian at work or a place to stay. I promise I'll do all I can to keep the dean off your back before I leave."

Val closed her eyes. "I'd appreciate that. When does it hit the fan?"

"You've still got a month before anyone else knows. Will that give you enough time to get things together and move back in town? I'll need help preparing the office for my departure."

"Yeah, that should be enough time. What will you need help with?"

"Just getting things in order since they have no one to replace me. So the whole office doesn't fall into bits when I leave."

"Aye, aye, captain. I'll keep the ship going. Me and Jorge. Wait, you aren't stealing Jorge, too, are you?"

Kim's eyes widened. "No, you can keep Jorge. Can you imagine him in rural Alabama?"

Val giggled. "I can barely picture him here, in rural Florida."

"Anyway, I can't stay too long tonight, but I wanted to tell you both outside the office. I won't be home tonight, as I've got to travel north to arrange things. I'm off to find Jorge."

With a startled nod, Val waved as Kim hurried away. She definitely seemed happier than she'd been in months. This decision must have taken a lot of worry off her shoulders. At least her granddaughter, Bailey, would grow up on a farm. She'd have a much better childhood than here.

Val searched through five different campsites before she spied Jorge talking to two blond men—one tall, lovely young man with long hair, and one tall with muscular shoulders. The slimmer man matched the description Jorge had given her before. He certainly looked the Icelandic part.

Jorge gestured her closer.

The thin blond man said, "I'll come by your camp later to pick that up, Hávaldr. See you then."

The muscular man waved and walked away.

57

Jorge clapped a hand on her shoulder. "Perfect, just the woman I was looking for! Vigdís, I'm pleased to introduce Snorri Sturluson, historian, poet, and law-speaker. If there is something he doesn't know about Icelandic life, I've yet to discover it."

Snorri bowed over her hand and she felt her color rise. "Pleased to meet you, Snorri."

The other man flipped his hand out in a gallant flourish. "The pleasure is positively all mine, my lady. I understand you are but recently inducted into the Kingdom of Trimaris?"

She nodded. "I'm new to the whole re-enactment culture. I mean, my husband has been doing Civil War stuff since long before I met him, but I never got interested in that period. Medieval Iceland, however, has caught my curiosity with a vengeance."

Snorri smiled, showing even white teeth. "Ragnar here mentioned that you might have a few questions beyond his own talents to answer, so I set aside some time to be available for them this weekend."

Jorge chuckled and clapped her on the shoulder. "I figured that would be a short introduction. Come on, I've got a small table set up at my camp. You can squeeze him dry of all his esoteric knowledge to your heart's content while I go in search of mead!"

Snorri held up a drinking horn dangling from a harness on his belt. "Payment for services rendered?"

Jorge took it with a smile. "Vigdís? Shall I fill yours as well?"

She handed him her drinking horn. "My first question is where did you get that sweet drinking horn harness?"

Chapter Three

More than a month later, Kim announced her departure, but at least that gave Jorge and Val time to plan a going-away party. In typical Jorge style, they headed to South Beach for a Friday night of alcohol and bad decisions.

After endless searching, they finally found a parking spot not too many blocks away and walked to the main strip.

This tiny enclave of glitz had become a bizarre phenomenon. Even during the day, a strange dichotomy existed between the resident extremes. Ragged homeless people walked next to stunning supermodels. Beautiful art deco architecture next to ugly modern block condos.

Val had been here before, but the area had grown in quickly over the last few years from boarded up derelicts to the current gentrified hot spot, a veritable den of iniquity and flash. Still, she didn't care to get shit-faced drunk. She enjoyed people-watching far more. South Beach was a veritable feast for any people-watcher.

When night fell, however, SoBe became a playground for sybaritic delight and outrageous flamboyance.

The neon lights drowned out the paler art deco colors with garish screams and brash flash. Drag queens strutted on stage in feathers and leathers. The Beautiful People gathered on every corner, smoking cigarettes, smoking joints, and brandishing fruity drinks.

Jorge had told them their goal for the night—a drag show. He pulled them along like a twisted kindergarten teacher on a field trip as they wended their way through the wandering sidewalk showcase and into a dim room, pumping with house music.

They'd found a small round table when the waiter came by. The muscular, ebony-skinned man wore bright red short-shorts and a white tank top that glowed in the black light. Jorge gave him a knowing smile and his phone number as he took their drink order.

A loud boom shook the room and Val whimpered and jumped off her chair, almost diving under the table. With a nervous glance, she noticed the stage lights raise and performers strut onto the stage. After giving a sheepish giggle, she sat again, trying to calm her racing heart.

Val drank her cocktail too fast and her face turned numb. Jorge called the waiter to refill her glass right away. They made several toasts, including one for Kim and her new venture, one for Jorge's newest one-night-stand-candidate, and one for Val, just because. Val pushed down tears for Kim's leaving, and for the most part, succeeded. The small splash of salt water didn't dilute her drinks appreciably.

The rest of the night became a deafening blur. She didn't even remember the cab drive home.

On Saturday morning, it took several minutes of reorienting to remember her new apartment in North Miami Beach, the place she'd just moved into. Yes, Karl lay next to her, snoring loud enough to wake the dead. Yes, she was positively hung over. In fact, her stomach told her in no uncertain terms she'd better stay close to the toilet.

With a groan and a hand on her temple, she stumbled to the bathroom and splashed water on her face. She stared at her expression in the mirror, drawn and ashen with bags big enough to haul an elephant under her still-bloodshot eyes. Wonderful.

She'd brought some work home, but it could wait until later. The college hadn't replaced Kim, so all her tasks were assigned to Jorge and Val. Now that Val lived back in town, she'd probably be working twelve-hour days just to keep up with the new workload.

She would definitely need something to escape the stress. Sure, she loved weaving, and the crafts Astriðr taught fascinated her. She met with her new friend to learn more things about Iceland in the twelfth century. She'd moved on from tablet-weaving to embroidery, calligraphy, cloisonné, and even learned basic Icelandic. Still, Val couldn't work on any of this in those waiting times at work, the time between getting the essential project into someone else's hands and the project getting back to her.

Her job was full of hurry-up-and-wait work, where she had to patiently anticipate others doing their part before she could finish her part. Val worked highly efficiently, but she never let her boss realize how efficient. Most days, she drowned in expense reports and payroll spreadsheets, until she cleared her docket; then she had to wait until more work came. She needed something to do in those in-between times.

She might write articles on the craft work, but that didn't really appeal to her. Could she write stories?

Not just one story. She should write a whole novel. They said everyone had a novel in them. She might even write a best-seller and become famous. Val had never considered herself a writer, but hey, how hard could it be?

Once she cooked and reluctantly consumed her breakfast, she told Karl she wanted to go to the library. She had some research to do on writing.

"On writing? Your handwriting is better than mine. Why do you need to research it?"

"Not handwriting, Karl. Writing. Like a book. A novel."

He furrowed his brow. "You want to write a novel?"

She shrugged. "I thought it might be fun to learn how, at any rate. Want to come with me?"

"Sure. I'll browse the Civil War section."

She checked out several books, including one by Dean Koontz and "Elements of Style." She'd also gotten lucky and found several books on Icelandic medieval life, one on living in the year 1000, and a basic language primer. That should keep me busy for at least the weekend.

Karl brought his books to the checkout desk, mostly filled with paintings of Civil War battles, and frowned. "Those look boring."

She shrugged. "Did you expect a lot of pictures when I'm learning about writing?"

He pointed to the Icelandic language primer. "What about this one?"

"Why not? I like learning new stuff. I might write a book set in Iceland."

Several hours later, she suspected he'd been right. The books didn't exactly make riveting reading. Luckily, she already had excellent spelling and grammar. Most of those rules she already used instinctively and didn't have to worry too much. She found the plot and structure information fascinating.

Character arcs, villains, tropes, beats; most of these were new terms to her, and she delved into the world of creating novels.

She picked up the next book in her pile, one on medieval life in Iceland. This one had several drawings of bucolic scenes around cooking hearths, farmsteads, and fishing boats. About halfway through, one illustration set her heart pounding.

The turf-covered roof of the farmhouse looked precisely like the one in her daydreams.

The house had been built in the exact same orientation, same size, same proportion. Three outbuildings ranged behind it, and a saucy sheep poked its head around the corner.

Karl poked her in the shoulder. It took her several moments to reorient her thoughts to the present day.

"What's for dinner?"

She shrugged and eyed the mail in his hand. "Sandwiches, probably. Anything for me?"

He shook his head. "Just a letter from Marjoree."

Val frowned. "What does she want? More money? We already pay her plenty for your son's child support."

"No, nothing like that. She wants me to come up for some play he's in."

"To Georgia? She wants us to go to fucking Georgia for an elementary school play? Is she serious?"

"Me. Not us. He is my son."

Val closed her eyes and counted to ten. In Icelandic. The count helped to calm her. "And how are you going to get up there? I need the car for work."

"I didn't say I wanted to go, I said he's my son."

She clenched her jaw and kept her tone measured. "I realize he's your son. I'm well aware that you have a child, Karl. You don't have to keep saying it. You have a child, and I don't. I'm also well aware that you have obligations to him. But this just isn't practical. If she lived anywhere near a real airport, I'd say you could fly up, but it takes three connections to get close to her in that backwoods town. We're talking at least five hundred dollars for airfare. Do you really think we have that sort of money now? After all the crap with the hurricane?"

He crumpled the letter and threw it at the wall. "Whatever. You asked about the letter. I didn't plan on saying anything."

He stalked off and slammed the door, making Val jump. After her heart calmed, she considered following him to continue the argument, but it wouldn't solve anything. His son remained a constant pain to her. She wanted a child, but Karl had seen to that. Besides, he already had his son.

With a clenched jaw, Val shoved aside the vision of herself holding a baby girl of her very own and dove back into the chapter on subtext.

Later, as she got ready for bed, Val tripped and hit her head on the side of the closet door. Her head exploded in a burst of white light and pain.

"Son of a bitch!" She had to sit down for several minutes as the world spun and her skull throbbed. Gingerly, she touched her scalp. The skin was tender and a lump already formed.

Carefully, Val pulled herself to her feet, using the wall as a bolster. She snuck by Karl, snoring in his recliner. After pulling several cubes of ice from the freezer, she stuck them in a plastic baggie and wrapped the baggie in a hand towel. She held it for at least a half hour before she decided she could sleep.

That night, her dreams filled with Iceland. The story played much more vividly than ever before, like a full cinematic production in Technicolor.

* * *

The next few weeks became a dichotomy of struggle and relief. Kim's absence threw the office into high-stress mode, but at odd moments, Val worked on her novel.

Details from the story came to her at night as she dreamed. Her writing became an exercise in transcription, writing the events that played in her imagination. She even secreted some of her research books in her desk drawer in case she needed information as she wrote.

Her first three attempts at the first chapter, she hated. She deleted the attempts in frustration and pique. The fourth time, though, she considered it good enough to let Jorge read it.

After waiting a good half hour for him to read the five lousy pages of her best efforts, she couldn't wait any longer. "Well? What do you think?"

"Iceland? I'm glad the SCA made such a strong impact on you."

She smiled. "I liked Astriðr and Snorri. Besides, who doesn't want to read a romance set in a barbarian society on the edge of the known world?"

"A romance? That's what you're writing? Wow, talk about irony."

She grimaced. "Shut the hell up. What do you think of the chapter?"

He frowned. "I'm no expert on romances, but this seems overly descriptive. You're describing the character, her back-story, her appearance, but nothing about her feelings, her actions. Shouldn't she be doing something? I mean, you've got her standing at the market while you talk about her. Have her pick up fruit, run into someone, get into an argument, step on a cat, anything. Make her accused of stealing."

"Hmm. Yeah, you're right. She's boring." Val frowned at the computer monitor and gritted her teeth, then pressed delete on the entire document. "Back to the drawing board."

"Why don't you ask Astriðr for some tips? She's written several novels."

"She has? I had no idea! I'll call her."

While Val wrote herself a sticky note, Jorge turned back to her. "Hey, Val? You didn't even give her a name."

She gave him a sheepish grin and took the pages back from him. "Oh, right. Well, it's Vigdís."

He rolled his eyes. "Your own SCA name? Self-fulfillment, much? Well, I can't wait to see what Icelandic barbarian hunk you match yourself up with."

She chuckled. "I'll make him sufficiently tasty, don't worry."

"I'm waiting with bated breath."

She got back to her work for the day. When she had a break, she glanced at her notes from last night's dream and dove into the story.

* * *

Iceland, 1103

Vigdís touched the leather with admiration. It appeared well-tanned and had exquisite designs tooled into its highly buffed surface. Behind her, the hawking cries of fruit-sellers, cheese mongers and metalsmiths faded into a cacophony of buzzing sound. She needed new leather gloves, and these fit perfectly.

She held up her coin purse to ask the seller the price. When he told her, she frowned. They cost more than she hoped to spend, but the sheep had chewed apart one of her old pair. With reluctance, she paid the price and put on her new purchase. The new gloves kept her hands warm and comfortable.

She turned at a shout behind her to spy a horse and cart running through the market at break-neck speed. She scooted behind a bench for protection as the riderless cart barreled through the area, knocking over tables of wares and people alike.

A large blond man jumped and grabbed the horse's harness, speaking to the beast in calm tones. At first, the horse reared, and Vigdís feared for the man's safety. With some cajoling, he soothed the creature with his rich, baritone voice. He walked the horse back to its owner, receiving several pats on his back for his heroic efforts.

* * *

Miami, 1992

A name. She needed a name for her hero. Her story already sounded so trite, so common. Still, this seemed a better start than her first four, so she ran with it. She grabbed one of the library books and flipped through, looking for name samples. One had several of the sagas, and she found one that rolled off her tongue. Hávarr Olafsson—that sounded heroic and hunky enough for her historic romance, right?

Val looked up the meaning of the name. The two parts meant "high warrior." Why not? Tall, blond, strong, and great with horses. What's not to love?

"That isn't a spreadsheet."

Val jumped at Jorge's words. "Damn it, Jorge. Warn a girl, will you?"

He patted her shoulder. "If I can sneak up on you, anyone can. You want the dean to catch you writing when you should be working?"

"You are well aware I can't do anything until that idiot Juana gets her part done. She's in the other room picking her nose while I'm waiting on the report."

"I know that, you know that, and I'm dead certain Juana knows that. But the dean won't know that. You don't want to get in trouble."

Val shrugged. "So, what'll she do, fire me? I'm the only one who knows how to do my job and Kim's job. With Kim gone, she'll be more than fucked if she fires me."

He wrinkled his nose. "That's as may be, but she wouldn't have to make your life pleasant, either."

"Fair enough." Val saved her work and closed the file. "So, when's the next SCA event? I've finally got my outfit sewn, except for the trim on the sleeves. I'm even learning Icelandic. 'Halló, hvernig ertu?'"

"Bara fínt, en þú? And you'll need to learn a lot more than a simple greeting to get by in the SCA."

She grimaced. "It's only been a month. I've got the basic conversation down, numbers, colors, and lots of vocabulary. My grammar sucks, though. Want to practice?"

"Not during work, darlin' girl. Now, pretend to be busy. Someone's coming." He scooted over to his desk and picked up a ledger as if he'd been examining it closely.

The dean didn't enter, but Juana came in with the reports. "Here. I'm going home for the day."

Val glanced at the wall clock, which only said three. She raised her eyebrows at Juana.

The other girl pressed her lips into a thin line and flipped her thick, dark braid behind her shoulder. "You aren't my supervisor. I don't have to tell you why I'm leaving early."

With a huff, she left. Val wanted to take the snotty girl down a few pegs, but she wasn't worth it. Besides, she'd have to take off early herself to drive Karl to the hospital. He had several tests scheduled that afternoon. She'd need to return after, but she still experienced guilt for her truancy.

Oddly, she got guilty for taking time off to take care of necessary medical procedures, but not for writing while at work. Other people waited for her work in the former case but not in the latter. Regardless, she pushed the guilt aside as she grabbed her purse and waved to Jorge.

* * *

Karl acted sullen and silent in the car. They weren't waiting on dire news from the test results, just another colonoscopy to check if his polyps had grown back. He'd been through a dozen such procedures in the six years they'd been married. Val wondered if the colonoscopies would ever prove Karl didn't actually have his head up his ass.

The lab walls were a sickly pale green and smelled of antiseptic. The nurse acted almost as sullen as Karl, and Val suddenly wished herself anywhere but here, playing nursemaid to a petulant, sickly husband, fifteen years her senior. How had she made it to this place in her life? She was twenty-four, educated and intelligent. With her accounting degree, talent in art, and evident talent in learning languages, she'd grown curious and effective. She wanted a family, a life, something that would carry on and be remembered after she died.

With Karl no longer able to father kids, her book would be her child, something others could read to glimpse her creativity and spirit when she'd gone.

While her husband had his tests, she outlined more of her novel. She added subplots, minor characters, and motivations, both for her main character and the love interest. What about a villain? A mother-in-law? No, that was way too trite. A father-in-law, instead? She'd read that some Icelandic men studied witchcraft, even in the Christian era

70

after 1000 AD. Val might make him a sorcerer. She made a note to find a book on Icelandic sorcery.

When Karl emerged, he looked less sullen than uncomfortable. With a pang of sympathy, she helped him hobble to the car. Colonoscopies were not fun.

After she got Karl settled at home with a protein shake and the TV remote, she hurried back to work, just to find Dean Danelli standing over her empty desk in an immaculate designer pink pantsuit.

"How nice of you to come in today, Val."

"I took Karl to a doctor's appointment. I only left for about two hours. Don't worry, I'll still be getting all my work done today."

She pursed her lips. "How many times is that this month? Haven't they figured out what's wrong with him yet?"

"It's not a matter of diagnosis. It's an ongoing genetic issue. He has to have regular procedures." She didn't really want to discuss her husband's health issues with the dean, but she didn't want to get in trouble, either. After booting up her computer, she shuffled papers busily so the dean would leave.

"Can't he take himself? Your husband's a grown man, isn't he?"

"He can't drive after the procedure. He gets sedated."

Dean Danelli made a guttural sound in her throat. "Well, he should just wait until it wears off. I need you here, working on those reports. The board meets tomorrow, and I'll need a chance to review your work before I present them."

She stalked off in a cloud of Chanel No. 5 and Val rolled her eyes. As if she would realize if any of the figures looked wrong to begin with. Dean Danelli was a political person, not a financial one. Val remained convinced the dean couldn't perform basic multiplication.

She'd have Jorge look over her work when she finished. A presentation to the board must be perfect. Her computer had finally warmed up and she glared at the black and green screen.

Several hours later, she cracked her knuckles and stretched her back. There, she'd finished. All sixteen slides of mind-numbing financial graphs. She made a copy on a floppy disk and placed it on Jorge's desk with a sticky note. Please check my figures first thing tomorrow. Thanks! Val.

She glanced at the enormous white clock. Eight. If she went home now, Karl would be asleep already in the recliner. Her evening would involve making dinner and going straight to bed. Instead, she opened her novel document and typed, trying to remember what last night's dream had revealed.

* * *

Iceland, 1103

Several women clustered around the tall, blond hero, but Vigdís held back, not wanting to be part of the crowd. When he finally escaped the throng, he walked to the baker's stall. Vigdís approached the stall with feigned indifference, picking up several barley loaves to sniff the aromatic herbs.

The baker, a dark, portly man, greeted the blond man with a hearty chuckle. "Saved the day again, young Hávarr? I swear, I sometimes think you create disaster just so you can avert it."

72

The man, Hávarr, gave the baker a half-smile. "That's me, a hero worth a thousand sagas. Have you any flatbread back there? My mother asked for yours, in particular. Are you certain you won't share your secret with her?"

The baker pointed to a basket of barley flatbreads and Hávarr took several out. Vigdís also pulled one out and sniffed it. She raised her eyebrows. "Thyme? And turmeric. Where did you find turmeric?"

Hávarr and the baker both stared at her. The baker put his fingers over his lips. "Shh. Don't tell anyone. The last trade mission from Orkney had a supply." The baker winked at her.

The blond man turned to her, one eyebrow raised. She hadn't realized quite how tall he was until she stood next to him. He made her feel like a child. "That's impressive. Are you a baker as well?"

Vigdís shook her head. "Not by trade, no. But I lived in Ireland and have come across several exotic spices in my time. My talents lie more in weaving."

With a gentle touch, he traced his finger along the trim on her sleeve, raising his eyebrows. "It's indeed fine work. I haven't seen trim so intricate before."

The warmth of his touch made Vigdís' heart race, and she lowered her eyes, certain her face flushed bright red at his attention.

* * *

Miami, 1992

Val stopped. She hated it. She hated it with a passion. The dialogue sounded so wooden. Still, if she kept scrapping her work, she'd never get past the first chapter. She'd read somewhere that a horrible first draft remained a thousand times better than no draft at all. Fine. She'd get this horrible first draft done and edit after. She did need to change the name Ireland. Somewhere in her research she'd read it had a different name in the middle ages. Hibernia? Eire?

A glance at the clock showed the hour already half past nine. Damn, I'd better get home. She saved her work and drove the ten miles to her apartment. As expected, Karl snored in his recliner, drool pooling out of the side of his mouth. She tiptoed into the bedroom, surprised to find he'd done the laundry. He'd even folded and put things away. Would wonders never cease?

Just for that, she'd cook him a nice breakfast in the morning.

Her bright, vivid dreams returned as she slept.

* * *

Iceland, 1103

Vigdís returned to her small turf farm, nestled in rolling hills and surrounded by ice-covered mountains and part of a large cluster of farms next to Mount Hekla. About forty families lived in the area, with a large, central farm. The main estate housed a family of at least twenty people, but she'd only met the local goði once, an older man named Olaf Squint-Eye, when she leased the farm.

She'd only come to this place a few months ago, migrating with one of the trading ships from the island of Eire. Her parents had perished from fever, and she met a young man who convinced her to try her luck in a new land.

While she had relative autonomy, she'd had to register as a single female without a male guardian with the priest, Father Ari. He'd been concerned about her safety, but she reassured him she had a blade and would use the weapon if anyone threatened her.

If she entered any contracts, like the lease on her farm, the priest would have to work on her behalf. In Eire, she'd had more freedom, but Connacht contained little arable land. Here in the south of Iceland, the loamy soil would yield better crops. The summer remained shorter, but the land offered more room to expand.

Vigdís unpacked her purchases from the day. She had several of the baker's flatbreads, trusting that Hávarr's mother had good taste. She wondered if they lived on a nearby farm. Several clusters lie within reasonable distance of the market. With a rueful chuckle at her romantic follies, she put the rest of her purchases away. The three good bone needles had been a godsend. Her last one had broken while she repaired her yellow apron dress. Five skeins of wool and one of lovely pale blue linen represented wonderful finds. She frowned at the loom next to the hearth fire. The small Eirish-style loom only made strips about a half arm-span wide. Still, it would serve until she could get a proper local loom.

She walked outside and scattered feed as her chickens clucked at her feet. The three piglets rooted around as she fed them. They looked small now, but they'd grow quickly. Until then, she'd have to purchase her bacon at the market.

Bacon! That's what she'd forgotten. With a curse, she considered another trip today. The market stood at least a two-hour journey from her farmstead. A glance at the sun, dipping halfway down to the horizon, told her another trip wouldn't be wise. She hoped there would still be bacon for purchase on the morrow.

Once she'd fed the animals and cleaned their stalls, she stoked up her dung fire and sat to her evening weaving.

She hadn't boasted about her skill. Her work had been renowned in Eire, with folks offering a premium price for her work, especially her fanciful embroidery. Perhaps she would have been better off finding a rich patron instead of escaping to this new land. But the man who had pursued her, Padraig, had been ruthless, determined, and cruel. She didn't doubt he would have followed her if she'd stayed in Eire.

Escape to another land had been her best option.

A knock on her door startled her from her reverie. Puzzled at who might visit her this late in the long, summer day, she carefully placed her project on the bench and walked to the door. With a frown, she grabbed her small knife and held it behind her back.

The open doorway revealed the tall, blond hero from the marketplace, Hávarr. Vigdís stood, open-mouthed, wondering how he'd found her. She also wondered why he wanted to find her.

His deep voice rumbled as he bowed his head. "Greetings to you."

Her mind worked quickly, recalling the proper etiquette. "Greetings to you. Please, would you like ale and bread?"

She opened the door more widely, inviting him in. He ducked through the low doorway, choosing a seat on the long, padded bench in the main room. She fetched a mug of ale from the keg and offered the flatbread she'd bought earlier. Discreetly, she put her knife down next to the keg.

He grinned. "You do have good taste."

She bowed her head. "I haven't eaten any yet. However, I bought them on your recommendation. If they're so good your mother sends you especially for them, they must be delicious."

Through a mouthful of crumbs, he mumbled assent. She took a bite of the other flatbread, and agreed with both Hávarr and his mother. The bread tasted freshly baked, well-ground, and while it was barley rather than wheat, had a light, fluffy texture.

"You are a difficult woman to find."

Apprehension gripped her stomach, and she had a flash back to another man's persistent courting. "You searched for me? But why?"

He held up his hands, ticking off his fingers. "First, I asked my mother, as she knows everyone in the area. She didn't know. Then I asked my father, as he is in charge of new tenant contracts. He said he'd set one up recently with the priest, so then I asked the priest. Finally, I found someone who knew your name!"

Her cheeks grew warm, and not just from the burning hearth or the ale. He'd gone to a lot of trouble to find her. But he still hadn't told her why.

"Now, I've learned your name is Vigdís and you leased this farm a month ago. The priest wouldn't tell me much else, so I came to find out more."

He sat, waiting for her to divulge her life story, as if he was doing her a favor. Well, she owed no man her story. She straightened her back. "As the son of the goði, you've every right to discover my name. However, I've heard of no law which require me to divulge my history."

Hávarr widened his eyes. "I am not asking for evil reasons, Vigdís. Instead, I hoped you would enter a contract with me."

She placed her hands on her hips and raised her eyebrows. "A contract? What sort of contract?"

* * *

Miami, 1992

The alarm crashed through Val's fogged mind, making her curse and jump up. She knocked it on the floor and cursed again as she scrambled to retrieve and turn it off. The jangling buzz was harsh and she deeply regretted it cutting into what might have turned into a lovely dream. She rubbed her eyes and grabbed, fishing her notebook from the nightstand drawer. With furious frenzy, she scribbled down the details of her dream before they drifted away with the morning routine.

The hot shower felt wonderful on her face. A contract. What sort of contract should she have them enter? Perhaps a livestock use contract? Something for her woven goods? None of that sounded good to Val. Neither seemed compelling enough, nor romantic. A romance novel turned out to be more difficult to write than she'd imagined.

Val dismissed the thought for the moment and shook Karl awake before she got ready for work. He never took as long as she did, but if she didn't start him early, he would just go back to sleep again. Since they had only one car, he would drop her off at her job before he went to his. Idly she wondered when the next SCA event would be. She had questions to ask Astriðr or Snorri which might help her with the next part of her novel. Had Jorge said when? The event might be this weekend.

Absently, she made a quick breakfast. She cleaned the dishes while Karl gathered his uniform and work badge. The room at Kim's had been great, but she appreciated the extra space they had. Two whole bedrooms seemed the height of luxury.

Memories of the house they'd rented in Country Walk seemed like another lifetime, far away. She tried not to think of that time.

Val had constant reminders of that life before the hurricane. Bills came in for credit card balances for items that no longer existed in this world. Her renters' insurance screeched to a halt in getting her any compensation for their loss. Most people her age didn't even bother with renters' insurance. She should thank her father for insisting she buy some.

She must fight tooth and nail with the agent. FEMA still owed them money. In addition, neither one took calls outside during working hours. She wasted her precious half hour lunch waiting on hold every day.

She'd catch hell if Dean Danelli caught her using the phone for personal business during working hours. With twelve-hour work days, she should have gotten slack, if the dean had been a reasonable human being. Val suspected the dean was, in fact, either a robot or an alien. That made much more sense. Perhaps an alien robot?

Val still stewed on the injustice when she got to her desk. The sticky note on her monitor said, "See me." See who? Santa Claus? The Purple People Eater? Whoever left the note, they'd need to come seek her out. She hadn't any psychic powers this week and her crystal ball had cracked.

A half hour later, Jorge strode in and saw the reports on his desk. He lifted them with a raised eyebrow.

She grimaced. "Dean needs them ASAP. Can you look over my figures, just so nothing glaring gets through?"

He nodded with a salute from his styrofoam coffee cup.

When nine o'clock rolled around, she'd just gotten the reports back from Jorge and paper-clipped the set as Dean Danelli stomped in with her fashionable heels. "Don't you have that report yet? Why didn't you come see me when you came in?"

Val handed her the folder. "I'd no idea who'd left the unsigned note. Here are your reports."

The dean glared at her and Val imagined she saw twin plumes of smoke coming from the dragon's snout. Her robot circuitry must have shorted out. The dean grabbed the folder, spun on her impractically high heels and marched back to her office, all the way at the other end of the hall. Val amused herself by listening to the diminishing clicks.

Jorge sipped his coffee. "Be cautious, darlin' girl. She ain't in a good mood this week."

"This week? As opposed to last week? Or last month? Or her entire life?"

He chuckled. "Be that as it may. She can't get a replacement for Kim, and it's pissed her off to no end. Neither of us are in for a gentle ride."

Val wrinkled her nose. Great, just what she needed. At least the situation gave her airtight job security, even if the dean caught her making phone calls during working hours.

"Jorge… SCA event this weekend, right? Near Pembroke Pines?"

He nodded, brushing his hand through his dark, gel-stiffened hair. "Come with your full kit."

When she finally got off work that night, Jorge dropped her off. She never knew how late she'd get off each evening. Karl drove fine during the day, but he got panicky at night.

She could eat a horse and hoped Karl had gotten dinner on the way home. She saw the Taco Bell bags and grinned with surprised delight.

"Karl, I'm home!"

He shouted from his workshop. "There are tacos on the counter!"

She sang the song Jorge had been playing in the car as she assembled her dinner. "Would you belieeeve… they put a man on the moon…"

A little bit of hot sauce, some sour cream, and voila! Wait, what's that green stuff? It doesn't look like lettuce…

"Karl, come here."

"Be right there, Val."

She stared at the taco for the entire time it took for Karl to come from his workroom to the kitchen. "Hey, honey." He leaned in to kiss her on the cheek, but she avoided him.

"Karl, what's that?"

He peered at the food and shrugged. "A taco?"

"No. What's that green stuff in the taco?"

"Looks like lettuce."

She closed her eyes and took a deep breath. "That is most certainly not lettuce. Karl, how the ever-living hell did grass get into my taco?"

He looked down and picked at his fingernails, but he didn't answer her.

"Karl."

"I only dropped them a little. I thought I got all of it out."

She wasn't hungry anymore. It would do her no good to yell at Karl for the mistake. He'd just do it again. Not the same thing; always some new and creative bumbling way to screw things up. She grabbed her notepad. "I'm going to lay down."

"Val, I'm sorry!"

She put up her hand to keep him from talking anymore. If he kept talking, she'd lose her temper, and she really didn't want to get more upset. She wanted to escape to her Iceland fantasy.

Notebook in hand, she decided that if her character wove, Val would need to study more about weaving herself, and not just tablet-weaving. Val had learned modern methods, terms, and equipment, but the medieval stuff was all new territory. She'd also have to learn about baking, spices, cooking on a spit, and surviving in the cold. She made a list of items to ask Astriðr this weekend. Oh, and dressing wounds? Definitely brewing ale. Crap, would she have to learn about slaughtering and butchering animals? Well, the essentials. She might learn about something and not have to practice, right?

A knock on the door interrupted her concentration. "Val?"

"What."

82

"Can I come in?"

Val sighed and put the notebook on the bed. "Fine. Come in."

She glanced at her list as he sat next to her. "I'm sorry."

"Thanks, Karl. Look, if that happens again, can you please buy new tacos? I don't want to eat stuff from the ground. People walk their dogs around here. I might be eating dog poop!"

"I didn't think about that."

She put her arm around him and hugged him. "You never do. But thank you for getting dinner anyhow."

"Want me to go get more now?"

"No, it's late. I'm not hungry now, anyway. Good night, Karl."

Val lay in bed with a growling stomach, eyes on the ceiling fan spinning slowly overhead. When she closed her eyes, she only saw the destruction which had become her former life. No matter what she did, she couldn't seem to settle in this new place. Karl had become more of a roommate than a husband. Her work sucked her soul dry. Nothing felt real to her any longer.

She pulled on her standby escape, her dreams of Iceland. The rolling hills, the cool, refreshing breeze, and the tall blond man.

* * *

Iceland, 1103

Vigdís placed her hands on her hips. "A contract? What sort of contract?"

Hávarr arched one eyebrow and shrugged his well-muscled shoulder. "A courting contract, of course! What else would I want with a beautiful woman?"

Her eyes grew wide. "A courting contract? We've barely met! You didn't even know my name!"

He shuffled his foot on the slate floor, looking like an errant child answering to an angry parent. The humility seemed rather endearing. "I spoke to the priest first. Since you have no father or brother to speak for you, the priest is the next option. But he said I should ask you before we set any terms." He looked up with an expectant grin.

The endearing quality dissipated. She clenched her fists, the anger rushing through her blood. "He thought so, did he? Well, that was considerate of him. Now get out! I need no stranger barging into my house and trying to lock me into a marriage when he barely knows my name!"

She whirled around and snatched the knife from the keg. When she turned back, he'd backed up several steps and raised his hands. "I don't understand. I don't expect you to marry me."

His words brought her up short. "You don't? Then why ask for the contract?"

He cocked his head. "If you put your weapon down, I'll explain."

Sheepishly, she glanced at the blade. Her fingers cramped from how tightly she held it. She placed it on the keg but stayed close. It remained in easy grabbing distance. "So, go ahead. Explain."

He eyed the knife and her still-angry stance. "A courting contract is not a promise to marry. It's permission to come and speak with you. Any woman of a good family must have such an agreement before she learns about her husband. It's the first step, but it doesn't mean you cannot contract others. I'm already in three contracts. Obviously, only one of them will ever become a marriage. The days of many brides disappeared with the pagan ways. Truly, courting contracts aren't popular, except it's a family tradition. Most marriages in other families are arranged without the bride or groom even meeting."

She still didn't want to relent, but his logic seemed sound. "Three others, huh? Three prospects aren't enough for you? Are you so sought after you need a wealth of choice?"

He glanced at his toes, blushing. "To be honest, they're all with women I've grown up with. They're distant cousins, but they feel like sisters. Sisters are no good to marry. But I would insult their families to not at least show I'm trying." His smile lit his face, showing a dimple in his right cheek. "But you, you're perfect! You come from far away, so we can't be related. Then, you've moved here alone, so you are brave and resourceful. You have intelligence and spark, or you wouldn't be threatening me with a knife, and you have baking talent!"

She waited, her arms crossed, resisting the urge to laugh at his frank assessment. He approached her cautiously, his hands out for hers. She reluctantly let him and looked into his eyes as he pulled her close.

"The ultimate reason is that the firelight dances in your hair and your eyes smile like the dawn."

Her urge to smile grew stronger, but with pleasure rather than laughter. The heat which boiled her blood now infused her face. He spoke smoothly enough when he tried. "Very well. I will talk to the priest about your contract. If he tells me it's a good idea, I may consider saying yes."

His smile glittered in his grass-green eyes. "Excellent! I'll wait for word from the priest." He bowed over her hand. "Until such a time as we agree upon a contract, we shouldn't kiss, so I will bid you good day."

With a bow and a swirl of his cloak, he left, not quite closing the door completely. She still stood next to the keg, trying to figure out what just happened, when a sheep nosed its way into the room through the open door and nuzzled her hand. A sudden gust of wind slammed it shut.

* * *

Miami, 1992

Val woke when the door slammed in her dream. With a mighty yawn and stretch, she glanced at Karl, but he remained comatose. Her alarm clock showed five in the morning, but she'd never get back to sleep.

As she relaxed under the shower, Val realized that her main character had a modern voice and a disdain for ancient sensibilities. She ought to make Vigdís a Cassandra character, someone who might see into the future. Or a time-traveler that skipped from time to time, sampling a bit of tasty history. The latter sounded more appealing to Val and it might keep the conversations from being as wooden.

She resolved to discuss the idea with Snorri when she next saw him. Between the historian and Astríðr, she'd gotten coaching, information, and a decent sounding board for her writing ideas. Her drafts got better each time, and they'd given wonderful feedback.

* * *

Val over-packed the car for her SCA weekend. Canvas tent. Check. Apron dress with ridiculous brooches and strings of beads. Check. Cooking gear, sort of. Last event, she'd found a beautiful carved bone bowl and a drinking horn, but she still needed a strap to carry the latter. She couldn't set the horn down without it tipping over. She'd bought a hand-forged fork and knife set with a lovely twist in the handle from the SCA blacksmith.

Loom, not yet. She needed to find a period loom as she wouldn't bring her modern one, with plastic bits and molded metal pieces. Last event, Astriðr had let Val use hers, but she should get her own. There might be vendors at this event who made them. She brought yarn she'd spun herself and the dye-stuffs Astriðr had given her. She might do her own dying this time.

She ran inside and grabbed her list of questions before calling to Karl. "I should be back late Sunday afternoon, Karl. Have you got a ride to the Civil War re-enactment still? Or do you want me to drop you off?"

He carried his canvas haversack into the living room. "Johnnie's coming for me in an hour. I'll be fine."

Val nodded and kissed him goodbye. "Have fun. Don't shoot anyone."

He laughed and tickled her waist before they parted.

She almost tripped going out the front door and looked down at her feet. Shoes. She still needed to get period shoes. She found slippers at Walmart which looked vaguely like medieval Viking footwear. While they had leather on the top and fake fur around the ankles, the bottoms were plastic. They wouldn't pass close inspection. Something else to put on the list—how to make shoes.

An hour's drive got her to the event site. She paid at the gate and parked her car, changed into her apron dress and set out to search for Jorge. He'd introduce her to the best vendors. She made certain her list remained folded in her pouch.

Instead of Jorge, she found Snorri.

"Vigdís! How fortuitous to see you. I've several people to introduce to you."

Val experienced momentary confusion at the name. *That's what I get for using my persona as my book's character!* With a genuine smile, she followed the tall, blond man to one trader after another. She found several things she needed, and more she didn't. Thankfully, her dad had just sent her a nice fat check for Christmas. The money went to excellent use.

Loaded down with more kit than she knew what to do with, she put most in her car before seeking Astriðr.

A few inquiries revealed her friend hadn't arrived yet, so she found several men practicing a song. Snorri sat next to her.

"What are they singing? I can only pick out a few words."

With a chuckle, Snorri cocked his head, listening for several minutes. "It sounds like one of the sagas. Gísla's saga? I heard his name twice and then Thorgrimm's. It's an outlaw saga and a love rectangle."

"Rectangle?"

"Well, there are six or more people involved, as well as a cursed sword, a brothers' feud, and lots of gossip. It's a true mess to rival any daytime soap opera."

Val held her hands in her lap and listened to the singing for several minutes. "I wish I understood them better."

"Keep learning the language. Oh, that reminds me, I brought language tapes for you to borrow, if you really want to learn."

She clapped her hands. "Oh yes, please! I'd love to borrow them!"

"Then I shall bequeath them upon you with due ceremony." He winked.

The singers stopped to discuss one line. Val turned to her companion. "Didn't they have any instruments?"

Snorri shrugged. "Pipes, horns, drums, perhaps bells or rattles. Possibly a lyre, but no complex stringed instruments. We don't really have any music from the early medieval era, just sagas. Sagas are more stories than songs, but some have put them to music."

Val took a sip from her drinking horn and found it empty. She scrunched her nose up in disappointment, and Snorri filled her horn. "I suppose reading the saga would be a good start."

"Sagas. Plural. There are lots of them and yes, that's an excellent way to learn about the culture."

"How many are lots?"

Snorri scratched his chin and glanced up at the clouds skipping overhead. "At least forty I can think of. Mind you, that's just the Icelandic sagas. There are also Greenlandic sagas, Vinlandic sagas…"

She threw up her hands. "Okay! Okay! I give up! Lots is lots. Can you at least recommend one to start? A simple one I won't get too confused with?"

"Hmm. Sturlunga Saga is shorter, at least."

"Sturlunga it is, then. Is it at least in English?"

He answered with a hearty laugh and a clap on the shoulder as he led her away from the now-arguing singers.

Later that evening, as she sat on a bench before the crackling fire, she wondered what had happened to Astriðr. Val swore her friend had planned on coming, but hadn't seen her all day. Snorri hadn't seen her, either, and Val got worried.

Astriðr had no family and lived in Lake Worth. She worked as an emergency operator, so sometimes got called in. Hopefully that's all that happened.

She stared into the fire, only half-listening to the discussion. They spoke of the Alþing, an annual parliament where the country's leaders gathered to settle cases, make speeches, decide on new laws, trade, and make marriage matches. Smaller Þings happened in each region, but this was the granddaddy of them all.

The flames danced to the staccato rhythm of the voices, and for a moment, she wasn't surrounded by a bunch of modern romantics talking about ancient customs, but by local goði, or chiefs, discussing the latest crops, or the newest outlaw, or a marriageable young woman. Olaf's querulous voice rose from the circle as other men laughed. She felt the icy Icelandic winter wind whip through the small space, biting her skin. Val shivered.

She shook her head to dispel the illusion, returning once again to the present day, albeit in traditional garb, eating a rustic meal on a bone plate.

I need air. With a nod to Snorri and Jorge, she sauntered out to the tree line. A few tents had nestled up against the edge of the forest, but plenty of space remained open. The stars shone bright and clear here, away from the light pollution of the city. She even saw the Milky Way, something she seldom saw in town.

She hadn't seen the stars so clearly since the hurricane.

With a shudder, she shoved that memory away, but she remembered Jorge's comment about how living rough wouldn't seem like such deprivation after that experience. He'd been right, of course. At least here she didn't need to eat endless cans of disgusting tuna. Instead, they had pickled herring. Snorri relished that particular delicacy. The herring she liked more than tuna, especially on the barley bread he made.

If she lived on a farm in Iceland, she'd have to get used to lamb stew, turnips, onions, and barley bread quickly. She likely would get little variety in what she ate. Luckily, she loved lamb. She probably couldn't slaughter one, even if she needed to eat, unless she raised a herd of suicidal sheep.

Her culinary skills were questionable. She'd baked chicken or made spaghetti, but cooking became so much easier with a microwave, she rarely bothered with 'real cooking' as Karl called it.

A cool breeze made Val shiver and pull her shawl more tightly around her. She glanced back at the fire. Everyone laughed at a joke and Snorri began chanting a song. The stars above her sparkled, mesmerizing her with sheer beauty.

Stars like this shone upon her characters in medieval Iceland, unchanged and eternal.

She should return to the party, but for now, the moonless sky beckoned.

* * *

Miami, 1993

Val sipped the soup and wrinkled her nose. It didn't taste bad, not really, but it definitely tasted bland. Leeks and onions were great, but when little else flavored the soup, it became boring. She needed garlic. Some pepper would help, but that would be expensive in medieval time, wouldn't it? Didn't it have to come all the way from the Mediterranean or something? Still, garlic grew plentifully, so she added more.

"What smells so good?" Karl came in from the living room, his hands covered in bits of blue and gray paint.

He reached for the spoon, but Val moved it away from him. "Wash your hands first. I don't want paint in the soup. Remember the grass in my taco?"

He made a rude noise, but dutifully scrubbed his hands in the sink. Most of the paint washed off, and he made a second attempt at the spoon. When she held it away with a smile, he attacked her midriff with a savage tickle. Her manic giggle made her drop the spoon, but he caught it and brandished it in smug triumph. Val rolled her eyes and gestured for him to try the soup.

"I'm trying to get a good recipe for a competition at the next SCA event. It's in Marathon next month. What do you think?"

He swallowed the spoonful and his eyes grew wide. "That's… that's a lot of garlic."

Fuck it. She'd never get this medieval cooking crap right. She resisted the urge to snatch the spoon back from Karl just to fling it at the kitchen wall.

Val had tried at least twenty different recipes, passed on to her by Astriðr. Recipes for roast lamb, stews, bread, root vegetables, all the things a good medieval Norsewoman would have learned to cook. She'd done well enough with the meat dishes, but her soups remained atrocious. She couldn't make them tasty without ruining them with too much of something. Her bread, at least, turned out tasty. Not the fluffiest bread around, but she might force it down with enough butter or jelly.

"I thought you liked garlic?"

Karl carefully handed her the spoon. "I do, but this much garlic would kill a dozen vampires from fifty feet away."

She blew a puff of air to get the bangs out of her eyes. Karl took this moment to kiss her, a quick peck on the lips. "But I will eat it happily because my lovely wife made it with her own two hands."

Val gave him a half-smile, in rueful respect for his comment. "At least I made bread. That might make the stew easier to stomach."

He picked up the flat bread and knocked against his head a few times. "More like a big cracker."

She rolled her eyes. "Medieval bread didn't leaven like modern bread. Wheat didn't grow well and barley isn't as fluffy."

He broke a piece and crumbs exploded all over the table, the floor, and Karl. With a sheepish grin, he chuckled. "'Fluffy' is definitely not the word I'd use."

"So, soak it in the soup."

Val grabbed the whisk broom and dustpan to clean the mess, but Karl took it from her. "I made the mess, I can clean it up. Go eat your soup."

He scooped up the crumbs and dropped them in the garbage can. Sometimes he acted so sweet, but then he'd do something like the grass in the tacos. She never knew from day to day if she would get Sweet Karl or Clueless Karl. She got Clueless Karl more and more often lately. She wondered if the hurricane somehow affected him as well. Eight months later and she still flinched at loud sounds.

The cooking practice had stressed her out. She needed to find a more relaxing pastime today. She should work on her novel. She might give Hávarr a brother, dark-haired and dangerous. Might he be a minor outlaw? Her mind spun with ideas for the next plot twist.

"I got another letter from Marjoree today." Karl's statement forced her spinning mind to a screeching halt.

Val put her spoon down. "What does she want?"

"Kris needs money for a school trip, so she wrote to ask me to send some."

Val's resentment over Marjoree's grasping ways—Karl paid plenty of child support that should more than cover such expenses—warred over her envy of having a child to send on school trips. She swallowed a sarcastic response and nodded. "How much does she need?"

He broke another piece of flatbread, careful to keep it over the soup. It mostly worked in keeping the crumb chaos contained. "She wants a hundred dollars."

Her sarcasm filter failed. "A hundred dollars? Where the hell is he going, Disneyworld?"

He shrugged, oblivious to her anger. "She didn't say. Can we send it?"

Val clenched her teeth. They had finally clawed their way out of the financial hole the hurricane had dumped then in, but only just. Still, she had spent about that on supplies for her SCA crafts, so she couldn't really begrudge Karl an equal portion for his son.

The analogy slammed into her stomach. The only things she created, the only bequests she'd leave to this earth, were bits of string or words glued together in a hollow mockery of legacy. How sad that her crafts would be the only offspring she'd ever have.

"Fine. Send a check, though, not cash. Marjoree would claim the cash got lost in the mail."

Val wasn't hungry any longer. She put the rest of the soup in a large Tupperware bowl and wrapped the cracker bread in tinfoil. She didn't quite slam the door to her second bedroom, repurposed as her office, but with the rest of the world safely shut away, she put her Icelandic music CD in and pulled up her manuscript on the computer.

What would be a good name for the outlaw brother? Val pulled out her book on the sagas, and scanned it for a reasonable name. It needed to be noticeably Icelandic. Several she rejected as too difficult to pronounce, and then her eyes alit upon Bergmar. The name had a faintly sinister connotation, for some reason.

Bergmar was tall, almost as tall as his brother. Long, dark hair, impeccably kept in braids, and a nice, full beard. Should she give him a rakish scar on his cheek? While he'd been outlawed, it had been minor outlawry. He'd only been exiled for three years, and was now allowed back in Iceland. Where had he gone? Norway was the most obvious choice. No, make it Eire. He would have something in common with Vigdís. Would he be a second love interest, maybe make it a love triangle? The concept was worth exploring. Conflict was good in novels.

What crime had he committed? She pulled out her copy of the Grágás, the medieval Icelandic laws. She skimmed through several chapters on violence, not wanting her character to be a brute or a berserker. When she found the section on wealth outlawry, she read more deeply. Letting your cattle graze on another man's land, in the amount of damage of five ells, or lengths of cloth, was subject to minor outlawry. Val nodded, pleased with a non-violent, non-greedy crime that might be an accident in the best light but still prosecuted in the worst light. A little ambiguity went a long way in making a bad boy into a misunderstood dark hero.

Her dream's eye filled in the rest of the details.

* * *

Iceland, 1103

Vigdís sat up from the now-shorn sheep and wiped her brow. Despite the cool summer breeze, sweat dripped down

Chapter Four

Miami, 1993

Val stopped and re-read what she'd written so far. Vigdís didn't sound medieval to her. She sounded modern and independent. Val didn't think she should be a simpering Jane Austen character but still, she ought to be more in tune with the norms of the time.

Maybe Vigdís didn't come from her time? What if Val made her a refugee of another era, in medieval times either by chance or by design? But she wouldn't have the skills to survive if she grew up in modern America. Well, unless she joined the SCA or grew up on a farm.

Val tasted the concept of time travel. How would she have done it? Maybe something simple, like a fatal car crash that propels her into the past? She would have landed in Eire, but made too many modern mistakes. The locals would consider her a witch or a devil, and she'd have to move to avoid notoriety.

The notion had merit. Her character's sarcasm and independence wouldn't be so out of place, then. With a determined grin, Val worked back through her manuscript, adding clues to the narrative so far. She made Vigdís into Valerie, the daughter of a farmer in Ohio in the 1960s, leaving home on a Greyhound bus to go to college. The bus crashed and she woke up in rural Eire at the dawn of the twelfth century.

Her initial confusion and fear would resolve into a determination to make her life work. She knew how to cook and care for animals, so she got a position helping at a local farm, working with the cattle and horses. Something must have happened to make her migrate to Iceland.

Back story, even if it didn't go in the novel, became important for the author to know. All the books on writing novels said so. Once she had the back story, she would implement the changes in the narrative and keep going.

She rewound the movie in her mind to where she'd left off in last night's dream.

* * *

Iceland, 1103

Vigdís held up two apron dresses. Neither were new, but both remained clean and in decent repair. She decided the blue set off her blonde hair better and pulled it over her head. She pinned on her best turtle brooches and draped the beads between them. Since she shouldn't need any of her sewing implements, she left those on the table. Her drinking mug, her horn bowl, and her iron spoon would be useful.

She brushed her hair and plaited it in a single modest braid, then covered her head with a linen headscarf, securing it with a tablet-woven headband to guard against the frigid Icelandic wind.

With a deep breath, she walked out the door.

The goði's farm lie about an hour's walk from hers, and luckily, the day remained fine and clear. She enjoyed the walk, despite the wicked breeze that played hell with her hair, even with the braid and scarf.

Her stomach became tied in knots about the dinner invitation. The custom for the goði to invite his farmers to dinner now and then made sense. Such a custom allowed them to air any grievances with him before the local ðing, when he would adjudicate any disputes. The meeting also let them to get to know him and his family, and vice versa. The evening should be pleasant and simple.

Still, she grew nervous. Surely, both the goði's sons would be there, along with the rest of his family. What would his wife be like? Vigdís scoured her memory for the woman's name. Senga? No, Siggi, Olaf goði had said.

Vigdís thanked her lucky stars she had a natural gift for learning languages and accents. She rolled the name in her mind to remember it. Would there be other tenant farmers tonight? She didn't know if she could handle a big crowd of strangers. She'd never done well with lots of people.

Almost five years ago to the day, she'd traveled by bus to college in 1968, from her father's farm in Ohio. A wrenching swerve and a cataclysmic crash remained her only memories from the incident, but when she'd woken, she opened her eyes to a new world.

The rolling, green hills of Ohio had disappeared, replaced by the rolling, green hills of Eire. How, she didn't understand. Valerie, which meant "strength" had become Treasa, an Irish name with a similar meaning.

Finding a way to earn her way in this strange time became essential. Farm work took a lot of strength and energy, but working on her father's farm had given her the knowledge she required. She had skill at sewing, and her embroidery gained her a reputation for fine skill. She stumbled through learning Irish with limited success. She'd already learned German and Latin in school, and surprisingly, the Latin helped with the Irish.

After several frightening encounters with a local man, she'd left both Eire and her persona of Treasa behind to find a new home in Iceland. She chose a new name, Vigdís, which meant "warrior woman," close enough to "strength."

Her foundation in German helped her learn the rudiments of the Icelandic language on the voyage. She supplemented that with working in Reykjavik through the winter before heading out to the countryside. By then, she'd amassed enough wealth and communication skills to rent a small farm hold in the shadow of Hekla, an enormous volcano.

The first few days, she'd eyed the volcano with suspicion but eventually learned to accept the dangerous beauty as part of the landscape. She worried about living in the farmstead throughout the Icelandic winter, but for now, she remained content to do her work and enjoy her solitude.

At least, she had enjoyed her solitude until the Olafssons meddled in her life.

If they made suit too strongly for her comfort, where would she go next, Greenland? She didn't even know if the Greenland colony still existed at this point in history. The semi-mythical Vinland must have been abandoned by now. She wished she'd studied this time and area back in

Hávarr's warm thigh pressed next to hers.

By this time, Olaf goði had carved several slices and Siggi made a plate for Vigdís. She piled on several onions, root vegetables, and a crowberry tart. The older woman added a thick slice of dark rye bread, slathered with sweet butter.

Vigdís stared at the meal, amazed at how much food she had to eat. With closed eyes, she savored the rosemary and lamb aroma once more before diving in. Since she'd had no stock ready to slaughter, she'd mostly been living on staples bought at the market, such as cured bacon and dried fish. Vigdís didn't intend to squander the luxury of fresh meat.

She glanced up after working through almost half the slice. Olaf goði asked Hávarr something about a horse while Fennja raised one eyebrow at her. "Does the meal meet with your approval, then?"

Vigdís grinned. "It's been so long since I've had fresh-cooked meat, I'd forgotten how delicious it tasted. What herbs flavor the turnips? It gives a nice, spicy flavor."

Fennja giggled. "That's the variety of turnip. My grand-mother bred them. The rutabaga has dulse in it, a seaweed."

"I'm familiar with dulse; we used it in Eire. Is there any way I can buy seed for this turnip? It's delicious."

Fennja nodded to her mother and kept her voice low. "You must ask Mother. She's the keeper of the seeds, and she holds her office seriously. She might part with the secret for someone my brother is courting." The dark-haired girl glanced at her parents, but they paid attention to their food, so Fennja winked at Vigdís.

Vigdís' eyes grew wide at this comment, but Fennja put a finger to her lips and winked again. So, the courting

109

remained a secret from the parents but not from the sister. Curiouser and curiouser.

Olaf goði's voice cut through her ruminations. "So, Vigdís, how are you handling the small farm? Do you need any help with the work?"

She hastily finished chewing the rutabaga she had in her mouth and swallowed, reaching for the mug of mead to wash her throat clear. "I'm doing well, thank you. It is hard work, but I can do it well enough so far."

The man studied her for several uncomfortable moments. Vigdís glanced first at Siggi and then Hávarr but still Olaf goði stared at her. Finally, he grunted. "Huh. I suppose you have too much wealth for me to buy you as a concubine. That's too bad. I'll bet you would be quite a challenge, too, with the muscles you've built."

Vigdís had no answer to this outrageous statement. Surely he must be joking? But he didn't laugh. Instead, he stared at her with his unnerving mismatched eyes. Hávarr shifted in his seat while Fennja looked at her food.

Siggi came to her rescue. "Olaf goði, stop. You're making the woman nervous. He can't buy you, Vigdís, not unless you fall deep into debt. You're safe from an old man's lustful fantasies." Olaf goði grunted again, this time in surprised pain. Siggi must have kicked him under the table.

That she might be bought, effectively enslaved, raised goosebumps on her arms and she resisted the urge to rub them away. If she truly came from this time, she'd be acquainted with the practice.

She'd seen slaves in Eire, but owners treated them more like indentured servants, working as part of a limited contract.

110

Danes had slaves, but she didn't know much about their treatment. She hadn't traveled to the Danish settlements in Luimneach or Weiseforth.

To hide her distress, she drank deeply of her mead. Siggi quickly filled it again.

A loud bang outside drew everyone's gaze to the door. It swung open and Bergmar entered, shaking his furry mantle. "The rain came out of nowhere! I would have arrived earlier, but my horse wouldn't cooperate."

Siggi frowned. "Well, you're here now, Bergmar. Do sit and eat, son. Have you met our newest tenant farmer, Vigdís?"

He nodded to her, noncommittal, and she nodded back. This added no information to their earlier frustrating meeting. The undercurrents of secrecy and family politics already made her head swim and she looked forward to when she might escape this dinner. Her small, isolated, and empty farm became more attractive every minute.

Fennja raised her eyebrows at Bergmar as she scooted over to make room on the bench. "Are you certain you didn't, in fact, shape-shift from that horse? You stink, and you've taken enough food to satisfy one."

He blinked at the well-laden plate he'd prepared. "I'm a young, healthy man. I need plenty of food to keep up my strength!"

Hávarr poked Bergmar in the ribs. "I think he's more like a bull. Full of blind rage and little sense."

Bergmar growled at his brother, but Vigdís sensed little malice in his reaction. Siggi frowned at each son. "This is no proper display for our guest. I'll thank you both to behave as a goði's sons should."

The brothers dropped their gazes to their plates, looking like nothing more than chastened children. Vigdís couldn't quite suppress a giggle, which earned her another short, fierce grin from Fennja. Finally, hunger overcame the men's shame and both dug into their meals with their previous gusto.

Vigdís stared at her own plate, surprised at how much she'd eaten. A few pieces of rutabaga remained, and though she could barely eat another bite, she made herself finish. She mustn't insult her hostess by not eating her entire meal. She hoped a dessert wouldn't be served apart from the delicious berry tart.

Olaf goði, finished with his meal, cleared his throat and announced he would relate a story, a saga from almost two hundred years ago.

Hávarr scooted closer to her on the bench and whispered in her ear. "You'll like this. Father is a master saga-teller."

The older man raised his mug in a formal speaking stance. "I tell you now of Gaukur Trandilsson, a man of exceptional bravery and gentle nature.

"Gaukur was well-renowned across the land, but despite his world-wide fame, he called this place, this farmstead at Stöng, his home. While many debate his existence as mere legend or myth, I count him among my own ancestors, as my great-great-grandfather."

Olaf goði drank deeply from his mug and let out a loud belch, settled his hands on his knees, and leaned forward.

"My esteemed forebear had a lovely wife, unmatched in her cooking skills. Friends came from the entire valley to sample her talents. His foster brother, Asgrimur, however, wanted to sample more than her cooking skills."

112

With the mention of food, Vigdís glanced at her plate, surprised to discover another berry tart had appeared. She looked at Siggi who motioned for her to eat more. With a fake smile, she sliced a small portion. The sweet treat remained delicious, but she would have to waddle home.

Olaf goði went on with the tale with bold arm gestures and sound effects and, while fascinated by the narrative, the effect of the unusually large meal made Vigdís sleepy. She wanted nothing more than to curl up by a hearth fire and take a nap. Too much mead and rich food meant she didn't relish the hour walk to her farm. Luckily, the summer sunlight lingered late, and she wouldn't have to walk home in the dark. Still, her own sleepiness might make the journey treacherous.

As Olaf goði finished his tale to the approving cheers of his audience, Hávarr toasted him and Vigdís hastened to do the same. She lifted her mug of mead, surprised to find it full once again. Icelandic hospitality might be the death of her. She unsuccessfully suppressed a yawn.

Siggi narrowed her eyes at Vigdís. "Our guest has become weary, Hávarr. Will you take her home on the cart?"

Bergmar jumped up. "I can do this!" He rushed outside.

Hávarr glowered at the open door. "It appears my brother needs more to do with his day, to have such energy by dusk."

Vigdís suppressed a yelp of surprise as, under the table, Hávarr squeezed her knee.

Olaf goði grunted while Siggi smiled. "He may imagine he needs to prove himself now he's returned from exile."

Exile? Vigdís wondered what his crime had been. His crime must have been a minor outlawry if he'd returned. Only serious crimes resulted in permanent exile.

When she walked outside, she watched Bergmar with interested eyes. To inquire about his outlawry would be horribly rude. He didn't seem comfortable sharing details of his shame.

* * *

Miami, 1993

A knock on her office door yanked Val back to reality. Her momentary panic resolved into annoyance. "Damn it all to hell with a cherry on top. I just got in the zone. What is it?"

Karl cracked open the door. "Kim is here."

"Kim? You mean my ex-boss, Kim? What the hell is she doing here? I thought she moved to Alabama to some god-forsaken alpaca farm?"

He shrugged. "She's here now. Are you coming out?"

"Just let me save my work."

When Val entered the living room, she had to admit that Kim looked good. She sat on the couch, tan, fit, with no bags under her eyes. She seemed more at peace and relaxed than Val ever remembered.

Kim rose and hugged her tight. "What a day from hell. I need human kindness."

Val stared at her sideways and sat on the couch. "And you came to me? You must be desperate. What's up?"

Kim sat next to her and thanked Karl for the gin and tonic he'd made for her. "I spent all day with the college lawyers."

114

"Lawyers. Right. Chug that. I'll call Jorge. This calls for a true night of pain relief."

* * *

Despite being Tuesday, Jorge worked his magic and found a comedy club with dollar margaritas.

In appreciation of his gift, Val toasted him with the first round. "If you bottled this talent for finding appropriate night life, you'd make a million dollars."

Jorge poured half the drink into his mouth, shook his head like a dog shaking water from his fur, and snorted. "If I bottled this talent, my places would become crowded by a bunch of idiots who can't find good times on their own. I think I'll hold this precious talent close to my chest."

He gestured to the waiter for another round, with a sly smile to the attractive young man.

"Fair enough. Kim, do you want to vent about today, or do you want to escape in debauchery and bad humor?"

Kim pressed her lips together, considering. "I think escape is imminent. Maybe later I'll drown you in my tears. For now, drink!"

They drank.

After only an hour, the party had devolved into a tearful chorus of "I miss you!" and "It's not the same without you!" When the show finished, they took a cab to Denny's for greasy food, coffee, and drunken reflection.

Kim sipped her coffee with a grimace, "The thing is, they know they're in the wrong, but they're trying to hide behind Byzantine regulations and faked performance records."

Jorge stuck his fork in a sausage and examined it before biting one end with exaggerated, suggestive relish. After a few chews, he swallowed and asked, "Faked? Don't you have copies of your staff annual evaluations?"

"You know I do, and I gave copies to the lawyer. They're arguing that their copies are the correct ones. They have me down for insubordination. Sometimes the note is for days I didn't even come in because I was at the hospital getting my cancer treatment!"

Val growled and dipped her toast into her yolk. "Seriously? They have balls, I'll give them that. What does your lawyer say?"

"Wendy says we've got them on the ropes and they're trying to throw anything and everything at us. If it gets too expensive for me, I'll stop fighting, so goes the theory."

With raised eyebrows, Jorge asked, "And? Will you?"

"My lawyer said she'll keep fighting even if I can't pay. She's more pissed than me and willing to fight to the death."

Val raised her coffee mug. "To the death!"

Jorge and Kim joined her toast, and they dissolved into a cacophony of drunken giggles.

* * *

When Val woke the next morning with a sour stomach and a throbbing head, she wished she dared call in sick. However, the dean had her on an urgent project, and would note any truancy. With a grumble and an enormous cup of coffee, she stumbled in and booted up her computer.

Jorge greeted her with a similarly surly grunt. His own cup looked as big as hers. They worked in sullen silence until the dean swept in.

"Val, have you finished with that slide yet? I need to show it to the board administrator."

Val stifled her yawn. "Just finished. Want me to print it or email it to you?"

"Print it. I told you I needed to show it to someone else. Did you not hear me?"

Val wanted to say, "Sorry, I don't speak idiot." Instead, she pasted on a fake smile and said, "Sure, give me a few minutes to warm up the printer."

With thinly disguised impatience, Dean Danelli tapped her foot and checked her watch a dozen times as Val turned the printer on, waited for it to initialize, sent the document to print, and retrieved the paper.

The dean practically ripped it from her hand. "I expect the rest of the slides by the end of the day."

Val didn't say the words out loud. Jorge did. "Fucking bitch."

"Right. Well, I'd already finished the rest of the slides, and she expects nothing else from me today. I'm working on my novel. To hell with her."

"Just be careful, darlin' girl. It doesn't take much for her to fire someone with extreme prejudice."

"I don't think she can fire me. I'm already doing my work and half of Kim's. You can't do all three jobs yourself, and no one else wants to work here because of her. Her reputation is well-known across campus."

"That doesn't mean she can't get someone in from outside. Just be cautious."

"Roger that."

Two hours later, Val stretched her back, making it crack.

Jorge looked up. "Ouch. That sounded painful."

"Nah, it felt good."

"How's the novel going?"

Val blew out a raspberry. "Not so great. I can't seem to get into the zone. Nothing I put down sounds tolerable. I've rewritten this same scene a dozen times now. I keep thinking of how they've screwed Kim over, and my train of thought gets derailed."

"Darlin' girl, I hear you. When I think of all the years she's put into this shithole, and how they treated her…"

They both jumped guiltily when Dean Danelli's voice cut across Jorge's statement. "The discussion of former employees is against this office's Code of Conduct. Both of you will have a notation in your file. And another for you, Miss Masterson, for using company time for personal pursuits."

After the dean left in a cloud of Chanel No. 5, Jorge whistled. "Damn. Damn it all to hell. If I didn't desperately need the income, I'd say we both walk out now and see how she likes the job."

Val let out a bitter laugh. "She wouldn't do any work. She'd let the art college fall into chaos before lifting a finger to work. Besides, remember? She can't even multiply. Not one line of her precious 'Code of Conduct' mentions 'discussing former employees.' She's so full of bullshit her eyes are brown."

"Regardless, I believe this is where I'm supposed to say, 'I told you so?'"

"Yeah, yeah, yeah."

* * *

Iceland, 1103

The constant summer rains had loosened an entire corner on Vigdís' turf roof, which necessitated back-breaking repairs. She'd need to cut several new pieces to replace the old ones. In the distance, her two cows lowed as if agitated, but a glance at the sky proved no storm came. What bothered them?

She'd just stretched her back after cutting her third piece of turf when he rode in on a black horse. The sturdy Icelandic horse stood stolidly while Bergmar, grinning fit to crack his face, leapt off and opened his hands wide. "You should not have to do this difficult work, Vigdís. This is man's work! Here, let me cut the turf for you."

As he grabbed for the shovel handle, she jerked it away. "I'm perfectly capable of cutting turf! Do you think I'm a babe born yesterday? I may not be a 'big, strong man' but I can dig in the dirt. I'm shorter, so I don't have to bend as far."

His eyes widened and then he laughed. Not the booming, hearty laughter of his father and brother, but almost a hysterical giggle, out of place with his deep voice.

As odd as the laugh sounded, it made her smile. She'd become well-versed enough in Icelandic not only to make herself understood, but to make jokes. She decided she'd reached a milestone and deserved a celebration.

"Very well, Bergmar. I won't allow you to do all the work, but you can help. In compensation, would a mug of sýra after we repair the roof suffice?"

"Such a sweet reward would be most welcome from your gentle hands, fair Vigdís. Almost as sweet as a kiss from your honey lips."

Vigdís couldn't decide whether she should slap him, kiss him, or laugh at him, so she bent over her shovel and dug it into the ground to hide her blush. When he spoke to her like that, with such intensity, she wanted to forget that she'd agreed to a contract with his brother.

Bergmar retrieved a turf-cutting adze from the stable and cut out the chunks of turf, so digging became easier. Soon they had a mound of turf pieces. He insisted on climbing the ladder to place the pieces while she handed each up to him. Once placed, she took over, tying the pieces down with twine wrapped around the pegs along the eaves until they grew into the existing root base.

As soon as she'd secured the last peg, her ladder shook. With a surprised glance, she checked to see if the base slipped in the mud, but it didn't move. Bergmar held the ladder firmly in place. Her own perch wobbled and she quickly descended the ladder. The ground felt no more stable than the ladder, but she wouldn't fall so far.

The basic truth of the earth being a steady, solid object rattled and broke within her mind, and she resisted the urge to grab onto anything that seemed solid. Nothing didn't move. The turf house, the stable, the cart, everything shook and rumbled, and her stomach dropped in a visceral unease.

First, the rumbling lessened, then the earthquake stopped and she sobbed with relief. She didn't know when Bergmar had wrapped his arms around her, but she became intensely grateful for his solid, reassuring embrace. His arms felt warm and sure and she didn't want to leave their safety.

"Is this the first earthquake you've been in? We get them all the time."

She shook her head and it rubbed against the fabric over his chest. "Once, in Reykjavik."

"Don't be afraid, they're common. We make a handsome team, Vigdís."

His voice sounded hoarse and she daren't look up at him. Instead, she extracted herself and cleared up the tools. She retrieved the adze, the shovel, and the ball of twine, taking them into the stable to clean and store them.

Vigdís hadn't realized he'd followed her until she turned and almost knocked him over. They stood much too close for comfort, but he didn't step back. Bergmar's breath misted warm in the small space between them. He put his hands on her shoulders. "Why do you run from me?"

She shook her head. "I didn't run. I tidied up the tools. Did you expect me to leave them to rust in the next storm?"

"You know what I mean. What's wrong? Do you wish me to leave?"

She both needed him to leave and wanted him to stay. She would speak of neither desire. To deflect the question, she asked a different one. "You didn't live here when I first came to this place. Where did you live before?"

He narrowed his eyes but didn't remove his hands from her shoulders. Instead, he squeezed slightly and gave her a sly smile. "I lived in Eire. I thought you knew?"

"How should I know? You tell me nothing, and Hávarr won't even speak of you."

"Would you like to hear my story? Perhaps over that mug of sýra you promised earlier?"

The first heavy drops of rain splattered on her head as they rushed to the house. Once inside, she coaxed the sullen fire to life and poured his drink. She sipped her own slowly, mindful of her earlier reactions. She must keep reign upon her emotions with this one. He grew too bold by half.

Bergmar chose the bench across from her, pushing aside the fur and reclining with one foot up on the wood. He downed half his mug and cleared his throat. "Three years ago I left my home, to sail the open seas like the Vikingr of old. I'd gone in fishing boats as a lad but never the big ocean-bound longships. I shall tell you, the idea of dying in the vast ocean frightened me to death."

For an Icelandic man to admit his fear, especially to a virtual stranger, was highly unusual. This wouldn't be the saga-like tale he'd tell a gathering at the Alþing. This would be a private tale for close family. Vigdís felt glad the dim light hid her face. She detested her penchant for blushing.

"When I arrived at the port in Reynir, I had a pack of clothes, a few coins, and a little food. My father paid for the passage. The ship was filled with traders going to Eire."

This must be when he'd been outlawed. He didn't offer that information and she couldn't ask.

"The midsummer nights remained bright as we crossed the miles. Five days it took to conquer the ocean. Five days of the long-burning sun and brief, blessed twilight—except for the last day."

Vigdís smiled at his poetic description, appreciating him as a talented storyteller.

"On the fifth day, as we smelled sweet land in the misted distance. Screeching gulls dove at our heads, a massive storm rose and threatened to swallow our boat. We all took turns manning the sails and bailing the water. The constant action kept us from despair. The fury of the sea frightened us all. The storm finally spit us into the emerald Eirish bay, soaked and exhausted."

Vigdís had been in a storm on her own voyage from Eire to Iceland. She hadn't taken part in any of the rowing or bailing, but had huddled, frightened out of her wits and constantly praying to God to deliver her from that wretched boat.

"Such a green land I had never seen! Massive, rolling hills of farms and lush trees as far as the eye could see."

He must not have landed near Connacht, then. Rock and stone filled the West Country as far as the eye could see. Bergmar must have seen her frown.

"Do you doubt me? You are from Eire, is that not true?"

"Yes, I came from Eire. But all the land is not as you describe. I lived in a barren and rocky area, making it difficult to scrape a life from the land."

He swigged his mug again and she refilled it for him. "Then perhaps you should have gone to a different part. The place we went, they called it Corcaigh, grew lush and dripping with life."

She laughed at the phrase, since rain remained an ever-present curse in Eire. "Dripping is exactly the right word for Eire!"

Bergmar grinned and joined in her laughter and soon they'd dissolved into giggles. As the last laugh died into silence, he gazed intently into her eyes and she suddenly grew uncomfortable. She stood and opened her pantry. "Would you like bread and cheese? Saga-telling makes hungry work."

He came up behind her, and she gasped as he put his warm hands on her hips. "I am hungry, it's true."

She removed his hands from her hips and strode to the door, ignoring her tingling belly. "Bergmar, I have chores to complete before night falls. I'm sorry, but it's best if you come back another time to finish your story."

"I can help you. Many hands make light work."

She shook her head. "Please, I must insist."

He watched her for several moments before he nodded. He took her hand and pressed it to his lips. Her belly grew warm and flipped. "I look forward to another time."

When he left, she let out her breath and closed her eyes. A man with intelligence who made her laugh remained a heady combination. He even listened to her when she asked him to leave. For a moment, she wished she had never agreed to Hávarr's contract, and thus remained free to enter her own.

* * *

Vigdís held the adorable, fuzzy lamb and buried her face in the soft fleece before she slowly grabbed the knife from the nearby stool. The scent of lanolin and wet wool filled her nostrils.

She swallowed her disgust at the slaughter and gritted her teeth. With a quick, sure stroke, she slit the lamb's throat, making certain to direct the flowing blood into the waiting bucket. The lamb struggled and cried but she held tight until blood spurt died and the creature went still.

By this time in her adventure, five years after waking up in the past, she'd had to slaughter dozens of animals. It never became easier to her modern sensibilities. If she hadn't grown up on a farm, she'd probably never be able to do it at all. This lamb had been one of triplets, and she must slaughter him or run out of fodder for the rest. Another lamb would have to go in a month. At least she'd have plenty of meat through the winter.

Once she dressed and hung the carcass, she glanced down at herself. Her slaughtering apron looked a horrible mess. Blood smeared up her arms and face, and her hair felt hopelessly tangled.

Naturally, Hávarr arrived at that moment. He took one long look at her and burst into laughter.

She growled and stalked to the water bucket, splashing chilly water on her face and arms. Finally, she lifted it up and poured a little over her hair, gasping at the cold shock.

By now, Hávarr had stopped laughing and set to work cleaning her tools and work area. She flashed him a grateful smile. "I must go in for a proper wash and to change into less bloody clothing. I won't be long."

He waved her away as he swept up the blood-soaked sand.

A man who helped clean was a treasure, especially in this antiquated time. While he had laughed at her disarray, he hadn't maliciously mocked her.

Once changed, washed and feeling fresh once again, she walked outside to discover Hávarr had fed the other animals and cozened the ewes, who had milled nervously after the slaughter. The mother ewe bleated for her lost daughter, which broke Vigdís' heart. She swallowed back silly sentiment.

With a hop to sit on the stone fence, she asked Hávarr why he'd come today.

"I came to invite you to the harvest celebration next month. Everyone helps with the heavy work at the main farm. We give a grand feast and five evenings of storytelling around the fire. The nights are long and full of drink and laughter. Please, say you'll come?"

His eyes held the endearing entreaty of a child asking for chocolate. Still, she didn't want to endure another intimate family dinner full of undercurrents and intrigue. "Who else will be there?"

"All the tenants. My family, Fennja's betrothed's family, Father Ari, and a visiting Bishop from Norway, according to rumor."

"Will the Bishop perform Fennja's wedding, or Father Ari?"

He shrugged. "They don't tell me details. The women discuss such things in secret, only to giggle and blush whenever I come near."

She chuckled at the description. "Your brother, will he be there? Or will he travel again, like last summer?"

The blond narrowed his eyes at her. "Why do you ask about my brother when we have a contracted courting? Has he been here? Are you looking to break our contract?"

She held her hands up but set her jaw at his jealousy. "I only asked. He has an air of mystery around him and I enjoy solving puzzles. Besides, is there anything in the law that a woman cannot be part of multiple courting contracts? Men may have several; why not women?"

He scratched his chin, looking off into the distance. "I've never heard of a woman having more than one at a time. Father Ari would be scandalized."

She lifted her eyebrows. "Have you told your parents yet about our courting contract?"

Hávarr gave her a half-smile. "Not yet. The time isn't right. They're busy with Fennja's wedding contract to Vigmund."

He reached out to caress her cheek, but she drew back, pushing his hand away. "The time isn't right. You've been using the same excuse for months, Hávarr. Every time you visit, you say the time isn't right. When will the time be right? When the moon turns green? When the ice on Hekla melts? When the sea swallows the island? If you are so reluctant to tell them, perhaps the contract is a bad idea."

"Fennja will marry at the harvest. Once she's wed, I can tell them."

She put her hands on her hips and glared up at him. "Am I so shameful, you can't tell them now?"

Hávarr took her hands in his and gazed into her eyes. "Shameful? There is nothing wrong with you but an over-sharp wit, Vigdís, which I relish. You are the one I wish to court, out of all my contracts." Hávarr stepped down from the fence and knelt in front of her. "You are the one who haunts my dreams at night and my thoughts in the morning. Your laugh is in every brook and your smile in every sunrise. You, my silk Valkyrie, are the one with whom I ache to make a home. This I swear to you."

Torn between pleasure and embarrassment, she tried to pull him to his feet, but he wouldn't budge. Finally, she threw up her hands. "Then why not tell your father?"

He stood, his head bowed. "My father wishes for me to marry my cousin, Enika."

"Enika? The little round girl? She's barely thirteen!"

He nodded. "Yes, but my father won't listen to my protests. He owes her father a great deal for his support at the last Alþing and wants to repay it by marrying me to Enika. I don't know what it's like in Eire, but in Iceland, parents arrange marriages, not children. Every time I tell him I don't want to marry her, he gets angry and threatens to curse me."

She laughed. "A curse? Seriously?" Then she remembered she no longer lived in the twentieth century. Medieval minds believed many things. Historic tales were full of curses and hexes.

A somber frown on his face, Hávarr nodded. "My father can work powerful magic. He vowed to leave his pagan ways behind when he married mother, but the symbols remain on his arms. He keeps magical artifacts in secret places. He still works the magic, when he chooses."

Vigdís ached to dismiss the conversation as worthless but must consider the notion that if someone believed in it, the curse might work. Certainly, real magic didn't exist. Did it?

128

Then again, if no magic existed, how had she ended up a thousand years in the past?

Her concern must have shown on her face, for Hávarr placed his hand on her shoulder. "Don't worry overmuch. I shall find a way to make this work."

She gave him a half-smile, unsure whether to trust this bluff, good-natured giant. "I'm still new to this barren island, Hávarr. I don't know your ways. If you say your father can work magic, are we wise to defy him?"

His eyes grew wide. "Barren island? Barren island! This land is lush with life!"

The change of subject made her smile in full. "Yes, barren, compared to Eire."

"I will make another vow, Vigdís of Eire. I shall show you the intense beauty of my island."

Chapter Five

Three months after the surreal dinner party at the goði's farm, Vigdís stared at her meager selection of clothing, trying to decide what to wear for the harvest celebration. She'd take at least two, as the activity lasted several days. Unlike some tenants, she lived close enough to travel home each evening, but she had the option to stay overnight. Which dress for the first day?

Hávarr told her the event encompassed both work, where everyone chipped in to bring in the fruits of the summer, and a celebration where they all drank and ate of the harvest. Since her own farm had only a modest plot of growing area with a focus on sheep, she had plenty of time to help.

Hávarr, as the goði's eldest son, had a strong chance of becoming the next goði, so no farmer failed to sue for his favor. Surely all his family must also attend. Olaf goði consolidated and strengthened his power, just like any medieval baron in British history.

Vigdís remembered studying the complex and warlike political machinations of the Anglo-Saxons of the pre-Norman era, full of minor kings and chieftains who lasted less than a year on their throne. Assassinations, usually by a cousin or even a brother, became commonplace. Assassinations may not be as common in Iceland, but politics remained strong.

Everyday corruption ran rampant and currying favor had been institutionalized in the Þing culture.

It took her a while to understand the concept of the Þing, but it represented, at heart, a democratic society. Free men took their grievances to their goði to ask for justice. If they didn't get justice from the goði, they took their case to the local Þing, or assembly. If the local Þing didn't satisfy the issue, any man might take their cause to the annual Alþing in Þingvöllr. The Alþing was a gathering of all the goði and free men across Iceland for stories, news, law, and justice. The gathering of the goði worked like a Parliament, the ultimate power in a land without a king.

Why should Olaf goði, a man with considerable political power, agree to let his heir-apparent marry an obvious no-body, an immigrant with no family and little wealth? Vigdís still didn't know enough of Icelandic law to determine if Olaf could forbid Hávarr to marry her. Even if law allowed it, societal pressure could be daunting. For instance, if Olaf goði threatened to evict her, Hávarr might relent.

Hávarr made her laugh and he respected her. He had a strong romantic streak and his smile brightened her day. When he spoke sweet words, her heart melted. She would never starve under his care and they'd surely have many healthy children. He maintained a positive outlook on life and had a charitable nature. Still, it might be better for her to reject his suit. She didn't wish to become a pawn in a family struggle for power.

Bergmar might be the safer choice in terms of family dynamics. Since he remained an obviously less-favored son, Olaf goði might not mind if he married a nobody. The darker brother intrigued her and they had fascinating discussions. She enjoyed arguing over silly things and matching wits. He'd been to Eire, so they had shared experience. While he didn't melt her heart, other parts of her responded more strongly to his touch.

Vigdís shook her head. She'd never figure this out worrying about it. For the moment, Hávarr had a claim on her, but that claim remained secret. Until he made it public, she must keep her own obligation hidden. A bit of harmless flirting on her part would be Hávarr's fee for such a secret.

Her rose-colored apron dress had been made of good, sturdy material, suitable for doing farm work while still looking passable. She dressed and prepared for the walk to the goði's farm.

Her bag, with changes of clothing, drinking mug, eating utensils and bowl, bumped against her back as she walked the well-worn path. A cloud blocked the sun, cooling the summer wind. She drew her cloak around her shoulders and shivered. While the cloud looked small, more ran across the sky and appeared ominously dark. Vigdís quickened her step and practically ran the last leg of the journey.

The first heavy drops of rain fell as she reached the door. About twenty other tenants milled about, some with their own tents set up in the field next to the smaller stables. One man waved to her, and she waved back. She recognized him from the market, but didn't recall his name.

While huddling under the door gable, she knocked, hoping everyone wasn't out in the fields. The musty scent of rain-soaked thatch filled the air as the drops became a torrent, splashing mud on her dress. The door opened to reveal a grinning Fennja. "Vigdís! I wondered when you'd arrive! Come in! I can't wait to show you my wedding crown."

Fennja pulled her into the enormous hall and into one of the many side chambers. The room burst with fabric, flowers, and four other chattering women, including Fennja's mother, Siggi. Vigdís recognized the mousy girl named Enika.

"Vigdís, do you know everyone? This is Dagmar, Atla, and Enika. Have you met Enika? Oh, good. Atla, help Vigdís find someplace to put her pack. Wait! First, tell me what you think of... this!"

The ebullient bride held up her bridal crown. The straw-woven creation had been festooned with summer flowers and colorful berries.

Vigdís blinked several times, searching for complimentary terms. "It's incredible. I've never seen anything like it."

Fennja grinned widely and bounced over to place the monstrosity carefully on the bench. "I've spent all week making this, with Enika's help." The younger girl blushed and lowered her gaze. Vigdís experienced a surge of maternal protection over the child. Olaf wanted Hávarr to marry this sweet little creature? He'd crush her with his first hug and she'd crumple like an autumn leaf.

She placed a hand on the child's shoulder. "Come, Enika. Can you help me clean the mud off my dress?"

Enika led her to the privy room, complete with bucket and scrubbing cloths. With a great deal of work, they got the worst of the mud stains out. Vigdís studied the child while they worked. Enika could be no taller than five feet and weighed no more than a hundred pounds. She'd barely developed a figure. How could Olaf even think about mar-

134

rying such a child off to a giant like Hávarr? Yet, she'd seen similar arrangements in Eire during her years in Connacht. Still, the actual marriages didn't take place until the bride had grown older.

At least the Eirish made certain the woman consented to the match. From her medieval studies, Vigdís remembered this wouldn't be a requirement in Anglo-Saxon traditions. Did Icelandic law require a woman's consent for marriage? Father Ari hadn't mentioned it, but he'd implied Vigdís had a choice. Perhaps only because she had no father or brother to speak for her. Who spoke for this child? Who wished to sell her off like an unwanted slave to a man three times her mass?

While tamping her anger down at the injustice of medieval society and its twisted norms, Vigdís wrung out the hem of her dress. "There, much better! Thank you, Enika. Where's the best place to store my pack during my stay?"

Once Vigdís changed into her work clothes and stashed her pack safely away, the rain had stopped completely. Enika and Atla took her outside to the hayfield where the rest of the valley had gathered. At least forty men, women, and children worked mowing down tall, golden hay swaying in the late summer breeze. Two or three people manned each iron scythe, working in rows and piling the hay in thin windrows to field-dry in the sun and the wind. Women would turn each row to keep it from getting too wet and developing mildew. At night, they would gather the rows under haycocks, and the next morning, they would spread the hay again to allow it to dry.

Billows of blown chaff tickled Vigdís' nose as they walked, sending her into a paroxysm of sneezing.

Atla helpfully held her shoulder until the spasm stopped, then offered a cloth to blow her nose. "I always sneeze with the hay. This season makes me miserable and unable to breathe."

Vigdís nodded. She didn't suffer from hay fever as badly as some, but her nose still itched.

Enika spoke for the first time, her high voice barely a whisper over the cries and laughter of those working in the field. "There are no more scythes for us to help cut. We should get rakes to help with the windrows."

Each armed with a wicked-looking iron rake, the women searched for a scythe group lacking help. Enika spotted the first and skipped to help while Atla found another place.

Vigdís searched for several minutes before she saw Olaf and Bergmar's scythe row. With a deep breath, she dived into the cloud of wheat particles to gather the cut hay into a thin line.

Several hours and at least a hundred sneezes later, Vigdís realized both men had stopped cutting hay. Past this point, all the hay had been cut by another group. A quick survey across the field revealed most of the area had been cut down.

Many hands did make short work.

Enika had mentioned six hay fields, with only one cut today. Tomorrow would be another day and another field, and so on. The mass of workers could now wash, drink, eat, and celebrate a good day of work done.

Bergmar's giggle caught Vigdís' attention, and she turned to see him smiling down at Atla, who returned his smile. She watched as the dark man caressed Atla's hair in a tender gesture. The seductive slyness of the girl's expression made Vigdís tighten her grip on her rake handle. A sudden clap on her shoulder made her shout and spin, her rake in a defensive grip.

Hávarr jumped back with his hands shielding his face. Despite his defensive pose, he laughed. "Stay calm, Vigdís! I mean no harm, I promise!"

She growled but lowered the rake to a less threatening level.

"Has Mother shown you a place to sleep tonight? Or will you go to your farm?"

She resisted the urge to glance back at Bergmar and Atla. "I don't know yet. It depends on how I feel after supper. The walk is longer if I drink too much."

His grin lit up his face and he bowed with a dramatic flourish. "Then my goal is to ensure you good cheer and drink tonight. If you feel you must return home, I'd be honored to escort you safely."

Olaf, with Bergmar, had walked up behind Hávarr. Watching his son's antics, Olaf frowned. "What's this?"

Vigdís raised her eyebrows, placing one hand on her hip, and glared at Hávarr. If he ever planned on informing his father about their courting contract, now would be the perfect time. She refused to look at Bergmar. The blond man sneezed, swallowed, and stared at his feet. Disgusted, Vigdís rolled her eyes and whirled, stalking off to the stable. She didn't care if she offended Olaf at this point. She'd better get the weapon out of her hands, or Hávarr would end up skewered and cooked for dinner instead of the traditional sow. Perhaps she'd skewer his brother for good measure as well. *How did I even get into this situation? I never wanted a husband in the first place!*

"Vigdís! Wait!" Bergmar ran until he caught up to her, but she didn't halt. "Did Hávarr say something to offend you?"

She stopped, planting the butt of the rake in the ground as she turned to scowl at Bergmar. She'd had just about enough of both Olafssons at this point. "What business is it of yours what Hávarr says to me?"

Bergmar took a step back at her naked anger, his eyes wide. "All I want is your happiness, Vigdís. If Hávarr has upset you, I'll challenge him to fix it."

"Challenge him. You mean, you wish to fight for me? Are you my father? My brother? No? Then what gives you the right to fight for my honor?" With each question, she took another step toward him, rake still firmly gripped in both hands. He took a step backward each time, his eyes flicking frequently to the sharp tines.

Finally, he planted his feet solidly and lifted his chin. "I have no right to fight for your honor. However, I'd like to contract for that right. Since, as you say, you have no brother or father, I must ask you. Will you enter a courting contract with me?"

Another one? She didn't even want one man courting her. What would she do with another one?

"I want no courting contracts. I plan on living and dying an old maid, never marrying or having children. I'll die a hermit on the hill, alone and unloved with many sheep and many cats. So I say, and so it will be. Go away, Bergmar! Go contract with Atla!"

She stalked off once again, mentally daring Bergmar to follow her. Sense must have crept into his thick skull, for he remained where he stood, arms still crossed but blinking with confusion.

Let him be confused. She wanted no contracts, no forced marriages, and no loveless mates. While she realized that in this time, young women married with little choice in the matter, she wasn't a medieval woman. She was a modern woman stuck in an ancient time, and she would be damned if she'd change her basic self to comply with expectations.

Even when she'd lived in Eire, Gaelic Brehon law required the woman's consent to any marriage. A father wouldn't force a husband upon his daughter. Even a servant or a slave might protest an arrangement, a fact which had saved her from marriage to the odious Padraig.

Icelandic law evidently didn't work the same way. Still, without a father or brother, no one could force her to marry where she didn't wish. Father Ari assured her he'd make no contract without her consent.

After she returned the rake to its wall and changed into her cleaner, fancier apron dress, she sought Siggi out. Fennja bubbled with her own bridal bliss and would be no fit confidante for Vigdís' problem. The older woman might offer insight.

With much searching, she found Siggi in the storeroom. Fennja's mother instantly recruited Vigdís to help carry several large wheels of cheese into the main hall. She realized Siggi would have little time to chat until the feast had finished and the cleaning done. The wife of a goði must be similar to the head woman of a castle.

Vigdís helped Siggi in the kitchen for another two hours before the food preparation finished and the tenants sat in the main hall. Even with the size of the place, it burst at the seams with fifty people crammed onto every bench and barrel available. The heat and closeness of the room made Vigdís want to run outside into the clear, cool, and wonderfully empty night air. She swallowed her anxiety and found a place at the lower corner of the table, wedged between two older men she'd never met.

The one on the right nodded to her. He stroked his white-streaked beard and grinned, showing several missing teeth. She smiled back, resisting gagging at his beer-laden breath.

She glanced at the man on the left, but he remained engrossed in conversation with the young man next to him. Vigdís did her best to squint at the other end of the table where Olaf lifted his drinking horn and offered a toast, but she couldn't hear a word he said. When he cried, "Skaal!" and drank, so did everyone else. She drank half her mug of mead and her heightened anxiety eased. The other half almost erased it completely. Instead, her head spun slightly and her skin grew warm. She'd better eat, and quickly, if she didn't wish to be half-insensible by the end of the evening. Already she had difficulty keeping her balance on the bench.

A touch at her elbow made her turn, almost unbalancing her again. She focused her eyes to find Enika.

"Would you like to walk?"

With a vigorous nod, Vigdís extracted herself from the bench. She jostled her neighbor, but nodded in apology to the bearded man. He dismissed her with a wave of his hand as she exited the crowded hall.

She needed to breathe the cool, clear outside air. Her mind cleared, and she stood on the earth again without tipping. She smiled down at Enika. "How did you know?"

The girl smiled shyly. "I don't like crowds. You looked uncomfortable, and it seemed like more than too many strangers."

Vigdís nodded. "You thought exactly right. I fiercely treasure my solitude."

The girl looked down. "I do nothing fiercely. I wish I could be fierce, but I have never had that temperament. My father thinks marrying me to a fierce warrior will give me fierce children, at least."

Vigdís sat on a bench and patted it so Enika would join her. "Do you want to marry a fierce warrior?"

Enika shook her head so hard, her hair escaped from its bun, her dark locks tumbling to her shoulder in the late summer sunset. "I don't want to marry a warrior at all. I want to marry… I… I can't say, because my father would kill me if he knew."

Her interest piqued, Vigdís took the younger girl's hand. Her skin felt cold. "I promise, I won't tell a soul."

Enika swallowed and gazed up at Vigdís, her eyes entreating. "You promise? On your ancestors' graves?"

Vigdís didn't know where her ancestors lived at this moment; probably somewhere in Germany or France. Her father had always told her the family had come from Alsace. She nodded.

Enika glanced at her toes and shuffled them in the dirt a few moments before she spoke in a voice so low, Vigdís barely heard her words. "His name is Nonni. He is studying with Father Ari. He's clever and gentle, and he promised he would wait for me."

A bookish lad made perfect sense for Enika the Frightened Mouse. She seemed a frightened starling. A priest-in-training made an excellent match, a much better match than the great lumbering force of Hávarr.

"I think Nonni sounds wonderful. Would he make you happy, do you think?"

Enika nodded but didn't look up. "But it will never be. My father is a goði. He will marry me to help his position."

A surge of anger heated Vigdís' blood. Enika lived in a different time and a different culture, she reminded herself. Marriages were arranged for wealth and power, not for love. Still, it pained her to watch Enika's despair.

"Do you know who your father has chosen for you?"

"I heard him telling mother. He's chosen Hávarr, but he'd settle for Bergmar."

Damn. Despite her earlier vow to die a spinster, she'd half-decided to accept Hávarr's suit to allow this innocent child to marry her beloved. But if her father didn't care, he'd simply choose another powerful man. Such a decision would only transfer the problem, though Bergmar would be less likely to hurt the child out of sheer exuberant strength.

"Can you think of no way to make Nonni more attractive to your father as a match?"

"He's the son of a Finnish slave, with no family, no wealth, and no land."

"What about his prospect to become a priest? That must be worth something, no?"

142

Enika let out a short, sharp laugh. "If he had already been a priest, it might help. He's but a student. Father has no use for writing or for books. He considers them a waste of time, nothing to produce food or wealth."

Vigdís thought about the sagas she'd read. The most powerful people would be the goði and the law-speakers. "Might he become a law-speaker?"

Enika cocked her head. "A law-speaker has great status, even more so than a goði. I hadn't considered such a path. Father would never call a law-speaker useless. I must ask Nonni if he would become one!"

The girl ran off to one of the larger stables, presumably to find her beloved, and Vigdís smiled. If she couldn't figure out her own dilemma, at least she'd helped the gentle girl with her own.

If Enika convinced her father of Nonni's worth, he would no longer push her into marriage with Hávarr. Still, he had other courting contracts and Vigdís didn't know the other women. Perhaps she'd already met them all.

She wouldn't solve this situation tonight. Vigdís' stomach warned her that she'd only had a mug of mead for supper and had worked hard all day. She needed more sustenance and quickly.

She snuck into the hall, now rowdy and boisterous with drink and cheer. Someone told a tale on this end of the hall while the other end burst into laughter at a joke. Surreptitiously, Vigdís grabbed a small loaf of barley bread and a hunk of cheese. She secreted her treasure and escaped back into the still-bright night to enjoy the meal.

Earlier, Siggi had shown her a place in the stable where she might sleep the night if she wished to stay. Her body urged her to take the soft straw bed, rather than walk an hour through the dimming landscape to her home, only to return in the morning. Once she finished her meager meal, she heeded the call of the warm straw and curled up, drawing the blanket over her.

Summer nights in Iceland barely existed. Vigdís had learned quickly to fall asleep despite the sun shining until all hours. At the height of midsummer, the sun only set for about an hour, and true night never came. Even now at first harvest, sunset turned to twilight turned to sunrise, all within a short time.

Vigdís managed a few hours of rest before the stables filled with farmhands on morning duty, milking cows and feeding horses. She tried to get back to sleep, but the cheery greetings and ribbing about drunken escapades the night before kept sleep a hopeless distance away.

Finally giving in to the inevitable, she threw her blanket off and stretched, whimpering when seldom-used muscles complained about yesterday's efforts.

Raised male voices beyond the normal morning shouts roused her fully. She wiped and shook the worst of the hay from her dress and relieved herself in the night basket before she went to investigate the disturbance.

Hávarr and Bergmar stood in obvious confrontation in front of the main hall. Olaf and Siggi both stood to one side, while Fennja watched from the doorway, her hand over her mouth. Vigdís scuttled closer to hear their words.

"You have no right to court her, Bergmar. I already have a contract in place. You can't have one at the same time!"

Bergmar narrowed his eyes. "You already have a contract? How many contracts do you need, brother? Will you court every woman in Iceland? Why be so modest? Why don't you take all the Northlands, and Eire as well? Skíta! Take all the Francian women while you're at it! There are plenty of women willing to fall for a blond, berserk buffoon with delusions of heroism!"

Hávarr's face grew redder. "Better than a sly schemer like you! You would talk the scales from a fish, with your twisted words and warped motives. Father should have named you Loki and been done with it!"

"At least I have no need to bribe women into contracts! Would you be so sought after if you didn't have Father's favor, Hávarr? Or would you be scrabbling around to find an ill-favored woman willing to bed you just to shut your endless chatter?"

Hávarr crossed his arms and cocked his head, giving his brother a nasty smile. "I don't know, Bergmar. Why don't you tell me what that's like? You're an expert in such matters."

Bergmar pulled the dagger from his belt, and Vigdís caught her breath. "You'll become nothing but a hearthfire idiot."

While his eyes flicked to the dagger, Hávarr laughed in Bergmar's face. "At least I'll have a hearthfire to call my home. You'll have nothing but dust and ashes left from your villainous plots."

Bergmar stuck his dagger into the ground between him and his brother's toes. "I challenge you, Hávarr. Under the law of the hólmgang. You are not a man's equal and not a man at heart."

"I am more of a man than you!" Hávarr lifted his hand in a rude gesture.

Bergmar retrieved his dagger and marched north. Hávarr stewed for a moment before stalking after him. Olaf followed both, staggering slightly.

Vigdís grabbed Siggi's arm. "What just happened? I've never seen either of them so angry."

Siggi closed her eyes and sighed. "Did you just arrive? Of course, you wouldn't know. The argument began an hour ago and escalated quickly. Bergmar just challenged Hávarr for the right to court you."

"Me?"

"Yes, you. And Hávarr with three courting contracts already. Olaf would be livid if he wasn't still so drunk from last night." The side of Siggi's mouth curled up slightly, betraying her amusement.

"Aren't you worried one of them will be hurt?"

She laughed loud. "I'm certain one will. I'm also certain neither brother will kill the other. This duel has been a long time coming, and may clear the tension between them. Come, let's walk to the hólm. Bergmar will need to mark the space out for the duel."

Vigdís' thoughts raced. A duel. Over her. Hávarr had finally let everyone know of their contract, at least. This was not precisely what she'd expected, nor wanted.

Siggi placed a hand on her arm. "How do you feel about this? I know you've spoken with both Hávarr and Bergmar.

Do you favor one over the other? Do you have someone else you prefer?"

"I… I'm not sure. I like both brothers, but I barely know them. Where I hail from, we have long courtships. Some betrothals take years to ensure the courters are suited to one another."

"I didn't realize Eire's laws were so different."

She must be careful. Too many anachronistic details might get her in trouble. "Perhaps only my town. We had odd traditions, but Gaelic law requires a woman's consent to any match."

Siggi nodded. "That's our family tradition, as well. Rumor is my great-grandmother hailed from Eire and perhaps that's why. However, men often pay little attention to tradition in matters of mating. If there's a challenge to a decision, the law-speaker must side with the man. Fortunately, I already cared for Olaf when my father chose him. He had a wealthy farm and cut a dashing figure in his youth, before his belly grew with ale. His magic made him dark and mysterious, though he's given all that up. Marriage to him hasn't been easy, but it's definitely not dull."

Vigdís doubted she'd be bored with either brother as a mate. She still didn't know if she wanted to marry at all, but the exchange had impressed upon her the impracticality of her determination in this society. If she didn't choose someone she cared for, she might lose her ability to choose, despite Father Ari's assurances.

They walked to the north field where Olaf had thrown a large cowhide on the ground, marking the corners with thin posts.

Siggi pointed to one. "Traditionally, the posts are hazel. We call this process skora a hólm, the scoring of the challenge. Once he wraps the rope around each post, the duel will take place within the höslur. Neither combatant may place a foot outside, else forfeit his claim."

"Do they fight with fists? Swords?"

"Swords and shields. They trade single blows, one at a time, until someone spills first blood. Then the challenge is finished."

Siggi's description didn't sound too bad to Vigdís. This seemed more like a prize fight to first blood than a duel to the death. She breathed more easily, her guilt at being the likely cause of injury fading.

One farmhand stacked three plain wooden shields on the north side of the höslur while another did the same on the south side. Both Hávarr and Bergmar stood beyond the ropes, still glaring daggers at each other. They became like angry bulls, ready to gouge the other with their horns, just waiting for the red cape to flutter.

With the preparations complete, Father Ari stepped to the höslur, one hand up in benediction. He spoke a blessing on each pole and one on both combatants. With a nod to Olaf, he backed away.

Olaf almost tripped over the rope but caught his balance. He hiccupped before he spoke. "Bergmar, you have challenged Hávarr to the hólmgang. Is that true?"

Bergmar nodded, his eyes fixed on his brother.

"Hávarr, you have accepted his challenge, is this true?"

Hávarr nodded with a grim frown on his face, putting his hand out for his sword. Once in his grip, he held it before

148

him with both hands. Olaf nodded to the farmhand next to Bergmar, who handed the darker brother a sword.

Olaf held his arms high, causing his sleeves to fall back. Vigdís noticed several strange symbols painted on his upper arms, like stylized snowflakes. They must be the magical symbols Hávarr had spoken of. Strange how she'd never noticed such things, but the older man rarely exposed his arms.

"This hólmgang will determine who has the right to a courting contract with the single woman, Vigdís. This hólmgang will end at the sight of first blood. This hólmgang will begin... now!"

Olaf dropped his hands and backed out of the höslur. This time he did trip, tangling his feet in the low ropes and falling on his backside. Titters rustled through the crowd and even Hávarr grinned before he carefully stepped over the rope, sword at the ready.

Siggi whispered. "As the challenged, he is permitted the first blow. Bergmar can block with his shield or parry with his sword but can't step beyond the ropes. Even taking a step back is cowardice. Two steps out of the ropes and he's considered fleeing from the fight and branded a coward forever."

The watching crowd grew silent as Hávarr aimed his first blow at Bergmar's left shoulder. The darker man easily deflected the cut with the wooden shield, though a large chunk of the shield broke off and flew toward Olaf. With a curse, Olaf ducked. Another giggle swept around.

Vigdís caught her breath as Bergmar lifted his sword in answer to his brother's blow. Instead of the straight, powerful cut Hávarr used, Bergmar feinted first high and then swung the sword low, aiming for Hávarr's thigh. Hávarr moved more quickly than Vigdís had expected, and jumped over the arc of the sword, neatly avoiding the cut.

With the first sally finished, each combatant crouched and settled into place.

The two brothers circled, each grimly studying his opponent. Fair and dark, they matched each other step by step in the small space. The crowd hushed as they moved, and Vigdís stood still, waiting for one of her suitors to win or get hurt.

Bergmar growled and the tip of his sword flicked toward Hávarr's shield. The blond brother didn't take the bait, though, and refused to answer the feint. After two more steps, Hávarr swept his sword at Bergmar's shoulder, but the shield blocked his blow.

Now Bergmar smiled with feral glee. Since Hávarr had taken a hit, Bergmar had his chance. He took his time, turning his head back and forth, contemplating each aspect of his brother's position, stance, and weapon. He stood slightly straighter, his shoulder muscles bunching for action, but then stopped before the sword moved more than an inch.

The crowd sighed in disappointment at the aborted action.

Before the sigh faded, Bergmar's sword jutted into the small gap below Hávarr's shield. If Hávarr hadn't shifted his leg, the tip would have sliced a good chunk of his calf. A bare inch of air kept first blood from spilling.

Now Hávarr had another chance.

Vigdís forced herself to breathe as her vision grayed from dizziness.

Once more, both brothers sunk into a battle crouch, intent concentration glaring across the hólmgang.

Olaf let out a primal scream and all eyes except Hávarr and Bergmar's turned to him.

The older man held up his own sword. "I want to fight for her, too! She should be my concubine. I saw her first, so I should have first claim!" He stepped into the ropes, whipping his sword at both his sons with a wild swing.

Hávarr didn't step back but ducked to one side to avoid his father's sword. Bergmar jumped back from the sword and shoved Olaf to the ground. "Stay out of this, old man! She's not for the likes of you!"

While Olaf distracted Bergmar, Hávarr placed his sword on his opponent's neck, pulling it gently to draw a fine line of blood. "I believe I have first blood, brother. Will you concede?"

Bergmar slapped Hávarr's sword away. "You use a cheap trick, Hávarr! Did you put Father up to this? Did you plan this all along?"

Hávarr shrugged. "How would I have planned this, brother? I didn't realize you'd issue a challenge. Now do you agree I've won the day? How do you rule, Father Ari?"

The priest stepped forward and held up Hávarr's hand in triumph. The blond gave Vigdís a self-satisfied smile so bright, it rivaled the sun.

Bergmar glowered and stomped off, flinging his sword aside and almost hitting the farmhand holding his third shield. Vigdís released her breath at the abrupt ending of the duel as Olaf stepped up, swaying slightly. "I disagree! I didn't get to fight for my right!"

Beside her, Siggi rolled her eyes. "I suppose I must retrieve my husband now. You should go speak with your champion,

Vigdís. You have plans to discuss. What I'll tell Enika's father now, though, I don't know."

Vigdís put a hand on the older woman's arm. "Perhaps ask her mother to listen to Enika. She should have a say in her marriage, don't you think?"

Siggi pursed her lips, studying Vigdís. "An intriguing idea. For what it's worth, I approve of you as Hávarr's choice." The older woman nodded with a half-smile and extracted her husband with soft words and whispered promises. She peeled him away from his sword and led him, stumbling, to the main hall.

Vigdís stared at Hávarr. He didn't do things by halves. His dramatic flair impressed her, despite herself. No, she'd never become bored if she took him to husband. Still, his sneaky win of the hólmgang bothered her.

Had this outcome been somehow fated? Had the first man to notice her in Iceland been destined to become her husband? She had never believed in fate before. Even her belief in God grew shaky at times. But what, if not destiny, had caused her to slip into a different time? What agency had pushed her through the veil of space and time from Ohio to Eire? What force had convinced her of Iceland as a destination when she needed to escape Eire? Did her own illusion of free will simply echo the idle doodling of some nebulous master of fate?

Shaken to the core, Vigdís took a deep breath. No matter what the intentions of the powers that drove her, she would make her own choices. She would take charge of her destiny.

As she approached, he turned to her, his smile broad and open. "See? I told you I would tell Father when the time seemed right! Now no one can deny our right to court."

She rolled her eyes and pulled his sword arm down, carefully. "Yes, you're quite clever. The announcement was sufficiently theatrical. Now come, let's eat. All this activity on an empty stomach will make me surly, and you don't want a surly wife, do you?"

He swung her around three times and kissed her before she squealed at him to put her down. He chuckled and patted Father Ari on the back as they walked toward the hall.

* * *

Miami, 1993

Val pushed away from the keyboard and stretched her back, moaning as it cracked from the unusual movement. She'd been working on this part of the story all Saturday and needed a serious break.

Karl had gone to a Civil War re-enactment, so she had a rare weekend all to herself. She used this precious gift to escape through her writing. She became more alive as her counterpart in the twelfth century than she did in real life. Psychiatrists probably had a fancy word for this. Projection, perhaps? Vicarious living?

Whatever it was called, writing remained more productive than reliving those horrifying hours, stuck in her bathroom as the storm threatened her existence. Val shuddered and shoved the memory back into the hidden pockets of her mind.

Her writing allowed her to enjoy an aspect of life she didn't have at home and gave her a sense of romance and adventure—a purpose. She must make certain her heroine married and had children—the ultimate vicarious living for her frustratingly childless self.

She opened the cupboard and pulled down the bread, grabbing jars of peanut butter and jelly. She'd miss this if she lived in another time—the sweet, salty satisfaction of a good PB&J. No fortified wheat or 7-grain, just nutritionally void white bread.

The gourmet concoction squished in her fingers as she sunk her teeth in. She savored the flavor while she put away the jars and washed the knife.

Hávarr and Vigdís must get married soon, she supposed. Bergmar didn't seem the type to accept his fate meekly and slink away. Surely he'd have something else up his sleeve. Olaf wouldn't be done with Vigdís yet, either. Where had she gotten the snowflake symbols from? She must ask Snorri if they sounded familiar. A glance at the calendar on the wall showed a craft meeting this weekend. While not a full event, Snorri sometimes attended the craft nights. Maybe Astriðr would recognize the symbols.

The mail truck slammed into the curb, making her jump. After closing her eyes and taking several calming breaths, she grabbed the stack of bills and junk mail. She frowned at a bill from Doctors' Hospital. Karl hadn't been in for a procedure in a while. What did they want now?

She opened the bill and stared at the total. Four thousand dollars? For what? A colonoscopy. Ridiculous. Insurance should have covered the whole thing.

The insurance office wouldn't be open on Saturday. She'd have to call during working hours to get this cleared up. Val noticed a letter addressed to Karl and instantly recognized his ex-wife's chicken-scratch handwriting. For a long moment, she considered opening it to see what the bitch had to say. She probably wanted more money. Val left the envelope, unopened, on Karl's nightstand.

Karl cost at least as much as he earned, and half again, between the medical bills, the child support, and his hobbies. In reality, she'd do much better, financially, on her own. Even when he stayed home, he had his nose in painting his models or watching yet another episode of Miami Vice. He'd become more a roommate than a husband. Still, she had her own pursuits and got as obsessed as he did.

Val wished she had girlfriends to hang out with. Not that Jorge didn't fill the shoes of at least three chatty women, but Val never really had close female friends. She'd always related to men far more easily.

She pushed her financial worries to the back of her mind and pulled a beer from the fridge. After she drank half down, she grimaced. The mead had spoiled her for beer. She now preferred the sweeter drinks to the hoppy flavor. Still, wasting alcohol would be a sin, so she finished the can.

Thus fortified, she sat at her keyboard and stared at it for several minutes. She re-read her last few paragraphs, trying to craft the transition into the next scene. Maybe she'd need to sleep again first? No, she must record what last night's dreams had brought.

* * *

Iceland, 1103

The next few days were full of work, food, and drink, and Vigdís didn't know how to react to all the activity. She preferred her solitary farm, with quiet evenings, weaving in front of the hearth, or watching the sun set. This constant industry and fervent celebration, not to mention the sheer number of people, set her teeth on edge.

Hávarr took her for quiet mornings away from the main farm. The first time he arrived at the stable, she rubbed sleep from her eyes to see the silhouette of the large man's shoulders blocking the morning sun from her face.

"Look, my very own eclipse."

His eyes went wide at her quip, but then he laughed. "But I don't predict seven years of drought and famine!"

She pushed past him, eager to wash her face in the rain barrel outside the stable. The hay dust caked on her skin each night, and she'd feel gritty until she could properly wash.

"May I take you to the river today, Vigdís?"

"To the river? Whatever for? We go to the river every day."

"Well, past the river, actually. I have something to show you."

Her eyes narrowed. His words sounded suspiciously like those of Tommy Jackson, in Ohio. Only he'd hoped to show her something a bit more intimate than a river. She'd rained on Tommy's parade by laughing at him, a strategy she used now. "We aren't married yet, Hávarr, and I've chores today, as do we all. Three fields still need clearing."

"Mother said I could steal you for the morning. Never fear, you won't get in trouble. The sight is truly spectacular, I swear to you!"

Her interest piqued, Vigdís reluctantly agreed. "Let me fill a waterskin, first. Is it a long walk?"

"About an hour each way. I have mead and bread." He patted the small bag slung on his belt.

Out of excuses, she nodded. "Then lead the way, my brave explorer."

He flashed her an endearing half-smile and took her hand, walking northwest toward the river. As they came to the river, he gave her a sly grin and before she realized, hefted her into his arms.

"Hávarr! Stop it! Put me down!"

"I'm only doing my duty and helping you across the river. Ow! Stop squirming! You're heavy for one so short."

When they got to the other side, she was torn between glaring at him and laughing. Instead, she turned toward the ridgeline in the misty distance. The looming horizon grew closer as they walked, coming into clearer view with each step.

When they finally arrived, Vigdís put her hands on her hips, somewhat breathless from the slight rise in the land. "Well? It's impressive, I grant you, but nothing so spectacular. I've seen mountain ridges before, Hávarr."

"This is not the spectacular part. Have patience, my silk Valkyrie."

She rather liked that nickname. He'd used it before, and the connotation of being both smooth and ferocious wasn't lost on her. Pursing her lips, she followed as he trekked toward a break in the ridge.

They wended their way through the narrow gap, the lava formations on either side seemingly writhing in frozen motion, caught forever into cooled rock. Several times, Vigdís imagined faces or animals staring at her from the sensuously twisted surfaces. A growing rumble made her think a low-level earthquake had begun, but she didn't feel the earth tremble at all.

Once clear of the ridge, they turned to the right, and Vigdís caught her breath.

There, in the shining sun, sparkled a rainbow above a magnificent roaring waterfall. The cascade must have been at least a hundred feet tall, falling into a churning pool below.

"Aha! I've timed it perfectly. A magical vision for my beautiful Eirish beloved."

He caught her hand and spun her around in a dance. She laughed in delight as he pulled her into his arms. Suddenly their faces were closer than they'd ever been, barely a hand span separating them. Vigdís breathed more heavily, uncertain what to do. Her stomach flipped and her face grew warm.

One moment became endless as she stared into his intense blue eyes, lost in the glittering depths of intense regard.

The tension became too much for her, and she broke away, her gaze drawn to the waterfall. She walked a few steps before she felt Hávarr's hands on her shoulders, and they both watched the water sparkling in the summer sun, the mist reaching out to form rainbows.

He almost whispered. "Do you regret our betrothal, Vigdís?"

She shook her head, still watching the mists. "No, not in the slightest. I still need time to get used to the idea of being betrothed. Our lives will change once we're wed."

"Indeed, they will, for the better. Will you still love me when I walk into the house with muddy shoes?"

She turned at the playful note in his voice. He waggled his eyebrows and gave her a goofy grin. She chuckled at his antics. "Of course, I will. As long as you promise to love me when I'm moody and waspish."

"We've a bargain, then." He hugged her close and she didn't want him to let her go. When they finally parted, they returned to the farm estate in silent agreement, holding hands as they walked.

This hadn't been the only time she escaped the throng of work and people. Over the last few days, she and Enika managed to chat together several times. She even carved a few moments with Siggi now and then.

Once Bergmar approached her, his face an intriguing mix of hopeful supplication. His charming smile made her heart skip a beat. "The day is warm, and you look flushed. May I walk you to the river?"

As tempting as his smile and his company remained, she must remain strong. "Do you really think that would be wise, Bergmar? After the hólmgang?"

His expression turned sullen and dark, and he stalked away, angry at her refusal, she stared after him. What did he expect? He publicly challenged for her and lost. Both their honor would be damaged if someone caught them walking alone. Hávarr would be upset and she dreaded disappointing him. Besides, Bergmar could court any of Hávarr's prior contracts now. Like Atla.

Hávarr piled on the charm after his triumph. He made a big show of weaving a wreath of wildflowers for her hair. When presented, he unplaited her hair and brushed it until it flowed free and long down her back, dancing blonde wisps in the Icelandic summer wind. He secured the wreath on her head and led her to a slow circle dance while Siggi watched, the older woman's hands clasped together in delight.

Fennja told her later it showed his mark of favor for courting, proving he'd chosen her as his preferred mate above all others. Vigdís hadn't expected to be so elated at this news, but she walked around with her head in the clouds. A brief talk with Enika assured her the young girl had no resentment toward her. In fact, the girl thanked Vigdís for removing one courter from her father's list. Enika also hinted her mother might try to help her secure a contract with Nonni.

Vigdís seldom saw Bergmar afterward. She only glimpsed occasional flashes of his dark, brooding face.

Fennja, her own wedding now complete, became full of plans and ideas for Vigdís' wedding. In fact, Vigdís had little to say about such planning, as Siggi and Fennja took over the preparations.

Fennja held up yet another fabric to Vigdís' face with an appraising expression. "We should have the ceremony at the last harvest. That would mean plenty of food, and you can stay warm all winter with Hávarr in your bed." Fennja's elbow jab made Vigdís grunt in surprise and not a little pain, but she grinned. She didn't wish to show how nervous the prospect of the wedding night made her.

160

Valerie had been only eighteen when she'd ended up in this strange time. While she'd been no angel, she'd only kissed boys. In Eire, she had held herself away from any men, afraid to get entangled in case she returned to her own time.

Six years later, she no longer harbored such a dream. She had become resigned to being truly stuck in this medieval world. She'd have to settle in and turn native. As a single young woman capable of bearing children, this meant getting married and having a family.

To have family, by necessity, meant having a wedding night.

Back in her native time, in the 1960s, her mother had sat her down on the bed one Saturday afternoon, after her father and brothers had gone to a baseball game. "Darling, there are things we must discuss, you and I. Woman things."

Valerie had rolled her eyes. "Mom, Natalie told me all about that."

Her mother had raised her perfectly shaped eyebrows. "Oh? What exactly did Natalie tell you?"

"Boys and girls go to sleep together when they get married. They have babies afterward."

With a low chuckle, her mother had put a hand on her shoulder. "She isn't wrong, but she left out a few salient details—that's what I'm here to tell you about."

The conversation had turned awkward, but eventually Valerie understood the mechanics. She didn't fear lying with Hávarr. With his ready laugh and beautiful body, she ached for his touch. Still, his height and weight made her feel tiny beside him, and she feared he might hurt her by accident.

"Vigdís? Vigdís? I asked what you thought of these." Fennja held up two sets of turtle brooches, one in bronze and one in silver. Both had intricate traced etching on them. The bronze had floral designs while the silver had cats.

Vigdís grinned. "I like the cats."

Fennja nodded. "You've made an appropriate choice. Cats are sacred to Freyja, and she is sacred to women during marriage."

"For a Christian wedding, there are a lot of pagan symbols."

With a laugh, Fennja placed the brooches on a growing pile of finery for the wedding. "Old habits die hard. Some of us cling to the ancient beliefs like a toddler on their mother's leg, loathe to let go or ever lose sight of them. Some day, perhaps, the last vestige will fade away."

Suddenly, Vigdís tried to breathe and couldn't pull enough air into her lungs. "I need to be outside, Fennja."

Without waiting for a response from the surprised woman, Vigdís ran down to the river. She sat on the springy grass along the bank, taking deep breaths as she watched the water flow by.

This whole marriage plan just moved far too fast for her. Her entire life became everyone else's to arrange and decide. How could she go along with this like a lamb to slaughter?

A chanting male voice wended around the riverbank, drawing her curiosity. The words formed a sing-song rhyme.

That sixteenth I know, if I seek me some maid
to work my will with her
the white-armed woman's heart I bewitch,
and toward me I turn her thoughts.

That seventeenth I know, if the slender maid's love

I have, and hold her to me
Thus I sing to her that she hardly will
leave me for other man's love

As Vigdís turned the corner, she saw someone hunched over a tree stump covered in small pieces of stone with markings carved upon them. Olaf stood, his hand shoving something into his pouch. "You look distraught, child."

She shook her head. "I needed to think for a while."

"Come, let us walk."

She didn't want to but didn't know how to refuse politely. He linked his arm in hers and led her to the nearby riverbank. She hadn't forgotten his drunken antics at the hólmgang and kept her eye on his hands.

He held a small package wrapped in black cloth. After he settled on the bank, he unwrapped it carefully and offered her the small loaf of bread, still steaming from the oven. She'd almost bitten it when she felt something on the bottom.

She turned it over and noticed inscriptions on the bread, forming an odd symbol. Two crossed lines, boxed in with marks that didn't meet at the corners. Four stylized pitchfork shapes surrounded the box, each with four tines.

"What's all this?"

"Oh, nothing. I draw things when I'm bored. Please, eat."

Vigdís remembered the symbols drawn on Olaf's arms, the ones she'd seen during the hólmgang. With a sinking feeling, she recalled Hávarr's stories of Olaf's sorcery and spells. Her throat grew dry.

"I don't think I'm hungry. In fact, I must find something to drink."

163

Before he could protest, she shoved the loaf back into his hands and ran to the hall. Thankfully, it remained full of people. She stopped to lean against the door beam and catch her breath, turning to the first person she found. Unfortunately, Bergmar's face glowered at her.

Her fear must have shown, for his brow furrowed. "What's amiss, Vigdís? You look as if you'd seen a spirit."

She glanced back to the river bank, but she didn't see Olaf chasing her. It allowed her to breathe easier. "I... Bergmar, can I ask you something? In private?"

He narrowed his eyes. "Are you changing your mind about Hávarr?"

She shook her head. "No, nothing like that, but I need your advice on something, as a friend. Can I trust you as a confidant? Despite everything?"

Several emotions flickered across Bergmar's dark eyes. Confusion, hope, resignation, and finally determination. He nodded and took her arm, leading her to one of the smaller, unused stables.

Once well away from others, she tried to regain her courage. After swallowing several times, Bergmar placed his hands on her shoulders. "Vigdís, please, whatever you need to ask, do so. I won't be angry."

She flashed him a grateful smile. "That does help, Bergmar. Thank you." She swallowed again before she dove in. "Your father—Hávarr mentioned he dabbled in sorcery. At the hólmgang, I saw the symbols painted on his arms. They looked painted in permanent ink. We called such marks 'tattoos' where I grew up."

164

Bergmar nodded. "He does magic, yes. Mother doesn't approve, so he doesn't do it often."

Vigdís blinked. She'd expected a denial or ignorance, not patent acceptance of sorcery. Still, she hadn't finished. "Today he tried to give me a loaf of bread with a similar symbol carved in the bottom."

He frowned. "What symbol? Can you remember? Can you draw it?"

She glanced around and noticed a thick piece of straw in the hay. In the dirt floor, she sketched what she remembered. The crossed lines, the not-quite-boxes around it, and the pitchfork shapes sticking out of each side.

As soon as she stepped back to show him, he looked wildly around, and scuffed the design into oblivion with his foot.

The panic rose within her. "What? What is it?"

"Nothing good. Come with me, quickly."

He pulled her arm and she stumbled after him. She squeaked in protest, but he hushed her angrily. After making certain no one watched them, he dragged her away to the small wooded area behind the chapel and Vigdís experienced a flash of alarm. Olaf was Bergmar's father. Her trust of him suddenly wavered.

Not many trees grew in Iceland, but a few copses remained. Considered sacred, none would cut them down or use them unless they fell by natural means. Once completely out of sight from the buildings, Bergmar took her by both shoulders and stared into her eyes.

"Tell me your name."

"My name? What in the name of all that's holy do you mean by that? Bergmar, let go. You're hurting me. You're also frightening me."

"Your name."

She glowered at him. "Vigdís."

He studied her face as she spoke and for several moments later. "Do you desire Olaf at all? Do you want to bed him?"

"What? Me, bed him? Are you insane? Don't be ridiculous. He's repulsive!"

He took a deep breath, closed his eyes, and pulled her into a long hug. "Good. That's good. It didn't work, then."

She struggled to extract herself from his arms. "Bergmar, do you mind telling me what you're talking about? What did he carve on that bread?"

He released her and sat on the forest floor and leaned his back to the beech tree. "A love spell. He tried to ensorcel you into loving him."

Despite her attempts at being circumspect, she burst out laughing, the sound echoing against the surrounding trees.

"Quiet, woman! Do you want people to find us? Hush!"

She wrestled her mirth to a low chuckle before she sat at another tree. "A love spell? Are you serious? Did he expect it to work?"

Solemn, Bergmar nodded. "The spell might have worked well enough if you'd eaten his bread. I'm relieved you were smart enough to refuse."

Her eyes widened. "You truly think it would have worked? Carved pastry as a magic spell? Bergmar, you're more intelligent than that, or at least I thought so."

He shook his head. "I've seen Olaf's spells work before, Vigdís. He's no priest, wishing for magic where none exists. He knows the old ways and can call upon them. There are still tales of how he convinced his first wife to marry him."

"First wife? You mean, he married before Siggi?"

Bergmar picked a clover from the ground and started shredding the leaves, tossing the bits behind him. "Isveig, a young girl, barely older than Enika. The story goes Olaf desired her with a burning passion, but she wouldn't even glance his way. One day, she completely changed her mind, and would accept no one else. They married within the moon."

"Where is she now? What happened to her?"

Bergmar closed his eyes. "That depends on who tells the story. However, most people old enough to remember say she simply disappeared one night. Some say Olaf and Isveig fought. Others say he wanted a divorce as she gave him no children and refused his bed. Still others say he already had an eye for someone else. No one knows for certain."

"The girl probably just grew tired of Olaf and ran away."

Bergmar shook his head. "No one saw her leave, and no boat took a girl of that description. Her father searched the entire island for her, without a trace. He thinks the Huldufólk took her under the hills."

"The Huldufólk? Those are like the elves, yes? Fanciful, magical creatures, not human?"

He nodded. "You have such beings in Eire, yes? They have different names but are similar in nature. Not creatures you wish to anger or insult."

Another chill shot down Vigdís' spine. "Bergmar, do you think Olaf might have killed Isveig?" He didn't answer right away, and she shivered.

"I don't know. It's a horrible thought, to accuse one's own father of murder. If he'd killed her, an accident, or even in anger, with others witnessing, he'd pay a weregeld to her father and the matter would be closed. But this would be a secret killing. A secret killing is always murder of the foulest kind. Only the most depraved Icelander kills in secret."

She swallowed again. What would she do if Olaf continued to try to ensorcel her into love? What would she do if he succeeded?

* * *

Vigdís straightened her back from collecting eggs and studied Hávarr as he curried one of her horses. He'd come by early that morning to help with her daily chores, despite Vigdís' assurance that she had things in hand. While it annoyed her he thought she needed help, it also tickled her that he wanted to help. He whistled, brushing the dun-colored coat, obviously enjoying the exercise.

She'd considered asking about Olaf's attempt but worried it would cause a rift between father and son. Telling Bergmar was bad enough, but Hávarr respected his father, by all appearances. To consider such an action might ruin that respect. Vigdís didn't wish to be party to such a rift.

Instead, she watched the impressive young man as he bent to wash the horse's fetlocks. His muscles weren't bulky like a weight-lifter's, but certainly exuded power and control. His

168

temper was even and almost jolly most of the time. Only a true transgression would bring out his temper, which quickly faded. Bergmar, on the other hand, simmered with sullen anger at any slight.

Hávarr stood, his hand wiping his face. "Have I manure on my forehead? Why do you stare at me so?"

She laughed and bent to collect the rest of the eggs. "No manure, I just needed a rest. You were a pleasant sight to rest upon."

Her comment brought the brightest smile she'd yet seen on his face, reaching his eyes with crinkled corners. He dropped the curry-brush and strode to her, taking the egg basket from her hands and placing it on the ground. Then he took both her hands in his and grinned even more deeply. "You have made this a delightful day, Vigdís, my Valkyrie."

Her face grew warm and for a moment, she felt trapped and wanted to pull away from his grip. However, she found it difficult not to relax and return his infectious smile. His hands squeezed hers and drew her closer, turning his head slightly and closing his eyes. Automatically, hers closed as well, and his soft lips barely touched hers. The feather touch of his kiss made her lips tingle, as well as other parts of her body. She reacted by moving closer, their bodies touching with tentative desire and shy wanting.

The horse neighed, and they burst apart. She swallowed and stooped to retrieve her egg basket, using it as a shield against her own longing. Hávarr cleared his throat and dipped the curry-brush into the water pail, attacking the horse's flank with renewed vigor.

She glanced at him several times as they worked, fully aware he watched her as well. They were betrothed now and allowed to kiss. Why did it seem so forbidden and illicit to touch? Perhaps because they weren't permitted to consummate until they married, the kiss seemed like a stolen treat, a promise which couldn't be delivered... yet.

The fragile balance convinced her to keep silent on Olaf's attempts. She mustn't soil this relationship with accusations about her betrothed's own father.

* * *

The simple, turf-roofed chapel had been built low to the ground, but long. Only the small iron cross on the crossbeams betrayed its sacred purpose. Father Ari sat outside on a bench, whittling a small piece of wood. He looked up as she approached.

"Vigdís! It's good to see your lovely face again. Come, would you like cool water? It's a warm day."

While she didn't agree his opinion of warmth—she had yet to be warm in Iceland—she came inside and let him pour clear water into a wooden cup for her. The cup gave her something to concentrate on while she tried to figure out how to broach the subject.

Subjects, to be honest. She needed to talk to the priest about Hávarr, about Bergmar, and most of all, about Olaf.

She sipped her water and studied the priest. He was young, tall, and thin with dark, curly hair. If he had been in her time, she might picture him in the Glee Club. He had a nervous artistic aura about him. She wondered if Enika's paramour was around, but Vigdís noticed no others in the tiny chapel.

"What can I help you with, Vigdís? Have you come to discuss the terms of your courting contract with Hávarr Olafsson?"

She nodded. "Yes, that's one thing I've come for. I also need advice on other matters if you have the time."

He lifted his small carving, a seal with a curved tail. "I've got little else but time, my dear. Come, sit with me and we'll work out your details."

A mind-numbing hour later, she'd learned more than she cared to about contract marriage in Icelandic tradition, her rights and responsibilities, her husband-to-be's rights and responsibilities, and the ceremony requirements. For a long-suffering moment, she wished Icelanders had a tradition for elopement.

When Father Ari finished his explanation, she tried to remember what else she'd wanted to speak to him about. Then the ominous symbol flashed in her memory. "Father, I'm concerned someone is trying to use sorcery against me."

She wanted to withdraw those words as soon as she uttered them. The priest's face filled with pity and contempt.

"Vigdís, my poor, dear girl. You must have faith that God, in His wisdom and power, will protect you from evil. You have faith, do you not? As a child of the church, you are safe in His hands. Don't think again on it."

"But his first wife…"

"His first wife left him, child. The woman became a faithless ingrate and deserves no notice."

"But what if he…"

Father Ari put his hand up, cutting off her protest "No, I'll not hear of it. Such subjects are forbidden to the faithful."

She considered, briefly, the weregeld she'd have to pay for punching a cleric. While she didn't know how much it would cost, the momentary satisfaction wouldn't be worth the extra cost.

With a curt nod, she left the priest, stewing the entire journey home.

Her putative father-in-law tried to put a love spell on her and the priest just waved it off as unmentionable evil. What good would that do? If Olaf had no real power, it still became an awkward situation. In addition, if he had murdered his first wife for refusing his bed, he remained dangerous. If, for whatever reason, he really had magical power, from whatever source… she must keep vigilant about what she ate and drank. Might he perform a different spell? She'd traveled in time, so she had first-hand evidence that unexplained things could happen. Who would she ask?

The only one who might tell her was Bergmar and being alone with him for advice had become too awkward.

* * *

Miami, 1993

The ringing phone dragged Val from her immersion in the world of Iceland, sorcery, and attractive outlaws.

"Hello?"

"Val? The event's over. Can you come pick me up?"

She glanced at the clock on the wall, which said two. Where had the time flown? She swore she'd just sat to write after she read the Sunday comics and finished her coffee. That had been five hours ago.

"Yeah, I'll be there in about twenty minutes. You're at the McDonalds, right?"

"Yup. Johnnie dropped me off on his way north."

"Go inside and have lunch. I'll leave now."

She saved her document and grabbed her purse.

When she arrived at the McDonalds, she didn't see Karl. She ordered a strawberry milkshake and sat in one of the chairs, aimed at the parking lot.

Someone poked her in the ribs, and she cried out, her heart racing. She jumped out of her seat and spun around, the milkshake spilling on her shoes.

"Karl! What the hell!"

Her shout echoed through the restaurant, bouncing against the plastic booths. Everyone glared at her. With a mumbled apology, she stalked to the napkin dispenser, leaving a trail of pink footprints.

"I'm sorry, Val. I was just trying to tickle you."

"Well don't, okay? You scared the shit out of me."

He pouted as he helped her clean up the mess. "You're so jumpy lately."

"You know, sneaking up on someone and then complaining they jumped is a bit stupid, Karl!"

"Don't call me stupid!"

Val glared, wanting to say a million things. She wanted to scream, to punch the wall, something, anything to get rid of this boiling fear and rage inside. Where the fear came from, she had no idea, but it simmered below the surface every day. It burst forth at the strangest moments. She couldn't figure out how to explain this to anyone.

Ignoring his comment, she finished mopping the shake. She replaced the lid over the rest of her drink. Karl bought his own milkshake and sat across from her. "I'm sorry."

She closed her eyes and prayed for patience. She forced herself to smile. "It's fine, Karl. Just don't do it again. So, did you have fun storming the castle?"

He frowned and took another sip of his drink. "No castle. We do civil war, Val. I've told you that."

She waved his comment away. "Yeah, yeah, never mind. How did it go?"

"One guy got burned because his neighbor didn't know how to use blank cartridges. He fired the thing right next to his face and the flash burned him."

"Don't you all take a training course before you're allowed to shoot any of the weapons?"

He nodded. "Either this guy ignored the instructions or skipped the class."

She sipped on her milkshake. "You got a letter from Marjoree."

He sat up. "I did? Is something wrong with Kris?"

"I didn't open it."

He stood, grabbing his drink and backpack. "We'd better go. You should have called me."

Val gritted her teeth and stood. "How would I do that, Karl? You were on a campsite in the middle of the Everglades. Last I heard, they don't have pay phones in the swamp."

He had no answer for her. She drove back to the house in silence.

174

Karl dropped his pack next to the door and rushed around the living room. "Where is it?"

"Next to your bed."

He ran into the bedroom and came out slowly, reading the letter as he walked.

"Well? Did Kris explode during the last eclipse? Or has he broken out in purple stripes?"

He shook his head. "Neither. He has a thyroid problem."

She resisted the urge to peer over Karl's shoulder to see how Marjoree spelled "thyroid." "Is he okay?"

"He will be, once he gets surgery."

Concerns about the boy warred with worries about their finances within Val's mind. Well, crap on a piece of toast.

"How much does she need?"

Karl didn't answer at first. He stared at the letter.

"Karl?"

"Four thousand dollars."

Val jumped up and paced, throwing her arms in the air. "Four thousand dollars? Are you fucking kidding me? Four thousand dollars? As in, a four with three zeroes after it?"

He nodded, handing her the letter in proof. She batted it away but then grabbed the letter and crumpled the paper, throwing it against the wall with all her strength. The letter fell on the carpet with an anticlimactic bounce.

"Karl, where the hell does she think I can pull four thousand dollars from? My ass? I don't have that kind of money. You don't have that kind of money. Doesn't she have health insurance on Kris?"

Karl shook his head.

Val clenched her fists. "What the hell is she doing with the child support you send her every month? Didn't the judge mandate she buy insurance with it? I'm certain I read that in the divorce decree."

"I think so. But she has none now."

Technically, because the court ordered her to buy insurance, Karl wouldn't be required to pay for anything her insurance covered. However, the legal details did little good for the child who needed surgery.

Four thousand fucking dollars.

They might take out a loan. What would they use as collateral? Their car already had a loan. They didn't own a house. Payday loans would never be for so much and came with exorbitantly high interest rates.

Her only option would be to ask her dad. She'd need to borrow money from her dad to pay for her husband's child's surgery, when the boy's mother had been ordered by a judge to carry insurance.

Val didn't want think about this right now. She needed to go walking or something. With an angry kick at the crumpled letter on the floor, she grabbed her purse and opened the front door.

"Val, where are you going?"

"Out. I need to think."

"I can come with you!"

She spun around. "No, Karl. You need to stay here. I need to think, alone. As in without you. Understood?"

The hurt-puppy-dog-look almost made her change her mind, but she needed to work out her options, and couldn't do that with Karl asking questions every five minutes. She turned again and slammed the door in his face.

She stalked down the street, dodging a loose dog at one point and a homeless man at another.

Val shouldn't have done that to Karl. Just because he had no hand in raising the child, didn't mean Karl didn't love his son with all his heart. Kris may have been a sweet kid, but with Marjoree raising him, he'd learned early to manipulate his father into getting what he wanted. Every Christmas and birthday resulted in dozens of gifts mailed to Georgia. Val secretly called them 'guilt payments,' but never said it out loud to Karl.

She'd probably think differently if she had children of her own. Not that her parents had pampered her. As an only child, she had crafted her own entertainment. A book or a set of crayons would keep her occupied for hours at a time. She'd created entire imaginary tea parties from some old plastic Tupperware containers and a table-shaped rock in the back yard. The apple tree became a medieval watch tower for Rapunzel. Not that the prince ever came to rescue her. She always had to rescue him.

Karl had never been her idea of a rescuing prince. He'd been the guardsman who came along while she waited for her prince. He'd been "good enough for now," someone to stave off the ever-present fear she'd never get married and grow old alone with a thousand cats.

Val came to the conclusion that being a cat-lady might have been the better option. In fact, that option would probably be less expensive and less frustrating.

If she included Karl in more of the decisions, giving him the opportunity to help manage their life, their finances, their free time, it might make things better.

The light dimmed and Val glanced up to see the afternoon's clouds forming. March heralded summer in south Florida, and with it came the afternoon downpour. Every afternoon around two, the skies opened and soaked everything in several inches of hot rain. She needed to run back to the house if she hoped to escape a soaking and subsequent sauna.

Val made it to the front door, panting and sweaty, just as a huge crack of thunder made her cry out. She yanked at the door but it wouldn't open, despite several tugs and sobs. A glance at the driveway showed her Karl had taken the car somewhere. At least he'd locked the door behind him this time. She'd yelled at him several times in the past for leaving the house unlocked and unoccupied.

Val sniffed back the tears and rifled through her purse, huddled under the small awning, but didn't find the keys. Drat! She'd left them on the kitchen counter when she came in from picking up Karl. She spied them through the window, glinting in the dining room light, taunting her.

Would the back door be open? Probably not. She didn't remember opening it today, and she always locked all the doors before she went to bed.

She'd have to sit here and wait for Karl to return, whenever that would be. If he'd gone looking for her, it would be hours before he admitted defeat. She huddled against the wall, holding her knees tight and rocking slightly each time the thunder crashed.

The awning didn't even offer enough cover for her to sit.

Fuck my life.

Two hours later, Karl pulled into the driveway just as the rain stopped. By that time, Val had gone through at least seven different stages of anger and self-pity, balanced by resolutions to treat Karl more kindly, pay more attention to him, or divorce him.

Karl carried two bags from Taco Bell. She supposed she should forgive him for tacos. Evidently, her honor was cheap.

Three tacos later, Val felt much more forgiving. Time to grab the problem by the horn and give Karl a chance to assist in the decision-making process. "Karl, the only option I've come up with for Kris' surgery is to borrow money from Dad. Can you think of anything else that might help? What do you think of that solution?"

He shrugged and chomped into his taco. A great blob of meat-like goop dripped onto his shirt.

Val sighed and closed her eyes, praying for patience.

* * *

"You're going to the library again? Weren't you there yesterday? And the day before?"

Val gathered her purse, the disk with her manuscript file, and her car keys. "Yes, and I'm going again. I have things I need to look up for my book."

He crossed his arms and stood in front of the door. "That's all you ever talk about. Your book, your book, your book."

She glared daggers at him. "It's all that's keeping me sane right now, Karl, and if you don't want me to snap into a homicidal rage, you'll let me past. Now."

"I don't understand how writing a book can help. It makes no money or puts any food on the table."

She took a deep breath. "The act of writing the story helps my mind work out problems when I get frustrated with other parts of my life. Like a husband who insists in getting in my way when I need to leave."

Karl backed up a step but still didn't move out of her way. "What's so frustrating?"

Val stared at her husband. "What's so frustrating? Oh, let's see. Hospital bills. Child care. A boss who hates me. A father who won't lend us money when we need it. And to top it all off, a husband who would rather play with toy guns and paint miniatures, and won't move when I need him to get out of my goddamned way. Now move, Karl, or I'll body check you."

He blinked owlishly but he finally stepped aside. She flashed him a parting look of sheer malice before she slammed the door and peeled out of the driveway.

Don't drive angry, Val. Don't drive angry. Accidents happen when people drive angry.

She forced herself to breathe slowly and take each corner carefully, stopping to let an older black man with a pronounced limp cross the street. When he'd passed, she resisted the urge to peel out again.

The past few weeks had gotten worse at every point. Her boss had threatened her job again. Her dad refused to lend any money toward Kris' surgery. She'd gotten a small loan from her retirement account, but she hadn't had a large balance in the account to begin with. For fuck's sake, I'm twenty-four years old. Most twenty-somethings didn't even have a retirement account. Marjoree had insisted she needed the whole thing to get Kris' surgery done.

Then, when Val had ever-so-sweetly asked Karl to have Marjoree send a copy of the medical paperwork, showing how much the surgery should be, he'd gone off the deep end. The screaming fight the night before had probably pissed off a few neighbors. Candles didn't make much of a mess when thrown against a wall, just a colorful spot of wax. Luckily, no one had called the cops on a domestic disturbance.

With all the stress, Val hadn't been sleeping well, despite staying in bed most weekends. She needed to be outside the house and away from Karl.

The library looked deserted for a Sunday. Everyone must be out at the beach. The April sun already burned too hot for her taste. She preferred air conditioning to melanoma.

She staked out a computer cubicle and went to find books. Today, she needed to find out more about medieval Icelandic wedding ceremonies. Feast preparation, clothing and traditions, anything would help.

Several hours later, the lights blinked on and off, alerting her the library would close soon. With a curse, she gathered the books she'd found and headed to the check-out counter.

The teenager behind the counter raised an eyebrow at her selection, but said nothing. Val almost wished she had, to give Val an excuse to yell at someone else. Instead, she took her selections and put them in the scorching-hot car. She should have remembered to leave a window open in the back. If she'd done that, someone would have shattered the window to break into the car.

Val hated this place. She longed for the cool, rolling hills of Iceland, where her heart felt free.

My God, that sounded hokey. Get ahold of yourself, Val.

She didn't want to drive home yet. Karl would be at home, and she didn't want to face him yet. She would just yell, and he didn't really deserve all her anger. She wished she had a physical hobby, like boxing or archery. Some sport that let her hit something to get her anger and frustration out. While she might get involved in the weapons training aspect of the SCA, that didn't really appeal to her. Such training required a hefty investment in armor and weapons, and those guys didn't hold back their blows. She'd seen people get hurt often.

Instead, she drove to the beach. North Miami Beach at night wouldn't be crowded and sometimes watching the water calmed her.

After she located a parking spot and trudged through the sand littered with seaweed, she found a relatively clear spot and sat. A storm brewed in the distance, creating a prematurely dark horizon. Val loved the gloaming, the time between day and night, the growing dusk. A twilight time when the world became mysterious, when the stark contrasts and shadows grew cloaked in secrets. Night became enigmatic and furtive, hiding stories and magic.

The rainstorm slanted from darkening clouds into the roiling sea, and the wind increased, whipping her hair and making her shiver. The scent of ozone and hot sand assaulted her. She should have brought her jacket, but who needed a jacket in Miami in April? Still, perhaps the better part of wisdom would be to return to her car.

And her home.

What would happen if she left? If she got in the car and, instead of returning to a frustrating marriage, she drove away, never to come back? They'd put the apartment lease in her name, and she'd lose her remaining childhood mementoes, but really, would she miss them?

Where would she go?

The obvious solution was her father's house. In April, he won't have headed to Vermont for the summer yet. He'd still be in Florida, both a blessing and a curse. Since her mother died, his drinking had gentled into a six-pack of beer a night. His alcoholism no longer resulted in screaming fights as her mother no longer lived to fight back.

If she moved in with her father, he would have someone to fight with.

Suddenly, leaving Karl didn't seem like such a viable option. In fact, avoiding those fights had been a strong reason for latching onto the first agreeable male she'd found.

She sat in her car as the rain fell, watching the abstract patterns of the heavy raindrops on her windshield, dreaming of another life to which she might escape. After a few moments of swirling dream memories, she pulled out her notepad from her purse and wrote.

Chapter Six

Iceland, 1103

Bergmar paced in the stable yard. "Vigdís, I can't dispute Hávarr won the hólmgang. However, I still believe you'd be much better with me as your husband. Hávarr can barely speak large words, much less hold your interest. You are a highly intelligent woman. Why would you mate yourself to a man with a head more bone than brain?"

Vigdís stirred the dye vat, unwilling to answer. He did not lie. She enjoyed her conversations with Bergmar much more than she cared to admit to anyone. He'd become more of a best friend than a lover. If Hávarr hadn't pursued her so single-mindedly, if Hávarr didn't stir her blood into a frenzied heat, Bergmar would make a wonderful husband.

However, she'd learned appearance and tradition remained indelible to Icelandic society. One broke the rules only with great consequences. One only had to listen to the great sagas to understand the lessons they gave.

In her situation, the hólmgang had made her choice for her. Hávarr had publicly declared his intentions and won the battle. His father, despite his drunken interference with the ritualized combat, had not objected to the match once sober.

The equivalent in medieval times would be reading the banns. In her time, her parents would publish an engagement announcement in the newspaper. Only dire circumstance could break the contract now.

While Vigdís had been born in modern times, it might mean her disgrace, or even her death, to ignore the social norms of her new era. A life with Hávarr would surely be better than a life of disgrace or worse. Even if it meant she wouldn't keep Bergmar as a friend and confidante.

She'd lost her best friend, Natalie, when she went to college and unexpectedly slipped in this time hole. Now she must lose another best friend by complying with what everyone expected.

"Why won't you answer me, Vigdís? Have I angered you? Disappointed you? Please, talk to me!"

She choked back an emotional plea of her own but forced herself to continue stirring the dye. The acrid stench of ammonia made her eyes water. Nothing else could be causing the tears.

Bergmar grabbed her hands, wrenching them away from the large wooden spoon. He spun her around to face him, but she kept her gaze on his boots.

"Vigdís, at least look at me! At least tell me why you've forsaken me! I can't stop thinking of you and us, living together in wedded bliss. Can't you feel the same? I've seen it in your eyes! Stop lying to yourself!"

He drew her so close his warm breath tickled her lips and her belly grew warm. She ached to kiss him but didn't dare.

"It's you who have lied, brother!"

Both Bergmar and Vigdís looked up, with guilty expressions, to see Hávarr stomping toward them. With one motion, the large man flung the two friends apart, Vigdís stumbling back and falling upon the pile of undyed wool cloth.

Bergmar held up his hands and backed away. "Brother, you misunderstand…"

"I can understand what I see with my own eyes! If I hadn't come when I did, my brother would compromise my betrothed. I challenge you, Bergmar, here and now. I beat you before and I shall beat you again!"

"You beat me with an honorless trick!"

Hávarr clenched his fists and stalked to where Bergmar had retreated. With a frantic glance at Vigdís, who remained where she'd fallen, he ducked as Hávarr swung a heavy fist at his left cheek. Bergmar backed several steps until his back bumped up to the stable. Startled, Bergmar stepped to the side, avoiding yet another punch from Hávarr. This one struck the turf-covered eave of the stable, and Bergmar used Hávarr's momentary grunt of pain to scuttle from immediate attack range. He ran until he stood in the clear space between the stable and storage shed.

"Hávarr, come to your senses. You saw nothing improper. I only spoke to your betrothed."

The blond man glowered at his brother and stalked him. "You were about to kiss her!"

Bergmar shook his head. "I admit I got too close. I tried to convince her of my point, but she wouldn't change her mind. She stayed adamant and loyal to you, I swear. If you insist on believing something happened, do not blame her for my impropriety. Vigdís is innocent of any wrongdoing."

Hávarr hesitated, glancing at Vigdís.

Emotions warred within her mind. While she felt furious at Bergmar for getting her into this situation, she also resented Hávarr's proprietary rage. Bergmar did his best to convince Hávarr she had no complicity in whatever Bergmar had done, and she appreciated the effort. If only Hávarr would believe him.

Bergmar snatched up a shovel, holding it before him like a quarterstaff. "Hávarr, if you insist on a complaint, we should take this to the Þing. This is not the proper place to settle this."

His brother growled but eyed the shovel with cautious respect. Hávarr searched the clearing for a weapon of his own, but only found the bright blue dying spoon. He stepped toward it with obvious intention.

Vigdís had had enough. She scrambled from the pile of wool and grabbed the spoon before Hávarr grasped it. She brandished it at her betrothed, making him take two steps back. Blue dye splashed on the ground near his feet.

"Stop it, both of you! This is a ridiculous and spurious argument. Bergmar, go home. You have no reason to be here, and you already know my feelings on the matter. Hávarr, nothing happened here, and nothing will ever happen. You don't need to beat your brother into a bloody pulp to win your case. I am betrothed to you, and that will remain true until we wed. I'll not have you breaking my good dye spoon just to satisfy your need to bash someone into submission out of misplaced masculine wrath."

Hávarr glared at Vigdís but didn't move until she nodded. She glanced to Bergmar, but he'd disappeared. She breathed a sigh of relief at the interrupted battle, relaxing her stance.

"Now, my beloved betrothed, will you help me with the dying? This whole situation has delayed my daily tasks, so I need your help."

Hávarr grunted and picked up a massive armful of wool with a sheepish grin. "Valkyrie, indeed. Where would you like this?"

* * *

Dozens of men, women, and children gathered for the local Þing. They converged like feeding fish on Olaf goði's huge farm to receive judgments, make complaints, and watch the entertainment afforded by all the above.

Three times, Vigdís had needed to dodge Olaf's grasping, pinching hands. The third time, Bergmar approached as she scuttled away from the older man. His raised his eyebrows, but she shook her head. The dark-haired brother must do nothing to defend her. Such a defense would merely cause talk; talk they could ill afford. At least she'd no longer discovered further attempts by Olaf to use sorcery to entrap her.

Vigdís hadn't attended the last Þing, though women often came to the local ones. Each district had a quarterly gathering where the goði settled disputes, assigned new positions, honored accomplishments, and settled debts.

As the local goði, Olaf had responsibility for such things in the Stöng valley area. He sat on his elaborately carved wooden seat, only used for this occasion, and made decision after decision.

Most of the disputes were over land or livestock, and Vigdís drifted into daydreams as the parade of disgruntled farmers walked up to the goði.

Hávarr stood by his father's chair, and Siggi sat next to Olaf in a plainer wooden seat. Vigdís hadn't seen Bergmar for hours.

A scruffy older farmer with a scraggly, thin, gray beard, spoke in a querulous voice. "He lets his cattle graze on my field every year! It leaves the grass short and useless. My own cattle cannot get enough to eat, and they grow scrawny and poor."

The younger man next to him, evidently the older farmer's son, nodded with vigor. "I chase them off every week, and the next day they are back. We've built fences, but they mysteriously fall down each night." The son glared at the defendant, a middle-aged man with black hair and a thick, braided beard. Several ornate silver beads decorated his braids.

The defendant stood silent as Olaf asked, "Is this true. Orinn? Do you allow your cattle to wander into this man's field?"

"I would never do such a thing, honored goði. This man cannot even grow a proper beard, much less proper grass. He wishes to find someone else to blame for his incompetence."

Olaf looked to the complainant. "And what do you say to this?"

The old man sputtered and stroked his beard, but his son said, "He lies! He is a liar. You should be more sensitive to cattle rights. Was your own son not exiled for the same crime?"

190

A collective gasp spread through the gallery. This had been the reason behind Bergmar's exile? Allowing his cattle to graze on someone else's land? She gazed at the crowd, searching for Bergmar's dark hair, but spied no trace of the man. Vigdís wondered if he'd committed the crime, or if he'd been accused unfairly. It didn't sound like an evil infraction, though with the short growing season in Iceland, she understood how precious good grazing grass would be.

Olaf sighed. "Have you any proof of your complaint, then?"

The son stepped up. "I have a witness. He has seen Orinn pull a part of the fence down at sunset."

Orinn gaped at the son, and Olaf waved his hand in a desultory gesture. "Bring forth your witness, then."

When Bergmar emerged from the back of the crowd, everyone gasped again. Murmurs flew across the group, quieting only when he reached the complainant.

Olaf squinted at his son. "Well, Bergmar? Are you here to bear witness for this crime? How ironic."

Bergmar flushed but stood straight. He clasped his hands and spoke precisely. "I have seen this man, Orinn, pull down the stone fence erected between the fields in question. He then goaded his cows into his neighbor's field. So say I."

Olaf stared at his son for several moments. Whispers in the crowd died as the regard continued, intense and unbroken. When Olaf broke the silence, a wave of relief spread across the gathering. "Orinn, I charge you with minor outlawry. You are sentenced with exile for no less than three years. Your sons may maintain your property while you are gone, and if you commit no more acts of crime, you are allowed to return at the end of your term. You must be on a ship leaving the island in no less than a month's time. So say I."

Orinn paled and stood silent until two tall adolescents, evidently his sons, led him away. The older farmer looked smug and bowed to Olaf. Then he and his son faded into the crowd. That left Bergmar standing in the open space.

Olaf frowned. "Bergmar, you've made your statement. Your testimony is no longer needed."

Bergmar still didn't move. "I have a complaint of my own to make to the goði."

The goði in question shifted uncomfortably on his carved wooden chair. He glared at his wife who gave the barest of shrugs. He then glanced at Hávarr, but his older son only had eyes for Bergmar. His thunderous expression spoke volumes to Vigdís. She suddenly wished to be anywhere but here. Even if it meant being back at her father's farm in Ohio, shoveling pig shit, she didn't want to be here at this moment.

"What is your complaint, Bergmar?"

The dark man clasped his hands. "I have a complaint against my brother, Hávarr. He stole a woman I already courted."

Olaf heaved a huge sigh and closed his eyes for several moments. His lips moved slightly, and Vigdís wondered if counting to ten for patience had been a common thing in this time. When he opened his eyes again, he glanced over his shoulder at Hávarr, but the other son stood perfectly still, staring at his brother. Vigdís wanted to shrink into the size of an ant. Several in the crowd glanced at her and whispered.

"Did you have a courting contract in place for this woman?"

"We had an understanding. I came to help at her farm often. We spoke of our future."

192

Olaf frowned. "But you had no legal agreement? Nothing vowed with witnesses?"

Bergmar looked down at his father's feet and clenched his fists. "I didn't know another suitor existed."

Olaf pressed his lips together. "So you have you lain with her?"

Vigdís waited anxiously for Bergmar's answer. Technically, he'd come close to kissing her. If Bergmar claimed he'd lain with her, she could never marry Hávarr. She'd not be able to marry anyone, including Bergmar. He might ruin her reputation with one exaggeration.

Hávarr growled and clenched his fists.

Bergmar hastily shook his head, putting his hands up in surrender. "No, no, I'd never do such a thing! She has never felt my hand, I swear!"

Vigdís let out her breath, grateful for Bergmar's honesty.

Hávarr took five steps to his brother until they stood nose to nose. "Swear to me this is true!"

"I swear it! I've not touched her!"

Hávarr's face grew red and thunderous. "You never think, brother, you assume! This time, your lack of thought has made a difference. You've lost, Bergmar. Go home. In fact, better yet, go away. Find a ship back to Eire."

Vigdís had held back long enough. She stalked into the open space until she stood between the two brothers, now glaring at each other and barely two feet apart. She placed a hand on each of their chests and shoved. "Both of you, stop it! I'm not a bone for two dogs to fight over. I'm a woman, and I will choose who I wish to marry!"

The crowd silenced instantly, but muttering rose again. Someone laughed and another person shushed them. The murmurs grew until a steady hum flowed across the crowd.

Olaf stood, silencing the whispers. A dog barked in the background.

"This is unseemly. Vigdís, child, this is Þing business. I realize you are but newly moved to our island. I don't know how your native Eire does things, but in Iceland, men decide important matters."

For a moment, Vigdís lost her ability to speak. Men decide important matters? War and taxes and governance, certainly, but her own marriage contract?

She took a long, shuddering breath and smiled with sickly sweetness at the older man. "Olaf goði, you are right. I am a stranger in a strange land. In Eire, a woman is never forced to marry against her will, even by her father. I have no brother, no father, no son to speak for me. Therefore, I must make my choice."

Before Olaf countermanded her declaration, she must make her choice clear. She mustn't waver nor leave a shadow of a doubt. With an instant of devastating regret for the friend of her heart, she turned to Hávarr. "I choose you, Hávarr, as my betrothed. Will you accept my contract?"

Behind her, Bergmar made a strangled sound. Don't turn around. Not only would it create doubt in her decision for those gathered, it might make her change her mind. Instead, she stared into Hávarr's eyes, willing him to be part of her performance.

He took her hands and smiled wide, showing strong, straight teeth. "Vigdís, you have made my heart sing. I shall treasure and cherish you until the end of our days."

Bergmar clenched his teeth audibly. "Brother, have a care for her."

Her muscles relaxed almost to the point she lost her balance, but Hávarr gripped her shoulder, holding her steady. Bergmar's footsteps faded away in the distance behind her.

* * *

Fennja frowned, holding up the blue apron dress. "But this isn't a new dress! You need something new for your wedding. I won't have my brother marrying a ragamuffin. Come, let me at least lend you something. Bergmar's last trading trip yielded some wonderful dyes."

Vigdís hadn't heard Bergmar's name in a fortnight and hearing Fennja casually mention him made her catch her breath.

Her very public declaration had made her marriage to Hávarr certain. Why, whenever a choice is made, do the alternatives look far more attractive? Still, no one had set eyes on Bergmar since the Þing, and Vigdís daren't ask where he'd gone. After the near-scandalous accusations Olaf had implied, the slightest whiff of interest in Bergmar would be disastrous.

Fennja clucked her tongue. "You have such lovely hair. Can I not convince you to let me arrange it in a complex style? I am skilled with complicated plaits. The summer has lovely blue flowers; we can weave them in with that blue silk ribbon Hávarr gave you."

Vigdís touched the ribbon in question, the lovely pale blue of the summer sky. "Fennja, you may do what you like with my hair. I'm useless at such crafts."

A knock on the door revealed Olaf. His clothing appeared considerably mussed. "Fennja, may I borrow Vigdís for a talk? I have details to discuss with her."

Fennja narrowed her eyes, but acceded. "Have her back in an hour! I need to take her measurements so her dress will fit perfectly. Two days isn't a great deal of time for alterations, but we can do it. Can you ask mother to come in? I need her help with the decorations."

He nodded and pulled Vigdís by her arm.

"Olaf goði, please, you're hurting me."

He glanced at her and lightened his grip, but didn't let her go. "We need to talk."

Vigdís truly didn't wish to be alone with the odious man. She tried to plant her feet as they passed the last stable. "We can talk here, Olaf goði. What do you need to know?"

When he tugged her arm again, she cried out. "Stop! Olaf, that hurt!"

"That is nothing to what will come on your wedding night! Do you not know that? And you must always call me by my name and title, even when you marry my son. Now come."

Fear made her skin crawl. "Why? Where are you taking me? I don't want to go anywhere."

He grunted and yanked, pulling her off her feet. She scrambled to stand but he dragged her away. "Stop, stop, Olaf! Help! Hávarr!"

Olaf smacked her across the mouth and she tasted coppery blood. "None of that, woman. Shut your mouth or I'll give you a reason to cry out."

Vigdís struggled but the older man remained too strong for her. When she tried to cry out again, he stuffed a rag into her mouth and pulled her by both arms, so she couldn't pull it out. She tried spitting out the filthy thing, but he stuffed it in again. The rag made her want to gag and cry at once, and she choked with panic.

Finally they stopped in the small woods, well away from anyone at the farm. He threw her down on the ground and lie on top of her. The gag remained firmly stuffed in her mouth.

"So, you think to steal away my son, so he cannot marry a wealthy daughter? You think to tease me and then lie with Bergmar? How can you expect to wed my first son with innocence and honor? You speak to the priest about Isveig? I'll show you what you're aching for, wanton girl. Hávarr won't taste this sweet honey until I've drunk my fill of your mead."

She wriggled underneath him, trying to win free, but he had both hands pinned above her head. She scissored her legs to keep him away, but he'd pulled up her dress with his other hand and fumbled at his own trews.

The tears and rage bubbled inside her, and she spit out a cry in anguish. The rag flew into his eyes, momentarily confusing him. She kicked with all her might at his groin.

Vigdís scrambled to her knees and crawled away, still sobbing from reaction. Once she regained her footing, she ran. She didn't choose a direction; she needed to escape Olaf. She dodged several birch trees until she came to a creek she didn't recognize. Following the creek downstream, she saw something in the distance that made her want to cheer. A thin curl of white smoke from a turf roof peeking out over the crest of the hill. With a backward glance to ensure Olaf didn't follow her, she ran to the farm house, panting with ragged gasps by the time she arrived.

The crabbed old woman who greeted her frantic knocking took one look at her, glanced around outside, and pulled her into the cottage.

"Who's done this to you, child? Are you hurt? Did he get away?"

Vigdís tried to speak, but her voice didn't work. The woman poured a mug of ale and made her sit on the bench. "Drink. Drink then breathe, child." She glanced at Vigdís' clothing. "I see he's torn your dress, but I see no blood. You got away in time?"

Vigdís sipped at the ale and nodded. The light, cool drink calmed her, and she finally found her voice.

"It... it was Olaf goði. He pulled me into the woods, and pinned me down, and... and..."

"Hush, girl, hush. I might have known who attacked you. Aren't you betrothed to his eldest, then? Yes, I thought so. You aren't the first that man has tried, and you won't be the last. At least he didn't work his magics on you."

Vigdís' eyes flew wide. "He tried, he did! But I saw the marks and wouldn't eat the bread."

The woman nodded. "Smart girl. I'm glad Hávarr chose you. Now, let's see what we can do about Olaf."

She lifted the next bench seat and rummaged around in the storage box beneath. Cursing under her breath, she dropped the seat and moved to the next. With a cry of triumph, she held up a white object.

"This! Yes, this is just what you need, child. Let me find a piece of thong and we'll tie it on with proper ceremony."

Bewildered, Vigdís watched as the woman pulled out a length of leather thong and strung the white object on, tying a knot in the ends. "Here, wear this at all times. It will protect you from his ministrations, unless he's gotten much stronger than he used to be."

The qualification made Vigdís' fear return, but she took the white talisman. The object looked cylindrical, smooth with a hole in the center. "But what is it? What does it do?"

"Don't you know, child? Oh, you aren't from here, are you? I thought you smelled foreign. From one of the Breton Islands, yes? Then that explains it. This, child, is the spinal bone of a great whale. Its strength is that of a thousand men, and the strength is yours as long as you wear it. Olaf and his witchcraft cannot touch you now. Just be cautious; magic doesn't always work the way you expect."

Vigdís gulped. Whether or not she believed in magic, this would be a powerful symbol. "Are... are you a witch, then?"

The woman glared at her, hands on her hips. "Is there aught wrong with being a witch, child? Despite what the priests say, magic is not evil. It's a tool, used for its wielder's purpose. It can perform acts of charity or cruelty, depending on intent."

"I thought all of Iceland followed Christianity now."

The crone turned and caressed a beam of wood on her wall, tracing her finger over several symbols similar to the ones on Olaf's arms. "Officially, that is true. For over a hundred years, Iceland has been dedicated to the Christian God. However, the old gods run deep. Many heathens kept their beliefs and continued to practice them long after the official dedication. The law allowed such practice, mind you, as long as ceremonies remained private. However, within a few generations, most parents raised their children as Christians. Only a few bloodlines kept the old ways, such as mine."

As the woman escorted her to the door, Vigdís turned to her. "Thank you… uh… I don't know your name."

The woman cackled several times before she caught her breath. "Haven't you heard of me? I'm Arnbjörg. Just you let me know if my nasty son pesters you again, child. Now, just down this way to the left, and you'll find Stöng again."

She closed the door, leaving Vigdís in the chilling evening breeze.

Olaf's mother? Vigdís reflected marrying into this family might not be the wisest move.

By the time she made her way back to the main farmhouse, Fennja had organized several of the servants to search for her. One girl spied her and set up a cry. "Fennja! Fennja! Over here!"

Hávarr's sister approached, limping closer. She looked Vigdís up and down and whistled. "What rock did you crawl out from under? There are twigs in your hair. What have you been doing? Did you find Hávarr in the woods for an early tumble?"

Vigdís swallowed and shook her head. "Not here. Can we talk in private?"

Fennja's laughing eyes suddenly narrowed. She gave a quick nod and pulled Vigdís into her sleeping chamber.

The redolent scent of dye and furs filled the room as Vigdís took a deep breath.

"What happened, Vigdís?"

How to tell her friend that her own father was a disgusting brute? Vigdís swallowed and opened her mouth, but no sound emerged.

Fennja tapped her foot. "Well? Someone obviously attacked you. You wouldn't be so reticent about falling in the forest. I remember precisely who dragged you away. Tell me what happened. I have few illusions about my father. I've lived with him all my life, you know. How do you think I earned this limp and scar? He's a monster, especially when he's meddling with his magic."

Hot tears pushed against Vigdís' eyes. Tears which didn't come when Olaf attacked her now threatened to burst forth at Fennja's instant understanding and acceptance.

Instead of answering the question, Vigdís fell into the other woman's arms, sobbing with sudden, uncontrollable violence. Fennja held her tight, stroking her back and murmuring reassurances.

Slowly, sense returned to Vigdís and the tears eased. Fennja took her by both shoulders and gazed into her eyes. "Did he succeed? Or did you escape?"

"I... I kicked him. I fled into the trees. I didn't know which direction to go. Eventually, I found a cabin, with an old woman..."

Fennja grinned. "Ah, you must have found Grandmother. Did she give you a charm?"

With a shy nod, Vigdís pulled out the piece of whale bone. Fennja examined it with a critical eye, turning it in her hand. "Aye, this should work well enough, especially if Father notices it. Prevention is worth more than a cure, true enough. Be cautious, though. Such charms lose power with time."

Stunned by the calm acceptance of having a serial rapist as a father, Vigdís tucked the charm back into her apron dress. The talisman lay warm and vibrant against her skin. She almost imagined it pulsed with life... or magic.

She gulped and pushed the thought away. Magic didn't truly exist. Perhaps these medieval people manipulated forces of nature as modern folk couldn't? Did they possess some esoteric knowledge that defied scientific explanation?

Vigdís had lived her entire young life being told that magic remained nothing but superstitious nonsense, stories made up by those who didn't know enough science to explain sunrises, plagues, or lightning storms. Magic or miracle explained the inexplicable, but never stood the test of scientific research.

Or did it?

Even the advanced science of 1968 left many things unexplained. Vigdís entertained no illusions that science had solved every mystery and unraveled every puzzle. Curiosities such as Bigfoot, the Loch Ness monster, aliens, Voodoo, people going into comas and waking up knowing another language—these things had no good, scientific rationalization, and yet evidence existed. She had traveled almost a thousand years and had no good, scientific rationalization for it, either.

Perhaps magical ability existed in some people. An ability to manipulate the forces of nature might be possible, beyond a scientific explanation. Magic may have existed in ancient times, but died out in modern times. After the medieval witch pogroms, anyone who had such abilities would wisely keep them secret out of self-defense.

Therefore, it is a distinct possibility that Olaf had possession of such arcane powers. In addition, he'd evidently become obsessed with Vigdís, and appeared willing to use his powers in pursuit of that obsession, despite her public engagement to his own son.

A cold chill caressed her spine.

Fennja hugged her. "Not to worry, Vigdís. I am aware and will work to keep Olaf from you when you're alone. Once you're married, he can't touch you."

"He can't?" Vigdís didn't think Olaf cared about such social conventions as being married if he tried to rape her in the forest.

Fennja laughed, shaking her head. "Once you marry, you have a strong protector in Hávarr. To slay his own father would be his duty, should Olaf violate his new wife. Such a situation has happened before in the sagas and the Grágás."

While recounting an act in the sagas and having a law about it meant the act had happened at least once, Hávarr would be a powerful guardian. With a silent, sharp nod, Vigdís pushed aside her worries and glanced at the sideboard where a beautiful bit of lace lay. "Is that for my wedding?"

With a conspiratorial grin, Fennja held it up to the light. The piece looked so delicate, the sunlight shimmered through the holes like magic. "Do you like it? I thought it would look lovely around your neckline. There should be just enough."

Chapter Seven

The days before the wedding grew frantic with activity and ceremony. Fennja had tried to warn her, but the reality became far more hectic than Vigdís had imagined.

The first day had been full of contract negotiations, actual documents drawn up on vellum, and no few heated arguments. With Father Ari as the only fully literate person for miles, his duties included recording all contracts, but he had little skill at mediation. Hávarr, Olaf, Siggi, Father Ari, and Vigdís engaged in several debates over her bride-price, her assets, expectations, and dowry. Since Vigdís couldn't yet provide the minimum dowry of eight ounces of silver, she must pledge part of her future industry, similar to a home mortgage. For the next three years, one quarter of her cloth production would go to Olaf goði for the privilege of marrying his son. This net amount would balance the bride-price Olaf must pay for his son to marry her. Since Hávarr's status and wealth stood so much higher than hers, she must pay more.

She brought one ell of cloth, the standard length of measurement in Iceland, to the wedding itself. It represented a down payment on the marriage price and a sample of her work quality. She'd chosen cloth dyed a lovely sky-blue.

Vigdís steamed at the prospect of paying to marry someone. It smacked of slavery. Would modern bride's parents paying for the wedding be any different? Still, when in Rome... she signed the papers. She had to trust Father Ari on what she signed as her facility with language included only speech. The written language still baffled her beyond her name and a few words.

With the negotiations completed, written, and signed, with six witnesses attesting to their terms, Hávarr took her hand for the official betrothal oath.

He grasped both her hands and gazed into her eyes. She resisted the urge to grin at his earnest manner, which would be an affront to this clinical, legal ceremony.

"We declare ourselves witnesses that thou bondest me in lawful betrothal, and with taking hold of hands thou promisest me the dowry and engagest to fulfill and observe the whole of the compact between us, which has been notified in the hearing of witnesses without duplicity or cunning, as a real and authorized compact."

Siggi assured her Hávarr would present her with the morgen-gifu, his own portion of the bride-price down payment. Such a custom still sounded like a mutual prostitution agreement, but at least she received the gift this time. He promised to include two kegs of mead and she looked forward to drinking herself silly. Siggi promised her the morgen-gifu would also include many household items, such as valuable iron pots, clothing, jewelry, and even livestock.

Once they completed the contract, Fennja spirited her away for her cleansing.

With men forbidden in the bath-house for this ceremony, the women entered amidst gossip and giggles. Vigdís recognized several of her attendants, including the old woman, Arnbjörg. The crone lifted one white eyebrow when Vigdís walked inside. With a half-smile, Vigdís lifted the cord from inside her apron dress, displaying the whale bone charm. Arnbjörg chuckled and nodded, returning to strewing herbs and petals into the bath.

Siggi, Fennja, and little Enika surrounded her as they slowly stripped off every bit of her clothing. They left the cord with the charm on it. Fennja brushed her hair out until it crackled against her fingers with static electricity.

The pungent odor of sulfur rose from the hot spring bath, so strong it almost made her gag, but Vigdís took a deep breath through her mouth to control the reaction. If she searched for ill omens, vomiting during her maiden ceremony would qualify.

While each of the female attendants stripped and joined her, they gave her advice on her upcoming change of status.

Siggi played with a piece of heather floating in the water. "Never marry a man who knows the meaning of fear."

Fennja laughed. "All men know fear, Mother. Some ignore it and do their duty anyhow. That's true courage."

Siggi smiled, but didn't argue the point. "These words are part of the traditional advice, daughter."

Enika spoke up next, brandishing a sponge. "There are runes said to ease the pain of the wedding night, and the pain of childbirth."

Arnbjörg snorted at this, but added no wisdom.

Dagmar glared at the old woman. "You must make his meals hot and his bed warm. Anything else is forgiven if those two things are always true."

Atla narrowed her eyes and frowned. "Not if he brings in a concubine. Then her bed will be warmer."

"Hush, Atla. If she keeps his bed warm enough, he will never search for a concubine. He'll be too busy!"

Enika giggled and Siggi rolled her eyes. "It matters not how warm the bed is, nor how acrobatic the first wife is. A man will stray when he wants to, and there is little a wife can do to stop it. Look at what happened with Isveig. Learn now, Vigdís. In fact, the more concubines a man has, the more peace the wife finds."

Arnbjörg piped up. "And the more a wife can find her own fun!"

"Hush, good-mother! That's not proper advice this day."

Atla splashed Siggi and giggled. "Don't forget to never be predictable! A man will stray if he knows what to expect from his wife. When he fears her reaction, he will behave better!"

Fennja stood, the water sluicing from her curves. "It's time for the final dunking."

Vigdís braced herself as the women led her to the vat full of ice-cold water. She held her breath as she stepped into the large container, hissing as the warmth of the hot spring fled. Her teeth chattered as Siggi ducked her head beneath the surface. For a moment, she panicked that the older woman knew of Olaf's attack and in a fit of jealous rage, she'd hold Vigdís under until she drowned. When Siggi allowed her to rise, Vigdís gasped for breath. Arnbjörg held out a fluffy sheepskin and Vigdís took it, gratefully wrapping herself in the warm wool. Few things felt as luxurious as a soft, warm wrap after a freezing bath. The aroma of the herbs infused her skin, despite the icy dunking, making her dizzy.

The women lay layer after layer of cloth over her shoulders. The layers showed her ability to provide cloth for her family, a basic measure of wealth. She'd only made two of the items with her own hands. Siggi and Fennja had lent her the others. An Icelandic girl worked most of her young life creating pieces for her wedding and marriage. By only recently immigrating to the land, Vigdís needed several basic items.

Arnbjörg, as the eldest, placed the bridal crown on Vigdís' head with a mumbled blessing. She barely saw the complicated construction on her head in her small hand mirror, but Fennja and Siggi both assured her she looked beautiful. Fennja had crafted the crown with elaborately woven straw and wheat, forming six tufts and decorated with yet more flowers. She wondered idly if they'd added a bird's nest or a squirrel to it. Her head seemed heavy enough.

Vigdís hoped no bird decided her crown would be an attractive perch until after the ceremony.

The time had arrived.

Arnbjörg handed her a rather thin sword, obviously ceremonial and of little practical use. She held it awkwardly in her hand, careful not to let the point touch her leg.

Every tenant farmer in the area must be here.

Vigdís studied the sea of a hundred faces, pale and tanned alike, in the gallery watching her, bedecked like a sacrificial cow, walk to the altar. Father Ari stood at the small platform with a frown, glaring at Olaf.

Vigdís had to step carefully, as she had no practice walking in seventeen layers of dress, nor with twenty thousand tiny autumn flowers braided through her unbound hair. In fact, she daren't move her head for fear the blossoms and the bridal crown would tumble to her shoulders.

All these details swam in her imagination as she made her stately progress toward the altar, where Father Ari waited to change her life.

Hávarr stood at the altar already, with his father glowering next to him. He dressed simply and carried a large sword, a symbol of his ability to defend his family. His face grew red and his eyes shifted from her to his mother with nervous frequency.

She scanned the crowd for Bergmar, but found no trace of the dark-haired brother. She took a deep breath. Just as well Bergmar had disappeared. She must keep to her decision at this point. Her fear had blossomed within her belly at each passing hour, and now threatened to burst forth like Hekla, the enormous volcano they all lived beneath.

A cloud passed in front of the sun, cooling the field with ominous shadows. Vigdís shivered and tried not to think about omens and magic.

Fennja had gifted her with a small, bronze amulet of the goddess Freyja, as a charm for fertility and luck with her marriage. She found the shape of the object in a pouch hanging from her belt and surreptitiously squeezed it. Oddly enough, the warmth of the bronze charm reassured her and the cloud drifted away from the sun.

As they approached the altar, the exchange between Olaf and Father Ari resolved into words.

"No, Olaf. I can't allow such a thing. This is a Christian ceremony. We are a Christian country now."

"But how can we bless a wedding without the proper sacrifice? Surely the gods will curse their line forever. This is my son. I can't let that happen."

Father Ari pursed his lips. "If you wish to dedicate the animal as a living gift—after the main ceremony, mind you—I will not object. It must be in private as per the law. No blood magic."

Olaf grinned and nodded. "A young goat would be perfect, a dedication to Thórr."

Father Ari held up his hand. "I'll turn a blind eye to it, but don't share the sordid details."

By this time, she'd come to the altar and halted, glancing at first Hávarr and then Father Ari, uncertain what to do next.

Hávarr lifted his sword and held it out to her. "With this sword of my ancestors, I gift thee, my bride. Hold it in trust for the sons you will bear me."

She cast a quick glance at Siggi, who motioned for her to hand her sword. She did, taking his sword in return. "With this sword I gift thee, my groom, with the power of my guardianship and protection."

Each sword had a large, complex wrought iron ring on the hilt. At Siggi's nod, she took hers and placed it on her arm, the cool weight at once reassuring and final.

She stumbled through her vows, repeated from Father Ari's promptings. Hávarr did the same, his voice quavering almost as much as her own.

Father Ari raised his hands. "With these swords and with these rings, the sacred compact of husband and wife is binding. The oaths are now made and let none break them asunder."

With a sidelong glare at Olaf, Father Ari dropped his hands onto each of their heads, and the watching crowd cheered. He raised his hands once again, calling for silence. "Let the feasting begin!"

* * *

Such a feast they had.

Vigdís had attended Fennja's wedding, but she remained a daughter of the house. Hávarr wasn't only the son, but the eldest son. The amount of resources used for his wedding feast put Fennja's celebration to shame.

The groom arrived first at the feast hall, a tradition which at one time involved an actual foot race, the loser being re-quired to serve ale that night. However, tradition dictated the groom must win, so Father Ari insisted they dispense with a physical race. When Vigdís arrived, Hávarr grabbed her hand and grinned, making Vigdís giggle with nervous energy. He led her into the hall, carefully leading her over the threshold so she wouldn't trip. Such a natural misstep would be another horrible omen.

Once she stepped inside, she became a proper wife, no longer a bride. Siggi had told her stepping into Hávarr's ancestor's home would be a pivotal moment in the ceremony.

Without warning, Hávarr lifted the sword she'd gifted him and with a great battle cry, drove it point-first into the roof-tree, the supporting pillar of the house. Vigdís let out an involuntary screech and jumped back, but Hávarr chuckled.

"The depth of the cut is the depth of our marriage luck. Look how deep the furrow is? We shall have enormous luck!"

She glared at him. "It would have been luckier to warn me first. I'm certain you shaved several years off my life with that scare! How lucky is it if your bride falls over from fright hours after you marry her?"

He pulled her off her feet into a bear hug, but she resisted, batting his arms. "Stop it, Hávarr! Stop! You'll make the crown fall off!"

Her groom chuckled and gently let her down. She snorted and glared at him, straightening her dresses.

Fennja caught up with her and carefully removed the crown. "Come with me and we'll get you out of most of this fabric. Then you can drink the mead-toast."

"Mead!" Hávarr lifted a drinking horn with his cry and went off in search of his quarry.

Siggi shook her finger at him. "Not yet, Hávarr! Your first drink must be with your bride. Have I not taught you correctly? We'll return with her shortly."

Hávarr pouted like a child, but sat on the bench, by all appearances behaving as a proper groom. The twinkle in his eye as he winked at Vigdís belied his façade.

Once she emerged free from her mountain of dresses, Vigdís imagined she might fly if she flapped her arms hard enough. She wondered at the reason for this part of the ceremony. The freedom from the weight of the crown and the costume gave her joy and energy. She hurried back to the feast hall, where she joined her new groom in their first taste of mead as a married couple.

She sat at the head of the table, conscious of all eyes on her. The entire crowd would never have fit in the hall. Only the head couple from each tenant farmer ate inside. The rest of the guests ate at trestle tables outside, in the dim autumn evening.

Siggi handed her a large bowl filled with honey wine. Handles in the shape of cat heads protruded from each side. Cats meant it must be sacred to Freyja, the goddess of fertility. Vigdís glanced at Father Ari, but he paid no attention to the decoration or the ceremony. He drank his own mead with single-minded determination.

Hávarr surreptitiously pulled out a small metal hammer-shaped charm and touched the cup. He tucked it into a belt pouch before Father Ari could notice. Hávarr then held the cup to her lips. She took a sip of the drink, redolent of summer flowers, and the warmth of the alcohol infused her blood. He took a sip from her hands, and Olaf said a blessing over them.

Siggi presented the roast lamb and Hávarr carved bits for each of them. Olaf took over the meat serving once the bridal couple had theirs. Dishes of cheese and honey, fruit, nuts, bread, and turnips passed by so often, Vigdís lost track of how much food she'd eaten. She didn't wish to get too full, but the mead had gone straight to her head. If she stood now, she'd stumble.

When Hávarr stood, holding his hand out to her, she stared at it, dumb. What now?

Siggi cleared her throat, and Arnbjörg waved her hand. "It's time, child. Go make your husband a man."

Certain her face burned bright red, Vigdís took Hávarr's hand, grateful for his steadying arm. He led her through a torch-lit hallway to a guest room, decorated for the ceremony with flowers and fruit on the branch.

Six men followed them, startling Vigdís. Did she need to perform in front of witnesses? Cold fear gripped her belly. She could never do such a thing.

Hávarr whispered in her ear. "Don't worry, Vigdís. There is a door to separate us. They must see us enter. They will return to witness us emerging in the morning."

Her breath returned, but she almost stumbled on the flagstones as he led her to the enormous bed. Without warning, he hefted her into his arms and placed her gently on the feather mattress. She gulped and glanced to the door. One witness, Father Ari, nodded to her and closed the door, separating the bridal couple from the intrepid observers.

Hávarr bent to kiss her, but a shout from outside stopped them. "Wait, wait!"

The door cracked open to reveal Fennja, the bridal crown in her hand. "She must have this on, and you must take it off. It's part of the ceremony."

Hávarr rolled his eyes. "Sister, you live to plague me. Give me the stupid crown."

He smiled as he took the bridal crown, and Fennja jabbed him in the ribs. "Just be gentle, brother. She's frightened enough as it is. If you hurt her, I shall find your tender spots and hurt you back, with a sharp knife if need be. Vigdís, remember your dreams tonight. Arnbjörg will want to know the details."

Once Fennja closed the door again, Hávarr hovered over her, his face inches from her own. "May I kiss you now, my bride?"

She forced herself to smile and show bravery she didn't possess. "Didn't I give you a sword that means you don't have to ask?"

"Just because I don't have to ask, doesn't mean I should assume."

With genuine humor, she said, "Perhaps you will make a good husband."

He caressed her cheek and his lips met her own. He tasted of mead and lamb, both sweet and savory. After a long, lingering kiss, he sat on the bed next to her.

Her cheeks burned again. Vigdís remained incredibly conscious of every place his skin touched her own. His thigh lie next to hers, and he leaned on one arm next to her shoulder. His other arm lightly touched her shoulder and along her arm, creating gooseflesh. She shivered and he smiled.

"Please, Vigdís, don't fear me. I vow, I will never hurt you."

"You may not be able to help hurting me. I've heard it's painful, no matter how gentle the man tries to be."

He frowned. "That may be true, and I cannot refrain or the marriage will not be legal. But I'll go as slowly as we need to."

She smiled, again putting on her brave face.

"First, I must give you the morgen-gifu. By the name, I should give this in the morning, but Grandmother says it's more effective before the first time."

She blinked, eyes full of innocence. "What, here? Now? Isn't there livestock involved? That might get messy, not to mention smelly."

He laughed, brushing his hand through his hair to tame the mess. "A token of the full gift now. The larger items come in the morning, after we eat." He bent over to the floor and fumbled with his clothing, returning with a small pouch in hand. After opening the pouch, he pulled out the hammer he'd touched to the cup at the ceremony and handed it to her.

The piece of jewelry glimmered with exquisite, intertwined decorations cut into the silver hammer.

"You should lay it in your lap for the blessing. This is to ensure your fertility."

She narrowed her eyes. "More pagan symbols?"

He dropped his gaze, glancing up meekly. "My father insists. He still follows the old ways, but the law says he must do so in private."

Vigdís traced the design on the hammer charm. "What must I do?"

"Place it here, like this. Now stay still while I bless the charm."

Self-consciously, Vigdís lay on her back with the hammer in her nether-region while Hávarr spoke in soft tones, too low for anyone outside the door to hear.

"Bring the Hammer the bride to bless
On the maiden's lap lay ye Mjolnir,
In Frigga's name then our wedlock hallow!"

He then kissed the hammer where it lay, and she giggled when his hair tickled her thighs. He looked up, grinned, and then buried his face in the area, eliciting more laughter.

When Vigdís could take no more laughter, she pulled his head up and stared into his eyes. He grew more serious, and gently nuzzled her belly, kissing his way down each leg, up her torso, along her arms and neck. Each butterfly kiss felt tender and fiery, making her ache to take him into her arms.

When she tried to embrace him, he shook his head. "Slowly, my bride. We will take this slowly. I can't avoid hurting you some, but I can make it easier if I go slowly, so my grandmother says."

Oddly comforted by the fact her husband had sought advice from Arnbjörg, Vigdís relaxed on her back and let Hávarr kiss her for what seemed forever. When the fire in her belly had grown to an almost unimaginable temperature, Hávarr lay on top of her, rubbing himself against her.

Vigdís arched her back, wanting to feel him. His manhood grew bigger than she'd imagined, but she refused to give in to her fear at the pain. Slowly, with great deliberation, he placed the tip at her now wet cleft, guiding with his fingers. She moved her hips, but he shook his head.

"Slowly, my bride. Slowly."

Rocking his hips in small, measured movements, he entered a little more each time. The tingling in her belly she'd previously only felt for Bergmar now threatened to engulf her entire body. She pulled herself to his shoulders, wanting to pull him in.

"Shh. Shh. Wait."

A little more, and a painful pressure began. Despite herself, she squeaked and he stopped.

"No, don't stop, Hávarr."

He moved ever so slightly, making the pain worse. She wanted to make him happy, so resolved to say nothing, no matter how much it hurt. However, when he pushed through her barrier, she couldn't help letting out a sharp whimper at the pain. The look of stricken horror on Hávarr's face made her give him a sad smile.

"It hurts, Hávarr, but keep going. It shouldn't hurt long."

He nodded, though his brow remained furrowed in worry. He continued to move slowly until she gritted her teeth and the pain subsided into a throbbing sting. The motion felt good but it still hurt.

Hávarr's face screwed up and turned red just before he grunted and shuddered. Suddenly he stopped his rocking and convulsed. For a moment, Vigdís thought he'd hurt himself, but then she remembered what Fennja had told her. Men appeared pained afterward.

From what she'd heard, most men now fell asleep, but Hávarr rolled to his side and caressed her. "I'm sorry it hurt, my love. Next time, it should be more pleasure for you."

Vigdís hoped he spoke the truth.

They spoke and touched each other, getting used to their intimacy for the first time. She played with his chest hair, many curly blond hairs, each one springy and pale. They trailed into darker hair below, where his manhood lay flaccid and spent.

He ran his hands over her breasts, and her buttocks, remarking on her pale, smooth skin and soft hair. His feather touch made her skin pebble and shiver.

When they tried again, her insides still ached, maybe even more than the first, since the tissues remained red and raw. Still, this time, Vigdís found her own pleasure.

* * *

Morning came much too early.

A plaintive mewing woke her from a sound slumber as the late morning sun warmed her face. Her body ached in places she'd never ached before, but a good ache, a stretchy ache.

Opening her eyes, she searched for the source of the mewing. A small, gray ball of fluff clawed at the bedding, trying to pull itself up the blankets. She smiled and scooped the kitten up, placing it on her chest.

"And who might you be, darling creature? Are you yet another wedding gift from my new husband?" She turned to study the man beside her. He lay on his side, facing her, curled in a fetal position with drool on his cheek. With a smile, she wiped it away, eliciting a small sound from him.

He'd tried so hard not to hurt her. Arnbjörg had done well teaching him how to treat a wife. The thought of her good-grandmother made her scramble for memory of her dreams. What had she dreamt? Vague flashes of her life in Eire and the odious Padraig swam through her mind, replaced with Olaf and then Bergmar. How had she dreamed about every man in her life except her new husband? But no, he had been there. He'd banished the others with a wave of his hand, like a magician with a wand. They swept into the ocean to drown, while Hávarr stood like a Nordic superhero, cape flapping in the wind, supreme in his victory.

220

Vigdís giggled, remembering the comic books her cousin had shown her years ago. Hávarr might have been a model for the Marvel character, complete with muscles and blond hair. He only lacked the cape and horned helmet.

The man in question moaned in his sleep and turned, bringing his face into the sun. Vigdís shifted and then winced, realizing several muscles hurt more than she'd expected. The kitten dug her claws into the blankets, grazing her breasts. Vigdís carefully extracted the razor-sharp claws and placed more layers between them. Then she experimented, stretching each leg and then her torso and arms, finding which hurt more.

"Mm. Keep wiggling like that, wife." Hávarr's eyes opened and watched her antics intently.

She stuck her tongue out. "You've done your duty for the night. Now I need food. You've worn me out, husband."

Hávarr helped her out of bed with random embraces and kisses. He convinced her to delay her dressing a little longer while the kitten mewed.

When they finished, sweaty and sated, Vigdís tried to stand to dress herself. "Is the kitten part of the wedding gifts as well?"

"Indeed. Another of your favorite pagan symbols. This one honors Freyja."

"I can't argue with that. However, I'm very ready for my morning meal." She'd grown ravenously hungry now, and the latest round of their love-making had made her even sorer. She sincerely hoped she wouldn't have to walk much this morning.

Once adorned, Vigdís turned to her husband. "When can we escape the celebration and go back to the farm? There are chores we need to attend if we don't want the harvest to rot in the fields."

He blinked. "Did no one tell you? Several neighbors will work our farm this week. We need concern ourselves with nothing but the festivities and ourselves."

Vigdís didn't like strangers mucking around in her farm, but she had to admit it made sense. Still, she looked forward to the time she could be alone without crowds of people watching her every move.

Once both dressed properly, she could think of no other excuse to avoid facing the witnesses and other people waiting to buffet her with advice, congratulations, and drink. At least she'd get something to eat.

Hávarr took her hand and squeezed, giving her a silly grin. They opened the door and emerged hand in hand, husband and wife, to the raucous cheers of the witnesses.

* * *

Miami, 1993

Val snorted at the Pollyanna saccharin of her narrative as she shook her hand out, waiting for her cramped fingers to stop aching. Whose wedding night is so idyllic? Her own had been far from perfect, with her mother insisting she didn't have to go through with the ceremony. She'd not been a virgin on her wedding night, though. She got married in the 1980s, not the 1100s.

Most romance novels she'd read seemed hopelessly naïve in that regard, making the first time a magical event, transforming the frightened virgin into a raging sex maniac. Never mind the physical effect of such efforts on a body, or the long day of ceremony before it. Romantic heroines were superheroes in their own right, able to leap tall wedding bowers in a single bound, and impale any evil villains with a parasol.

Val snorted at her own fancy and shook her head. While she preferred to read realistic books, she knew over-the-top heroes and heroines remained more popular. She would need to decide if she wrote for herself or for a market.

Watching the heavy drops splatter against her car hood, flashes of the wind and rain from the hurricane blanketed her mind. With a shake of her head, she stuffed her half-filled notebook back into her purse and started the car. Karl must be worried about her. The car coughed and wheezed a few times before it roared into life, giving her a moment of panic. She really didn't want to be stuck here in the rain with no way to get hold of Karl.

When she finally got into the house, soaked to the bone in the short sprint from the parking lot to the open hallway of her apartment complex, Karl slept fast in his recliner. With a sigh, Val grabbed his blanket from the bed and pulled it gently over his snoring body. He would sleep better than in their bed. He complained the bed was too comfortable and he didn't toss and turn as much, so his bones ached from being in the same position too long.

After a hot shower and a cold sandwich, Val took to bed herself. She lay in bed, staring at a stain on the ceiling. With each breath, she remembered a new thing she had to take care of, a new thing to remember, to manage, to fix. Karl's inability to do anything made her angry and frustrated. He couldn't even keep track of his own doctor's appointments. If she didn't have them written on her calendar, they'd miss one.

Val paid all the bills. Once, only once, had she asked Karl to take care of paying the bills. This small attempt had resulted in disaster, despite her patiently showing him how to balance the checkbook, go through the stack of bills from the mail, write out the checks, stamp the envelopes. That first month, she'd checked all his work. He'd written the check for the power bill with the amount due to the car insurance. The check for the doctor's office had been for twice what it should be, because both a bill and a statement showing that bill had been in the stack. She'd corrected them and given up letting him handle the bills.

The next time she'd tried to delegate the garden. She figured maybe Karl would be better with some hands-on tasks rather than financial ones. Val realized many people had no talent with numbers.

Back when they'd rented the Country Walk house, she'd helped him dig up last year's garden plot, bought the seeds, showed him where to plant them and how to do so, and let him handle it.

Nothing sprouted. Val didn't know how he'd screwed it up. She ought to have double checked his work, but she'd gotten caught up in cleaning the kitchen, and forgot. As a result, they had a lovely dirt garden all year.

Val glanced at the bedside clock. The green numbers shone balefully in the dark, reminding her she only had six hours left to sleep before she must wake up for work. She didn't want to go to work the next day, but what choice did she have? All she really wanted was to stay in bed, curled up in the covers and sulk. Maybe get some sleep. Sleep would be nice.

The buzzer from her alarm startled her awake and she moaned, reaching over with exhaustion to slap the button off. If she got over four hours of sleep, she'd be surprised. Val rubbed her eyes, grimacing at the grit which crusted her eyelashes.

With half-open eyes, she went to the bathroom to go through her morning routine. While she normally woke cheerfully, being a morning person, lately she'd been reluctant to leave the somnolent bliss of each night. Her dreams had become more interesting and intriguing than her real life. She supposed that might be true of most people, but hers had become peculiarly intense lately.

Going through the motions without paying much attention to the details, she showered, shaved, brushed her teeth and pulled on a reasonable work outfit. Then she remembered Karl.

Crap, if she didn't get him awake and moving, he'd be late. That meant she'd be late, as they shared one car.

She ran out to the living room, but Karl no longer slept in his recliner. She found the blanket, balled up on the floor. Karl had disappeared.

Val searched the apartment for any sign of her husband, but he had disappeared. She didn't see his wallet where he normally dropped it on the kitchen counter. With a cold fist in her stomach, she opened the door to peer out into the parking lot.

No car.

Fuck, fuck, fuck. Karl took the car, her only mode of transportation. She frowned up at the sky, cloudy but no longer raining. Running back into the kitchen, she noted the time and tried to remember the bus schedule. Two busses would take her to work, but to catch the 6:30am run, she'd have to book it.

She grabbed a piece of bread and slathered it with peanut butter, stuffing it into her mouth as she fetched her purse. After a moment's frantic thought, she also took the small collapsible umbrella. If those clouds decided to rain upon her, she didn't want to be standing at the bus stop in a downpour.

The air seemed cooler than most April mornings. Cool remained a relative concept in Miami. Cool meant eighty degrees rather than ninety-five. Miami had nothing on Iceland for cool mornings.

Val just made it to the stop, panting from her jog, as the bus pulled in. She quickly peered at the front to verify the route and jumped on, pulling out her purse. She dropped several coins in the counter and glanced at the seats. All seats looked full so she grabbed a pole and braced herself as the vehicle lurched forward.

Fuck Karl and fuck him again.

The older man behind Val rubbed up against her, and she inched away. He stepped closer to her, despite the dirty look she flashed him over her shoulder. After he groped her butt, she spun around. "Keep your hands off me, asshole!"

He leered at her and stepped back. She entertained herself by glowering at him for the rest of the trip until her transfer stop. As she stepped toward the door, his hand groped again, but she wouldn't risk missing her second bus to deal with the creep.

Her resentment simmered as she waited for the second bus. She glanced at her watch, praying the second bus didn't run late.

In a cloud of black exhaust, a bus pulled to the stop, but for the wrong destination. She waited impatiently as people got off, craning her neck to see if a second bus pulled in behind this one. When the wrong bus finally left, she saw another large vehicle in the distance down the busy street.

This bus had relatively few people on board, and she gratefully took a seat near the front. Her feet hurt from standing too long on the other bus, bracing against unexpected movements.

When the stop near the college loomed, she pulled the cord. The bus enveloped her in another cloud of exhaust before parting.

She coughed several times, wishing Karl was here so she could yell at him. Instead, she stalked to her building just as the campus clock chimed eight.

Once she addressed her immediate work tasks, she considered what had happened to Karl. Her husband rarely did anything spontaneous. He normally behaved mostly biddable, if somewhat dense, and rarely took initiative for anything. She hadn't seen a note or anything, but to be fair, she'd rushed out of the house like a bat out of hell once she realized she'd have to take the bus.

She glanced at her desk phone, but no message light blinked. A phone message at work meant Karl must remember her work number. The conundrum bothered her through two mind-numbing administration meetings, several routine tasks, and one minor crisis involving paychecks.

Jorge raised his eyebrows when she turned down his invitation to lunch. "You're in a fog lately, darlin' girl. What's going on?"

She shrugged. "Stuff. Crap. The same old same old. I hate my job. I fight with my husband. This morning he left with the car without telling me."

He whistled. "How did you get to work?"

"City bus."

"Oh, ick. Those things are filthy, Val."

"This from a guy who enjoys camping in the dirt?"

He fluttered his hand in dismissal. "There is filth and there is filth. Natural dirt is much less filthy than the City bus. You can't imagine what people get into or when they last washed before they sit in those seats and touch those bars."

Val found no fault in his statement. Surreptitiously, she wiped her hands on her pants, even though she'd carefully scrubbed her hands when she arrived at work.

"But where did Karl go? Did he leave a note? Have you called his job?"

Val opened her mouth but shut it again. "I hadn't even considered that. Did he go to work early?"

She dialed the number and put on her professional voice when someone answered. "Hello? May I speak to Karl Masterson, please? This is his wife."

The girl on the other end hesitated. "I'm sorry, Karl called in today. He said he'd be out for several days due to a personal emergency?" Her response sounded like a question rather than a statement.

Not wanting to appear to be an idiot, Val extemporized. "Oh, that's right. I'm sorry, I forgot about the arrangements we'd made. Thank you."

After she hung up, Val bit her lip. "Not at work. He called in for a personal emergency for several days."

Jorge narrowed his eyes. "Wouldn't you be aware of any personal emergency?"

Her mind racing, Val considered. "In an ideal world… oh, fuck it all, that's where he's gone."

She opened her drawer, searching for a paper, slammed it shut and opened the next. With growing rage, she placed the letter on her desk.

"He must have gone to her. To Marjoree. That woman wants to bleed us of four thousand dollars and he's taken the stupid car and driven up to her stupid house in stupid Georgia."

"I didn't realize all of Georgia lacked intelligence. Or does she act like a stupidity black hole, capturing the stupid in a stupidity gravity well so it can't escape?"

Val had to chuckle, despite her fury at Karl's betrayal. For a long, horrible moment, she considered just letting Karl go, let him go back to Marjoree, let him have the car, and file for divorce. It would make life so much easier to be free of him. His medical bills, his arguments, his idiocy…

"You're considering letting him go, aren't you?"

She stared at Jorge. "Is it so obvious?"

He nodded with pursed lips. "He's no good for you, Val. You're miserable with him, surviving solely on sarcasm and momentum, and the few times he makes you laugh aren't enough payment for the crap you have to go through. Seriously, chica, you need to cut him loose for your own sake."

Fear bubbled up within her. Fear of being alone, against the world. Fear of dying alone, an old woman, unloved and unwanted by anyone. Karl made her feel needed, at least. He needed her to help him survive. He valued her even if he didn't always show it.

Jorge took her by the shoulders and shook her gently. "Stop arguing yourself out of it, Val. Stop it, I can see it."

In a tiny voice, she said, "I can't face life alone, Jorge. I just can't."

He pulled her into a hug. "Val, if I liked women, I'd snap you up in a minute. I'd never let you be alone. I promise I'll always be your friend and stay by your side. Isn't that enough?"

Her friendship with Jorge remained strong, and it helped more than even he realized. Jorge was the one person in the world she could talk about such things to. The one person she admitted her fears to. She didn't even talk to Karl this way since he depended on her to be the strong one.

"It should be enough, Jorge, but…"

He hugged her more tightly, almost hurting her, but she didn't mind. The tears dripped on his shoulders and she sniffled, not wanting to burst into a full-on cry session at work.

He pulled back, staring into her eyes. "You get yourself to the bathroom, my friend. Wash your face, cool your eyes, and come back. You don't want the dean to come in and witness your humanity, do you? She'd never let you live it down." He grinned. "No sense giving that witch more ammunition than she needs, right?"

He pulled her into a brief, fierce embrace once again before he spun her around by the shoulders and pushed her toward the hallway.

She glimpsed Juana on the way to the bathroom, turning her head so the other woman wouldn't see her red eyes and wet cheeks. She barely made it into the sanctuary of the stall before the tears burst out again.

Karl left me. Left me for his manipulative ex-wife. It didn't matter if his betrayal turned out to be temporary or permanent. Val didn't want to think so far into the future. She'd grown weary of planning, of forecasting, of being the adult. She needed to let go, to let her emotions run free awhile.

With muffled sobs, Val indulged her sorrow for only a few minutes before she pulled herself together. Heaven forbid Juana or Dean Danelli walk in and heard her weakness. She blew her nose, splashed cold water on her face and scrubbed it red. Gazing at her image in the mirror, she judged herself reasonably presentable. Tonight, when she sat safe at home, she might let herself cry again. For now, she had adulting to do.

* * *

That evening, when Jorge gave her a ride to her empty apartment, he insisted on coming in.

"There is no way I'm letting you stew alone tonight, darlin' girl. You know me better than that. Get your glad rags on. I'm taking you out for some fun. Remember, everyone needs a night of alcohol and bad decisions."

She sighed. "Jorge, getting drunk and finding a fling isn't the answer to every ill in the world. I'm exhausted. I need to figure out how to get a new car. I need to find out if I'm right about where Karl went. I need to make plans."

He snapped his fingers at her. "Are you arguing with me? That's no way to treat your best friend. Chop, chop! Glad rags, now. Something sparkly and sexy. Let's go, Cinderella!"

"I've got to at least call the bitch to make sure Karl's there and not dead in some ditch at the side of the road."

"Fine. One phone call. Then we're hitting the clubs."

Val rolled her eyes and looked up Marjoree's number. She dialed it, counting out four rings before someone picked up.

Karl's voice crackled. "Hello?"

"Well, I guess that answers my question."

"Huh? Val, is that you?"

For a moment, she wanted to scream. Modulating her tone, she said, "Yes, it's me, Karl. What did you expect? You leave without a word in the night. Did you imagine I wouldn't notice? Did you think I wouldn't care?"

"But… but I did leave you a note!"

"Where, Karl? Where's the note? I didn't see a note."

"On the fridge."

She hadn't even looked at the fridge. After craning her neck, she saw a white paper stuck with a white magnet on the white appliance. Her anger fled, replaced by chagrin. "Oh. I see it now."

"Yeah. So have you read it?"

"How would I have read it if I just saw it? Hold on."

232

She walked around the counter and grabbed the note, Jorge peering over her shoulder. In Karl's shaky block letters, the note read, "Marjoree needs me in Georgia. I'm taking the car. Be back soon."

Val shook her head and grabbed the phone receiver. Jorge put his hand on hers. "It's not worth it, Val. Just let him go."

She swallowed. While she didn't want to admit failure, he had a point. She didn't want to let something she'd built crumble, even if she didn't particularly care for it any longer.

She didn't want to admit her mother had been right all along.

With another gulp, she picked up the receiver. "Karl, I've read your note."

"Good. I'll be back in a couple days."

Marjoree's harsh voice cut in. "No, he won't! He's stayin' up here wit' me and Kris! You can't have him back!"

Karl must have covered the receiver because his voice muffled, but she still heard him. "Shut up, Marjoree! Let me handle this!"

Val took a deep breath. "Karl, Keep the car. I'll sign it over to your name, and the payments will be up to you. Stay with your family."

Before he answered, before she changed her mind, she hung up the phone and burst into tears.

The phone rang, but Jorge kept hold of her hands, refusing to let her answer. "Let it be. Let it be. You know it's better this way."

She did. That was the problem. Val knew damn well she was better off without Karl. He'd been far better than the cretins she'd dated before, but that still didn't mean they were good for each other. She'd treated him poorly. Unconsciously, she might have been trying to make him leave. Well, she'd succeeded at that.

Jorge pulled her in for another hug, holding her for a long time. By the time her tears finally dried, she'd grown exhausted. She simply wanted to curl up in her bed and be miserable.

"Are you ready to go out on the town, darlin' girl? You need a night of alcohol and bad decisions."

"Absolutely not, Jorge. I can't face people right now. How about we do our drinking here? I have vodka and orange juice."

He grinned. "I can get behind that idea. Tonight, at least, but only because it's Monday. Come Friday, you have no excuses left, mind you."

She managed a smile of her own as she pulled two glasses from the cabinet. "Oh, yes I do. There's an event this weekend, isn't there? No time to go Puttin' on the Ritz when we have camps to set up."

"Ah, Christ on a cracker, I forgot about that. Well, there's plenty of mead and stronger stuff at a Viking camp, never fear. I won't allow you to drink alone."

She chuckled. "You seldom do, my friend."

When Val woke the next morning, her head pounded mercilessly. She moaned and slapped the alarm, shuffling to the bathroom with one eye cracked open. She really didn't want to face the world today. She should call in sick.

In the living room, she spied someone sleeping in the recliner and for a moment, didn't remember who it was. Karl had left, hadn't he? Then she remembered insisting Jorge shouldn't drive after five screwdrivers. He'd finally admitted her wisdom and curled up on the chair.

"Jorge, wake up. Time to get ready for work."

He startled awake, eyes shifting around to take in his surroundings. "Oh! Val. Okay, sorry. I didn't remember where I fell asleep."

She raised her eyebrows. "Do you often wake in strange apartments?"

He chuckled. "Not often enough for my taste!" He groaned and massaged his forehead. "Would Dean Danelli suspect something fishy if we both called in sick today?"

"The same thought crossed my mind and yes, I'm sure she'd realize something was suspicious. Especially as we both seemed fine yesterday. One of us might get away with it, but not both."

He stretched his long, lanky frame with a few cracks and pops of his joints. "Well, the answer is obvious. You have no car and I do. I'll drive to work, but only if you promise me you'll spend the day getting things done. Find a new car, get rid of the one Karl has, get paperwork for the divorce, whatever you need to do."

"How am I going to do all that without a car?"

He considered that and frowned. "Crap, fair point. Let me consider the options. Can I use your shower? That's where I think the best."

She nodded, pointing to the bathroom. "Extra towels are in the closet."

She made breakfast while Jorge took his shower. When he emerged, a towel wrapped around his hips, he smiled. "I have the solution!"

One eyebrow quirked, Val handed him a plate with bacon and eggs. "Do you, now?"

"You drop me off at work and take the car to do your errands."

"And what happens when the dean sees me dropping you off?"

He snorted, shoveled a huge bite of fried egg into his mouth. "Since when does she show up this early?"

"Fair enough. And Juana? You know damn well she's a prime snitch."

He shrugged. "We'll take the chance. You can drop me off around the corner."

Val tried to find another argument, but nothing came to mind. "Fine. Any idea where I can find a car for, uh, two thousand?"

"Total, or down payment? Cash?"

"I took a loan from my pension to help with Kris' surgery. That money is much better spent on a new car. I'd rather not have car payments if I can help it, but that won't buy much car."

"Well, you won't get a Coupe de Ville, but you might get an old banger for that. I know a guy." He winked.

Val narrowed her eyes. "A legal car?"

Jorge opened his eyes wide and placed his hand on his chest, the perfect picture of offended innocence. "You doubt me, darlin' girl? Tsk, tsk. You should have more trust in the Jorge."

"The Jorge? You are a title now? C'mon, if I need to drop you at work before Juana shows up, you've got to get dressed. Move it."

He grabbed the last piece of bacon, flourished it like a magic wand, and chewed on it as he returned to the bathroom. Her head still ached, but the food had helped. Val cleaned up and made a list of things she needed to do with her surprise day off.

They had three credit cards in both their names. She'd have to fix that. They'd put the car in her name as she had better credit. Where would she get divorce papers, the courthouse? Phone calls would be the first step. Marjoree meant she'd absolutely need a lawyer. Crap, how would she pay for a lawyer? Her pension loan might be needed for that. She'd rather buy a car since Miami had such horrible public transport. Val really didn't relish depending on busses for the foreseeable future.

Maybe this wasn't such a great idea.

That lonely farm in the middle of nowhere looked so appealing right now. Val glanced at the few things she'd acquired since the hurricane. A few pieces of furniture, some clothes, damned few sentimental keepsakes. Stuff was just stuff; the hurricane had taught her this cruel lesson. If she wanted to, she might pick up and just disappear, go wherever she liked. Nothing held her here anymore. No husband, holding her down like the proverbial ball and chain, needing her care and resources.

As if she had enough money to travel and buy a farm.

The farm brought the memory of her manuscript to mind, and for a panicked moment, she worried she'd left her notebook with the latest chapters in the car. After rifling through her purse, she sighed in relief to find it there, safe and sound. She'd hate to have lost all that work. She shuddered at what might have happened if Marjoree had gotten her hands on it. Not that Val imagined the woman could read, but Marjoree wouldn't scruple at holding it for ransom.

"Stop it. I can see you reconsidering."

Startled, she turned to see Jorge perfectly groomed, as if he wasn't wearing the same clothes from yesterday. "How the hell did you get the wrinkles out? You have no right not to look rumpled."

He grinned, flashing his too-white teeth. "I hung my clothes in the bathroom as I showered. It steams them straight."

Val snorted. "Too bad that doesn't work on gay men."

He grimaced. "That would make my life much too complicated. Now, have you made a list? Let me see."

Grateful to surrender control, even in this tiny manner, to someone else, she let him see the list.

"Hmm. Good, good, good. I can help with the lawyer, too. The divorce papers are at the courthouse, yep. Okay, here." He handed the list back. "Courthouse first, then lawyer. Those are your priorities. Intiendo?"

"Yeah, I understand. Let's get going. Those eggs are threatening a revolt."

Chapter Eight

Val had gotten a lot done in her one day, including a fruitful meeting with Jorge's cousin, a lawyer with a downtown firm. She'd gained a lot of information on contested divorces, uncontested, and the differences in cost and time. Since they had no children and few assets after the hurricane, the process became simple.

She hadn't transferred the car title or found a new car, but one step at a time. Next week would be soon enough and Jorge remained willing to drive her to work each day. While she detested relying on someone else, at the same time, the coddling made her feel treasured. Someone cared enough to help her, which soothed her bruised and battered psyche.

On Thursday, Karl's boss called her, demanding to know when Karl would return. Val wanted so badly to curse them out, or to say he'd never be back. Instead, she took the high road and said he remained busy with a family emergency.

On Friday morning, she pushed aside other thoughts and got things ready for the SCA event that weekend. She packed her gear, her garb, and her bottle of mead. Monday night aside, she looked forward to getting squiffy with intelligent, nerdy friends who wouldn't care less what her soon-to-be-ex-husband had done.

As the work day ended, she turned to Jorge. "Hey, I had a horrible idea. Are you going to have enough room in your little car for your gear and mine?"

He shook his head. "Normally, no way in hell. However, I've got one of those space pod things to put on top. Both our tents should fit in that, leaving the interior plenty of room for the rest."

She smiled. "Clever man. You consider everything. Are you sure you won't turn straight, just for me? I could really use a competent, thoughtful man in my life."

Shaking his head, he waggled his finger. "Sorry, darlin' girl. You ain't got the right equipment."

Val raised her eyebrows. "They sell things like that, you know."

After a moment of pregnant silence, they both burst out laughing. Val's eyes teared and they laughed until Juana came in, demanding to know if they were high.

Val shook her head, still chuckling. "Oh, go away, we're not bothering you. Don't you have a cauldron to stir or something?"

Juana left in an indignant huff. Jorge frowned at her retreating form. "Be careful, Val. She's had that look in her eye lately. She may be in a mood to file a complaint."

With a roll of her eyes, Val waved her hand. "Let her. Max in Human Resources adores me and thinks Juana's a tedious bitch."

"Just the same, I'd hate to see you fired. They might move her in with me, and that would be dire."

They drove back to Val's place, loaded everything up, and then drove to the event. After paying at the front gate, they drove through the site, looking for a spot to settle. They passed three large, colorful tents and the feast hall before they chose a quiet spot off near the tree line for their campsite.

Val had waved to several folks during setup, but didn't stop to chat until she'd set up her tent. She didn't quite want to face strangers yet.

She dressed in her kit, her SCA mask, the façade behind which she could hide, shivering from strangers while her persona took on the heavy lifting of being social. Her off-white underdress, her blue apron dress, a turtle brooch at each shoulder. A long, bead-decorated chain draped between the brooches, which also held chains for her sewing tools. At her belt hung a drinking horn, eating knife, and various other things. Her new boots were comfy and warm as she wiggled her toes.

Jorge took longer to set up than she did, so she relaxed and contemplated nothing for about twenty minutes. The nothing morphed into idyllic images of her farm in Iceland, complete with her hunky blond hero.

Jorge's words dragged her back to the present. "Ready for the first day of your single life, darlin' girl?"

"I'm not single until the divorce is final, Jorge, and that's barely begun."

"That's all legal detail. You're single in your heart as of this week, and we're making certain your body knows it."

She raised her eyebrows. "I thought I didn't have the right equipment for you?"

"Not me, silly child. I'm but the matchmaker."

"Pimp, Jorge. You're the pimp."

"And you will fetch a high price, my dear. Come, let's mingle with the customers." He crooked his arm out for her to take.

Val glared at him for a few seconds before donning her mask and accepting his proffered escort.

She sought Astriðr first but her friend and writing mentor hadn't arrived yet. However, Snorri was in evidence, with a few of his language-nerd friends.

When he spied her, Snorri rummaged in his shoulder bag, brandishing a small, black square. "I have something for you, sweet Vigdís!"

She smiled. "What's that? A computer disk? How dare you brandish such an obvious anachronism!"

Snorri chuckled, handing it to her. "Astriðr didn't know if she'd be called in to work. Therefore, she entrusted me with this."

Val blinked a few times, looking for a clue on the label. "But what is it?"

"Notes on your manuscript. She said you gave her an electronic copy. She read through it and gave you a detailed critique."

Val clutched the disk to her breast. "Thank you, blessed Snorri! I shall treasure this gift forever!"

He raised his drinking horn, and she raised hers in response, as did his friends. "Skaal!"

After several drinks of mead, she practiced her Icelandic on them, and they helped her with Icelandic pronunciation refinement before Jorge rescued her.

"Come, I've someone for you to meet. Bring your drinking horn." He nodded at the horn in question, which lie on a stump next to her. She retrieved it and hurried after him.

"Who am I meeting? Anyone interesting?"

"Would I drag you away from an enclave of linguists for someone boring?"

She chuckled. "You might, if you decided the person in question would make me forget about Karl."

He stopped, hand over his heart. "I'm shocked, shocked I say. Am I so base in my motivations? Have you so little faith in me?"

She grimaced. "Jorge, you are the very definition of 'base motivation.' When you open the dictionary to the phrase, your picture is there, in full color with a plethora of notes and captions."

"Mm, plethora. Great word, that. You're becoming a true author."

"Shut up. Who am I meeting?

He pulled her arm. "Someone."

She stopped. "Tell me or I walk no further."

"Women in medieval Iceland shouldn't be so willful, Vigdís. Their mothers trained them to listen to the better judgment of the men in their life."

She smacked at a mosquito that landed on her arm. "And if you were a man, such logic would apply."

"Shocked, shocked I tell you."

"Jorge."

"Fine, fine, fine. He's working on a project in West Palm Beach, and he's Icelandic, a historian by trade. I told him of your interest in the medieval period. His name is Hávaldr."

She halted again, peering at Jorge in the deepening twilight. "Are you fucking kidding me? Hávaldr? How close is that to my book's main character, Hávarr? Is this your idea of a sick joke?"

"Your book? Oh! Right. Well, that's pure coincidence. There are only so many Icelandic names. They keep recycling them."

She remained unconvinced. It would be just like Jorge to set up a fake 'this is your imaginary life' jest, though why he'd do it now when she felt so fragile confounded her. "What does he look like?"

Jorge just tugged at her arm. "You'll see in a moment. Come on."

She finally gave in and let him lead her to the feast hall, brightly lit with torches and hung with vibrantly colored banners representing the households and companies in attendance. Two thrones stood at the front of the hall, and three long trestle tables filled the interior. No one served a formal feast on Friday night, just a huge soup pot and a pile of bread for people to eat as they wished.

Several knots of people sat around the tables, one in the corner practicing with some musical instruments, laughing and playing a few chords. Another worked on a sewing project, while a third was playing a game of some sort involving colorful cards.

Jorge passed each of these groups and pulled her to the fourth one, near the thrones. Two men and a woman sat at the table, a huge book open between them. One glanced up as they approached, a big man with long, blond hair and a beard. Val stopped, stunned. He looked so much like how she pictured Hávarr in her mind, she had to glance at the modern fixtures on the wall to ensure she was, in fact, in the twentieth century and not in the twelfth.

Realizing she'd stopped, Jorge turned back to her. "What? What's wrong?"

"Uh, nothing, nothing at all. Sorry."

When they reached the group, Jorge made introductions. Naturally, the gorgeous blond man turned out to be Hávaldr.

Jorge put a familiar hand on the other man's shoulder and smiled. "And this rather pedantic gentleman is known as Tomirr, is that right?"

The stooped man with glasses and sandy brown hair nodded. "Aye, that's me. Welcome."

The pretty brunette woman put her hand out to shake. "I don't believe I've met either of you. I'm Helga."

Val shook her hand and smiled. "Very nice to meet you all." She looked to Jorge for a clue as to why, precisely, she'd needed such a precipitous introduction.

"Vigdís is working on a novel set in medieval Iceland. I figured since, between Hávaldr and Tomirr, you have, what, five degrees in Icelandic history, that you might be a valuable resource for her research. Hávaldr lives in Iceland and works at university in the research department. Mingle."

Jorge flapped his hands at them and sauntered off.

Val's smile grew more genuine and she glanced at the book they'd been studying.

Hávaldr smiled at her. "Want to see? It's a book of genealogical charts, recounting the sagas, as best they can. What's your favorite saga?"

She didn't hesitate. "Hrolf Kraki's Saga."

He raised one eyebrow. "Oh? Why that one?"

She shrugged, her hands held wide. "Who doesn't love a half-elven necromantic princess raising an army of dead criminals and monsters to steal her half-brother's throne?"

This elicited a laugh from the others. Tomirr slapped Hávaldr on the shoulder. "Who, indeed? She's got you there, brother. The woman knows her sagas. She's brave enough to back a villain, too. Have a care."

She bent to examine the book, accidentally brushing Hávaldr's arm. "Do you have that saga listed in your genealogy?"

They studied the book for over two hours, lost in a sea of Thorsteins, Thorvalds, and Knuts before Snorri joined them. "Vigdís, I've been looking for you! Astriðr called, and she can't make it to the event."

Val's face fell. She'd been pushing the pain of Karl's perfidy from her mind and truly hoped to speak with Astriðr. Jorge had been a fantastic friend, but gay or not, he remained a man. She needed a woman's sympathy.

Snorri stared at her. "Right. Gentlemen, will you excuse us? I must borrow Vigdís for a while."

With a hasty apology to her new friends, Val allowed Snorri to pull her away from the bright modern lights of the feast hall to the warm summer night. He made her sit on the small log in front of a modest fire.

"What happened?"

Val swallowed. She had no confidence she'd be able to relate all the facts without crying. Snorri didn't understand the history of her marriage. How would he appreciate the emotions flying through her mind? Her husband, the man who had rescued her from her alcoholic childhood home, had abandoned her. While she'd considered leaving him many times, she'd never acted on such thoughts. The guilt of those thoughts just made it worse. Logic had no part in her rampant emotions.

She said no words, but her tears betrayed her. Snorri held her in his arms and let her get his shoulder wet with sobs.

As her tears subsided, he patted her back and held her by the shoulders, looking into her red-rimmed eyes. "Your husband?"

Val nodded. "He left me for his ex-wife, without a word. He even took the car!"

Inexplicably, this made her laugh, but it turned into a hiccup. That heralded another set of tears, interrupted only when yells at the toll gate commanded their attention.

With a mighty sniffle, she turned to discern the fracas. Snorri kept his hand on her shoulder as they walked toward the shouts.

Karl stood next to her car. He argued with the man at the front gate who wouldn't move from in front of the car.

"I need to speak to my wife, let me in!"

Val noticed a shape in the car. A shape which looked like Marjoree.

The large man crossed his arms and planted his feet. "Sorry, man. Unless you pay the gate fee, no one gets in. C'mon, it's only ten dollars a person. Don't be cheap."

"I'm not here to camp or eat, I just need to talk to her. Val! Val, I know you're here! Come out and talk to me, now!"

Val wanted to run, to hide in the woods and never emerge. She wanted to flee to Iceland and find a farm to live forever alone. She definitely did not want to have it out with her husband in front of the entire kingdom of Trimaris.

Snorri squeezed her hand. "Would you like me to hide you? I have no problem doing so. I've never met your husband, but he doesn't sound like he's in the mood for reasonable discussion."

She gulped and nodded, not trusting herself to speak. For all her bravery and all her competence, suddenly she wanted nothing more than someone else to make decisions. She needed to not be in charge of this mess.

"Come on, then. I have just the place." Snorri led her into the darkness, along a wooded path to a small lake. The sounds of her angry husband faded into the trees as the crickets and mosquitoes sang in the dark starlit night. The almost-full moon reflected in the water, a slight ripple marring the image.

Someone had placed several logs around the lake, and they sat on one. Snorri didn't relinquish her hand.

"I'm familiar with extracting yourself from a toxic marriage, Val. You don't have to worry about a thing. I'm here for you, whatever you need. Silence, if that's what you crave. Discussion if you would prefer. I'll even make certain he leaves the site, though it's better if site security deals with that. Your wish is my command."

His selfless kindness brought her tears back. Her throat closed and she nodded.

Nature's symphony surrounded them, enveloping them in a quiet, velvet solitude only a hot Florida night can offer.

* * *

The next morning, Karl had gone. Val had mixed feelings about what she'd done the night before. Maybe Karl did want to come back. Maybe he really had only left to help Marjoree and hadn't meant to leave her forever.

"Maybes seldom are," as her grandfather used to say.

Maybe she made excuses. Maybe she didn't care to admit to herself she'd just wasted seven years settling for a barely suitable husband.

Maybe she needed to take a deep breath and get on with her real life.

Maybe she should just crawl back into her sleeping bag and deny the day's existence.

An overly cheerful voice outside called her name. Did she want to face anyone this morning, much less the painfully optimistic Jorge?

"Up and at 'em, darlin' girl! I have coffee and bacon."

Evidently, bacon was the magic word that swept all the maybes away.

As they sat around the smoldering ashes of last night's fire, Jorge pointed to her with a piece of crispy bacon. "Karl said pretty nasty things last night before he left. Would you like the highlights, or do you prefer to live in blessed ignorance?"

She sighed, pushing the runny scrambled eggs around with her fork. Flecks of char peppered the eggs, and she preferred hers well-done, but runny eggs tasted better than none. "Sure. Give me the Cliffs Notes."

"He said, and I quote, 'she is an ungrateful, bossy bitch who had no heart.' He also mentioned your parents, your ancestors, and a particular tendency toward being an ice queen in bed."

"Fan-fricken-tastic. That's precisely what I wanted the entire Kingdom of Trimaris to hear."

"Oh, ye of little faith. We had an entire coterie of hecklers throwing it back at him, never fear. Between Tomirr, Hávaldr and I, we baffled him with words of over two syllables and made him retreat in confusion."

"But they barely met me!"

He shrugged, chomping on his last piece of bacon. "It matters not. You're one of us, darlin', and we protect our own."

Her blood warmed from the unconditional acceptance and the actions of the men. She felt, for once, protected and cared for. Perhaps she didn't need a hapless husband barely able to hammer a nail.

"Now, what are your plans today, Val? Have you signed up for any workshops or classes?"

She nodded, taking a sip of her scorched coffee. "There are several I'm interested in. There's one in women's roles in medieval England, and how they used both hearth tools and weapons."

He grimaced at his own coffee and set it on the log. "Sure, makes sense. What else?"

"Snorri is doing a lecture on Icelandic law in the year 1000, which will be invaluable in my book research."

"Sure, I plan on going to that one myself. Nothing crafty?"

She gave him a sidelong look. "Sure, I'm taking crafty classes. An advanced tablet-weaving class is after lunch for Pebble Weave, a leather-dying class, and a tin-smithing workshop."

Jorge scraped the rest of his runny eggs into the ashes, which sputtered in protest at the offering. "Not the class on Viking Age clothing embellishments?"

"I took that one last event. Oh, I'm also considering the one for making rune staves."

"To carve the rune staves or to read them?"

"Both, I believe, according to the description in the flyer. Either way, I'm fascinated. I came up with some odd symbols in my book, and I'm not sure where the idea came from. I'm hoping the teacher can give me some insight."

"'Came up with?' What do you mean?"

She shrugged, putting her own empty plate on the log. "I wrote and in my mind's eye, I saw some magical symbols. I can draw what I imagined, if you'd like."

"Show me."

She found a stick and drew the symbol for the love spell, with the pitchforks and the not-quite-closed box. Jorge frowned. "You said you imagined this in your story?"

"Yeah. I was just writing and this flashed in my mind, so I described it in the narrative. The character used it as part of some love spell witchcraft."

"Witchcraft? Val, what are you getting into?"

She snorted. "I'm not getting into anything. I'm drawing a made-up symbol from my novel. There's no power in it."

He brushed the marks out with his foot. "Symbols can have power, Val. You may not believe it, but they do. Look at the power of the swastika or the peace symbol. For good or ill, symbols mean something."

"Now you're just being silly. You aren't seriously going to tell me you believe in ancient Icelandic sorcery, or that somehow my mind extracted this symbol from the ether to use it properly in my novel? It's just a doodle."

"Val, even in this modern age, there are things science still can't explain. Voodoo. Past lives."

"All right, all right, Leonard Nimoy, this isn't an episode of In Search Of."

"Stop being flippant. I'm serious. You know I'm Cuban, right?"

She blinked several times at him. "No, Jorge Carlos Barrenechea-Hernandez. I had no clue you were Cuban. Not a single one."

"Stop being a snippy bitch. Whether you believe it or not, lots of strange crap goes on in Santeria."

"I'm being a bitch? Since when is questioning rank superstition being a bitch?"

"When you're being an idiot and meddling in things you don't understand!"

They both stood, glaring at each other for several moments. The tension broke when the nine o'clock bell rang.

With a glance at her tent, Val broke the deadlock. "I'll have to hurry to get to the tablet-weaving class."

"Fine, go. Just… just go."

Val grabbed her craft bag and stalked to the tent where her class was held. She barely paid attention to the instructor, instead steaming about Jorge and his archaic ideas. Santeria, seriously?

When her class finished, she found the rune-maker before his class started. It turned out to be one of the men she'd met the night before.

"Tomirr, I'm glad to see you. I have a question for you on a symbol. It's not a rune, but it might relate to Icelandic magic symbols. Can you look?"

He grinned, showing a gap between his front teeth. "Absolutely! Draw it and I'll tell you what I can. I'm no expert on Icelandic witchcraft, but I've studied a few books."

She sketched out the box and pitchfork shape. He frowned and turned it around several times. "I'm sure I've seen this before, but I can't recall… oh, wait, yes I do! Hold on for a moment."

He sifted through several books he had in his bag, and pulled out a small, black, hand-bound hardcover book. The title read Galdraskræða by Skuggi, no last name. He flipped through several pages covered in Icelandic handwriting until he found the page he wanted. He turned it around to show her. She couldn't make out what the Icelandic description said.

"Is this it?"

Val's skin chilled as she recognized the symbol. It's exactly what she remembered in her mind. How had she known it?

"Vigdís? Val? What's wrong? You've gone pale! Here, sit down, have some water."

She drank the proffered mug and sat, numb, as she stared at the symbol.

"Tomirr, I've seen this symbol. I saw it in my head as I wrote. I described it in my narrative as a love spell. How could I have done that? Is there any way I could have come across this in casual research before? Just reading about medieval Iceland?"

He shook his head. "I doubt it. This is rather esoteric stuff. They do think this symbol was used for love spells.

You're writing a book, right? Have you checked out any books from the library?"

She nodded, still staring at the book.

"Still, I don't think this book is available in libraries. I had to get it in Iceland, and I had to search hard for it there. Even in modern times, Icelanders remain wary of putting such symbols in public use."

Suddenly Jorge's arguments seemed much more relevant.

* * *

She apologized to Jorge when he arrived for the rune class, but he brushed it off. "It's no big thing, darlin' girl. I realize you're stressed about the mess with Karl. I shouldn't have gotten so uppity."

"No, I should have listened to you. Hey, what are you doing next weekend? I don't trust myself to be home alone the whole time."

He narrowed his eyes. "There's a craft show. Remember the hat bands I make? I've got a stall at the South Miami Rotary Fair this weekend."

She sighed. "Right. People. Well, in a choice between being alone to stew in my stupid spinsterhood and hanging out with you and dealing with idiot craft shoppers, I guess the latter is the lesser of two evils."

Jorge clutched at his chest. "Be still my heart! Darlin' girl is getting social, and on purpose, no less!"

"Not so fast, Speedy Gonzalez. How long is this show? What do you need me to do?"

"If you want the full experience, you can help me set up, sit in my booth all day, be nice to customers, watch the place when I take a bathroom break, and then help me break down. Luckily for your first time, this is just a one-day show."

She considered saying no and sequestering herself with her manuscript. However, she didn't want to risk her still-raw emotions taking over and making her into a crying mess. That had already happened too many times lately.

"Fine. What time and where?"

"You still don't have a car. I'll pick you up Saturday at six."

"Six AM. As in six the morning? Christ on a piece of toast, Jorge! That's no decent hour."

"Since when have I ever claimed to be decent?"

That week, Val buried her misery and her troubling revelation about the witchcraft symbol in the daily routine of work and writing. Most evenings she spent at the library, taking advantage of the word processors and the ready resources for spot research requirements. She stopped often to research what herbs they used in cooking, or what process they used for tanning leather, which broke her narrative flow. Having the resources on hand helped immensely.

She should sleep in one of the library cubicles. Such a move would save her bus fare, though by Wednesday, Jorge had come through with a clunker car. The ten-year-old Mitsubishi looked ugly and sported several colors, thanks to replaced panels, but it started and it got her to work each day.

After the first few days of ignored messages on the answering machine, Karl stopped calling. She filed her divorce paperwork quickly. A huge weight fell from her shoulders as she left the lawyer's office. She felt like skipping but she satisfied herself with a broad grin.

After Jorge picked her up on Saturday morning, she cradled her coffee mug to keep it from spilling as he drove.

"How long does your setup take?"

He slammed the brakes and flipped off the guy who cut him off. Val cursed both idiots and wiped the hot coffee from her leg. At least she'd worn shorts. Instead of stained pants, she only had third-degree burns on her thighs.

Jorge handed her a napkin. "Normally, by myself, about two hours. With your help, it should be, oh, about two hours."

She glared at him. "So, I'm no help at all? Why the ever-living hell did I get up this early, then?"

"You won't be a big help the first time, no. I'll spend more time explaining how to do things than you will save. However, next time, you'll be much more useful."

"Next time. Right. Let me survive this first time before we go crazy."

"I think you'll enjoy this more than you think. We play bingo."

"Bingo? At an art show?"

"Just wait. You'll see."

She sipped what remained of her coffee and grimaced. "I'm waiting with bated breath."

The dawn had barely broken when Jorge pulled into the street, blocked off with traffic barriers and manned with bored-looking volunteers. Jorge waved a colored piece of paper, and the volunteer waved him in, moving the barrier slightly so he could get the car through.

People moved like ants along both sides of the street, carrying boxes, tents, and sipping life-giving cups of coffee in the dim morning light. Some had obviously either been here for hours or set up the night before as they already hung product on their tent walls.

Jorge pulled in front of an empty spot. "Right, this is me, H33. First job, unload everything in the car. Stack it on the sidewalk behind the booth space. Once that's done, I'll go park the car."

Even though the morning felt relatively cool, it remained April in south Florida, and the humidity already approached maximum. Within moments, Val dripped with sweat and regretted agreeing to this labor. Still, she owed Jorge an awful lot. He's the only reason she hadn't descended into a morass of self-pity and depression and if this helped repay her debt, so be it.

Maybe if she'd been more appreciative of what Karl had done for her, he wouldn't have left her for his ex-wife. Maybe if she'd been a better daughter, her parents wouldn't have fought so much.

Maybes seldom are.

They finally unloaded the tent, chairs, tables and boxes from the car, and Jorge went to park. "Don't set up the tent until I get back. It's much easier with two people."

"Isn't it an EZ-Up? Aren't they designed for one person?"

"Yep, but it's easier with two. We're not in a hurry."

He drove slowly away, slaloming through the various other artists and their vehicles in differing states of unpacking. Val surveyed the pile of stuff and eyed the tent. It looked easy enough.

She placed the folded tent in the center of his space and inched the corner pillars apart. They dragged across the pavement with frustratingly slow progress as she went from pillar to pillar. With a flash of inspiration, she ducked under the center and pushed up, making the four legs move apart with satisfying ease.

Once she got it mostly unfurled, she studied one corner, and then pushed the mechanism until it clicked. She repeated at the four other corners.

Jorge returned with two steaming plastic cups of coffee and handed her one. "Well, I see you're following directions, as always."

Val shrugged. "Did I do it wrong?"

"No, no you did it right. Here, let's raise the roof, so to speak."

He showed her how to raise the tent legs until it topped out at seven feet. They moved tables into place, covered them with bright Caribbean-print fabrics. He laid them out so they layered diagonally, placed his hat stands on tiers, and set Val to placing the bands on the hats.

She still sweated profusely, but at least she could do this part sitting in a chair, rather than lifting and carrying boxes. The sun had risen fully now and beat down on the pavement with relentless heat. Why would they even hold an art show in the full of summer? Sure, late April didn't technically count as summer for most of the country, but south Florida had summer from March through November.

"Right. All done with those? Here's another box."

With a sigh, Val handed him the finished stack of hats and pulled the new ones out. "When does this shindig get started?"

"Ten. It's open from ten to four. Usually the rain closes us down around four anyhow, so there aren't many customers."

Val grunted. Rain in the afternoon was a given on any Florida summer day. She could probably set her watch by it.

Jorge laid down a tarp and affixed a clear plastic tent wall to the back of the tent, placing all the empty packing boxes between them. He covered this with another colorful cloth. "Out of sight and camouflaged, but still protected from the deluge. Okay, darlin' girl, it looks like we're ready to roll."

She glanced at her watch. "It's barely nine thirty. I could have slept another half hour."

He shrugged. "Better early than late. See? There are already women out with their canine jewelry."

"Canine jewelry?" Val craned her neck to see what he meant by that cryptic phrase.

He handed her a sheet of paper that looked like a bingo card. "Here, you get one and I get one."

She glanced at some of the spaces. "Canine jewelry," "Sticky hands," "Close talker," "My daughter makes these," and "Look at my work" all made her chuckle.

"This, darlin' girl, is Art Show Bingo. Each space represents common art show attendees, ranging from the mildly amusing to the downright nasty. Canine jewelry is when a woman carries around a tiny dog like an accessory or a handbag rather than walking the poor creature. Bonus points if he's in a stroller."

"A dog in a stroller? Are you kidding me?"

He shook his head with a wide smile. "Oh, how I wish it were so. You would be amazed at what some of these people do. Just keep an eye on the kids. They have a habit of yanking at the hats, and their parents usually couldn't care less what Precious Junior destroys in his mad quest for entertainment."

"Roger that." She sat in her chair and surveyed her view. Jorge had placed them at each back corner of the tent, so they had a good cross view of the space. He had placed the cash box, bags, and invoice pad between them.

The first customers trickled in as she sipped the last of her coffee. One woman had a baby in her arms and jiggled him so much, Val thought the child would explode like a can of soda. His little cheeks bounced and bobbed like Jell-O.

Val made a few sales while Jorge watched to get the hang of it. He nodded when she finished the third one. "You've got the gist. I'm off to find a bathroom. Can you hold the fort for a few? I'll spell you when I return."

"Only if you can find bagels or donuts. I'm starved now that the coffee is working."

"Your wish is my command."

As soon as he left, five customers crowded into the ten by ten booth, and Val had to juggle several transactions before they all filtered out. Then she spent several minutes resetting the hats the way they had been, less those that sold. The last customer had to try on every single hat in the booth, over forty, before she finally decided on the first one she'd considered.

Jorge came back with a brown box. He opened it with a dramatic flourish, revealing a box full of crullers, round johns and chocolate donuts. "Milady's breakfast has arrived!"

"Give me five minutes. Where's the bathroom?"

He pointed to the left and she quick-stepped, suddenly in great need. She wove through clueless patrons, narrowly missing tripping over a dog leash, a stroller, and a set of twins.

The port-o-potty smelled and looked disgusting, but she didn't care. That coffee had done far more than wake her mind up. She sighed with relief as the pressure eased, trying not to touch the filthy seat.

Funny how she had no problem peeing in the woods but port-o-pottys made her skin crawl. Natural dirt and human filth did not engender the same reaction.

She shuddered as she spied a cockroach in the corner and hastily finished her business.

The booth stood empty except for Jorge when she returned and sat, wiping her hands with some water and a napkin, then taking her selection of the sugary confections. "What do you do when you haven't wrangled a friend into helping you? Do you work the booth alone?"

Jorge nodded, taking a bite of his round john. The white crème filling dripped on his cheek, but he caught it with a flick of his tongue. "Usually I work the show alone. Some days are long, ten hours or more. I make friends with my neighbors, and we watch each other's booths if we need to. Some shows offer booth sitters, but most don't."

Val glanced at the neighbor to the right, a loud man with photos of wildlife and seascapes. His booth almost always swam with people. She'd already heard his sales spiel a dozen times, and already grew sick of his forceful, piercing voice. "Pandas! Pandas are where it's at. You can't go wrong with pandas. Wouldn't you love an adorable panda on your wall, young lady?"

The woman on the left had knitted and crocheted items, mostly in pastel colors. Val hadn't even seen anyone go in her booth. She didn't seem to have a sales pitch, but worked on her craft behind a table all day long.

Jorge finished his donut and rested his hand, with his elbow on his knee, and gazed at her. "So, today you're avoiding reality by helping me, which is fine, but what about tomorrow? And next week? What's the plan?"

She swallowed a gulp of water to wash down the sugary goodness of the glazed cruller. "Write my book. Work. Research other jobs I might enjoy more. Pack up some of Karl's crap so he can come get it. I'll be damned if I'm paying to ship his shit to him in Georgia, not after giving him the car."

"Good plans, good plans. Want help with the last one? I'll be more ruthless than you."

"Maybe… but you've done so much for me. Don't you have your own life to ruin?"

He sighed. "You would think so, wouldn't you? I had been dating someone… but he decided a younger model would be more exciting."

"What about the man at the SCA event last weekend? Tomirr? I saw the looks he gave you during his class." Jorge blushed, dropping his gaze. "Oho! So you do like him! I knew it. Who would have thought The Jorge could blush! Well, what can I do to help this along?"

He shook his head and munched on another donut. "He's too smart for me. Tomirr needs someone who can keep up with him academically. I'm just a brainless fashion slut."

"Did he say this? Or are you assuming? And since when did 'brainless fashion sluts' learn Icelandic?"

He glared at her as a customer walked in. He turned to the older gentleman, all smiles, and jumped into his sales spiel.

Many sweaty, exhausting hours later, the clouds rolled in, temporarily cutting the heat with impending rain. Hastily, Jorge and Val packed the hats and bands into the boxes ahead of the daily deluge. She'd accidentally bumped the tent pole of their loud neighbor with the wildlife photos.

"Watch it, little lady. Don't want to knock things over before Mother Nature gets her chance!"

Val bristled at the hated phrase, "little lady," but decided he wasn't worth her rage. She packed three more boxes before his voice intruded on their work again.

"Hey, you packing up already? It's against the rules."

She glanced up to the sky, now almost black with rain clouds. "We'd rather not let the stock get ruined."

"Pah. That's what insurance is for. If you pack up now, all the customers will think the show is over and go home."

Val and Jorge both made a show of looking up and down the street. One lonely patron walked their dog across the street.

Val narrowed her eyes. "Yup, I can see how that would be a problem. Did you not make enough money from the throngs of panda-lovers today?"

The man, who stood at least six feet tall and had wide shoulders, came out from behind his cash register, his finger out as if he scolded a child. "Listen, missy, you don't have to take that attitude with me. I'm telling you the rules."

She raised her eyebrows. "Attitude, is it? I've had to listen to your stale sales pitch all day long, at high, grating volume.

They could hear about your fucking pandas halfway down the block. Don't you realize other vendors would love to hear their customers, too?"

Jorge tugged on her shoulder. "Val, it's not worth it. Leave it. I'll go get the car, just watch the boxes. We'll pull the tent down when everything's safely packed in the car."

Her friend rushed off, keys in hand, glancing at the roiling clouds above with obvious trepidation.

"Listen to your precious husband, chickie. Go run home and make him a sandwich."

For one horrible moment, all of Val's anger and frustration at Karl bubbled up inside of her. Jorge had it right; this toxic asshole wasn't worth her rage. She still needed to vent the pressure. With a primal scream, she kicked one of his print boxes so hard the plywood splintered just as a crash of thunder rolled down the street. A whoosh of wind followed the thunder, and suddenly the entire street scrambled to pack their artwork.

Their neighbor stared at the splintered box. She kicked again, harder. Her foot hurt, but she'd gone past caring. She kicked over and over, splinters of wood flying.

"Hey! Hey, stop that, you crazy bitch!"

Val couldn't stop. She needed to kick and kick until Karl's abandonment didn't hurt any longer. Her kicks continued until the print box became nothing but splinters. She aimed at the next one, but something held her back.

Jorge and their other neighbor, the knitting woman, pulled on each of her arms, dragging her away from her targets. She struggled, but her rage-filled strength was no match for both.

"Who's going to pay for my boxes, huh? Huh? You'd better get your wife in a strait-jacket, man, or fuck her more often. Jesus Christ, is she on the rag or somethin'?"

Val growled and tried to launch at him, to punch his chauvinistic smile off his god-damned face, but Jorge had a strong grip on her, and shoved her into the car. He slammed the door and locked her in. She felt too angry to figure out how to unlock the stupid thing. She stewed while he packed the car, racing against the approaching storm.

When the first heavy drops of the storm splatted against the windshield, startling her out of her angry fugue, Jorge hopped into the driver's seat. "Thanks for that, Val."

"Sorry. If I got out again, I'd have punched him in the face."

He wrinkled his nose. "Yeah. That. He acted like a twat-waffle, but that doesn't give you the right to destroy his shit. You realize he could sue us? Chances are I'll be next to him at another show."

"Sorry, sorry. Crap, what can I do to help? I lost my mind there. I kept imagining the wood to be Marjoree's smarmy face."

He chuckled. "Not that I didn't silently cheer you on. How about we go out for my favorite treat?"

"Alcohol and bad decisions? For once, I'm on board with this plan."

* * *

Val didn't remember much of Sunday, but she definitely paid for her alcohol and bad decisions. Still, she managed to get in some writing between bouts of worshipping the porcelain god. That evening, she self-medicated with the hair of the dog that bit her, and regretted nothing.

As Monday rolled around, she stumbled in to work. She might have damaged something in her foot, as it hurt to walk. Every heartbeat accompanied a pounding which had more to do with her blood-alcohol level and less with the thin blood pumping through her brain.

Jorge shot her a tired wave, looking just as rough as she felt. He cupped his forehead over a steaming cup of coffee with his eyes closed.

Juana bustled in, slamming a stuffed file folder on Val's desk, making her jump. "Here. These are all the expense reports you've been nagging me for all week."

Val glanced up, blinking through bleary eyes at her co-worker. Juana had too much make-up on her eyes, making her look like a rabid raccoon. "All week? You mean the stuff the dean wanted two months ago?"

"Whatever. It's done." Juana rolled her eyes and flounced down the hall. Val groaned and put her head down on the desk. The massive file made her arms uneven so she shoved it aside. The folder fell to the ground, scattering papers everywhere.

Jorge looked up from his coffee sauna. His eyes looked as bloodshot as hers. "Must you set off a bomb so early in the morning? A guy needs his beauty rest."

"Last night you weren't a guy, you transformed into a flaming queen. You flamed so hard, I got sunburnt standing so close to you. Did you at least get his name before you stuck your tongue down his throat?"

He managed a tired smile. "Names, schmames. I got hold of his butt, which was all that mattered." He took a sip of his coffee and closed his eyes in bliss. "I didn't see you complaining when that Irish lad kissed you."

Val couldn't remember an Irish lad. Hell, she could barely remember her own name last night. She grunted and scooted her chair over so she could pick up the papers.

The click of high heels on the terrazzo floor heralded Dean Danelli's appearance. Jorge straightened his back as she entered, but Val kept picking up the papers.

"What's this mess? Valerie, I swear, if you don't act more professionally, I'll find a replacement. It shouldn't be difficult to find someone who at least looks human."

Val sat up from her labor and lifted her eyebrows, waiting for the dean to announce the reason for her intrusion.

Dean Danelli glared at them both. "Which one of you is in charge of the monthly expense reports? Personnel is asking me for them, and I can't find them in my files."

Val pointed at the papers on the floor. "Juana just brought me her work. I've been bugging her for weeks to complete it. I still have to summarize the data."

The woman nodded once and glared at Jorge. "What are you smirking at?"

He schooled his expression. "Nothing at all, Dean. That's simply my natural demeanor."

"Well, fix it."

She turned and left, heels clicking away. Val's head renewed its pounding. With a sigh, she bent down to finish her task.

"I really need to find a different job, Jorge."

"You and me both, darlin' girl."

After she compiled the summary of the expense reports and handed it to the dean, Val had no urgent work for the rest of the day, so she opened her manuscript to continue the story. She had to read the last scene to remember where she'd left off, but soon she got back into the rhythm of the tale. She decided the wedding would be a great time to jump to that winter, about five months later.

Her dreams showed every day in this imaginary life; the boring, simple days and the exciting, seminal events, as if she lived in the other time every time she slept in this time. Her job, as a writer, was to pull out those interesting events and make it into a story line. She dredged her memory for details of the wedding.

* * *

Iceland, 1103

The Icelandic winter hadn't even hit with full force, and Vigdís already wished she could move back to Eire. Better yet, back to the Ohio of the 1960s with central heating and electric blankets.

She shivered as the freezing wind tried to knock her over. The cows had better appreciate her coming out in the dark to milk them. Earlier that year, she'd noticed another farmer had built sheltered walkways, not much more than fences with a wicker roof. She'd scoffed at them before, as they'd do little to keep out the cold, but now she fully understood their value.

She'd asked Hávarr to help her build some, and they'd dug out a line of postholes for the fence. However, they'd barely begun the project before the winter freeze made the ground impossible to dig. She walked carefully to avoid twisting her ankle in one of the dark holes. As she passed the last one, though, she caught a glint of something inside.

Kneeling to get a closer look, she brushed aside the dirt to see a white object. With a little digging and prying with icy fingers, she dislodged it to examine it closer.

It looked like a bone.

With shaking hands, she turned it over. Familiar now with the shape of sheep and cow bones, this bone didn't match. Instead, it looked remarkably like a human femur.

There must be some reasonable explanation. Perhaps the people who lived here before decided they lived too far from a church to bury their dead in a churchyard. Perhaps they'd been pagan, and didn't need consecrated ground. She swallowed and shivered, tucking the bone into her cloak. Hávarr might have some insight.

Once she'd gained the relative shelter of the stable building, she shook her coat to dislodge the ice. Hávarr looked up from his milking stool and frowned. In an attempt to use humor to hide her shock, she put her hands on her hips. "What? I'm here, aren't I? Despite it being as black as sin outside. Does the sun never rise in the winter here?"

"It does in the summer. Night is the winter's lover."

She glanced up to smile at her husband, casually leaning against the stable doorway. "Come in and close the door. The cows will stampede in protest."

"Two cows can't stampede. Here, let me help you." He bent to grab another bucket and sat next to the second cow.

She squinted at him. "Your father would yell at you for doing women's work."

"My father never learned how to make a woman truly happy. I've been fortunate enough to learn from his mistakes. Also, I listened to my grandmother."

Vigdís smiled at the thought of Arnbjörg. The older woman had visited several times since they'd married, giving invaluable advice on keeping the home, preparing for winter, and a few salacious bits of wisdom about keeping a man happy. Vigdís had grown to love the old woman. Both of her grandmothers had died before she'd been born. A special place in her heart kept ever-warm, like a hearth fire, for the tough old witch and her unquestioning protection.

"Hávarr, I found something in the yard."

"That sounds intriguing. Did you find Huldufólk treasure?"

"I'm not certain."

Her flat tone erased his joking manner and he stood. Taking both her hands, he asked, "What did you find, wife?"

Silent, she removed the bone from inside her cloak and handed it to him.

He turned the femur several times. His face turned pale in the dim winter light.

"Is it human?"

He nodded.

"Who lived here before I took tenancy?"

Hávarr gazed into her eyes, his own sad. "From what I remember, it has lain empty for many years. Ever since Ísveig disappeared."

"This was Olaf's first wife's farm? What about her family?"

Hávarr shook his head. "When he married Isveig, they moved north to Akureyri. She still stored her personal things here, and escaped when she could, from what the rumors said. Then she vanished." He gazed bleakly at the bone in his hand. "Show me where you found this."

She drew him to the post hole, showing the darker spot where she pulled the bone from the dirt. He fetched a spade and dug further into the earth, chipping away at the frozen earth until a huge hole full of nothing gaped in the yard.

The wind blasted them and they hurried back to the barn. Hávarr replaced the spade on the wall with a shake of his head. "No other bones, at least not here."

"Then we can't know whose bone this is, can we?"

"That's true, we can't know."

Unconsciously, she touched the bit of whale bone she still kept on a string around her neck, the charm against Olaf's attentions. Whether it worked magic or Hávarr's father had finally given up on pursuing her, she couldn't tell. Either way, the effect remained the same; Olaf hadn't tried to touch her since that day.

Her hand moved lower, to her belly.

"Do you feel kicking?"

She shook her head. "Not yet. Grandmother said it would be a few weeks still. But he's there."

Her husband's face lit up with a joyful smile, and suddenly, Vigdís didn't care if the sun had risen yet or not. The warmth of his grin started a fire in her heart.

"Are you finished there? Let's get back to the house. I want to be warm again."

He gave her a sly smile. "I can make that happen."

He carried both buckets but when she opened the door, Vigdís heard a crash in the pantry.

She glanced at Hávarr, who carefully put both buckets down and grabbed the axe from the wall. He put a finger to his lips and motioned her to stay silent.

Vigdís grabbed his old seax from the wall. She gripped the short sword and walked behind him, careful to stay out of swinging range in case he forgot her. If Olaf somehow discovered they'd found a bone…

Another crash and a streak of black ran through her legs. She shouted and Hávarr whirled, then laughed.

She turned to see their kitten, Bragi, scoot under the table. Bragi had been a typical Icelandic bride gift.

With increasing trepidation, she glanced into the pantry. At the sight of the chaos, she closed her eyes and prayed for patience.

When she opened them, she glared at the mess. "It looks as if our plans are delayed this morning, kæri eiginmaður minn. Instead, we must clean the cat's decoration efforts."

Hávarr took her seax and replaced it on the wall with his axe. "When you call me 'my darling husband,' I always expect I'm the one in trouble. It's nice to hear someone else get the short end of your temper once, kæri kona mín."

She picked up a wheel of cheese that had rolled to the end of the room. "If you help me, we don't have to procrastinate our earlier plans for too long."

He took her into his arms. "You make an excellent argument."

"But if you don't let me go, we must wait longer."

272

The cat emerged from under the table with a plaintive meow, and Vigdís crouched to pet him. "If you would stop trying to destroy the house every time we leave…"

Hávarr scooped spilled dried beans into a jar. "He must have been chasing a mouse. It's his job to protect our food from vermin. You can't chastise him for doing his job, that wouldn't be fair. That reminds me, we must visit father next week. The quarterly rent is due."

She eyed her loom. "Do we have enough cloth? I'm almost finished with the ell I'm working on."

He nodded. "We should have plenty. He reduced it this quarter, based on the quality of your last payment, remember?"

"Your mother mentioned reducing it, but your father argued the point."

He frowned. "Without proof about the bone, we can't bring it up to Olaf. You understand this, yes?"

She nodded.

"Then let me deal with him. As for my mother, she recognizes the higher craft of your work. He cannot argue with her on cloth."

Vigdís sighed as she hung a braid of onions. "I hope so. It takes me longer than others. I've not practiced weaving all my life like most Icelandic women."

He placed the small barrel of butter on a top shelf and took her hands. "You do wonderfully. Your work is already well-renowned across the valley. Every bride wants some of your fabric for their wedding."

She smiled. "You are kind to say so, my husband. Still, I'll be glad when we've made the payment. Will we stay the night?"

273

"When the whole day is a night? What else would we do?" He grinned to take the sting out of his sarcasm.

Vigdís longed for the seemingly endless Icelandic summer days, when the sun barely dipped below the horizon each night and it never got darker than twilight. The payoff for that brilliance became the Icelandic winter. Icelandic midwinter sun barely rose into a sullen, dim orb, hugging the horizon for a few hours around noon, before returning to its long nightly slumber. The sky remained full dark from at least mid-afternoon through mid-morning, leaving them countless hours of starlit skies.

At least she could see the Milky Way in all her glory. Their farm in Ohio had been too close to Akron to see the stars well. The light pollution had dimmed the brilliance to mere bright points.

Now, however, despite her growing intolerance of the long nights, she still marveled at the stunning cloudless panorama above her.

Vigdís packed for their trip to the goði's farm. An ell of cloth measured about a half yard, the distance from her elbow to her fingertips. She still had to think about the conversion to make sense of the price of things. While they might pay rent in butter, cheese, or skyr, a thin, sour cheese, most paid with ells of cloth. With twenty sheep and ten goats, Vigdís and Hávarr had plenty of wool to weave with. The limitation came from her time available for weaving. Since they only officially became a married couple in the autumn, they had an extra month before their first quarter-rent came due.

The quarter-rent for a married couple cost higher than for a single tenant, but not double. She had been glad to learn that. At least with a husband to help, she spent less time on chores, and Hávarr helped more than most Icelandic husbands did.

When she'd asked him why he helped so much, he had raised his eyebrows. "If I didn't help, what should I do? Sit around and let my wife serve me? You're my wife, not my slave. I'm happy to work. Otherwise I would become bored and smash things just for excitement."

Conversations with Fennja proved Hávarr to be unusual among Icelandic husbands. Fennja's own husband disappeared for days without notice, leaving her to wonder where he went, when he'd be home, and what trouble he got into. Once, he'd returned with a barrel of fish, saying he'd been to the coast to be part of a fishing expedition. Since his barrel seemed well-salted and dried, she doubted the tale, but she didn't argue with the bounty. Without wheaten bread, Icelanders often buttered slices of dried fish to eat. Vigdís rather liked the odd, crunchy treat.

Still, Vigdís didn't like to leave the question of the bone to him. While her husband had heart and strength, he didn't possess a particularly clever mind. He paid little attention to the dark undercurrents between people. She believed it would take more than bluff and brawn to solve this.

Hávarr had gone out to muck out the sheep pens, leaving her to tally their goods. She'd completed twenty-three ells of cloth toward their rent. She had one more almost finished so that would make twenty-four. Along with the small barrel of skyr and three wheels of cheese, the goods should be sufficient for the quarter-rent.

The pile of goods near the door looked like a meager testament to all their work for the last three months, but she reminded herself that her larder burst with food, ready for the long winter nights. Her animals had plenty of fodder and warm stables to weather the cold. Her belly grew and it would be summer by the time she gave birth. She offered thanks for small miracles.

She rubbed her stomach again, a faint smile on her lips.

The door opened behind her, and she turned, expecting Hávarr to hug her with wind-chilled arms. Instead, Bergmar stood in the doorway, his face a naked mask of pain and hope.

Vigdís gasped, one hand going to her mouth and the other to the wall, to keep from falling. She'd long since thought Bergmar had died, perhaps lost in a sea storm. Could he be a ghost, back to haunt her for her decision against him?

She chided herself for such silliness. Just because she now lived in medieval times didn't mean she must adopt medieval superstitions.

Bergmar shivered under thick furs and a sealskin coat. Over his shoulder he held an enormous bag. She stared at him until he shook his head, dislodging several chunks of ice from his beard. "Well? Will you invite me into your home, good-sister?"

She gulped and gathered her senses. Still, her tone remained flat and wooden. "Of course, of course. Greetings to you and welcome to our home." She stepped back to allow him room to enter.

He swung the bag from his shoulder and it fell to the flagstones with a heavy thump. Her vision turned to gray and she sat on a bench before she fainted.

"Vigdís? Vigdís, you've gone pale. Let me get you some sýra."

She shook her head. "No, no I can't stomach that stuff right now. Water, just get me some water."

He scooped a mug into the water barrel and rushed back to her, crouching beside her. He stared intently into her eyes. "Vigdís? Are you ill?"

She touched her belly again, and his eyes grew wide. "You're with child?"

She nodded, searching his expression for anger. She only found delight.

"Then I have gifts for my niece or nephew! All the way from your homeland of Eire!" He turned to his bag and rifled through before brandishing a small package wrapped in cloth. He held it up like a torch.

Vigdís managed a weak smile. "You brought a gift?"

He chuckled. "I brought many gifts. At first I thought to woo you away from my idiot brother. However, if you're already married and breeding, it's much too late for that."

She dropped her gaze, suddenly ashamed at her role in the brother's enmity. "I'm sorry, Bergmar. I had to choose to end the feud. It's not that I don't care for you… but Hávarr…"

He put the gift on the bench and took her hands. "Shh, Vigdís. Shh. I don't fault you for your decision. Hávarr is better for you. I can see the glow his love gives you. You are more radiant than ever, and any fool can see this."

Bergmar's eyes grew wide and something pulled him backward. Vigdís looked up to see Hávarr, his face full of thunder and rage.

"How dare you come here, brother? Can I not turn my back for one minute without you trying to seduce my wife?"

Even during the hólmgang, Vigdís had never seen Hávarr so furious as she did just now. His eyes had disappeared into burning points in his flame-red face as he threw his thinner brother out the front door and into the blowing snow.

"Wait, Hávarr! He only brought a gift!"

Her words fell upon deaf ears as Hávarr followed Bergmar out the door, slamming it into Vigdís' face. She tried to open it again, but it stuck. She heard the two men outside, shouting at each other over the gale, but the words remained muffled.

She pounded helplessly on the solid wood and grew dizzy again. As her world spun into gray, she sat heavily on the floor, holding her head to keep from fainting. Outside, the shouts had devolved into sounds of fighting.

"Help! Hávarr, I need you!" Her voice sounded pitifully weak against the stout wooden door and the howling wind, but the fighting noise stopped. In a moment, the door flung wide and her husband loomed in the doorway. He looked around frantically, finally spying her, now lying on the flagstones.

"Vigdís! Oh, sweet Freya, what have I done!"

He tenderly lifted her and carried her to the bedstead, gently laying her on the feather mattress. His face grew stricken, with one cut over his eye dripping fresh blood.

"Send Bergmar… I need grandmother…"

His face clouded for a moment, but then he nodded. In clear, crisp words, he told his brother to get Arnbjörg, and to waste no time.

Hávarr rushed to her side, a mug of sýra in his hand. "Here, kæri eiginmaður minn, drink your milk. Get your strength."

With a violent shake of her head, she pushed the sýra away. "No, it will make me vomit. Fresh milk."

He drank down the sour whey himself in one gulp and returned with a mug of milk, still slightly warm from the cow. She took a sip to test her stomach, but it behaved, so she drank more deeply.

"What's wrong, Vigdís? It is the baby?"

"I don't know. I'm just dizzy. Arnbjörg will know." She fell into a fitful sleep, her gaze filled with her agonized husband's face.

Sometime later, Vigdís drifted into consciousness at the sound of Arnbjörg ancient voice.

"She'll be fine, but you must let her rest. I've seen this before. Hávarr, you must do more around the farm. Don't let her lift, carry, reach, none of that. Pamper her like a newborn child."

She tried to say, "but he does!" but it only came out as a croak.

Hávarr hurried to her side, her hand in his. "Don't speak, Vigdís. Just rest."

Arnbjörg nodded. "Good. You'll do. Bergmar, can you take me home on your horse? The weather isn't fit for man nor woman out there."

Bergmar threw a concerned look at Vigdís, but she only closed her eyes. The door slammed and silence fell.

"Vigdís? You should eat. Arnbjörg cooked some nice, meaty broth for you. Will you have some?"

Instead of speaking, she nodded, and Hávarr spoon-fed her until she felt ready to burst. She lay back on the bed, annoyed with how little energy she had. Would she be like this until the baby came? She'd go stark, raving mad, if she did nothing for seven months.

"Hávarr…" she cleared her throat, trying once again. "Hávarr, bring me my small loom, will you? And help me sit up? I can at least keep my hands busy."

After a long, measured look, Hávarr nodded and brought the small wooden loom, fixing several pillows behind her back to keep her upright. He piled four fur blankets over her before she protested. "I'm weak, not fevered, Hávarr. I don't need seventeen layers on top of me."

Sheepishly, he removed two blankets and placed them on the bench near the door. He picked up a small object. "What's this?"

She swallowed. "Bergmar said he brought a gift for our baby."

Hávarr frowned. "How would he know of our baby? He left immediately after we wed. Did he say where he'd been?"

"Eire, evidently. That's where he said the gift came from. I don't think he bought it specifically for the babe, but when he realized I was with child, Bergmar pulled it out and said it would be perfect for him. That's when you came in." She dropped her gaze, unwilling to accuse him of being pig-headed after his obvious solicitude.

He let out a short bark of laughter. "My brother offers our child a present and my first thought became him try-ing to steal you away from my hearth. I'm so sorry, kæri eiginmaður minn, I jumped to a horrible conclusion in the heat of jealousy."

With a half-smile, she patted his hand. "I can see why you would make such an assumption, but he simply said how inappropriate such a thing would be with us wed and a baby coming."

"I'm a fool twice over, then. When we see him on the quarter-day, I shall offer my apologies for my boorish behavior."

Vigdís pointed to Bergmar's cloth-wrapped bundle. "What should we do with that?"

Hávarr considered the gift for a few moments. "I think I should bring it back to him. He may no longer wish to gift it after how I treated him. I will leave it to him to decide."

* * *

Hávarr wouldn't let Vigdís even carry her own bag as they loaded the cart with the quarter-day rents. The clear weather made her grateful for the respite as he worked.

He waggled his finger at her. "Sit. Sit and watch. Do nothing. Direct me if you must do something, but if I see you lifting one piece of straw, one piece of fish, I'll… I'll…"

She glared at him. "You'll what?"

"I'll…" his eyes flickered around the front hall for inspiration. He looked at a barrel and grinned. "I'll pour that entire barrel of skyr over your head!"

Vigdís raised her eyebrows. "You wouldn't dare. There's no call to waste all that food."

Still wearing his foolish grin, he picked her up, hefting her over his shoulder. "Then I shall drop you in the skyr!"

She struggled to get down while trying not to laugh, pummeling his back with mock rage. "Hávarr! We don't have time for this! Put me down!"

He gently placed her on her feet and held her shoulders, cocking his head. "No, I believe you look much more beautiful without skyr in your hair. This time, I will let it pass. Next time, though…"

"Come, my silly husband. We're due at the goði's farm and the light will fade soon enough."

The weather luck held until they arrived, and they even got faint beams of low sunlight skidding across the hills as they crested the last rise.

Just as they reached the door, however, the clouds roiled across the sky, dimming the already setting sun with silver menace. With hurried industry, Hávarr grabbed several farm thralls to help him unload their rents while he shooed Vigdís into Arnbjörg's stern care.

"Have you been resting? Do you still get dizzy? Did you drink the tea I left you?"

Vigdís nodded at each of the woman's rapid-fire questions. "Yes, grandmother. I've obeyed all your orders. I feel much stronger now. I even brought my small loom so I can sit quietly and weave while I'm here."

Arnbjörg narrowed her eyes and studied Vigdís' face, smelled her breath, and listened to her heart before nodding. "Good. You can listen to your elders. Now, Fennja has a surprise for you. Walk, mind you, don't run!"

Like a chastened child, Vigdís hid a smile and deliberately strolled slowly to the main hall where her good-sister waited for her.

"Vigdís! Oh, I'm glad you arrived before the snow. Wait just a moment." She reached behind her on the bench and pulled out a small iron piece, in a stylized snake form, almost forming the letter C.

"It's exquisite! Who made it?" Vigdís didn't want to admit she didn't recognize the object, but the workmanship on the iron looked striking.

"Don't recognize the style? I asked for something made in Eire, so it would be familiar to you. It took too much time for the trader to find a fire-steel from Eire, though, so I had our blacksmith make one instead. Do you like it?"

A fire-steel! Vigdís remembered seeing Siggi use one. The iron implement was designed to hold the flint while striking it to start a fire. A precious gift, as iron remained difficult to find in Iceland, with even good iron pots being scarce.

"Thank you, Fennja, thank you so much. This will make my day easier."

She hugged her good-sister tightly, staving off the threatening tears. Why did she cry so much lately? She'd never cried like this in Ohio. Not even in Eire had she been so subject to extremes of emotion. Perhaps allowing herself to love allowed her emotions to run rampant, no matter who evoked them.

"This should have been a gift at your betrothal, and I'm so sorry it took so long. At least I got it to you before the babe came. That would have been dire luck, and grandmother wouldn't have allowed such a breech."

Vigdís, for the first time, experienced a moment of doubt about the impending birth of her child. Her belly hadn't even grown yet, and she'd almost fainted from some unknown weakness. How would she survive seven more months without modern medicine? Women died of childbirth all the time, even in her own time.

Fennja must have seen her trepidation, for she hugged her once more. "I have a secret to share."

"What secret?"

The raven-haired girl smiled, her eyes glistening brightly. "Your baby should arrive a month before mine!"

Vigdís drew in a sharp breath. "You're pregnant! That's wonderful!" She hugged Fennja tightly.

"Shh! Not so loud. No one else knows."

Vigdís lowered her voice, barely whispering. "I'm so excited for you!"

"I can't wait until we're both mothers. Our children will be close-cousins, and will grow up loving each other."

Suddenly, Vigdís' life and future seemed richer than she'd ever believed possible.

"Is this a private conversation, or may a brother join?"

Vigdís turned to see Bergmar. His eye had puffed purple and yellow, a trophy from his fight with Hávarr. She ached to touch it, but pulled back when his eyes widened. Suddenly ashamed that he'd been so hurt by her husband, she dropped her gaze.

He pulled her chin up so she looked into his eyes, full of obvious entreaty and sorrow. "Vigdís, none of this is your fault. Hávarr sought me out and apologized for his temper. We've made our peace, I promise you."

"If only that peace stays true. Why do you men fight so much? Are you not content with the things in your life?"

284

As soon as she said the words, she regretted them. Bergmar's lovely dark eyes turned bleak, and he swallowed. This man, who had declared his affections for her, had no woman, no family, no child on the way. Bergmar, who had been in and out of Iceland, his only home, many times in his short life. Partly because of her decisions.

Hávarr came up behind his brother and slapped him on the back. "I hoped you'd be here, brother. I've a favor to ask of you. Can we speak?"

The two men withdrew, and she glanced at Fennja, who had raised one eyebrow at her brothers. "I've never seen them so jovial, Vigdís. Perhaps you're good for them."

Vigdís shook her head. "It won't last."

"You're too young to be so pessimistic. Come, we have preparations to make for feast. Will you help mother and me?"

Amidst the women of the farm, including Siggi, Arnbjörg, Enika, Atla, and several of the farm slaves, chatter turned to gossip about eligible men, local scandals, and advice on a variety of subjects. When Siggi brought up Vigdís' condition, she blushed and rubbed her stomach, making all the women laugh.

Arnbjörg waggled a finger at her. "You are too innocent to be a mother, granddaughter. I must give you some instruction before the babe arrives. Can you come to my cottage once a month for a day? There are many female mysteries to learn before your day, lessons a man shouldn't hear."

This only made Vigdís blush more. What had changed her so? She'd never blushed so much in her native time. Perhaps the ever-present possibility she might commit an act of horrible rudeness, all unwitting, kept her so circumspect and modest. In Ohio, she'd thought nothing of wearing a bathing suit to the lake. Now, to have exposed so much skin in the view of men would horrify her.

What if she lost all memory of her young life? What if she forgot her parents, her friends, her school?

Would that be such a horrible thing? So far as she knew, she'd never return to her time. She lived in this time, in this place, and with these people. Her survival depended upon her assimilating completely into their society. If she clung to her native beliefs and morals, she might make a terrible mistake, and pay for it with her life.

Upon such dour, doomed thoughts, Arnbjörg held up her arms. "Stop! All of you stop your chicken chatter."

The silence grew deafening, except for the drip of water from the wash bucket. The old woman stared at Vigdís, eyes intent and head cocked as if listening.

"Child, you must come with me now. We have things to speak of."

Siggi furrowed her brow. "Mother, we need her help and yours. There is so much to do before feast tonight!"

"You can manage without two pairs of hands, I have faith in your ability to overcome anything. Now, Vigdís, walk me to my cottage."

Utterly confused and more than a little apprehensive, Vigdís glanced at Siggi, but the other woman nodded. She removed the washing apron and grabbed her cloak, walking with Arnbjörg.

They said nothing on the trail to her cottage on the edge of the woods. When they entered, the older woman stoked the fire to a cheerful flicker and sat on the padded bench.

She waved her hand to the other seat, so Vigdís sat, hands in her lap. What did Grandmother want?

"You aren't from here."

Startled at the obvious statement, Vigdís nodded. "That's true. I thought you knew? I traveled from Eire over a year ago with…"

She raised her hand. "No. Not Eire. That isn't what I mean. You aren't from here, now, this time."

Fear bubbled up into Vigdís' mind. Arnbjörg admitted to being a witch. Did she somehow discover Vigdís came from the future? She sat with her mouth open, staring in amazement.

"Future? Past? You have the stink of another time on you. I detected an odd odor last time, but I assumed it was because you came from Eire. Bergmar freshly returned from that land, smelling of Eire, but you have something else. Something I've only noticed once before."

Vigdís finally found her voice. "Once before?"

The older woman nodded. "Long ago, in another lifetime, when I remained young and beautiful. A traveling trader came, and he had wondrous inventions. He knew far too much for this time, and he shared secrets with me." Arnbjörg closed her eyes in reverie, perhaps remembering her young man. Had he been a lover? A friend? Vigdís suddenly grew curious about the traveler. Had he been Olaf's father?

"You have a hint of the gift yourself, I see. Yes, Sven was Olaf's father, and this may be why Olaf has the gift of sorcery. Only those that can travel truly have the gift. My grandfather also had it. He came from a time far in the past."

Vigdís breath grew short. She put her hand on her unborn babe and thought about what the child might inherit. The cottage suddenly seemed too close, too small, too crowded. She sprung to her feet and grabbed her cloak, rushing out of the front door.

Once in the clear, frigid air, she drew in several deep, ragged breaths until her throat grew raw from the cold. Arnbjörg joined her.

"You are not stupid, Vigdís. You have survived a full year with no one discovering your secret. I see no reason you shouldn't continue to do so, your entire life."

"Is there a way... back? Do you know?"

The witch shook her head, sorrow strong in her eyes. "Not a way Sven ever discovered. He searched his entire life for a passage back to whence he came, and he died without success."

The small blossom of hope which had formed within Vigdís heart died. Suddenly she missed her father with a burning intensity. Her throat closed and though she tried to stop them, the tears poured forth.

Arnbjörg held her and whispered reassuring words until she had spent her tears. "You may never see your time or your old life again, Vigdís, but you have found a new one here. We shall hold you to the bosom of our family."

Unable to speak, Vigdís merely nodded.

The other woman fixed a mug of sýra and Vigdís drank it, grateful for the sour drink her pregnancy craved. "Now, will you satisfy an old woman's curiosity? From whence did you travel? How?"

"I didn't make it happen. I rode in a bus on the way to college—"

"Bus? College? I don't know these words."

Vigdís smiled. "Of course, you don't! I'm sorry, Arnbjörg. A bus is like a large wagon, but instead of horses or oxen pulling, it moves itself. A college is where people learn things, like one big building full of apprentices."

The old woman looked thoughtful. "You worked no magic?"

"I can do no magic I know of. The bus crashed into something, I remember that. Then nothing but blackness until I woke up on a hillside. Not a nearby hillside, but in Eire. My home..." Vigdís choked for a moment, suddenly overcome with homesickness for her mother, her father, her best friend. The familiar smells of her home farm, different from these. The trees and valleys of her home town of Alliance, Ohio.

Arnbjörg hugged her. "You miss your home. Tell me of the place, keep it alive in your story."

Vigdís spoke of the dairy farm, the local market where her father would send her for groceries, and the Saturday night dance where she first kissed a boy. They chatted of the details, the small bits of modern magic which fascinated the old witch and made Vigdís homesick for her life as Valerie.

"This place you lived, it lies to the west? West of here?"

Vigdís nodded. "We are taught the Vikings had a saga, recounting a settlement in a place called Vinland. Some people think they settled in America, my land, but no one has discovered any evidence for this. It's been a thousand years."

The witch looked out into the distance, a dreamy expression on her face. "A thousand years. What truly wondrous magic. Yes, child, Vinland existed. The Greenlanders settled there, but ended up turning back. Too many skrælingi."

"Skrælingi?"

Arnbjörg nodded. "Savages. Local folk, though the idiots who tried to settle imagined them as supernatural. I'm sure they only defended their land. Enough about the past, tell me more about the present. You woke in Eire. Why did you need to leave? Did you not make a life for yourself there?"

"I became a servant, but my talent with weaving gained a reputation. It seemed to be a good life until the owner's son came home from his fosterage.

"Padraig was the farmer's son, and he was a bully. He'd decided the new farm help needed lessons, intimate lessons only he might teach. I complained to his father, but the man simply shrugged. Evidently, 'boys will be boys' is a universal truth throughout history."

Disgusted, Arnbjörg snorted. "Olaf and Padraig seem to be woven from the same cloth. I tried to raise the boy to respect women, but he defied me every point of the way. His stepfather's abuse may have made it worse. If Sven had stayed, I would have married him…"

The faraway look returned to Arnbjörg's eyes, and Vigdís smiled. She must have truly loved her traveler to remember him so fondly after so many years.

"Regardless, done is done. You're here with us now, and I shall do my best to ensure Olaf doesn't run you off like this Padraig did."

Vigdís felt within her dress for the whale bone amulet, and Arnbjörg nodded. "That has helped, has it? He's not tried again?"

"I've seen the look in his eyes as I pass, but he's not tried to find me alone again."

"Good, good. The magic may fade with time, so let me know and I shall renew the spells."

Vigdís swallowed, mustering up her courage. "Arnbjörg…"

"You call me Grandmother, now, child."

"Grandmother, then… Hávarr and I found a bone in my farm."

"A bone? Why would that be so strange? You slaughter livestock every season."

She shook her head. "Not an animal bone. A human leg bone. Buried in the stable yard."

"Did you, now? That's most interesting. What did you do with it?"

Vigdís glanced at the door, wishing she had magic to conjure the artifact for Arnbjörg to examine. However, it remained at their farm, buried under several lengths of cloth in the storage room. "Hidden away. We thought it might be part of…" She swallowed before continuing. "Isveig."

The old crone narrowed her eyes and tapped her lip, also glancing at the door. "That is an intriguing idea. Most intriguing and concerning. I shall have to think upon that and see the bone myself. Bring it next moon when you come for your marriage lesson. Now, I suppose Siggi will be peeved with me if I keep you all day long. Will you walk back with me?"

* * *

Vigdís felt certain she'd never been so tired in her life. Even the harvest gathering hadn't been as exhausting, and that had definitely been more physical labor.

She had no experience at weakness. Valerie in Ohio had always been a physically fit young woman, able to run, jump, swim, whatever she liked. Illness seemed to skip her and she'd never suffered a serious injury.

This pregnancy, though, drained her strength so quickly, it alarmed her. Even Arnbjörg kept a close eye on her, holding out a hand to steady her whenever she swayed. What would happen on her own farm if she collapsed?

She'd brought the mysterious bone to Arnbjörg's home and the woman had clapped her hands with glee, but she'd not heard a peep from the woman about it since. Vigdís remained reluctant to bring the subject up, but she itched to know if the old woman discovered any information.

Siggi finally made her sit in the corner and shell peas while the rest of the women worked in the kitchen. Vigdís felt excluded from the bustle and camaraderie, but she really shouldn't complain. Soon enough this child would come and she'd return to her former level of activity.

Vigdís shelled her peas in the chilly, empty room. Tonight, it would be full of tenant farmers and their families, but for now only she sat in the corner, shelling peas into a large bowl.

The door swung wide, and she glanced up to see who brought in the winter wind. With a shiver for both the cold and the visitor, she recognized Olaf's bulky form.

With a desperate glance to the other door, which led to a hall to the next room, beyond which a dozen women stood laughing and gossiping, Vigdís forced herself to continue her task. As Olaf stepped closer to her, she smelled his stench, stale alcohol and dried blood. He must have been drinking in the slaughter barn. She hid another shiver and swallowed, wishing she had something on hand to use as a weapon.

She touched the whale bone briefly, not wanting to make it obvious.

"Who would leave such a lovely flower alone, growing in the dark?"

Vigdís glanced up as if surprised to see someone looming over her. "Siggi should be back shortly. I'm almost finished with my task."

He chuckled, a nasty, oily sound. He placed his hand on her shoulder and she flinched. She had no strength to fight him off, and he blocked most of the passage to the door. She placed the bowl on the bench next to her, in case she spied an escape route.

"Why do you shrink from me, Vigdís? I'm your good-father, not some random stranger. I'll treat you kindly, I promise."

No longer caring about being obvious, she yanked out the whale bone and clutched the talisman, praying with all her might that its magic remained strong.

Olaf laughed. "Oh, so this is what Arnbjörg gave you? Let me see. My, it's a pretty thing, isn't it?" He took it from her, turning it over in the dim light, examining the carvings. He chucked it over her shoulder and she heard it clatter on the flagstones. His eyes glittered as he stared at her. She stopped breathing, waiting for him to move.

Her husband's father, the honored goði in this valley, leaned in close, his sour breath hot on her face. She had nowhere to run, no more room to shrink back. He had her trapped in the corner, and she had no escape.

"I'm no monster from the sagas, Vigdís. I will show you pleasures my son has never learned." His hand stroked her thigh, pulling at her dress until her knee lay bare. Gooseflesh crawled along her skin at his touch. He reached higher until he reached her cleft, and she gasped when he plunged his fingers within her. She tried to pull back, to push him, to cry out, but his other hand pressed against her mouth. She bit him, but to no avail. He shoved his fingers into her hard, his nails scratching her. His body pinned her in the corner and she cried, wishing against wish that someone would come look for her, come save her.

Olaf kept his hand on her mouth and his body on hers, but now he pulled his lower hand away. For a moment she relished the reprieve, until she realized he only withdrew to untie his breeks.

Blessed cold air flooded the room and light flashed at the door. It slammed with the wind and Olaf turned to see who intruded. Vigdís could just make out the dark hair and glowering eyes of Bergmar.

With one motion, Bergmar pulled his father off Vigdís, slamming him against the long wooden feast table. The solid oak shifted on the flagstones, making it screech in protest. Olaf let out a growl and leapt at Bergmar, hands out for his face. With a duck, Bergmar tackled Olaf in the middle, pushing him once again against the wood.

Vigdís scrambled to escape the room and get help, unable to think of anything else coherent.

She fled down the hall and into the next large room. When she flung open the door to a ring of astonished female faces, she fell without a word. Siggi glanced at Arnbjörg while the older woman gathered Vigdís and sat her on a bench.

"Enika! Get her water. No—mead! She needs something stronger. Atla, get a wet cloth. The poor girl is faint with fear."

As the women hurried to obey orders, Arnbjörg peered into her eyes. "Where is the charm, Vigdís? Didn't it work?"

She shook her head. "He… he took it and threw it away."

"Fire and fury. He's grown stronger than I realized."

Siggi returned and shouted orders. As much as Vigdís tried, she made no sense of the words her good-mother spoke. Arnbjörg's face swirled in her vision, and the world turned gray.

Vigdís slept through that night and most of the next few days. She roused several times to see Hávarr's solicitous face, or Arnbjörg's sympathetic wrinkles, but she drifted back again into the arms of slumber.

She tried to speak to Arnbjörg when she woke, but the woman wouldn't let her. "Hush, child, you must rest. Drink this tea, it will help. I won't let you end up like Isveig, I promise."

No one would tell her what happened to Olaf and Bergmar. Had one killed the other? Did anyone realize what happened? The soothing, warm drink brought the gray again, and Vigdís descended once again into oblivion.

Her body ached and her head felt full of cotton. When she opened her eyes, Hávarr's anxious face hovered over her own, so close she might kiss his nose. She managed a weak smile.

She tried to say, "Hello, husband," but she only croaked. He handed her a mug of milk and helped her sit up. After a few sips, she attempted again. "Hello, husband."

He smiled, sadness and fear fleeing from his gaze. "Hello, wife. You frightened me out of several years' growth. Please, don't do that again! Grandmother has been by your side for a week, keeping you from death's gate."

Vigdís blinked. "A week? I slept for a week?"

"Not sleep, no. You barely breathed when I arrived. Grandmother refused to let anyone but me near you. She cleaned you when you soiled, and poured broth down your throat every day. If you had slept, I might have wakened you. You lie closer to death than to sleep."

The sorrow had returned to his eyes, and Vigdís ached to wipe it away again.

With a gasp, she touched her stomach, her eyes growing wide. "Is the babe alive?"

He nodded, and the tightness around her chest eased. "Grandmother said the babe should still be fine. He might even move soon."

His smile matched hers and he caressed her cheek. His hand felt warm and rough against her skin.

"What happened after… a whole week…?"

He dropped his gaze and glanced to the door. In a whisper, he said, "It's been a rough week, my silk Valkyrie. Bergmar almost beat our father into an early death. When he could speak, Olaf claimed you seduced him, while Bergmar claimed it was the other way around. We all believed Bergmar but as goði, Olaf's word prevailed."

Vigdís struggled to rise, but Hávarr placed a hand on her chest, keeping her in place. She had no strength to fight him. "Where is Bergmar? He saved me, Hávarr. Olaf attacked me and…"

He shook his head. "Olaf banished Bergmar with minor outlawry. His own father."

"But that's unfair! He came to my rescue!"

"Fair has little to do with a goði's judgment when he is in the wrong, Vigdís. This is part of Icelandic law."

She shook her head. "No, no, that's not right! You and Bergmar had finally become friends again. He did nothing wrong! This can't be happening! Where's Olaf? I'll punch him between the legs. He can't do this to us!"

He held her down as she struggled to rise. "The only thing I can do is appeal at the Alþing, but until then, the judgment must stand. It is our law."

"Damn your law, Hávarr. There is law, and there is justice, and this is not justice. What redress do I have for Olaf's attack on me?"

"It's the only justice we have for now. Next year, when all the goðr gather at Þingvöllr, I can make my case to revoke the judgment. Until then, we must bide in my father's rule."

Vigdís hated this with all her strength, such as she had left. Bergmar had come to her rescue and received punishment for his heroism.

For now, she must wait.

Chapter Nine

Iceland, 1104

As Vigdís' belly grew, the date of the Alþing came closer. She became concerned her pregnancy would keep her from traveling to the event, but Arnbjörg had reassured her the whole family would take part in the journey this year.

"You'll not have a comfortable journey, as the cart will jostle and bump for days, but you can be there if you wish. If you prefer not to, though, I am happy to remain with you."

She shook her head. "Bergmar needs my word to testify to the truth of his rescue. They will believe Olaf if I am not there to speak against him."

The older woman nodded. "You do not lie. Still, this injustice can wait until next year if need be."

Vigdís refused. "I will not allow Bergmar to remain in exile any longer than he must when my actions can clear his name."

With preparations for the journey almost completed, the baby kicked almost constantly as she directed Hávarr. He wouldn't let her lift a thing.

While she hadn't grown ill again, Hávarr still refused to let her do any heavy work or farm chores. He had been full of solicitous help and stern commands when she tried. Finally, she surrendered to his demands and sat on the bench as he prepared their travel packs. He'd just had to slaughter the second lamb of the triplets, so their remaining fodder would last. The carcass hung in the drying house, the ominous image seared in Vigdís' mind like a scene from a serial killer movie.

At least they'd have their own wagon and horses. To travel in Olaf's wagon would have been horrible.

The trip would take almost three days in the wagon, three days of rough journey over faint trails across the Icelandic hills.

Just as they packed the wagon, and Hávarr offered his hand to help Vigdís into the seat, the ground rumbled. By this time, she'd experienced a dozen minor earthquakes, and she'd learned to ignore them. This shake lasted longer than usual, but didn't even threaten her balance, even awkward with child.

With a somewhat nervous chuckle, Hávarr held her hand as she stepped into the wagon, settling herself on the cushioned bench. Her husband joined her, grabbed the reins, and clicked at the two horses to move.

They'd discussed traveling with his parents' wagon, but Vigdís convinced him they'd be happier on their own. Olaf knew they'd brought appeal against his judgment and relations had grown strained.

To pass the time on the trip, Vigdís told Hávarr stories. She'd discovered a flare for storytelling, and no one, except perhaps Arnbjörg, realized she stole the tales and plots from her own time. They loved her tales of an investigator who possessed an unnaturally keen eye for detail. She named him Sigrun rather than Sherlock, as the name meant "secret winner," an appellation which would have appealed to Sir Arthur Conan Doyle.

After recalling a movie from her childhood, she told of a Roman slave who created a revolution against his oppressive masters. Hávarr had been skeptical of the tale, but she assured him the ancient saga was well-venerated.

Try as she might, she hadn't figured out a way to make one of her favorite books, "To Kill a Mockingbird," into an Icelandic saga. The reliance on law seemed appropriate and prejudice against foreigners or slaves worked. However, the idea of killing a law-speaker for doing his duty would be anathema to an Icelander.

As an expert on the law, the law-speaker became a highly respected person in society, more so than any goði. Icelanders lived and died by their laws.

By the end of the first day, Vigdís already regretted her decision to come on this trip, but she refused to let Hávarr know of her weakness. He already considered her a delicate flower, and she'd needed to enlist Arnbjörg's support for him to even agree. Fire and earth wouldn't allow her to complain now, despite her body's ache.

The day's pain felt worth the privilege of sleeping under the twilight sky in the Icelandic summer. She gazed at the bright, full moon nestled in the deep azure light above her, holding Hávarr's hand as she remembered her journeys. She'd come so far in both distance and time. What would be happening under this sky in Ohio now? Natives hunted and loved, lived and died in the valley, long before European settlers found them.

Vigdís recalled Grandmother telling her of the Vinland sagas. She now lived long before Columbus had made his voyage, but there had always been rumors of Vikings coming to the Americas before him. No evidence had proven this theory and likely they'd never know. The Vinlandic sagas she'd heard here named no landmarks Vigdís recognized. As if an ancient Icelander would say, "Hey, I found Maine! Let's eat some lobster."

She giggled at the fancy, and Hávarr, asleep and nestled against her side, groaned. He placed his hand on her distended belly, caressing it as he shifted. She covered his with her hand and he opened his eyes.

"Are you still awake, my wife?"

"Mm. The moon is staring at me, so I can't find sleep."

Hávarr glanced up at the moon, its baleful face gazing upon them. "Have you ever heard the story of the children and the moon?"

She shook her head and he settled back to tell the tale.

"A man named Mundilfari had two children, a brother and sister named Hjúki and Bil. Both children were fair to look upon, so he called them his Sun and his Moon. This vanity angered the gods, so they determined to rob Mundilfari of his children.

"The gods called Hjúki to drive the horses that drew the chariot of the sun, while they called upon Bil to steer the course of the moon, to determine its waxing and waning."

Hávarr's soothing voice, as he spoke of ancient tales, finally lulled Vigdís into sleep.

In the morning, the mist swirled strong around them. Hávarr frowned at the bare trail they'd been following.

"I've ridden this path many times before, and I know it breaks ahead, near a waterfall. I hope the fog lifts before that. I'd hate to take a wrong turn and miss the opening days of the Alþing."

"What happens if we miss the first day?"

He shrugged. "Nothing momentous, just seeing friends and feasting. Still, that's the day we should file our request for appeal on Olaf goði's ruling. Fennja told me she will file if we aren't there, for whatever reason, but the appeal will hold more weight if we are the ones to file. Especially if Father brings a large retinue of tenants for his cause."

"Tenants for his cause? You mean, the law-speaker might decide in his favor because he brought supporters?"

He nodded. "Icelandic law has many strange rules, and popularity is a strong voice. That's not to say all he brought will stand by his side. Some may side with us when the testimonies are complete. However, we can't count on any of their support, either."

Vigdís hadn't expected true justice, not in medieval times. During her studies in school, she'd read more than a few texts on the horrific excuses for trials in medieval England. Often they served as vehicles for corruption and theft by a powerful person, stripping the defendant of any meager holdings they might have.

She'd hoped Iceland, with its strict code, would have been more equitable, yet it still seemed like a high school popularity contest rather than a true trial. No central government administration had some disadvantages.

Vigdís, in her earlier life as Valerie, had never been one of the popular girls in school. She'd had friends in the popular groups, but she'd also made friends with the band nerds. She hadn't really identified with one clique. Even the 4H and the FFA agricultural types didn't completely accept her.

Now she wished she'd paid far more attention to the lessons those agricultural classes and clubs had offered. She'd kill for a Farmer's Almanac or a copy of Gray's Anatomy.

She must have finally fallen asleep, for the sun shone bright upon her face as the wagon jostled over a rut in the path. The fog had finally burned away and the grass sparkled with dew, making the landscape a magical panorama which took her breath away.

Views like this made her remember both Ohio and Eire, both unique in their beauty, but equally breathtaking. Suddenly gripped with an intense bout of homesickness, she swallowed hard, trying to keep from crying.

The track grew wider as they drew closer to the Alþing. Another wagon traveled far in front on the track, from the clouds of dust the wheels kicked up. Vigdís glanced behind her and saw several horses pulling another wagon.

The crowds gathered amongst the dust and the horses. All the powerful men in Iceland came to one place for the Alþing.

Would she have the strength to stand up before all these people, all these powerful men, and denounce one of their own for an attack upon her? Especially as she'd denounce him as a liar, an oathbreaker. These would be serious charges against any man, but more so against a goði. A goðr's duties included keeping his valley profitable and peaceful. While he had incredible autonomy within his area, he still must answer to the law of the land. The Alþing is where that law would be decided and enforced.

If the only thing at stake had been her own body, she might forgive herself for letting the matter go. Hávarr had kept her from physically attacking Olaf for his actions, while sympathizing with her visceral need to find satisfaction for the violation. The matter should be settled by law, not by physical violence.

However, this matter didn't just apply to her body or her honor. Bergmar's freedom also stood in the balance, and she owed it to him, not only as his good-sister and his friend, but as her savior from further violation at Olaf's hands.

She shuddered at the memory and clenched her fists, once again wishing Olaf stood here, now, in front of her, so she might punch his teeth in. Odious creep.

The sound of horse hooves behind them grew louder. She twisted around, and noticed they'd come much closer.

"Hávarr? Should we pull to the side? They seem in a hurry."

He nodded and clicked at their horses, pulling them to the side of the track. The grassy verge held some purple clover, and the horses took this moment to grab a treat as they waited for the other wagon to pass.

Instead of going past, though, the wagon pulled to a halt. A gnarled old man with a long white beard and snaggled teeth held his hand up as he reined in. "Hail, friend. I have need of your help."

Hávarr handed her the reins and dismounted. "Certainly, honored elder. How can I help you?"

"One of my horses needs attention, but I'm too old to bend that far. Can you check their hooves?"

The left mare, a lovely sturdy roan, held her hind hoof at an angle, as if unwilling to put weight on it. Hávarr took his belt knife out and picked at the hoof, dislodging a large stone. He flung the offending object away and studied the hoof. "It's tender, and she'll not want to walk on it much. We'd be happy to wait with you if you wish to rest for a while."

The old man shook his head. "I'm obliged, but I need to get in to the Alþing. My grandson has a case I must help in." He clicked his tongue to move the horses, and Hávarr scrambled out of the way before he got trampled. The mare limped a bit, but she seemed sound enough.

Hávarr frowned, pulling at his beard. "He should have rested her. At least a half day travel lies between us and the site, still, and he may permanently injure his horse by pushing on."

Another wagon came toward them at great speed. Hávarr moved to jump out of the way, but he tripped on the gravel, falling onto his face. A sickening crack and a seep of blood told Vigdís he'd hit his head. He didn't move.

With a gasp, Vigdís tried to get out of the wagon, but her bulk betrayed her. She couldn't get to him in time. Instead, she stood on the seat, yelling and waving her arms for the oncoming wagon to stop or slow. Surely, they saw Hávarr's figure lying prone in the road?

Clouds of dust, noise, and terror filled her world. She couldn't see anything before her, and she daren't move for fear of her babe's safety. The only thing she could do is watch and wait.

The wagon didn't slow until it had passed. Several other wagons behind it slowed, and as the dust settled, Vigdís finally disentangled herself from the reins and lumbered out of the wagon. She hurried to Hávarr's side.

The red had been covered with trail dust. Everything showed dismal pale brown and she coughed, trying to feel his neck for signs of life. Was that a pulse? A faint movement under her fingers gave her a surge of hope.

"Help me! Someone, please help me get him off the road."

Several figures jumped from the lead wagon, and the swirling dust parted to reveal Fennja and Siggi.

"Help me pull him, Fennja. I can't shift him myself."

Fennja yelled for her own husband to help, and the four of them got him not only off the road, but into the back of their wagon bed. Vigdís poured water onto a cloth and sopped away the worst of the dirt on his left temple, a knot already growing round and purple. A small slit seeped red, but not gushing enough to cause her alarm.

However, when she looked at his chest, she clearly saw a forming bruise in the shape of a horseshoe on his chest.

Olaf's voice cut through the settling clouds, and Vigdís straightened her back to glare at her good-father. "This is your doing! You ran over your own son, Olaf!"

"Olaf goði, girl. Always use my title."

The dust settled, but now red swam in her vision as she confronted Olaf, stepping close to him. "I spit on your title! Your son might be badly injured! I don't know what sort of internal injuries he's gotten from your idiocy. Must you attack every person in your family? Do you think you can get away with it?"

Her babe protested her rage and action, performing a tumble in her womb. She placed a hand, urging the child to be at peace. She refused to think of Hávarr's chances of surviving. What if he bled inside?

Torn between a need to heal her husband and rage at her good-father, she flicked her gaze between the two, confused.

Olaf went to his son, examining his wound, his chest, nodding several times. He sent a servant to fetch something from his wagon and hummed a chant under his breath.

"Fennja, what's he doing? I don't want him hurting Hávarr more."

"It looks like he's performing a healing spell. I've only seen this once before, when one of the tenant farmers got injured."

She didn't want this sorcerer performing possibly evil magic on her husband, the father of her baby.

With three steps, she grabbed Olaf's shoulder and pulled him around. Startled, he looked down at her, a frown on his face. "What? I'll tend to you later, girl. I've work to do."

"No, you won't perform magic on my husband, I forbid it!"

He laughed at her, a guffaw so hearty he held his stomach. "You forbid it, do you? Oh, that's rich. I didn't realize you had such humor, good-daughter." He turned back to his ministrations, now that the servant had returned with a wooden box. The older man placed the box on the wagon, pulling out two stoppered bottles and a bag of herbs. He sprinkled the herbs, along with three drops from each bottle, onto a rag. Several other wagons had pulled up to watch the scene, but she didn't care about the spectators. She only cared about Hávarr.

Vigdís turned to Fennja. "Can't you help me stop him? Is Siggi here? What about Arnbjörg?"

With a quick shake of her head, Fennja dropped her gaze. "Arnbjörg didn't feel strong enough for the journey. Siggi won't say anything against him. They had a fight earlier today, and he… I guess he won the fight. She has no fight left in her."

Vigdís turned back to watch Hávarr's ashen face. He barely breathed, but that he breathed at all gave her hope. Hope gave her strength and will.

She pulled at Olaf again, but he resisted. When she pulled a third time, he spun around, smacking her across the face.

The sharp pain flashed in her cheekbone and she staggered back with a cry. Fennja caught her, but Vigdís hadn't finished. She stood with both feet braced apart and pointed at her good-father. With all the power of anger and frustration within her, she made her voice carry across the gathering audience.

"Olaf, I call upon you to stop this foul work! What you do is not Christian. What you do is wicked sorcery, beloved of Satan."

The murmurs flew across those watching, and the crowd parted to reveal the one person she most hoped to summon with her words, Father Ari.

With an audible sob of relief, she almost collapsed. Once again, Fennja kept her from falling and led her to a bench. The priest strode forward, peering at Olaf's preparations. The two men consulted quietly for several moments before the priest nodded. With a reluctant frown, he turned to her. "I see nothing evil here, child. He's just preparing a concoction to help his blood to heal."

Vigdís shook her head. This couldn't be right. Why did everyone believe Olaf, whatever he does, whatever he says?

Has he performed obedience spells on everyone? She stood again, with every intention of making her case once again, but she staggered. Her lack of physical stamina betrayed her, and her legs folded beneath her.

Someone else came through the crowd, someone she hadn't expected to see.

Once again, Bergmar came to her rescue. He walked past Father Ari, who tried to stop him, but Bergmar gently pushed the priest aside. As he reached his father, he spun him around, as Vigdís had tried. However, Bergmar had much greater strength and Olaf didn't shake him off so easily.

They stood, nose to nose, father to son. "What did you do to my brother, old man?"

Vigdís yelled, "He trampled him with his wagon, and now he's trying to ensorcel him!"

Bergmar glanced at her with the barest flicker of a smile and raised his eyebrows at his father. "Is this true? Did you run my brother over with your wagon?"

Olaf raised his hands in protest. "The girl is hysterical. She's ready to give birth. You know how hysterical women can be at that point. She wouldn't have seen a thing, anyhow, with all the dust. Surely, he's only out due to the blow on his head. Even the girl will admit that happened before we arrived."

Bergmar glanced at Vigdís. With growing trepidation, she answered his unspoken query. "Yes, he hit his head before Olaf arrived, which is why he lay in the road. I tried to get Olaf to stop, but he drove his wagon right over him! There's a hoofprint bruise on his chest, if you don't believe me!"

With a sidelong frown at Olaf, Bergmar lifted Hávarr's tunic to peer at his chest. In one swift motion, he spun and punched Olaf square in the face. The older man fell into the dust and silence fell upon those assembled.

Vigdís resisted the urge to jump to her feet and cheer.

* * *

A brief hug of thanks for Bergmar was all Vigdís allowed herself before they secured Hávarr in the cart.

Only a half day of journey remained to reach the Alþing. Bergmar drove the wagon while she sat in the back, holding Hávarr's hand. The gathering would have plenty of healers, using true herb lore and medicine rather than dangerous sorcerous dealings.

Bergmar would have to deal with the consequences of his actions, but at least this time plenty of people witnessed the event. His case would be much stronger with the protection of his brother and herself.

More carts joined them on the road, which widened now as they approached the site. Alþingr had been held in this valley, named Þingvöllr in honor of that event, for almost two hundred years. No one questioned its importance or sanctity. Through a shift from heathen beliefs to Christianity, the Alþing remained sacrosanct.

After the land had been settled, a rather remarkable system had been set. The common system of kings and overlords of their native lands had been left behind, in exchange for a republican system of local Þingr. Anything not dealt with at the local Þingr would come before the Alþing and subject to

311

the judgment of his peers, a national assembly of freemen. Vigdís felt surprise at how closely the model resembled early America.

The open plain, dotted with rocky outcroppings of lava formations, already held countless camps, wagons and teams of people. Vigdís estimated at least seven hundred people swarmed in knots and groups. Several vendors had set up market stalls already, peddling their wares to the huge crowd. A wide, meandering river ran beside the massive campsite, lazily wending its way next to the steep canyon beyond. Several bathers soaked in the water, washing away dust from the road. Near a small stone church, the Law Rock loomed in the afternoon sun, jutting out into the sky like one of the monoliths in Eire's stone circles. This rock would be where the law-speaker would recite a third of the Grágás, the law of the Free State. He recited one third each year so none professed ignorance of the law.

The sheer mass of people, after so many years in an isolated community, made Vigdís wish for her lonely farm, away from the throng.

She tightened her grip on Hávarr's hand, and he squeezed back, weak but awake. "Are we there yet?"

With a half-smile against her memory of asking her father the same question on countless road trips, she nodded. "We've arrived. Bergmar will find a healer for you as soon as we stop, I promise."

He smiled, his pale face grimacing from his pain. Wrinkles she'd never noticed dug deep around his hollowed eyes.

Vigdís let Bergmar and Fennja find a healer, find a place to camp, and arrange their búðir. Her concern focused on her husband and his health. She trusted them to do their best for Hávarr as long as Olaf goði had no part in the decision.

Her rage at her attacker bubbled inside her and her hands clenched, eliciting a whimper from Hávarr. She relented, but remained furious. How dare he interfere yet again in their lives? She ached for the chance to banish him from Iceland for his crimes against her and his false witness against Bergmar. While she realized the trial wouldn't be what she hoped for, perhaps justice might prevail.

In the meantime, she must help her husband to heal.

A strange voice near the wagon made her glance up to see Fennja leading an old woman toward them. The craggy face and white hair instantly reminded Vigdís of Arnbjörg, and she wished again the old woman had been with them. Still, anyone who had lived so long must have wisdom, and if Fennja had chosen her from all those available, she must have skill.

Reluctantly, Vigdís relinquished Hávarr's hand to the newcomer's regard. She watched as the woman, introduced curtly as Margit, smelled Hávarr's breath, poked his bruise, examined his eyes, and asked him several rapid-fire questions. She reached for Fennja's hand, unable to handle her fear for the future alone. Her good-sister stood by her in silent support, a true gift.

Margit's poking and prodding had elicited grunts and one whimper from Hávarr, but he grew more coherent than he'd been since they'd arrived. She wrinkled her nose at one point and bent to search through her bag. After a few minutes, she laid out several items: a small stoppered glass bottle, three bags of herbs, a mortar and pestle, and a stone with a rune carved on it. The symbol looked simple, an upside-down U with a small mark on one prong.

Vigdís shoved down her now visceral reaction against magic of any sort. This woman didn't rely on magic. She mixed herbs with oil from her bottle. The aroma that drifted from the concoction grew pungent but pleasant. Margit applied the compound on the open wounds Hávarr sustained, both the one on his forehead and minor cuts on his body. Then she cleaned her mortar thoroughly and brought out a different group of medicines.

As she mixed up the new batch, she called Fennja to help. At her direction, Fennja obtained clean linens to wrap around Hávarr's chest. Margit dipped the bandages in her new mixture, astringent, garlicky, and sharp. She wrapped the long cloth several times, knotting it at his chest. She then rubbed the runestone over each injury, grumbling magical blessings.

With a sharp nod to Vigdís, the woman murmured something to Fennja and left.

The woman quickly disappeared in the throng of people passing by. Vigdís turned to her good-sister. "That's all? Now what?"

Fennja shrugged. "Now we set up camp. Bergmar said he'll set your búðir for you. Stay near Hávarr. I'll bring food and water."

Vigdís didn't mind sitting with Hávarr. It alleviated her guilt for avoiding all the people. In Ohio, she'd been in crowds bigger than this. Her father had taken her to a Cleveland Indians game once, and there were thousands of people in the stadium.

These people were, for all intents and purposes, strangers to her in culture and language. While she'd become fluent in Icelandic, she remained a foreigner in both time and place. The idea of losing Hávarr reminded her of that every moment. If he should die, a part of her heart would die with him. If he should die, her child would have no father, and she'd have no protector.

Bergmar touched her shoulder. "Your búðir is ready, Vigdís. Let me help you get Hávarr settled inside."

They carefully moved Hávarr onto a cot inside. She looked around in surprise. The búðir, or booth, seemed surprisingly comfortable and cozy. It had a stone foundation reused each year, with a temporary fabric roof over the top.

"I don't remember packing this many furs, Bergmar."

He dropped his gaze. "I added a few of my own. Hávarr needs them more than I during this warm weather. If I get a chill, I get a cold and get better. If he gets a chill while he's healing…"

They both let the words trail away without comment.

"Fennja said she'd bring you some food and drink. Would you like me to watch my brother while you wash? There is a bend near the church where the women prefer. It's sheltered like a cave. Fewer prying eyes to see."

Suddenly, a bath in a cold river sounded incredible. She nodded and took a clean dress to change into, with soap and a cloth for drying.

She had underestimated the distance to the river and her feet ached after several days of inactivity on the wagon. She waddled toward the church, using the small, square building as a beacon for her eventual comfort and relaxation.

Only ten other women bathed and some left as she arrived. She nodded to them in greeting and undressed, stepping into the water.

She'd expected an icy cold river, as streams that led from glacier melt-off covered the land. The warmth of the water surprised her with a shock, and she closed her eyes in pleasure. There must be a hot spring fissure nearby to keep the river so warm.

Vigdís sighed in relief and ducked her head. Her hair hadn't felt clean in ages, and she eagerly scrubbed herself from head to toe for once in a long time.

She normally bathed on her farm every few days. A small shed covering a hot spring hole lay on the outskirts of the stable yard. However, the hole remained small and difficult to climb into while gravid. She'd not availed herself of the luxury in several months.

After sending a brief thanks to whatever God might listen the Icelanders valued bathing almost as much as modern Americans, Vigdís scrubbed the rest of her body with the harsh lye soap, grimacing when it stung a cut on her hand.

After she had gotten as clean as one long soak would make her, she reluctantly emerged from the warm water and dressed in her clean yellow apron dress. She didn't need to attach the beads and chains immediately, not to walk back to her búðir.

No one required her today, so she remained by Hávarr's side. Fennja had told her she'd file the appeal with the allsherjargoði. This man became a goði above the others, but not like a king in the classic sense of the word. Instead, he became a final arbiter, like a Supreme Court judge.

Her good-sister would file the appeal and add the events that occurred on the journey to the Alþing. Vigdís would only need to arrive when the trial asked for her testimony. Most of the proceedings would be closed to her and the other women. Only freemen and their goði attended the court itself.

Fennja had assured her, however, many people watched from secret places. While she wouldn't be able to hear all the words, she could watch how the trial went by the body language of those involved.

Vigdís' urge to see Olaf goði brought to his knees through harsh judgment felt both primal and unrealistic. The urge remained strong within her as she sat by her husband's side, willing the healing herbs to work.

* * *

Three days passed before Fennja brought word about the trial. In those three days, Fennja and Bergmar helped her with every detail of life. They brought her food, drink, a few visitors, and the daily gossip. Several times they watched Hávarr for her so she might escape the confines of the small búðir.

Slowly, she became acclimatized to the crowds of Icelandic goði, Þingmenn, freemen, families, and servants. New foods, sights, and odors permeated the market area, and she made several judicious purchases. To her surprise, an Eirish trader had set up a stall, and she spent a great deal of time chatting with him about luxuries he'd brought from his island. She bought several to tempt Hávarr's palate.

When word finally came, she remained nervous, but ready. Hávarr had recovered enough to sit up and walk short distances, though he did so with a grimace of pain and a bloodless face.

Bergmar and another man carried Hávarr to court several hours before Vigdís would need to appear. Fennja took her to a place to watch, hidden by one of the craggy lava formations which dotted the region.

The men assembled in three concentric rings of benches, with a tall rock to stand on in the center. One man stood there, his arms gesticulating as he spoke. Vigdís only heard snippets of the words as the wind snatched them from her.

Fennja whispered, "That's the law-speaker. He's giving his annual recitation of the Grágás."

"Wouldn't he have done so two days ago, when the Alþing started?"

She nodded. "He recites a piece each day. It saves his voice and allows those who cannot be here on time to catch some of it."

Vigdís nodded, watching him gesture as if stabbing someone. Then he pantomimed being stabbed, and she giggled. He looked like a one-man Greek tragedy in a silent movie.

Fennja elbowed her in the ribs, but she smiled. "Shh. It's not respectful to laugh."

As the law-speaker finished his speech, he jumped down from the rock. Three others assisted an older man climb the rock. This older man had a long gray beard, plaited in three braids, several colored beads and glints of metal making it sparkle in the sun. His floppy green hat ruffled in the wind.

He spoke with somnolent low tones which reached Vigdís in her hiding spot. "We have gathered here today to hear the appeal of Bergmar Olafsson against his father, Olaf goði Sigurðsson. Bergmar Olafsson, do you have new evidence to bring to the quarter court?"

Bergmar stood, as did Olaf. Together, Vigdís realized how similar they looked, separated only by time and belly fat. Their personalities remained so disparate, she hadn't made the comparison earlier.

Now the law-speaker called Hávarr forth, supported by two men. He gave his testimony, but his voice sounded so faint Vigdís didn't even hear a murmur of what he said.

Siggi gave her account of events after Hávarr, and Fennja tugged on Vigdís' sleeve. "We should be next. Come, we must be ready."

They clamored off the lava sculpture and made their way around to the crowd of people standing away from the official court area. When a runner came for them, they both stepped forward.

With slow, deliberate steps, Vigdís walked, hand tightly clasped in Fennja's, through the three rings of goðr. Each one stared at her as she made her way through to the center of the court. Bergmar flashed her a quick, nervous smile. Hávarr sat again, his face gray with his effort. His eyes closed and she hoped he'd not pass out from the strain. He remained so weak from his injuries.

The law-speaker called her name, and she stepped forward. "Vigdís Erinsdottir, what say you on this matter?"

Since she hadn't been able to speak at the first trial, she'd considered her response many times over the last several months. Siggi had warned her she needed to be concise and objective. None of her fear or hysteria should shine through her words or actions.

She swore an oath that what she claimed was true and seen with her own eyes.

"This man physically attacked my body on two occasions. He attempted to take me once on the day of my wedding and again two months later. When my good-brother, Bergmar, discovered the latter attack, he pulled Olaf goði Sigurðsson from me and punched him several times. Despite his gallantry, his father tried him for this rescue while I lay ill, and sentenced him to minor outlawry.

"On the journey to this Alþing, a half day from the site, we stopped our wagon. Hávarr had tripped and fallen in the road, hitting his head, and didn't move. I saw a wagon approaching at great speed. I couldn't get out of the wagon in time to pull Hávarr due to my advanced pregnancy. I tried to wave my arms to stop the wagon, but Olaf goði Sigurðsson ignored me and ran his horses over my husband. As you can see, almost a week later, his injuries are still so severe we fear for his life yet."

Vigdís hesitated, considering what else she might say. Fennja had warned her she mustn't bring up anything other than her own experiences. Still, to deny Isveig a mention seemed cruel. "Olaf's first wife disappeared. We found her bones."

A collective gasp came from the watching men, and Fennja grabbed her arm with a hiss.

The law-speaker rapped his staff against the rock three times, quieting the whispers. "You are only to speak of your own matters, woman. Have you aught else to say on your behalf?"

Vigdís shook her head. She had proof for nothing else. She couldn't testify to anything she hadn't seen. The murder and the effort to ensorcel left no good evidence, so they had no place in this court.

The law-speaker dismissed her, and she kept her back straight as she walked away, with a brief, anxious glance at Hávarr. He opened his eyes again, whispering in Bergmar's ear. Vigdís breathed a sigh of relief.

Along with Siggi and Fennja, Vigdís awaited the decision. The thirty-six goðr sitting in judgment at this Alþing must now agree upon a verdict. Several hundred goðr lived throughout Iceland, but not all came to the annual assembly each year. Of those that attended, the same would not sit in judgment next year or the following year. This way justice was more evenly applied, and no one goði garnered too much power. Even the allsherjargoði had little true power, except to lead the Alþing.

Two hours later, after much deliberating and discussion, Vigdís and the others got called back to the circle. She sought her husband and held his hand. He smiled at her and squeezed, but said nothing.

With three raps of a highly decorated ceremonial staff, the law-speaker spoke. "We have come to a decision. Bergmar Olafsson and Olaf goði Sigurðsson, please step forward to receive our judgment upon your appeal."

With a sidelong glance at his son, Olaf strode to the front with all the confidence in the world. Bergmar stepped more circumspectly, bowing his head in deference to the assembled goðr and the law-speaker.

After clearing his throat, the law-speaker said, "Bergmar Olafsson, come forward for your judgment."

Bergmar raised his head and watched the man on the rock with apprehension.

* * *

Miami, 1993

Dean Danelli stomped past the office door, and Val hastily closed her manuscript on the computer. Instead, she pretended intense concentration on the spreadsheets she had next to her keyboard, positioned for just this subterfuge. Jorge glanced at her and shook his head.

Since the Dean might be back at any time, she resolved to do no more writing for a while. Instead, she pulled out the newspaper, open to the want ads. After circling several options in red, she sighed. None of them seemed a great fit, but something had to be better than this crappy job. When she finished, she wrote down the information and handed the newspaper to Jorge. "There's a few here you might like."

He rolled his eyes. "What I like is sitting on a beach with a lovely man on my knee and a sweet, alcoholic drink in my hand, perhaps with a jaunty paper umbrella. What I don't like is needing to work. Even worse is searching for a new job. I've been here for years and, despite the Evil Dean, there are worse jobs."

Val shook her head. "I can't handle her any longer. Nothing I do is right, and the constant worry about being fired is giving me an ulcer. It's not like I can't move wherever I want now that Karl's gone."

He raised an eyebrow, perusing the circled ads. "Historical research? Seriously?"

"What? Isn't that what I'm doing anyhow for my novel?"

"Yes, true, but that's a subject you're fascinated with. I will guarantee you, if they have to pay someone to do the research, it will be the mating habits of the tapeworm, or a scintillating subject like that."

She shrugged. "I can deal with tapeworms more easily than Dean Danelli and her Chanel No. 5."

He waved his hand. "It's your life, darlin' girl. I will miss working with you, but you must fly as your butterfly wings allow."

"I'm not going just yet. First, I've got to get a different job."

He pointed at her word processor. "First, you've got to finish that chapter. Are you done yet?"

She frowned. "Yes, but I haven't edited it yet."

"I don't care. I want to find out what happens to Olaf. Give, girl!"

She chuckled. "Have I got you hooked on the Exploits of Vigdís and Hávarr, then?"

With a sidelong glance, Jorge spoke slowly. "Not if that's your title. If it is, I'll put you in front of the Alþing for judgment myself, and ask for nothing less than full outlawry."

Val laughed, handing over the disk with a copy of her updated manuscript. "No, that's just a working title. I haven't figured out a good title yet. Maybe I'll ask Snorri or Astriðr the next time I see them. They've been invaluable help as readers, pointing out flaws and rough spots."

"And I'm the copyeditor. I see how it is. Low man on the totem pole."

She grabbed her purse and shut down her computer. "The most important man is on the bottom. All those above him rely on his strength."

He laid the back of his hand across his forehead in a melodramatic pose. "Oh, the suffering I must endure for the sake of art!"

"Oh, stop hamming it up and take me out to dinner. I want to celebrate that chapter."

"You want me to pay for your dinner, when I can't even read it yet? What is this, torture? Slavery?" Despite his protests, Jorge picked up his keys and the disk, opening the door for Val. "How about Denny's?"

While she ate her Grand Slam, Val picked at her eggs, swirling the yellow yolks into patterns like she'd seen in Norse decorations. Jorge slammed down his coffee mug. "Wake up, sunshine! I swear, you're away with the fairies more often than not lately. What has gotten into you, darlin' girl?"

She shrugged and munched on a piece of toast. "I don't know. Really, I just don't want to be here. I don't know where I want to be, but it isn't here, it isn't now. I don't even have anyone to be here with."

He placed his hand on hers. "That's not an unusual state, Val. Many of us go through this life alone even if we're lucky enough to find partners now and then."

She shook her head. "It's not just that Karl left. I mean, yeah, it hurts he abandoned me, but I thought of leaving him even before that. I seem… disconnected from this world in a way I've never been. Like I'm a traveler, watching a TV show. I have no real effect on the things around me."

He sighed and patted her hand. "I feel that way, too. My therapist says it might be the first sign of depression. Are you seeing anyone?"

She glanced up. "How the hell do you afford a therapist? Our health insurance is crap."

He gave a wry smile. "I have a cousin who's a psychology major. I get to talk to her for free."

Val rolled her eyes. "Got it. No, I can't go see a therapist. Expenses are tighter than I expected with Karl's income gone."

Back at her apartment that evening, Val dove into her manuscript once again, picking up where she left off, the trial of Bergmar. The memories from the night before shone vividly in her mind, and she rushed to scribble the details on her notebook.

* * *

Iceland, 1104

"We cannot verify you attacked Olaf goði Sigurðsson with malice or intent of injury. We find you not guilty of assault, and therefore not sentenced to outlawry of any degree. However, as Olaf goði Sigurðsson sustains injuries from your actions, he is due payment of one sheep."

With a respectful bow to the law-speaker and the assembled goðr, Bergmar stepped back to stand with Siggi and Fennja. His mother squeezed his hand and smiled at him. His own face had grown pale but he smiled back.

"Olaf goði Sigurðsson, come forward for your judgment."

Vigdís stopped breathing as the man stepped up to the Law Rock. Her entire world shrunk to just herself and the two men near the rock. Nothing else intruded upon her focus.

Olaf gazed around as if he owned the world.

"We have determined that you have misused and abused the Grágás when you convicted Bergmar Olafsson of minor outlawry. For that, we have sentenced you to full outlawry. We strip you of your status as goði and you have three months to find a ship and take yourself away from Iceland, never to return upon pain of death." He rapped the staff three times on the rock, the staccato report ringing across the valley.

Vigdís cried out in delighted surprise before she covered her mouth. Hávarr's eyes widened. Siggi turned pale and Fennja hugged her mother. Bergmar sat on the ground, evidently stunned by the judgment.

Olaf didn't seem to have heard the sentence. The older man blinked several times, staring up at the law-speaker. He glanced around at the three circles of goðr around him, perhaps looking for some sympathy or assistance, but he found none. Several burly men approached to escort him from the assembly of his former peers.

With an animal cry, Olaf suddenly burst into action, hopping away from their grip. He bounded toward Bergmar, a rictus of pure rage upon his face. Bergmar stood, Siggi and Fennja next to him, stolid and strong. This stance brought the charging Olaf up short, but then he turned to Vigdís.

"You! You caused this. Everything here is your fault, you wanton witch!"

He launched at her, his hands like claws reaching for her face. Startled, she whipped out her long knife and backed several steps until she bumped into Hávarr, still sitting on the bench. She held the blade out in front of her, her eyes daring Olaf to advance.

Vigdís didn't want to live in fear any longer. She'd had enough of this man and his harassment. Tightening her grip on the hilt, she gritted her teeth. "Come for me, you repulsive worm. Do you still want to drag me to your bed? I'll skewer your member and feed your liver to the pigs."

He took a half step forward, and she adjusted her grip on the knife, angling it toward his crotch. No one else said a word as the two faced off.

"You've created this yourself, Olaf Sigurðsson. No longer the proud goði, are you? Now you're nothing but a repulsive outlaw, an exile to everything you've ever known. Now leave, maggot, and never trouble this family again."

Olaf's squinting eyes shifted wildly between her and Bergmar. The dark brother stood beside her, a united front against the crazed older man. "Listen to her, old man. You are no longer my father. You are outlaw. No one will punish Vigdís if she stabs you. In fact, many of us might cheer."

Fennja and Siggi joined them, the bitter disappointment apparent in the latter's eyes.

Olaf's escort caught up with him and yanked him away from the small tableau. His screeching disappeared into the rise of voices, muttering of the scandalous scene.

Fennja led Siggi away with a backward glance of steely disgust at her father. Bergmar helped Vigdís return to their búðir, finally secure in the knowledge they had won the day against evil.

Before Hávarr fell asleep that night, he held her hand tight. "You, my ruthless beauty, are my own silk Valkyrie. I am proud of your strength."

Siggi traveled back with her husband, but Vigdís believed her good-mother would rejoice when he left the island.

While a few of his Þingmenn stood by the former goði, most of them ignored him. Any Þingmann had the right to choose his goði, and the status didn't pass from father to son. This custom stood to avoid just such abuse of power as Olaf had exercised. They might change every quarter, if need be, though a Þingmann who changed so often would be seen as fickle.

Several men came to Hávarr after the trial, sat by his sickbed, and offered to pledge to him as the new goði in the valley. Hávarr said he wasn't yet strong enough to take on such duties, but he would consider it. While a son might take up his father's duties as goði, such a progression never became guaranteed.

With a light heart, she helped nurse Hávarr back to health. His recovery proved slow, and the journey back to their farm didn't help his health. The road dust alone made him cough so much, his ribs ached. Bergmar and Fennja traveled with them, offering help and support.

More men approached Hávarr on the trip and yet more when they arrived at the farm. Hávarr turned each supplicant away with firm assurances he didn't yet want to shoulder such responsibilities.

To each one, he said, "Give me time to heal and for my child to be born. I shall reconsider at the next quarter-day."

Each man nodded and withdrew, but a few pulled Vigdís aside. They urged her to speak to her husband and influence his decision toward taking the office. When they returned, the farm hands who had worked the farm in their absence helped her move her husband into his bed.

Vigdís didn't think she wanted to be the wife of the goði. She had no interest in replacing Siggi at the large farmstead where the goði and his family lived. While Fennja assured her they had no obligation to evict Siggi from the farm, Vigdís remained reluctant to even consider the prospect.

After a few weeks, Hávarr walked again, albeit with the help of a stout wooden stick. He ambled around the farm, doing more chores each day. Bergmar still helped, but he split his time between their farm and his mother's homestead.

Olaf hadn't used his full three months to leave Iceland. He'd found a trader the first week after his trial finished and vanished from their lives. Vigdís sincerely hoped she'd never see his oily smile again. She sympathized with Siggi, left alone to run a huge estate.

As she milked the cows that morning, Vigdís noticed them stamping their feet more than normal. With a glance outside, she saw clouds roiling on the horizon, near Hekla. They might be in for some nasty weather later in the day.

She picked up the milk pails and lugged them to the main house one at a time, careful of her distended belly. If a storm came in, she'd need to make certain the sheep stayed close. She fetched her walking stick and herded them into the rough enclosure, a task which took a good two hours. Then she needed to check on Hávarr.

She'd set him to household chores. Despite being women's work, it required less back-breaking labor than the outside chores, which Bergmar had been helping with. The cleaning, organizing, and mending taxed Hávarr's weakened constitution less and he'd only complained once a day of becoming a weak woman.

When she entered the main house again, he sat meekly on a bench, spinning red-dyed wool into yarn. His yarn was lumpy and rough, but would work well enough for a blanket. She grinned at his attempt as he proudly showed off his work.

"See? A man can do anything a woman can."

"Sure, that's so. Except this, perhaps." She caressed her belly just as the child gave a mighty kick. The kick heralded a sudden, painful ache in her back. Vigdís groaned and dug her hands into the small of her back, hoping to relieve the discomfort, but it only intensified.

Hávarr rose, putting a hand on her shoulder and peering into her eyes. "Vigdís? Are you ill? Is it the babe?"

She shrugged. "My back hurts, but I can't tell if it's time yet. This is my first baby, remember."

His eyes shifted around the room and led her to the bed. "You lie down. I'll fetch Grandmother."

"She's miles away, Hávarr. You haven't the strength for such a journey. Bide awhile, please? Bergmar said he'd be back around mid-day to help with the fence repair. He can go get her if I'm still in pain."

He frowned but didn't run out of the house, so she relaxed. The ache didn't go away but spread down into her legs and up to her belly. The child remained still now, so still it felt eerie.

Outside, cows and sheep gave voice to their own discomfort. Why should they react to her impending birth? They might be upset by the weather. Trust her to have a child in the middle of a fierce summer storm.

The ache intensified, and suddenly she had trouble breathing. Her belly felt as if a hand pushed down on it from the inside, a pressure that grew with each passing moment. As suddenly as the pain came, it disappeared again, making her pant with relief.

"Vigdís, I've seen labor pains, and you just had a labor pain. I saw your belly ripple under your dress. I'll get both Bergmar and Grandmother, and maybe Fennja." He held up his hands. "I'll take the horse, never fear. She moves much faster than I can walk."

She wanted to argue, but her last pain convinced her. The birth had begun and she needed Grandmother. With a sharp, quick nod, she sent Hávarr to fetch Arnbjörg.

Wind whipped the door shut as he left, and she'd glimpsed the darkening sky. This late into the summer, the sky only grew dark for a few hours each evening unless clouds covered the sky. The heavens looked like late night twilight, darker than it ever got in the summer nights.

The sturdy turf-covered farmhouse groaned with the wind and Vigdís shivered, wishing she'd had a different option. She truly did not wish to be alone at the moment, but she also needed Grandmother. Hávarr fetching the healer would be the only choice.

Another pain shot through her lower back, twisting her abdomen and spine for a minute before releasing her. She spasmed once and lay, spent, on the bed. With a sudden craving for something hot, she swung her legs to the edge and carefully waddled to the pantry. She put some dried lavender in a mug and filled it with hot water from the hearth, willing it to steep quickly.

How long would it take Hávarr to travel to the main farm and back? The journey took an hour to walk, but on horseback maybe a third of that. Would Arnbjörg come back on horseback? If so, it might be a full hour before he returned. If not, then perhaps three.

Vigdís groaned as another contraction rippled through her body. Suddenly, she needed to use the necessary. She hobbled to the small vestibule and relieved herself.

Her tea should be ready now. She peered into the dark mug, swirling it before blowing on the steaming water and taking a sip. It still scorched her lips, but the warmth soothed her throat.

Once again, the house creaked in the strong wind. After putting her mug down, she opened the front door to witness the violence of the weather.

She'd always loved watching storms back in Ohio. The frenzied energy of wind and rain fascinated her, and she would watch thunderstorms for hours. Tornadoes required hunkering down in the storm cellar, but anything less than a twister and she remained glued to the window, watching the fury in the skies.

The dark gray of swirling clouds looked odd. Iceland had different storm patterns than Ohio had, but she'd seen nothing like this. She almost discerned a funnel shape over the mountain, but it didn't look like a tornado, just a darker column of cloud.

At first, when the ground rumbled beneath her, she imagined she'd had another contraction. However, the vocal alarm of the sheep convinced her otherwise. The earthquake didn't seem strong, but it lasted a long time, making her queasy and concerned. The air stunk of sulfur and she glanced toward the hot spring pool. Steam shot through the cracks in the small building over the pool, looking for all the world like a teapot about the whistle.

Something didn't feel right. Storms didn't make animals cry, hot springs boil, or the earth shake.

With a horrible wrenching in her stomach that had nothing to do with labor pains, Vigdís looked at the long ridge known as Mount Hekla. Hekla, she reminded herself, was actually a volcano, and had the nickname of the "gateway to hell." While the monster had never erupted since people lived on Iceland, evidence of earlier eruptions surrounded the countryside in old lava formations, fields of volcanic ash, and the crater on the volcano itself.

Vigdís had never been in a volcanic eruption, but she'd heard the stories. One saga told of the eruption of Eldgjá, a volcano several days' travel west, over a hundred and fifty years before. A tale called the Völuspá told of apocalyptic occurrences from that time, and may have convinced Icelanders their pagan gods had abandoned them, convincing them to convert to Christianity.

"Dark grows the sun, and in summer soon come mighty storms."

Vigdís found no fault in the ancient story-teller's description. Her skin turned cold as she watched new billows of white smoke move starkly against the soot-gray storm clouds.

Small ash particles fell on her face, and she blinked several times, unwilling to believe her fears confirmed.

"The sun turns black, earth sinks in the sea.

The hot stars down from heaven are whirled;

Their farm stood too close. If ash already fell, the lava might reach them. Hot stones spewed forth from an angry earth might destroy everything they knew, including their lives. The fire of the earth that killed ancient gods would pulverize mere mortals.

Fierce grows the steam and the life-feeding flame,

'Till fire leaps high about heaven itself."

Vigdís remained rooted where she stood, unable to move, unable to stop staring at the dusky plume on the horizon.

Another rumble in the earth broke her from her transfixed fascination and drove her into action. They must leave, and would need supplies. They'd need to take anything they daren't leave behind. She grabbed the small store of gold they had and stuffed preserved foods into a sack. Cured meat, aged cheese, dried fish, unleavened bread, all shoved together and tossed into the wagon. No matter they had only one horse to pull the wagon, since Hávarr had ridden the other to find Grandmother. When he returned, they'd waste no time and leave instantly.

She bent over, struck down by the sudden pain in her belly. Unable to stand, she sat abruptly on the ash-covered grass until the contraction passed. She tried to think of how long each contraction lasted and how long between, but the exercise became futile. She had no midwife training, so the time would mean nothing to her.

Clothing, her loom, any iron tools, her cooking pot. What would they do with the animals? The sheep bleated at her, panicked at the shaking earth. If the lava made it this far, nothing would help them. However, if all that fell on the farm was ash and rocks, the stables might shelter them from the worst.

With a stick and increasingly hysterical shouts, she penned all the sheep into the stable with the two cows. They complained about the close quarters, but their bleats grew less terrified.

The goði's farm lay even closer to the volcano than hers. Vigdís prayed to whatever gods, Christian or pagan, that might listen, that Hávarr might evacuate the whole family away from the estate. A whole wagon train might hurry toward her. She must be prepared to avoid any delay.

The ash layer now grew to an inch thick or more. Should she lead the cows with the wagon train? They'd be too frenzied to control if they ran. Frightened beasts caused injury, perhaps even death. After Hávarr's near-trampling, she'd learned to respect the power in all hooved beasts, domesticated or not.

Once again brought to a halt by a contraction, Vigdís leaned heavily on the wall and cried out for her husband. Instead of her husband's voice, though, the thunder of hoof beats answered her. At first, she imagined it to be another strange sound from the volcano. She turned to see Bergmar riding toward her on his own horse, hell-bent with dark hair flying. He reined in next to her as she slid down the wall to the ground.

"Vigdís! Vigdís, are you hurt? Hávarr sent me when he saw Hekla."

She shook her head and gasped out against the pain. "It's the baby. He's coming."

He leapt off his horse and tried to help her rise, but the ache wouldn't let her. Finally it eased and she stood steady once again. "Help me into the seat. I've got it loaded with what we can take. Once Hávarr returns, we can go."

"No, he sent me to get you. He's heading east with the rest, but knew he would be of little help to you as he's still frail. My horse and yours can pull the wagon."

Once he'd hooked up both horses, she glanced back to the stable, full of guilt for the livestock.

"They'll either be fine or they won't. If we let them free, they'll break their legs trying to escape. You've done right to give them some shelter."

Vigdís took a deep breath and nodded. Bergmar had lived in Iceland all his life, under constant threat of volcano, blizzard and other natural hazards. He would know better than she would.

Bergmar hefted her, despite her bulk, into the seat. He glanced at her and then grabbed several furs from the wagon to shove under her. "Get ready for a bumpy ride. I'd spare you if I could, especially if you're in labor, but there's no time."

She nodded and gripped hard to the frame. She gritted her teeth as he clucked and slapped the reins, making the horses move out.

Ash already covered everything in the wagon. Bergmar's hair had turned prematurely gray. Small bits of rock fell to

336

the surrounding grass, sizzling with tiny plumes of smoke. Vigdís knew they'd only get larger as the eruption continued.

The jostling grew agonizing. Every bump in the road shot red-hot pokers through her muscles, her spine, and her joints. Contractions came at random intervals. She'd lost the ability to count or keep track of how long each one lasted.

One chunk of steaming rock landed on the wagon seat between them, and Bergmar swept it off quickly, scorching his hand. He waggled it a few times before she grabbed his wrist. "Hold still. I'll get water."

He grimaced as she poured cool water from her water skin. An angry red blister already formed on the skin.

"Leave it, Vigdís. I need both hands for the reins. The road is bumpier ahead."

Her spine informed her the road felt plenty bumpy already and then her abdomen added to the argument. She clutched her stomach and bent over, unable to suppress a moan at the agonizing contraction.

The wagon slowed, but Vigdís glared up at Bergmar. "Don't slow for me! I'd rather be in incredible pain and further from the deadly volcano than be in slightly less pain and die in a rain of fire!"

He eyed her with one eyebrow raised, then nodded. "As you wish!" He slapped the reins on the horses' back and the journey became an endless ordeal of movement and pain.

A mere change from intense pain to mild discomfort proved impossible, but she daren't ask him to stop. She held tight and endured. Endured through one more contraction, one more throbbing ache, one more fierce wave of agony.

Something rose in the distance, on the road before them. Vigdís couldn't focus her eyes well enough to discern the shape. A cloud of dust, perhaps? How could she tell in the dim atmosphere of ash and smoke?

As they drew closer, more hoof beats clumped on the ground, punctuated by falling rocks and rumbling earth. The dust slowly resolved into darker forms, and she recognized Fennja's long, dark braids. She sat in the back with Hávarr. He sat up and waved at her, foolishly grinning, but his hand gripped the side with tight determination. With all the ash in the air, she had no way of telling if he looked pale or weak. However, it spoke volumes about his condition that he didn't insist on driving.

Vigdís now saw that Siggi and one of the farm hands drove. Another three wagons ran in front, presumably with the rest of the workers. Each looked loaded with household goods, haphazardly packed and shoved into place. Rope tied most items fast, but a few shifted alarmingly as wagons bounced along the rutted path.

Another contraction hit, and she doubled over, gripping the bench for strength and steadiness. She no longer repressed her groans and let out a scream. No one heard her now, anyhow, nor should they care. The pain simply existed and then it eased. Nothing in between mattered.

The ash fall intensified until she barely saw the path before them, a blizzard in gray and black. The entire world contracted into the moment. No future or past existed, simply now. Now became dim, painful, and indefinite. Nothing permanent or steady existed in her life at this moment, and this moment lasted for an eternity.

North they rode, away from the angry fire of a furious earth goddess. North they rode, from the ash and the grit, the stones and the lava. North they rode, from everything they knew and everything they owned.

Vigdís had no way to tell time. As far as she knew, they'd always been riding in this wagon. She'd always lived with this intense pain which radiated from her lower back and through her belly, around her spine and down her legs. She'd always clenched her muscles against the oncoming agony of childbirth.

The ash grew thicker, but fewer large stones fell. As the stones grew smaller, the sound decreased, though the earth still growled and grumbled beneath their feet.

The wagons in front slowed, and Bergmar pulled in on his reins. He placed a hand on her shoulder, lifting an eyebrow.

Vigdís' throat had grown dry with ash and screams, but she croaked out a reassurance. "I'm fine, I'm fine. Keep going."

"We're stopping soon. I know where we're headed."

She glanced at him. "How can you know where we even are? Nothing looks the same."

"I know this path and where it leads, Vigdís. There's a ridgeline ahead and it should offer shelter. The lava is unlikely to come this far and if it does, the ridgeline will halt it. There are caves and grottoes within the ridge we can shelter in until the ash stops."

She stared at him, remembering the day, a lifetime ago, when Hávarr took her to the waterfall along the ridgeline. Ash fell on her tongue and she instantly regretted the action, coughing and choking.

"Did…" she coughed, "Did you have a place planned?"

He nodded. "Every Icelander who lives in the shadow of a volcano has a plan, Vigdís. We live in constant knowledge that on any given day, in any given hour, the world may explode in a cloud of fire. Dotted throughout the landscape are escape havens. Some even have supplies laid by, in case it isn't practical to bring a wagon."

Vigdís remembered Ohio residents and their storm shelters for tornadoes. Basic logic dictated natural disasters happened everywhere. If one was lucky enough to know what sort of natural disaster normally happened nearby, one planned accordingly. She'd fallen into a modernist's trap of believing medieval people to be less intelligent, less world-wise, than their modern counterparts. This wouldn't be the first volcano to strike the Icelanders, and it wouldn't be the last.

The wagons had gathered, and more came behind them. A dozen, at least, pulled up to a narrow pass in the ridge. The path led through the ridge to the other side. One by one, the wagons drew into the pass, every feature erased with gray ash.

When her wagon came out the other side, the north face of the ridge seemed oddly absent of the ever-present gray. Oh, some flakes clung to flat surfaces, but the mostly vertical cliff remained verdant and green, a stark contrast to the gray which filled the rest of the world. Still, despite the ash, she caught a glimpse of a beautiful waterfall to the right and recognized it as the place Hávarr had taken her to show off the beauty of Iceland.

Slowly the wagons drew around to the west, along the green and gray karstic landscape. Vigdís now counted over thirty wagons, far more than Stöng alone would account for.

Farms from the entire valley must have targeted this place as a haven. She only recognized a few faces from those she discerned beneath the ash.

She glanced at Hávarr's wagon, but he lay down again. Fennja appeared unconcerned, so Vigdís trusted Hávarr only rested. Siggi stood and peered into the gloom, perhaps searching for their destination. One wagon in the far distance ahead seemed to disappear.

Bergmar pointed. "There, it must be ahead."

"Will there be room enough for all these people?"

He grinned, a macabre mask beneath the ash stains. "You'll see."

One by one, the wagons vanished into the cliff face. As they grew nearer, the cliff cut away, forming a huge green and gray upper lip, the black mouth below gaping and hungry for more.

The cavern soared above her head, easily larger than the stadium in Ohio. Echoes from the people already inside bounced against the stone walls, drumming against her ears after the strange pyroclastic sounds outside. Another contraction chose this moment to strike, making her cry out in surprise and misery.

Bergmar's voice rose above the din. "Grandmother Arnbjörg! Come, quick. Vigdís needs you!"

Vigdís' awareness of the people dimmed into a sea of voices, darkness, and gritty ash in everything. Vaguely, she felt someone lift her from the wagon, and lay her upon something soft and furry. Pain shot through her back and down her legs, and she doubled to steel her muscles against it, but Arnbjörg's cracked voice whispered in her ear. "Relax, child. I'm here, and I will help you and the babe."

Arnbjörg held a cup to her lips and tipped it, forcing her to sip the warm tea. How had she warmed water this quickly? The stink of sulfur answered her question. This cave had a hot spring. Vigdís became torn between an incredible urge to wash the gritty ash from every part of her body and wanting to shed her painful, useless body completely. Again, the pain ripped through her, punctuated by wetness and slime between her legs.

"Good, good, perfect timing."

Perfect timing? Vigdís wanted to laugh at Arnbjörg's assessment. Perfect timing, to give birth during a volcano? Still, the sagas sometimes spoke of children born during a natural disaster, and they became heroes in the tales. She must give the child a properly heroic name.

As another pain rippled down her spine and rolled forward to her belly, she hoped she'd survive the ordeal to name the child at all.

Arnbjörg draped a cloth blanket over Vigdís' lower half and rubbed something between her legs, something soothing and soft. Oil, perhaps? The aroma wafted spicy and sweet. Someone held her hand and she looked up to see Hávarr's face, brow wrinkled with concern.

Vigdís smiled at her husband. "You made it, my love."

He nodded, squeezing her hand. "I wanted to come for you myself, but Mother forbade me."

Vigdís nodded. "Bergmar found me."

A tear cut a black track through the ash on his face. "I have my brother to thank for your life and our child's."

She brushed the tear away. "You should go wash, minn kæri eiginmaður.

He pressed his lips together and glanced toward the back left corner of the cave. "There is a line of people waiting to do the same. I can wait for a while."

Vigdís tried to smile, but the pain hit again and she cried out. The sound echoed again, earning several concerned glances from strangers. She hadn't particularly wanted to give birth in full view of the entire valley, but it seemed she had little choice in the matter.

Arnbjörg shooed Hávarr away. "Go, now, and get me some things. I need more hot water, several furs, and my medicine bag. It's on the black wagon, next to the iron pot. Go, make yourself useful."

Reluctantly, Vigdís let go of his hand and he walked away, still watching her. He stumbled and with a laugh, paid more attention to the ground than his wife.

Arnbjörg pressed against her belly in several places, frowning.

Vigdís experienced a cold stab of fear as a counterpart to her labor pain. "What's wrong?"

The older woman shook her head and dipped her hand into a pouch, pulling out several carved runestones. She rubbed two across Vigdís' belly, and the third between her legs. Then she took the bag Hávarr brought her, shooing the man away once again.

Strange how Olaf doing this would have made her skin crawl, yet when Arnbjörg performed obvious magic, Vigdís had nothing but trust for the woman. Intentions were stronger than superstition, evidently.

She set up the mortar and pestle, combining several ingredients, and created a paste. This paste she rubbed on Vigdís' belly and once again, between her legs. Once again, she frowned. The low sound of chanting confused Vigdís at first, but then she recognized Arnbjörg's voice. The woman stood with her eyes closed and her hands held out flat over Vigdís' stomach.

More pain kept Vigdís from concentrating on the older woman's actions for several moments. Vigdís focused on the roiling ache in her belly.

When Vigdís drew breathe again, Arnbjörg appeared more drawn. Her wrinkles seemed deeper, but Vigdís blamed it on the ash stains.

Grandmother's voice definitely sounded hoarser. "The baby is breech. I need to turn it. This will hurt."

Vigdís gulped but nodded. She closed her eyes, unwilling to watch. The older woman only massaged her belly in several places. She hummed and chanted as she worked, pushing here and there. Nothing hurt, though the pressure grew uncomfortable.

Just as the pressure from outside stopped, another contraction twisted inside, and Vigdís cried out in weary pain.

When it passed, Arnbjörg asked, "Can you walk, child?"

Vigdís' eyes grew wide, but the older woman amended her question. "Just a few steps, to the hot spring."

She considered the journey and gave a tentative nod. Arnbjörg helped her to her feet.

The line of people at the spring had dwindled, and only a few waited. They moved readily enough as the older woman led Vigdís to the long, low pool of steaming, sulfurous water.

"Now, lie down as best you can on your back, as if you're floating. Can you float?"

With a hint of her normal humor, Vigdís replied, "I don't know how buoyant I am with this rock in my belly, but I'll try."

This elicited a chuckle from the healer, and she smiled. "Once you are in, see if you can plant your feet and raise your belly up, like a curved bridge."

Vigdís complied with Fennja holding her shoulders to keep her head above water. The stretch became oddly comforting. Her back must be relieved for the hot water after hours of bouncing in the cart.

Arnbjörg pressed her belly again, applying gentle pushing to one side of the baby, and it twisted within her.

The shift made her gasp and Fennja almost dropped her.

"There! Much better." Arnbjörg definitely looked more haggard now, even with the ash washed from her face. Vigdís imagined she looked even worse herself.

"We can stay here. The water will be easier on you and the babe both."

Sweat and water dripped from her face and Vigdís found a small ledge to sit on, remaining in the warm, soothing water. The ground still rumbled, but not nearly as violently as at their farm.

In an attempt to concentrate on something outside her immediate pain, she wondered how their animals fared. Had they remained in the relative safety of the stable, or had they panicked and escaped? Either way, she had few illusions they'd find them unharmed. Would they even be able to return to their farm soon? Would they ever return?

Another contraction rolled through her belly, but it didn't come as painfully as before. Vigdís didn't know if it was the warm, therapeutic water or the proper position of the child, but she felt grateful. Perhaps the old woman did have magic within her chanting and runes to ease the pain.

Eased, but not gone. She moaned as the ache radiated to her legs. Arnbjörg rubbed the rune against her belly and down each leg, again chanting under her breath. The pain pulled from Vigdís as the rune passed over her skin, under the water, and up her stomach. Arnbjörg stumbled, but Fennja steadied her. "Grandmother? Did you trip?"

Arnbjörg shook her head. "It's nothing, child. My concern now is the child. She's not had an easy entrance to the world so far, and it's unlikely to get much easier."

Vigdís gulped at the words. What would be worse than a mad ride across the countryside in an unpadded wagon, escaping the fury of a fiery volcano?

With every push and every cry, what strength she had slipped away. Arnbjörg held tight to her hand through each of them, and Vigdís drew strength from the older woman's determination. Each time, the old woman paled more. The dim light of the cavern must make strange reflections on human skin to make her look so white. Hours passed like this and Vigdís imagined she would trade anything for a modern hospital with an epidural.

Arnbjörg had her lay back, Fennja once again supporting her shoulders as the healer examined between her legs. The healer's voice sounded pained and faint. "Push now, child. Push hard. Push so hard the baby will bounce off the walls."

Vigdís squeezed so hard, her vision spun behind closed eyes. When she opened them, she swore the old crone glowed with a blue light. Her mind must have lost its grip on reality.

"Again!"

The pulse of her blood pounded behind her temples, and she heard nothing but her own inarticulate grunts.

"There, the head's out! One more time."

Vigdís had nothing left, but she still pushed. She drew strength from the surrounding women, from Fennja's support and Arnbjörg's magic.

With a final cry of triumph, Vigdís heard the reed-thin squall of her child. Fennja gently laid her back against the rock and brought the tiny baby, bawling with indignant screeches.

The wisp of Arnbjörg's fading voice caressed her ears. "One more for the afterbirth, grandchild of my heart and then we are truly done."

Vigdís pushed once more, but she didn't hear Arnbjörg's voice. Something slimed out of her and into the hot water, so it must have worked.

Tears and sweat dotted Fennja's face as she handed Vigdís her child. Her good-sister tied off the cord so it would die and fall away. The world now became her baby daughter's face, red and angry, full of rage at the cold, cruel world.

Fennja smiled sadly at her new niece. "What will you name her?"

Vigdís looked for Arnbjörg. "Where's grandmother? I want to ask her a good name."

Fennja shook her head. "She can't help now, Vigdís."

"What?" She struggled to sit up, to see the rest of the pool. The steam obscured so much around her. Where had Arnbjörg gone? Why didn't she come?

Her good-sister pushed her back into a prone position, a grim frown on her face. "No, Vigdís. She's gone. You can't help any longer."

Vigdís didn't think she had any tears left after a day and a half of labor, but she'd been wrong. Her heart grew ready to burst with heartache. "No, she can't be gone! What happened? What did she do?"

Tears streamed down Fennja's own face as she explained. "She gave her life-force for you, for the babe, her great-grandchild. I saw her do it, Vigdís. The chanting, the runes, the glow, they all tied her magic to you. She did so willingly for you, the granddaughter of her heart."

Chapter Ten

Miami, 1993

Val looked up from the manuscript with a sigh. The volcano had been a wrenching scene to describe. Flashbacks to the hurricane had haunted her throughout, though the details of each disaster remained different. Her own experience at cleaning up afterward would be useful in describing the aftermath of this cataclysm for her characters.

She glanced at the clock and realized it would be dawn soon. Evidently, she'd been up all night, writing furiously on her manuscript. She'd be a zombie all day at work. This called for copious amounts of coffee.

After showering and getting dressed, she picked up yesterday's newspaper. She might as well check if any new jobs had been posted. As she flipped through, her eyes lit upon a travel agent ad, touting cheap fares to Iceland.

She laughed, thinking how silly it would be to leave everything she had on some mad adventure in a foreign country.

Would it be so silly, though? She had a passport, thanks to several trips back to the UK to visit her grandfather. What did she have here that she would miss if she left? A horrible, dead-end job? A bunch of mismatched third-hand furniture? The few mementos she'd salvaged after the hurricane sat in a single box, safely at her father's house in central Florida. Her friends? Sure, she'd miss Jorge, but was that enough to keep her here?

With shaking hands, she tore out the tiny advertisement and shoved it in her purse.

On her way to the car, she grabbed the mail she'd forgotten about last night. She'd sift through the inevitable bills once she got to work.

Traffic remained horrible, but typical for Miami. When she finally found a parking spot, after trailing behind several meandering students, she jogged into her office and planted her butt in the seat just as the clock struck eight.

"Good morning, darlin' girl. I see you decided to join us. Late night?"

She chuckled and rubbed her eyes. The first coffee hadn't been nearly enough. "No night. I stayed up writing."

"All right, John Grisham, you can surface from the life of a best-selling author now. This is a side project, remember? Not your entire life."

She rolled her eyes. "Anything worth doing is worth doing right. I read that somewhere."

"'Doing well.' Get your grammar right if you want to be an author. And that's from some British noble."

Val waved the trivia away and went to the coffee machine for a refill.

He followed her with his empty cup. "Val, I'm serious, don't brush this off. You might lose your job if you aren't careful."

She poured in too much non-dairy creamer. "What if I don't care about this job, Jorge, did you ever think about that?"

He spun her around to face him. "What else would you do, Val? Go off and live in a cabin in the woods? Even then you have to buy the land and get food."

Instead of answering, she clenched her jaw, breathing heavily.

He jammed his hands in his pockets. "All right, let's have it. What's the grand plan, Val? Have you got some honey ready to take you in his arms and be your sugar daddy?"

She turned back to her coffee and stirred in the excess creamer. She took a sip and grimaced at the overly chemical taste, but she remained too angry to make another carafe.

"Is your plan a secret? Or don't you have the details ironed out yet?"

Val still refused to answer him. Instead, she took out her mail and looked at each envelope. Bill. Bill. Letter from some lawyer. Something from FEMA. Letter from Karl.

She was sorely tempted to pitch the last into the shredder but she opened it, expecting the signed divorce papers.

Instead, she received a letter in his scrawled, dark printing. It begged her to understand. He needed to be with his son and he wanted her to wait for him. Kris would be eighteen in just three more years and Karl would return to her then.

She should have shredded it when she'd had the chance. Val dropped it into the garbage bin, but changed her mind and retrieved it. She wouldn't put it past Juana to dig through people's garbage, looking for gossip. It wouldn't be the first time.

Jorge watched her stalk to the shredder. "What?"

He jumped up and snatched the letter from her hand. "Well, that's icing on the cake. Is he serious?"

"Dead serious. He has no clue how ridiculous he sounds."

"Here, let's shred it together. It'll be cathartic."

She felt better when the machine had reduced Karl's idiotic plea to nothing but strips of worthless paper.

Back at her desk, she glanced at the lawyer letter, but she didn't recognize the name. She opened the FEMA envelope first. For a moment, the information didn't register. She stared at the check for several minutes before Jorge said, "What, did someone send a spider and they bit you?"

She shook her head, still staring at the check. "FEMA just sent me four thousand dollars."

He got up and came around behind her desk, letting out a low whistle. "Damn, darlin' girl. You're in the money!"

She read the Determination Letter in the envelope, which detailed damages to her property destroyed by Hurricane Andrew. She stared again at the check. "Well, that definitely made my day better!"

Jorge frowned. "Logically, that means the third letter should be more bad news."

She eyed the third, unknown envelope like a snake ready to strike. With slow moves, she ripped the back of the envelope open and pulled out the thick wad of papers.

"A will?"

Jorge peered at the paper. "What? Who left you money?"

"I don't know. Give me a minute to read this. It's all legalese."

Kim's name jumped out at her. She steadied her gaze and read more carefully. In a dead voice, she said, "Kim. It's Kim. The cancer came back."

"Oh, crap. God damn it."

Val choked back tears, unable to read any further. Kim had been her mentor for several years at her job. She'd opened her house to Val and Karl when the hurricane destroyed theirs. She'd been more of a mother than her own had been for so long. Guilt for having lost touch with her in these last few months pounded on Val's heart, making the tears burst through.

Jorge held her while she cried, shedding plenty of tears himself.

When the dean entered, she shouted, "Hey! None of that in here, you disgusting perverts!"

Val spun so quickly, Jorge didn't have time to stop her. She swung her fist straight at the dean's face. All the power of frustration and rage over Karl, her job, and now Kim, drove her fist. Kim, whom the dean had pushed out of her job and out of town for the last precious few months of her life. Kim, who had died alone in another state, without her friends.

The sickening crunch of Dean Danelli's nose sounded like music to Val's ears. Her screams became a symphony.

Jorge finally managed to pull Val back, but much too late. The dean screeched for security. Jorge grabbed Val's purse and pulled her out of the building before the campus guards responded.

"Well, now you've done it, darlin' girl. You'll have to find that cabin in the woods."

Val nodded, stunned at her own actions and the now-dawning consequences. "Jorge, I need my stuff. The letter about Kim. The check from FEMA. The disk with my book! No, wait, that's in my purse."

He put his hands on his hips. "Well, at least you've got your priorities straight. I'll see what I can do about keeping you from jail and gather your things, never fear. It's still early, but you go home. Have a good cry. Think on what's next. I'll come over at lunch with your stuff. Deal?"

She nodded, unable to speak. She took his hand and squeezed thanks before he walked back into the college.

* * *

Iceland, 1993

Despite being mid-summer, the wind gusted with chilly force as Val and Jorge stepped off the plane. The jetway hadn't been insulated against the wind and she longed for the sweltering summer heat and humidity of Miami.

They didn't speak much as they collected their rental car and headed for Reykjavik. Jorge drove as Val opened, read, re-read, and folded again a letter she'd finally received from Hávaldr, the Icelandic man she'd met so long ago at that SCA event. He lived and worked in Iceland, at the Árni Magnússon Institute for Icelandic Studies. He'd invited her to come and examine historical records for her book research.

The money Kim had left her wouldn't be enough to retire on, but it might be enough to get her through a couple years of sabbatical. Jorge had taken his own leave of the college shortly after Val had been dismissed for assaulting the dean. He'd refused to bear witness against her with the police, so they'd left together. After they both threatened to report the dean for several violations of workplace safety, she'd dropped all charges. Dean Danelli had screamed bloody murder, but

Val thought the arrangement would be the best revenge she might have engineered, for Kim's sake. Now the Dean had no one who knew how to run that office.

Val had sold her clunker of a car to a college kid, liquidated what remained of her worldly goods, and left her few mementos with her father. Then she bought a plane ticket and Jorge insisted on coming along.

"Surely Iceland has places for alcohol and bad decisions and perhaps a hunky Viking or two who likes batting for the other side. It's time take this show international!"

Jorge had suggested contacting Hávaldr. She'd felt self-conscious writing the letter asking for his help. As a true historian, he'd replied that he'd be delighted to show her around a real medieval farmstead for her book research.

Val gaped at everything they drove past, trying to catalog the differences between American and Icelandic architecture, people, clothing, whatever she could see. Everything she saw looked disappointingly similar except when an Icelandic word on a building popped out at her.

She'd expected something exotic, foreign, something other than the pedestrian, everyday life. Sure, buildings appeared constructed differently due to a colder climate. People dressed in jackets and sweaters, even in June. The temperature felt fine when the sun shone and the wind didn't blow. However, a hint of breeze and she became grateful for her new Icelandic knit sweater.

The three-story building rose, square and white, from the manicured lawn. A group of houses sat on one side, with other university buildings on the other. Jorge squeezed her hand and they got out of the car.

Val didn't know what made her so nervous about this venture. She wanted to find something real, something she might sink her teeth into about medieval Iceland.

Through several dismal gray corridors, they found Hávaldr's office. Val knocked lightly, almost wishing he wouldn't answer.

When he opened the door and greeted her with a hearty smile and a strong handshake, she gathered her courage.

"So, are you ready for a small adventure, Vigdís—I mean, Val?"

She nodded, unable to stop from grinning.

"Grand! Let me get my jacket. You have sweaters, good. It might be chilly up at the site. The drive is about two hours, so we'll have plenty of time to chat about your project on the trip."

As Val clambered into his enormous 4X4 Jimmy, she eyed the huge, knobby tires and decided that Americans, with their love of monster cars, had nothing on the Icelanders.

Jorge and Val both remained glued to the windows as the city quickly dropped away, leaving rolling green hills dotted with small, white farmhouses and their corrugated steel walls.

"So, Val, what got you interested in Icelandic history?"

After tearing her gaze away from the bucolic countryside, she grinned at her host. "The SCA, thanks to this reprobate in the back seat. He blackmailed me into attending an event, and hooked me with a steady diet of crafts."

Hávaldr shot a grin back at Jorge, but the other man remained fascinated by the passing view. "And what about writing the novel? What made you do that?"

She shrugged. "I needed something to escape to, I guess. Something to take my mind off daily stress."

He nodded, calmly down-shifting to accommodate the flashy car which pulled out in front of him. Val carefully removed her fingernails from the handle over the glove compartment and forced herself to breathe again. If they hadn't had tires the size of a small apartment, they might have skidded on the road.

"Did it work? Helping with the stress, I mean."

Val considered the question for a moment. Her novel really had helped alleviate a lot of stress. The work had distanced her from Karl, and so Karl had left her. That removed one major stress from her life. Jorge would probably agree that the novel had also contributed to her leaving her job, and thus indirectly funneled her life into the simple quest she now pursued.

"The novel got me past a lot of bumps and created others. In the end, I think it worked. Now it's brought me here."

She shot him a shy smile, and he grinned back. "Indeed it has, and it's delivered you to my tender mercies. I shall endeavor to handle you with care. Now, you set your novel in the twelfth century, correct? Early or late in the century?"

"It starts in 1103 and ends a year later."

His eyebrows shot up. "Did you realize the place to which I'm taking you had been abandoned just then, after Hekla erupted?"

Her grin deepened. "I did! In fact, the eruption is the climax of my novel. I haven't finished it yet, though, because I haven't found data on whether the residents ever went back to their farm, or if they had to rebuild somewhere else."

He frowned, stopping the car as a line of horses crossed the road, their wrangler waving as he passed. "That's a matter of some debate in academic circles. There is evidence of farming after the eruption, as they can date the cultivated pollen in the strata of ash. Hekla has erupted regularly, so we have a nicely defined timeline of the surrounding area. However, it's difficult to determine how quickly they returned. It might have been the same year. It might have been ten years later."

Val considered her options for the novel. The absence of evidence allowed her, as an author of historical fiction, to fill in her own details. As long as she found nothing in the historical record to contradict the idea, it might have happened.

"Still, for your novel, you might go by modern eruptions. Usually it takes several years for the land closest to the eruption to become usable. The thick layer of ash, if it's over fifty millimeters, might take a generation to become arable again."

"Forgive me for being a horrible American, but how much is that in inches?"

His laugh filled the car. "No forgiveness necessary. About two inches."

"Two inches? That's it? And it ruins the land for years?"

He nodded. "Not only does the ash seep into the water supply, it covers the grass, which is the fodder for your animals. No animals, no nitrates from their waste. No sunlight on the soil, no crops. Iceland already makes it tough to grow food due to a short summer, so any change can be catastrophic. You can plow the hell out of the land, mixing the ash with the soil underneath, but that still thins out the arable soil. Usually it's easier just to move."

She considered her characters and their resources. Siggi would have had considerable wealth at her disposal. She might have found other land in the wilds of Iceland. Maybe closer to the coast.

They pulled past a large horse farm, and Val became entranced by the small, sturdy animals and their long manes flowing in the wind. Their manes and tails looked stylized, something from a fashion magazine.

Hávaldr turned one sharp bend and the Jeep climbed to a highland with several buildings covered in turf on the crest. A large rocky ridge loomed beyond it, wreathed in the mist.

Val stepped out of the Jeep carefully, transfixed by the buildings on the plateau.

Jorge stepped out and put his hand on her back. "Val? Are you okay? Did you get carsick or something?"

She waved him off, not taking her eyes from the farm. "I'm fine, Jorge. I'm fine. I just… I know this place. I've dreamt of these buildings many times. This is where Olaf goði's farm stood."

"What? Come on, Val. Drop the Psychic Hotline crap. You must have seen a picture of it or something."

She shook her head. "No, not a picture. I know the inside. If you go into the house, the main room is to the left, then a kitchen area past that. Straight forward would be the bathroom. Down the main room and to the right is a massive pantry."

Hávaldr raised his eyebrows. "The lady is correct in her description, Jorge. Shall we go see?"

Val's throat had grown dry. The weight of the centuries pressed upon her chest, forcing all breath out of her lungs.

"Come on, Val. Let's see if you're right."

Val pulled a deep, ragged breath, shrugged, and forced herself to smile. "Right. Maybe I am full of it."

The wooden door stood in the middle of the long, rectangular building, the carved wooden beams forming a peak above it. The turf covered not only the roof, but most of the walls, almost to the ground. Stone foundations peeked out from under the turf near the ground.

The gloom of the interior was relieved only by the cheery fire in the main hearth, placed right where she remembered it. The flickering glow chased shadows across the timber-framed ceiling. Iron pots hung from the ceiling, well above the fire, far enough away to ensure nothing in them would cook.

Jorge examined the fur covering the benches. "What is this, arctic fox?"

Hávaldr shook his head with a half-smile. "Synthetic, but that's what it's meant to be. It appears, my dear Val, that your memory has been precisely correct."

Val nodded, silent. After wandering through each room, she pointed to the lower part of the pantry. "They used different wedge stone construction there, I think. I can't remember exactly, but those seem wrong."

Hávaldr frowned. "I remember someone saying they'd changed it so it looked like a different farm's construction, but for the life of me I can't remember the details. Still, I'm duly impressed. Oh! Come here, tell me what they used these for."

Jorge stopped Val from following the Icelander. "Don't tell me you're buying into this hokum, Hávaldr? Do you seriously believe Val had a vision of the past?"

The blond man shrugged. "I have no other explanation of her knowledge, Jorge. Most of the research has been published, but only in Icelandic or Norwegian. I don't think Val speaks it fluently enough to have read the papers, much less gotten hold of the papers from America. Most of the theses are only here in the university library."

Jorge rolled his eyes. "Fine. You go play at being witches. I'll explore the grounds."

Hávaldr pulled Val into the pantry. "Can you tell me what they stored in those barrels? There are three theories, but I won't tell you yet."

She closed her eyes, trying to remember. "One definitely held salted fish, at least when I visited. The other may have been pickled vegetables. The third held skyr." She made a face, and Hávaldr laughed.

He stared at her for a long moment before breaking into a cheerful laugh and giving her a quick, fierce hug. "Well enough. Those are the prevailing theories, from what I've found. Do you have any theories yourself? As to why you know these things?"

She narrowed her eyes at him. "This really isn't proof, as it could be deduced with logic and guesswork. You seem to be taking the possibility of some supernatural cause awfully calmly."

He shrugged. "Americans don't believe in magic and have denied it for many years. Icelanders are more open-minded. We still dare not disturb the homes of the Huldufólk. You never know when one might get angry at such a violation."

Val had no logical explanation for her knowledge. "I dreamt scenes and wrote them into my story. Movies played in my head, complete with setting, dialog, characters... I transcribed what I saw into my novel. I thought I made it all up as I went, but perhaps that's not the case. Maybe an ancestral memory? A former life, with reincarnation? A rip in the space-time continuum? Doctor Who kidnapped me in the TARDIS?"

"But you saw yourself as the main character, yes? Married to the man who ran this farm?"

"His son, actually. The goði who ran this farm is my villain."

He lost his smile, and Val felt an instant chill in the air. She didn't know what had caused this censure, but the urge to bring his smile back grew strong.

"You don't believe me."

He folded his hands and steepled two fingers, placing them against his lips in contemplation. "It's one thing to entertain such a fancy. But I've been an historian my entire life. I've dedicated my years to the study of medieval Iceland. For you to claim to have memories from such a time, an actual life lived amongst the very people I've studied... this idea will take some getting used to."

She wracked her brain, trying to think of some way she could prove, without a doubt, her story. The image of Isveig's bone floated across her mind's eye and she shuddered.

"What? What have you thought of, Val?"

"The proof may not exist but... I, uh, she, Vigdís, I mean, found a bone at their farm, before the eruption. She never looked, but the skeleton may have been her step-father's first wife. There was a mystery about her disappearing."

He narrowed his eyes and tapped his lip. "Not here at Stöng?"

"About an hour's walk northwest."

Silently, they collected a still-sullen Jorge and climbed in the Jeep. Val directed their journey with some hesitation, as the landscape looked much different from her memory. However, basic landscape details of cliffs and rolling hills felt familiar. She directed Hávaldr to stop by a bend in the deep-cut river.

"Here. This is where the main farmhouse stood. Barns were over there and there." She pointed to several hilly spots covered in purple lupines. "Hávarr was building me a covered walkway between the main house and the horse barn, which would have been about here."

Jorge glanced around. "You brought us from one God-forsaken wilderness spot to yet a further God-forsaken wilderness spot? For what?"

"Stop pouting, Jorge. We're trying to find some sort of proof of my memory."

Hávaldr heaved a sigh and opened the trunk of the Jeep. He pulled out two shovels. "This area hasn't yet been surveyed or excavated. I'll get in trouble for digging without permission, but we need to know. We don't need to find your bones, but if we actually find evidence of a farm, I'll be convinced. If you're certain this is the spot, let's find a homestead."

Val wasn't certain if she wanted verification that her dreams were real memories. She held her shovel and swallowed, watching Hávaldr's form as he grunted with effort. He dug several times before he stooped to examine his work. He straightened, shifted slightly to the left, and dug again.

Closing her eyes to bring up the image, Val turned toward Hekla, looming in the distance behind a wreath of cheery white clouds. She stepped to where she remembered her front door, the entrance to her short, happy lifetime with Hávarr. With more fear and apprehension than determination, she stuck the shovel into the loamy earth.

A half hour later, with dirty sweat streaming down her face, she regretted her efforts. They hadn't found anything yet. Jorge had watched them for several minutes before going to Hávaldr's first hole to brush aside the dirt, searching for smaller discoveries.

A clang of metal against rock shook her arms and she dropped her shovel. She told herself there was nothing to get excited over. Iceland was made of rocks. Just because she found one where she'd hoped to, meant nothing.

She glanced up to see both men watching her. As one, they converged on her spot, stopping to brush away the loose dirt.

Jorge caught his breath as the obviously dressed curbstone came into view. "That is no natural formation, is it, Hávaldr?"

The Icelandic historian shook his head. "No, it's not. Come, let's concentrate on this area. Jorge, can you take over from Val? She looks ready to topple."

Her friend picked up her shovel and attacked the spot with vigor while Hávaldr made her sit. He fetched some cold water from the Jeep and bade her supervise. "You've done the hard bit, finding the right spot. We'll do the heavy work."

"Did I just get promoted to management?"

This earned her another dazzling smile and she dropped her gaze, her face growing warm with flush.

Within two hours and several breaks, they'd cleared the corner of a farmhouse.

Hávaldr wiped his brow and surveyed the site. "If we don't stop and let the Archaeological Office play now, they'll flay me alive. We must stop."

She looked over the violated land, ugly piles of dirt staining the purple lupines. Her memory applied an overlay of the farm house at its peak, with animals and playing children. Hávarr's laughter echoed in her ears. Tears fell down her cheeks, streaking the dirt.

Jorge had his arm around her shoulders instantly. "Darlin' girl! Don't cry, don't cry."

The Icelandic man looked nonplussed at her outburst and leaned on his shovel. "Val, I wish to offer my abject apologies for doubting you. You had no way of knowing about this place, and it's obvious you have some memory of its history."

She shook Jorge off and closed her eyes, shaking her head. "It doesn't matter. It doesn't prove anything."

He clapped his hands. "I know! Let's search the genealogical records from the time. Perhaps we can find familiar names. I have extensive records at my office."

Val gaped at him "You can't really believe we'll find names that match my imagined characters."

The tall man gripped her shoulders. When she glanced up, she noticed how intensely blue his eyes shone, sparkling in the sun. "We can't know until we search, Val. Stranger things have happened in life. 'There are more things in heaven and earth, Horatio, than are dreamt of in your philosophy.'"

She shook her head and gave him a wry smile. "I can't believe you just quoted Shakespeare to me when we're talking about medieval Iceland."

They drove back to the university where Hávaldr enlisted help. A tall, middle-aged man with a ready grin and a quiet voice led them to the library.

"Jorge, Val, this is Thorsteinn. He's helped me with much of my research and is likely the most intelligent man I know."

Thorsteinn ducked his head and ran his fingers through his shoulder-length red hair. "You flatter me, Hávaldr. I'm simply doing my job. The work is my passion."

Val elbowed Jorge in the ribs and whispered. "Stop staring, Jorge. You'll let the flies out of your mouth."

"Hush, darlin' girl."

She glanced between Thorsteinn, who had flashed a shy smile to her friend, and Jorge, who actually blushed. A glimpse to Hávaldr confirmed he noticed the instant interest as well.

"Hávaldr, once we find the ledgers, we won't need Thorsteinn's help, right? We might let him show Jorge around the place?"

The historian nodded, his own grin wide. "Ja! In fact, once we get the appropriate records out, I don't think we'll need either of them for the rest of the day."

Val suppressed the urge to giggle at the glare Jorge sent her, a mixture of dark resentment and cautious hope. Thorsteinn seemed intelligent, trustworthy, and steady—exactly the partner Jorge needed to counteract his own flightiness.

Several hours later, with seven musty journals spread out across the solid oak table, Val found a name she recognized. With a sharp gasp, she pointed at it. "Hávaldr, see? There, it's my main character's name. Hávarr Olafsson. There's his brother, Bergmar, and his sister, Fennja."

Her lungs didn't seem to work. She tried to draw in a breath, but it caught in her throat and her heart pounded in her ears. Hávaldr's hand rubbing her back helped, but she still couldn't breathe.

"What about his mother's name, Siggi? Is that what you remember?"

She rubbed her temples. "But it can't be, can it? I can't have a memory of lives from a thousand years ago. It's not possible."

He arched one eyebrow. "Obviously it is. Who's listed as Hávaldr's wife? Can you make out the writing?"

Val examined the smudged mark, barely deciphering the name. Vigdís.

She shoved the book away, her hands shaking. "No, no, this can't be right. This can't be true. This is some surreal nightmare, right? A sick university joke?"

Val pushed back from the table and stood abruptly. The chair clattered to the tile floor, the crash echoing in the quiet research room. Several people studiously reading glared at her.

She needed to be elsewhere, and right now. Hurrying out of the library, she suddenly missed the comfort of her life, her former reliance on a crappy job and a crappy marriage. At least then, she might predict her future. She knew what the day would hold for her. At the moment, she stood in a swirling, chaotic realm of a thousand possibilities, none of them safe or predictable. Her future and past had become fungible, malleable, something erratic and volatile. Nothing made sense any more.

Down several dim corridors, she finally found the door outside. The sun shone, but dark clouds swept the sky and quickly blocked the warmth.

Val took several deep breaths, anxious to stop the constriction that gripped her heart and lungs. The fear and panic returned, pressing hard upon her chest.

Hávaldr emerged from the university and approached her cautiously.

"Val? Can I help?"

"Help? What help is there for insanity? Surely this is what it feels like. Nothing is making sense, Hávaldr!"

He gathered her into a tight hug. She struggled at first, but his arms felt warm and strong. The tears came unbidden. A cool wind made her shirt flutter in the breeze and she shivered. He squeezed her and held her at arms' length. "This must be extremely frightening, Val. I'm here, though. I'll help you figure it out."

The first drops of rain fell on her head. Hávaldr led her back into the university and had her sit in his office. He fumbled in his desk for a few moments and emerged with two small plastic cups. After he splashed some clear liquid into each one, he took one cup and handed her the other. "Drink, Val. This will help you for the moment."

She sniffed, and the strong alcoholic odor of caraway hit her brain. She wrinkled her nose and downed it, the fiery warmth soothing her knotted muscles.

"Do you get this often?"

"This? What, an impossible revelation about my life in medieval Iceland?"

He waved his hand. "No, no, not that. Yes, that's intriguing and warrants investigation, but I mean your panic attacks. When you can't breathe. My mother suffers from them, ever since I was a boy. Her doctor gives her medicine, but sometimes she has to run away. Too many people make it worse. Is this the same with you?"

She swallowed and nodded, unwilling to speak. He understood exactly. Why had she never been able to explain this to anyone? It seemed so simple.

"The attacks are frightening, but they can be treated, I promise you. I'll find out the medicine she takes for them, so you can speak with your own physician."

At that moment, she decided Hávaldr was a bigger hero than any of those in the sagas.

"Now, about this historic revelation. We shall make a plan, yes?"

Her head swam, either from the strong alcohol, the panic attack, or from the shock, she didn't know or care. "What plan? I don't understand what I need to do."

He leaned back in his chair, crossing his arms. "From what I understand, you have set yourself adrift from your life in the United States. Am I correct?"

She grimaced and nodded.

"Then you are free to find a new life!"

"A new life? I screwed up the last one I had, Hávaldr. I don't deserve a new one. I'll just break it."

He stood and crouched in front of her. For a moment, the position felt horribly patronizing, but when he took her hands, she realized his eyes were the same intense blue she'd imagined Hávarr's to be. She swallowed with fear and anticipation.

"Val, in the short time I've known you, I've witnessed amazing things. You've created a whole world, drawing from the past and weaving an amazing tale. You're strong, intelligent, and any man's dream.

"What I'm trying to say is that I would like to help you build a new life. Here. With me. If you only want friendship, I will be disappointed, but I'll understand. But will you consider letting me be your partner?"

"Partner? Do you mean a business partner?"

"My English sometimes betrays me. I mean love partner. Boyfriend? Is that the American word?"

She giggled somewhat hysterically and nodded. "But you live here. I—"

"Will you help me with research, here? I have strings I can pull and get you a visa for the university. I can help you research your story to discover why this has happened, maybe even how this happened. In the meantime, you can be a research historian assistant. I only have one confession."

Val's imagination went instantly wild as to his confession. She waited to discover if he had previously been a woman, or lived with his mother, or picked his nose. He watched her expression and let out a booming laugh.

"Nothing so dire, I assure you! No, you'll have to like both cats and children."

Her heart sunk. He already had children. Just like Karl, he already had a family and wouldn't want more with her.

He gave her a half-smile, showing a deep dimple. "I already have the cats, but am hoping to have a large family, with children and grandchildren running around my feet. However, I need a complicit lover to help me with this goal."

Her relief burst into a grin at the image. She'd been so careful to sever all her ties to Miami. Now that she had such an attractive offer, what else should she do? Her fear of actually finding happiness kept her silent.

"No need to decide now, though. First, we need more alcohol than I can fit in my desk drawer, and a hearty Icelandic supper. I'll go find our friends and we shall paint the town."

She found her voice, though it remained barely a whisper. "Alcohol and bad decisions?"

Hávaldr grinned. "Excellent notion! I approve!"

After far too many drinks, jokes, and silliness, Val crawled into her hotel bed. When it finally stopped spinning, she slept and dreamt more vividly than she ever had before.

* * *

Iceland, 1114

Ten years passed before Vigdís and Hávarr returned to their farm next to Hekla. They'd gone back after the ash cooled to salvage a few items from the wreck. A few sheep had survived the blast, but they'd not lived much longer, despite the care lavished upon them. Some iron pieces they hadn't been able to pack remained usable. Not much else.

The new farm, much closer to the coast, had plenty of room for them, Siggi, Fennja and her family, and Bergmar. Several of Olaf's former Þingmenn had pledged to Hávarr when Olaf had left Iceland per his outlaw verdict. Not all of them—some chose different goði—but enough for Hávarr to build a respectable farmstead.

Despite raising three children, Vigdís helped Hávarr with his duties as a goði, and he often sought her advice on thorny problems. Together, they developed a reputation for good and fair goðr, and their influence grew.

She'd just chided Hávarr for waking her too early that morning. "The children keep me awake enough, minn kæri eiginmaður. I need to sleep for the new babe on the way."

He traced his finger down her nose and kissed the tip. "But I'm your husband, not your children. You vowed duties to me as well. Must I wait in line behind a ten-year-old girl child?"

His finger traveled down her chin and through the center of her chest, pausing to encircle her breasts, one by one. His touch tickled and she flinched away.

"Do you wish me to stop?"

She shook her head and traced her own finger through his blond, curly chest hair. His hands moved to her back, caressing the curve of her spine as she kissed his neck. His need pressed hard against her belly and she shifted slightly so it didn't poke the baby bump.

The house remained quiet in the early dawn hour as they made love, careful not to wake the children.

After they'd spent their passion, he cupped her cheek in his hand. "Do you remember when I said you were any man's dream?"

She nodded, suddenly apprehensive.

He smiled, his blue eyes intense. "I never had magical dreams, like Grandmother. And yet, I cannot imagine dreaming up someone more perfect for me than you have become, my silk Valkyrie."

She smiled at the memory of how they'd kept their vows, the warmth of the renewed desire flushing her cheeks.

Her eldest daughter, Arnbjörg, the child born during the eruption, ran toward her, a baby lamb in her arms. "Mother! Mother, see? The ewe finally had her baby!"

After pushing her loom aside, she affixed her beloved daughter with a stern look. "Arnbjörg, what did I tell you? You must leave the baby with her dam. Come, I'll take you back."

"But Uncle Bergmar said—"

Vigdís cut off the child's words with a flip of her hand. "Your Uncle Bergmar likes to make trouble for its own sake. Now, pick the lamb up gently; her bones are still soft from being born."

"Bones are soft? Were my bones soft?"

For a moment, the mention of bones brought to mind Ísveig, Olaf's lost wife, and the bone they'd found in her old farmstead. She'd always meant to search for more bones, but life had intervened and they'd never searched. With a smile, Vigdís nodded to her eldest child. "Indeed. You were born in a hot springs, so a very soft baby."

"I'm a water baby!"

She patted her child on the back and they walked to the stable where the ewe bleated for her lamb. This ewe was the last of the triplets from Vigdís first herd, the one spared from the slaughter.

A strange sound made Vigdís spin, her heart pounding. Every loud noise frightened her, despite being ten years since the eruption. She automatically glanced into the sky, searching for falling rocks before she chided herself as silly. No earthquakes heralded another eruption, and they'd settled this farm far from any of the volcanoes.

Another noise followed the first. An anguished cry cut through the wind, a cry in Hávarr's voice.

"Arnbjörg, give the lamb back and fetch Grandmother Siggi."

The child, her eyes wide with alarm, scuttled off to do her bidding. Vigdís ran to the storage shed.

So much blood. Where had the blood come from? A cow lay on her side, the thick fur matted with blood. Vigdís heaved a sigh of relief. Then she saw his legs.

The cow heaved and mooed, struggling to rise. Hávarr's legs jutting out from under the massive beast trembled as his moan drifted from under the beast. She ran around the other side of the cow, trying to find Hávarr's head, his chest, his arms.

Siggi came running, the child close behind her. "Arnbjörg, go find Uncle Bergmar, Uncle Vigmund, send them here. Any men you can find, child, run!"

Vigdís didn't want to touch the cow, for fear Hávarr still lived beneath the bulk of the animal. Any struggle the beast made trying to rise might easily squeeze away his remaining life and breath. She cast around for something, anything she might do on her own, but found nothing. The cow panted, her chest heaving with pained gasps. Her mooing grew faint and anguished.

The sound of running feet made Vigdís spin, relieved beyond measure to see Bergmar and three other burly farmers pelting toward her. She didn't need to say a thing. The men saw the situation and instantly took charge, gently pushing her aside as they worked.

Vigdís gripped the turf covering of the stable so hard, her nails bit down to the wood beneath. She didn't dare watch, so she screwed her eyes shut, listening with all her might for Hávarr's voice, no matter how faint.

Bergmar shouted directions, a hint of panic in his voice. "No, Vigmund, gently! The cow mustn't crush him further. Now, Erlar, pull the head. Tromm, you pull his feet. No, you idiot, don't yank! Gently, gently."

Vigdís cracked open one eye to see Hávarr's limp body emerge from under the now panicked animal. The cow mooed one last time, her eyes white-rimmed with fear, and collapsed again. This time, however, the men pulled Hávarr clear and left the cow to die.

She wanted to go to the animal and help put her out of her pain, but she daren't move. Until she knew Hávarr's condition, she remained glued to the stable wall.

The men gathered around her husband and together, they carefully carried him into the farmhouse. Siggi must have arrived during the extraction, as she hurried in after them, healing bag on her shoulder.

With a brief prayer to Grandmother Arnbjörg's spirit, Vigdís removed her grip from the turf and woodenly made herself enter the farmhouse. The house where she had made a life with Hávarr. The house where she had borne their two other children. The house where she finally felt at home and at peace.

Everything had changed with the sight of Hávarr's motionless form under that cow.

She should help Siggi. Fennja arrived, doing the older woman's bidding, while Enika took Vigdís' daughter and young sons to Fennja's house for minding.

The actions of the healer became blurred in her sight. Bergmar's voice lurked somewhere behind her, muffled and confused. Her mind's eye filled with Hávarr's strong face, ashen and utterly still. No spirit inhabited his body. He had left her alone.

Bergmar moved to his brother's side, pressing a seax in the dying man's hand. He curled Hávarr's fingers tightly around the sword's handle, holding it as tears fell down his cheeks. This small gesture gave a place in Óðinn's hall in Valhalla for a pagan warrior.

Why couldn't she cry? She wanted to. The grief threatened to burst from her with wailing intensity, and yet, nothing came. A stone wall separated her from the relief of tears. Her back against the wall of the house, she slid down until she sat on the cool flagstones, still staring at her lifeless husband.

Siggi stood then, finally admitting defeat in her healing efforts. She pressed a small dagger into his other hand with a whispered prayer to Óðinn, to take this warrior into his hall. She then closed her son's eyes with her fingers and crossed herself.

Fennja embraced her mother, and they shed quiet tears, yet still Vigdís did not cry.

Even when her good-sister tried to lift her from the flagstones, Vigdís wouldn't move of her own volition. She moved as if a lifeless puppet herself, directed with strings and words of command.

The men returned, and Bergmar held a fine blanket of white linen. He tucked this around his brother, covering Hávarr's face.

Vigdís jumped up, reaching for the linen to tear it away. "No! No, you mustn't! You can't!" Bergmar and Vigmund held her, despite her mad struggles. "Please! He can't be gone. He can't! Stop it, let me go!"

Bergmar shook his head, holding her arm tightly. "He's gone to the next world, Vigdís. We could have done nothing more. He'd departed before we had a chance."

Now the tears came, and she didn't care. They ran down her face until her vision dimmed. She wailed and screamed, uncaring of who heard.

Someone carried her to the bed, but this made it worse. She recognized their marriage bed, where they'd lain in joy and love for many years. Fennja's voice murmured something and they carried her outside.

Still, Vigdís cried and screamed, unable to accept her loss. When she finally slept, her eyes and throat had grown raw from grief and pain.

She woke, but didn't want to. She kept her eyes closed, but someone placed their cool hand on her forehead.

Bergmar's voice cracked as he spoke. "I know you're awake, Vigdís. It's been two days, but you must be thirsty."

Her own throat rasped as she tried to speak. He lifted her to a sitting position and handed her a cup. The cool, sweet water tasted more delicious than anything she'd ever drunk.

She glanced at the dark brother. He had deep, red rims and new lines around his eyes. "We must place Hávarr to rest, Vigdís, and we need you to preside over the ceremony."

"Has anyone found out what happened? Where did the blood come from?"

He shook his head. "Someone speared the cow and pushed her. Outlaws, perhaps? It may have been a deliberate attack on Hávarr, or it may have been a horrible accident."

She sat up straighter and regretted it as her muscles ached. "An attack?"

"Shush, Vigdís. I'm sure this wasn't on purpose. Likely some idiots out for mischief."

She tried to stand up, but Bergmar wouldn't move out of the way. She shoved him aside. "An attack! Why would anyone kill a cow, Bergmar? Cows are valuable."

Siggi entered, a bowl of steaming broth in her hands. "Bergmar, what are you up to? She need healing, not agitating. Go, now."

The woman sat next to Vigdís and made her eat, refusing to answer her questions. When she finished the broth, Siggi allowed the younger woman to rise. "Dress in your best, Vigdís, to honor my son. We will put him to rest this afternoon. Father Ari is here but you must be part of the ritual."

The word "ritual" made her spine tingle and Vigdís remembered Olaf and his sorcery. She shivered as she remembered his oily smile and squinting eyes. He'd been outlawed for over a decade.

In her ten years in Iceland, Vigdís had attended several funerals. The details of this one remained clouded forever. Each vision jumbled with another into an incomprehensible mess. She stood when told, spoke the words she must, and buried her husband in the cold, unforgiving ground. Then she slept.

She slept for days, ignoring the entreaties of her children and family. Fennja and Bergmar worked the farm and constantly begged her to return to life, but she refused.

Better she fade away here and now than to live life alone. Hávarr waited for her in Valhalla. She held onto the small knife, the same one Siggi had pressed into her son's hand. A warrior who died with his weapon in his hand would be assured of a place at Óðinn's feast hall after death. Vigdís might be a warrior. She'd fought against the volcano and won. She'd fought against Olaf and won.

Now she'd grown tired of fighting.

Arnbjörg's plaintive voice filtered through her grief. "But I don't want to play with the new lamb. I want to see Mamma."

Bergmar's voice murmured something, but she couldn't hear. She didn't care.

Fennja came in with more broth. She'd grown sick of broth. Vigdís turned her head, refusing to eat.

"Come, Vigdís. You must eat. You've become a stick. How can you attract a new husband if you're a stick?"

Vigdís shoved the bowl away so hard it flew, splashing the liquid on the wall. Fennja frowned. "Stop it, Vigdís! I miss Hávarr deeply, but life must go on. You have three children to care for, and we can't help you forever. Do you hear me?"

She stared at the wall again.

Bergmar murmured again and someone left, shutting the door.

Her good-brother's voice intruded upon her once again. "She's right, you know. You must live again, Vigdís."

He placed his hand on her back, rubbing gently.

"Go away, Bergmar. I'm not yours to inherit because your brother is dead."

Her angry words halted his hand. "I never assumed such a thing."

"Then why are you here? Leave me alone. I don't want comfort." "Perhaps I need comfort. I've lost my only brother."

She flipped around and stared at him. "You need comfort? You, who travels wherever he likes, and beds women in every town? What sort of comfort would you need?"

He raised his eyebrows. "And where do you get these lies, Vigdís? If I slept with so many women, why haven't any come to me for care of their children?"

The rumors never had such details. She had no answer, so she scowled.

He picked up her hand, but she snatched it away. He gave her a half-smile and bowed his head slightly. "I have no women, no lovers, no children. This I vow to you."

"Why do you vow this? Why would I care what you do?"

He shrugged. "You seemed incensed that I should grieve my brother due to my many lovers. I am letting you know you have incorrect ideas about my personal life. Now, would you at least allow me to escort you to the baths? You need a long, hot soak."

Suddenly, hot springs appealed to her intensely. With a sigh and a nod, she allowed Bergmar to help her to the bathhouse.

She needed the help. Her muscles, unused to walking, betrayed her several times.

The new farm had a large bathhouse, large enough for a half-dozen people to bathe comfortably at once. They'd carved out passable steps into the water. Bergmar stripped to his tunic and led her carefully down into the steaming, sulfurous water. She sighed and closed her eyes, grateful for the heat and steam.

She scrubbed away the grime of several weeks, along with her melancholy and despair. From the hot water seeping from the very earth that destroyed her first home, she drew in the courage and determination to live once again, despite her loss.

Vigdís emerged from the hot spring a new woman, and Bergmar waited to take her in his arms. As he dried her off, he grimaced as if from pain. Confused, Vigdís watched as he crumpled to the ground.

Behind him stood Olaf, a gaunt shadow of the man he'd once been. Rake thin with wild, white hair, his eyes danced with shrieking madness. He held a large club in his hand and a wicked grin on his haggard face. "Did you forget me, woman? I'm here to claim my spoils!"

Vigdís screeched at the top of her lungs, the sound echoing in the bathhouse as she kicked Olaf between the legs with all the rage and frustration she could muster. He'd twisted, but she still landed a glancing blow, enough to make him double over. She snatched the club from him and slammed it on his head once, twice, three times until he lay utterly still. The crunch of his skull left her no doubt she had finally vanquished him, but she couldn't relax until she saw the blood seeping from his brain. She panted as sweat dripped from her face, watching his body, daring him to rise again so she might kill him.

He didn't move. Vigdís heard a moan, but it came from Bergmar. She helped her good-brother to his feet, and together, they went to fetch the other farmers.

An outlaw had returned, and his justice would be swift.

Epilogue

Val put her head down on her desk, cradled in her arms. So much paperwork, and so little in English. Certain she'd well over-stayed Hávaldr's patience, she became determined to puzzle out the bureaucracy herself. Jorge had no problem asking his new boyfriend's help with everything, despite his greater fluency in the language. Why must she be so stubborn?

A warm hand on her shoulder made her glance up into Hávaldr's smiling eyes. He placed a mug of coffee on her desk and she grinned.

"You looked like you needed an afternoon boost to your caffeine addiction."

She took an appreciative sip. "At least Iceland knows how to make excellent coffee."

He laughed, sipping his own mug. "We have the best water in the world, filtered through lava."

Val glanced down at her papers, wanting to ask his help while dreading it.

"Yes, I will help. This is difficult enough when Icelandic is your native language. Why won't you ask?"

She chuckled. How like Hávaldr to know exactly what she thought. He continued to amaze her, even after they'd been together for four months. "I'm a modern, independent, capable woman who doesn't need a man's help with anything. Also, I'm stubborn."

"And you don't lie in the slightest, especially on the stubborn part."

She grinned and shoved his shoulder at the backhanded compliment. "I need a break after this. What would you like for dinner?"

"Is it too early for alcohol?"

"Normally, I'd say it's never too early for alcohol. However…" She glanced down at her stomach and caressed it, smiling. "I don't think that's a good idea in my condition."

Hávaldr's eyes grew wide and his smile answered hers. "Truly? Yes?"

When she nodded, he whooped and lifted her into his arms, twirling her around. She laughed as she grew dizzy.

"Then we must celebrate! No alcohol… but good food is a must. First, I have something to show you." He carefully placed an ancient tome on her desk, open to aged paper covered in faded scribbles. She squinted at the writing and shook her head. "I can't read that, Hávaldr. Even if it had been written in English, I don't think I could decipher it."

"Never fear. I have read and translated it. It's a document from thirty years after the genealogy we found before. A death entry. Such entries remained rare in those days as no central government existed to keep track. However, a few families kept bibles, and noted births, deaths and marriages in the fly leaves."

Val sipped her coffee and arched her eyebrow. "And? Are you going to keep me in suspense or tell me what you found?"

"Patience, my American rose. I found one of your names, Bergmar. The brother in your dream, yes?"

All sarcasm and kidding flew as she put her cup down. "Thirty years later? A death entry then, I imagine?"

He nodded. "What I found more interesting was the listing for his wife at the time."

"Oh?"

He pointed to the bottom of the left-hand page. "See here? Names aren't of one language. You should be able to make it out."

She squinted at the faded brown ink.

"Bergmar, eiginmaður Vigdísar."

She closed her eyes to quell the rising nausea and slow her heartbeat. Bergmar, husband of Vigdís. She married Bergmar after all. Every flutter of her stomach at the darker brother's clever words and feather touches rushed back to Val's memory. It was as if someone had punched her in the gut.

Hávaldr rubbed her shoulders and bent to whisper in her ear, bringing her back to the present. "I'll try not to be jealous. It appears you have more dreams to transcribe. And perhaps another book to write."

* * *

No matter where the watch hands turn, she'd rather remain home. But with every time-traveling trekker's life at stake, can she stop a deadly clock?

Time Tourist Outfitters, Ltd. is the intriguing first book in the Toronto Time Agents science fiction series. If you like feisty heroines, beautiful landscapes, and astounding adventures, then you'll love this explosive tale.

Buy *Time Tourist Outfitters, Ltd.* to
race against the bell today!
www.greendragonartist.com/books

Thank You!

Thank you so much for enjoying Past Storm and Fire. If you've enjoyed the story, please consider leaving a review to help others discover the magic of Iceland.

If you would like to get updates, sneak previews, sales, and contests, please sign up for my newsletter.

Monthly Newsletter Signup and homepage:
www.greendragonartist.com

Other Books by This Author

Author's Note

The night Hurricane Andrew hit was probably the strangest night of my life. I don't really remember a lot of fear, but that probably meant I just didn't understand the danger. I wasn't a child, or anything. I was 23 and living for the first time on my own in an apartment, but I still had that mental superpower most young people have where they believe themselves immortal. I've since learned better.

The Stöng Farmhouse in Iceland is a real place, a reconstruction of an historical site in that place, destroyed by a volcano in the 12th century. We visited that place when we traveled to Iceland in 2015 and became enchanted with the history.

For pronunciations, the ð is a soft th, like in 'this.'

If you enjoyed the book, please leave a review!

About the Author

Christy Nicholas writes under several pen names, including Emeline Rhys, C.N. Jackson, and Rowan Dillon. She is an author, artist, and accountant. After she failed to become an airline pilot, she quit her ceaseless pursuit of careers that begin with the letter 'A' and decided to concentrate on her writing. Since she has Project Completion Compulsion, she is one of the few authors with no unfinished novels.

Christy has her hands in many crafts, including digital art, beaded jewelry, writing, and photography. In real life, she's a CPA, but having grown up with art all around her (her mother, grandmother, and great-grandmother are/were all artists), it sort of infected her, as it were.

She wants to expose the incredible beauty in this world, hidden beneath the everyday grime of familiarity and habit, and share it with others. She uses characters out of time and places infused with magic and myth, writing magical realism stories in both historical fantasy and time travel flavors.

Combine this love of beauty with a bit of financial sense and you get an art business. She does local art and craft shows, as well as sending her art to various science fiction conventions throughout the country and abroad.

Social Media Links:
Blog: www.GreenDragonArtist.net
Website: www.GreenDragonArtist.com
Facebook: www.facebook.com/greendragonauthor
Twitter: www.twitter.com/greendragon9
Instagram: www.instagram.com/greendragonartist9
TikTok: www.tiktok.com/@greendragonauthor

Printed in Great Britain
by Amazon

26765209R00229